As We Lay

ALSO BY DARLENE JOHNSON

Dream in Color

As We Lay

A Novel

DARLENE JOHNSON

ONE WORLD
BALLANTINE BOOKS • NEW YORK

2009 One World Books Mass Market Edition

Copyright © 2003 by Darlene Johnson

Published in the United States by One World Books, an imprint of The Random House Publishing Group, a division of Random House, Inc., New York.

ONE WORLD is a registered trademark and the One World colophon is a trademark of Random House, Inc.

Originally published in trade paperback in the United States by Strivers Row/Villard Books, an imprint of The Random House Publishing Group, a division of Random House, Inc., in 2003.

ISBN 978-0-345-51070-9

Printed in the United States of America

www.oneworldbooks.net

OPM 9 8 7 6 5 4 3 2 1

To everyone who is not afraid to live,
then tame the wildness

ACKNOWLEDGMENTS

FIRST, I give honor for the blessing of being able to write this book and share it with you. What a journey this past year has been! I've said hello to a new city and friends and good-bye to old ones. Thank goodness my family managed to stay the same: crazy as ever, and always giving me something to write about.

I have to give a special hug to my nephew Lemarn Sally, Jr., for braving the move to the Wild West, "Beverly Hillbillies style" and on a wing and a prayer, and persevering with me. I'm proud of you, and I know that you will be the success that we all know you are capable of achieving. There's no telling what adventure I'll get us into, and you're right there with Malcolm, Doug, and me, experiencing it, living it, and probably loving it.

I have to recognize the people who have come into my life the past year and have brought new meaning to it, especially Dr. McLean Geo-JaJa, who has stepped forward and unwittingly become that wise voice that is a constant reminder of my worth, urging me to keep pushing forward. Also thanks to Ozwald Balfour, for opening up Salt Lake City to me; Keith Debus, for introducing me to a new path and being an integral part of the internal and external journey; and Rodger Lee, for giving me wonderful encouragement, support, and unconditional friendship without judgment (even when I screw up). You set a wonderful example of what it is to be evolved enough to admit that we're not perfect and it's okay. I have deep spiritual love for a wonderful host of new friends that have opened their arms, hearts, and homes to my boys and me: Sonia James, Simone Fritz, Sister Maryam, Deanna Blackwell, Heidi Hart, and Cherrone Anderson. With all of you, I'm learning to live in each moment and embrace the experience. I want to send a huge thanks and hug to my good friend Reginald Greene, who manages to stay connected with me throughout the years no matter where I move.

Thanks to my wonderful editor at Random House, Melody Guy, for keeping my words true, and the copy editors, who won't allow me to overlook even the simplest of things in their attempts to achieve perfection. I offer a large hug to my agent, Peter Miller, and the people at Peter Miller Literary and Film, for working hard at keeping me literarily employed. I also have to thank the great writers of AOL's writing chat—Litt, LadyJune, Quill, Duff, and Bride—for being faithful, patient, and a great support. I look forward to chatting with each of you every week.

I take this time to thank all those who have read *Dream in Color* and took the time to write me and gave me such wonderful feedback. I loved reading all of the e-mails from you; THANK YOU for taking the time to write. So many of those e-mails brought tears of joy to my eyes. Thanks to Minga Suma Book Club in Los Angeles, Atlantic Bookpost, and all of the other book clubs that read *Dream in Color* and sent wonderful words of encouragement. Thanks to the producers of *Dawson's Creek*, which showed *Dream in Color* on one episode; you helped me reach a totally different audience that wouldn't have read and loved the book otherwise. I want to thank my number one fan, Francine Yates, who always has a kind word to say. And I have to thank Daniel B. Aaron, a special fan who instant-messaged me just to say how much he loved the book. That was a first. Thanks.

I'm sure I've missed some names, and if I did, it is regretfully. I can't possibly name all those who have been instrumental in my life and reminding me how extremely blessed I am.

ONE

THE WORKPLACE attire in the small, three-person office Breck leased each month was business casual or whatever you happened to put your hands on that morning. When it came to style, Breck was the worst. Most mornings she strolled into the office wearing the jeans she had thrown over her bedroom chaise the night before. Her secretary, Tachi Tanaka, Chi for short, was the fashionable one. Her name was pronounced "Kie"; however, most people who only saw it written said "She." Whether or not Chi corrected them was determined by their importance. "It's not worth the breath," she explained to Breck one day when her name was called for a table at a restaurant.

Chi was blessed with the type of beauty and petite frame that always made her look good no matter what she wore. She had both women and men falling all over her and throwing credit cards and gifts at her just to take her out. She accepted the gifts, of course, but it was only the women she was interested in. She never deceived the men about her sexual preference, but most of them still vied for the chance to be the one to "convert" her. The ones with the largest egos insisted that after one night with them she would never look at a woman again.

Even with her flawless beauty, Chi was extremely self-conscious about her breasts, or lack thereof. So she took a two-week vacation and had the problem rectified. "What Mother Nature didn't give me, Dr. Anderson did," Chi sang as she pulled her shirt tight around her enlarged bosoms.

Breck hired Chi straight out of junior college, where she'd received an associate's degree in business administration, but the only thing the school had prepared her for was a high-level administrative-assistant position. Chi knew how to use all of the office software programs, write business letters, and run an office efficiently, thus making her perfect for the position. The initial interview lasted over six hours; she and Breck ended up leaving the office together and headed to a local martini club for a drink.

The third person in the office was the part-time CAD specialist, Jonathan Franks. By day Jonathan was a computer operator. He'd taken the extra job to support a wife and three kids. He worked nights during the first part of the week, and Breck hardly saw him. The only evidence that he even existed was the computer-image file he left for her.

BRECK SAT in her office overlooking the canal. Every time the phone rang, her pulse hammered until Chi verified it was not the call she was hoping for. Was Eric Warren ever going to call her back? It had been nearly a month since he'd phoned her after she had been recommended to him by one of her other clients. Breck had spoken with him briefly then about designing a convention center in Mansfield, Massachusetts. His voice sounded formidable as he questioned her about her previous work. Nothing she had done in the past was on the scale of what he wanted. But she had convinced Mr. Warren to look at her designs, and he had invited her to visit him and his partner, Stephen Peterson, to go over the ideas for the center and see the actual building site. Naturally, Breck had accepted. She would have been a fool not to.

Breck had flown to Boston and shown up at the Warren & Peterson Property Management office dressed in a brand-new Donna Karan business suit, only to be greeted by Eric Warren's fashionable secretary, Gloria, with the news that he had been called away on an emergency and would not be able to make it. Stephen Peterson would accompany her to the site and answer any questions. Gloria escorted her to Mr. Peterson's office.

The contemporary interior decorating coupled with an impeccable view of Boston Harbor made the Warren & Peterson offices extraordinary. You could see the ocean from all the east-wing offices. The firm was located on the top floor of a downtown Boston tower, where each employee enjoyed the luxury of a private office. The staff was kept small, which accounted for the vast wealth racked up by the two partners.

Breck waited for almost thirty minutes outside Stephen Peterson's office. Occasionally his secretary would glance up apologetically as she sorted through the barrage of mail dumped on her desk. The wooden nameplate on her desk read "Amy Snow," prominently scribed in gold-plated lettering. Several times Breck had to stand up to keep the sweat from staining the underside of her skirt. Finally Ms. Snow took an incoming call and announced that Mr. Peterson was ready to see her.

Peeling the back of her thighs from the leather chair, Breck stood up and flattened the wrinkles in her skirt with the palm of her hand before the secretary escorted her through the oak double doors.

"Have a seat, Ms. Larson." Stephen Peterson motioned her to the chair in front of his impressive oak desk. As she walked across the thick mauve carpet, his eyes remained fixed on the computer monitor on the left corner of his desk. He was more than six feet tall, with a protruding midsection that revealed that his after hours were not spent in a corporate gym. She sighed when she saw she would have to do battle with yet another leather chair. She sat and placed her portfolio case next to her.

Stephen Peterson still did not look up. Breck folded her arms across her chest and looked around the uptight office. The sun streamed through the large windows and bounced off his bald head. In the center of each impeccably papered wall hung paintings by contemporary artists in frames that probably cost as much as the artwork itself. A collection of miniature bronze and copper statues was displayed on the oak file cabinet behind his desk.

"I'll be right with you," he mumbled, seeming reluctant to draw his attention away from the computer screen. After several minutes he finally swerved his chair to the center of the desk. "Eric's been called away on an emergency," he said, repeating what Gloria had already told her. He reached inside a desk drawer, pulled out a massive folder, and flopped it on top of the desk. "He asked that I see you get all the information you need when you visit the site. Gloria will be accompanying you and should be able to answer most of your questions. If not, perhaps you can find the answer in this." He pushed the folder toward her and settled back in his chair, waiting for her to respond.

"You won't be joining us?" she asked. If he wasn't taking her, then why in the hell was she still here?

"This is Eric's project," he said, throwing up his hands and waving them as if the whole thing were a big inconvenience. "Gloria knows what Eric wants done more than I do, so I'm handing you off to her."

Getting rid of me sounds more like it, Breck thought as she flipped through the papers of building specifications and zoning requirements. "When is Mr. Warren due back?" she asked, hoping that he would at least be available to talk with her before she returned to Indianapolis.

"It's hard to say at this time, but it's very doubtful he'll return before you leave."

Breck sighed and tried desperately not to lose her cool. She'd spent over a thousand dollars on her suit and canceled several appointments to travel to Boston, only to be put off and discarded.

"Excuse me," he announced, reaching across his desk and picking up the telephone. He pressed three buttons and waited. "Gloria, are you ready to join Ms. Larson?" he asked, spinning his chair to look at the panoramic view of Boston Harbor. "Wonderful. She'll be waiting for you in my lobby." He turned to face her again before replacing the handset.

That was her cue. Not only was the bastard not taking her to the site, but he'd just politely kicked her out of his office. And not a moment too soon, she reasoned, standing and tucking the portfolio case underneath her arm. "Where should I leave this?" she asked.

"What is it?"

"My portfolio."

"Give it to Gloria," he said, then returned to his computer. He didn't even bother to say good-bye.

Breck eyed him, biting back the urge to snap at him for his callous demeanor. She turned and quickly exited the office before she lost her cool. Gloria was approaching her in the foyer from the opposite corridor.

"Are you ready?" Gloria asked, slipping her arms through the sleeves of a thin sweater.

"Yes, but I don't want to lug this around with me," Breck said, holding up the giant case.

"Are those your designs?"

"Yes."

"We can leave those in Mr. Warren's office. He'll want to look at them." She headed back down the corridor, with Breck following close behind.

Another set of double oak doors was on the opposite end of the corridor. Breck assumed this was Eric Warren's section. Like Amy's desk, Gloria's desk was placed a few feet in front of the doors. Anyone wanting to see these gentlemen would first have to get by their gate-keepers. Gloria opened her desk and pulled out a large set of keys, rifling through them until she found the one that unlocked the office.

Eric Warren's office smelled of wood polish. Breck stood in the doorway feeling as though walking into his office would somehow invade his space.

"I'll take that." Gloria took the portfolio case and walked across the plush carpet toward the enormous oak desk. As evidenced by the carpet, Mr. Warren hadn't been in the office that day. The triangular designs left by the cleaning staff's vacuum were still fresh on the carpet. Each time Gloria lifted her foot, a pointy-toed shoe print remained. From the doorway Breck noted that in contrast to his partner's office, Mr. Warren's had friendly pieces of childish artwork framed on the walls—handprints and what appeared to be a child's first attempt with paint and a paintbrush.

"Interesting artwork," Breck said, smiling. At least one of the Warren & Peterson partners seemed like an empathetic human being.

"Mr. Warren is a family man," Gloria said, placing the portfolio case on the desk. "His son made the paintings, and his wife decorated the office." She rejoined Breck and locked the door.

"So, what is he like?" Breck asked as they headed to the elevator. Even the elevator door was oak-paneled.

"Nothing like *him*. Believe me." Gloria motioned her head toward Stephen Peterson's area.

"That's good to know." The two ladies took the company's limousine and driver to the Mansfield site, where they met with Martin Stone and his partner, Brian Ramsey, who owned the construction company responsible for building on the empty lot. It turned out that the two men were longtime friends of Eric Warren's and Mansfield was the small community they were all raised in. Over lunch Breck learned that the convention center would be part of a broader community-revitalization project. Warren & Peterson owned most of the vacant buildings and old homes in Mansfield, with Eric having the controlling interest. Their motive didn't seem to be making money since most of the sales were well below market value.

"Warren and Peterson doesn't need the money," Martin explained. "Eric is doing it to fulfill a promise. He throws Stephen a few crumbs so he doesn't complain too loudly."

With growing curiosity about the guardian angel of Mansfield, Breck left Boston feeling better about the possibility of working with Warren & Peterson.

IF IT weren't for the dance floor, no one would ever know that the Alley was one of the hottest gay clubs in Indianapolis. Men and women mingled in small groups like at any other nightclub. It wasn't until you looked at the dance floor and saw same-sex dancing that it became clear.

To further baffle Breck, the men and women were the most gorgeous she had ever seen. The selection at Jump, the so-called heterosexual hot spot in town, could never top the men who walked through the door of the Alley. These men were prime catch: doctors, lawyers, and hard-bodied construction workers who kept women driving in circles. Some of the sharpest-dressed men she had ever seen turned up here—with other men.

"Look at him," Breck said, lifting her Long Island iced tea in the direction of a brown-skinned man, perfectly groomed and wearing a pair of fitted jeans and a sweater that fit just right, showing off the reward of hours spent in a gym working out his upper body. "He can't be gay," she said, shaking her head.

"Hey, William!" Chi yelled across the room, waving the man in question over.

"You know him?" Breck asked.

William was upon them before Chi had the chance to answer her. "Hi, Chi." He leaned forward and kissed her on the cheek.

"Where's Richard?" Chi asked, proving a point to Breck.

"He's working. He has an important case coming up, so he's stuck at the office."

"Oh, bummer. I haven't seen him in a long time."

"Well, he's trying to make partner, so he's been working his ass off. He thinks he has a shot at it this year."

"Good. You're handling it okay with him being gone so much?"

William shrugged. "What can I do? He's a hardworking man, but he does take good care of me." He and Chi laughed at the sly joke.

"Well, hang in there." Chi squeezed his hand. "William, this is my good friend and boss, Breck."

"Nice to meet you, William." Breck reached across the table to shake his smooth, well-manicured hand.

"Give me a call if you need to hang out," Chi said, and kissed him on the cheek.

"I will." William walked away and rejoined his mixed group standing at the bar. Breck shook her head.

"What?" Chi asked.

"He could have any woman he wants. I don't get it."

"He can't have me."

"He could if you wanted a man," she said, looking at her petite Asian/black friend who could easily win any beauty pageant. Breck abandoned trying to understand how two beautiful people such as William and Chi would want someone other than a member of the opposite sex.

She took a long sip from her drink and settled back into her seat.

"You're nervous about the Warren & Peterson contract, aren't you?" Chi asked, taking a sip of wine and placing the glass gently on the table.

Breck nodded. "This could be my break. If I get this contract, I'm in."

"What do you mean, 'if'? The contract is yours. You've done everything they've asked, including putting up with Stephen Peterson for even five minutes."

Breck rolled her eyes, remembering her short and heartless moments with the partner. "I don't know. I wish Eric Warren could have been there so I could have sold him on my ideas instead of being stuck with his rude-ass partner."

"Forget about him."

"But it's been a week and I haven't heard if they liked the portfolio. I blew it."

"You didn't blow it. You've worked hard on this and it's going to work out for you. I can feel it." Chi squeezed her hand. "Now, when are you and Quentin getting married?" She grinned.

"Married?" Breck coughed. "Probably never." She took a sip of her drink.

"It's been eight months. I thought things were working out pretty well for you two."

"They are, but something is missing. I don't know what it is."

"How's the sex?" Chi asked candidly.

"Great, but like I said, something just isn't there." She took another sip.

"What do you suppose it is?"

Breck shrugged. "I don't know."

"Do you love him?"

Breck shrugged again. "I don't know."

"You work too hard. You just need to loosen up." It

was one of Chi's simple answers. As good as her answers sounded, the solutions were never quite that simple.

"No, what I need to do is talk to Eric Warren and get this damn contract finalized. This could be the start of a brand-new life for us," Breck said, taking a deep breath.

Chi was finally able to convince Breck to forget about War-ren & Peterson and concentrate on having fun. After another glass of Long Island iced tea, Breck ventured out onto the floor with Chi and danced.

The best thing about dancing with Chi was letting loose and being wild. Many times they exaggerated how close they really were, especially when a woman was trying to pick up Breck. Instead of going through the trouble of trying to explain that she was straight even though she was sitting in a gay bar with a lesbian, she and Chi would just dance together. She could get as funky as she wanted with Chi and know that Chi would never take it outside of the bar.

"Have you ever kissed a woman, Breck?" Chi had asked her after one of the first times they'd danced together at the Alley.

"Oh, yeah," Breck answered, and took a sip of her Tanqueray gin and tonic. "Melissa. She was a friend of mine in college."

"College is the best time to explore your sexuality. Was she your best friend?"

"No, not best friend, but a good friend."

"What did you think of kissing a woman?"

"She was a great kisser." Breck laughed. "But I was nineteen and I'd only kissed about three people in my life." The smile on Breck's face stretched wide. "It was a crazy night. It was Melissa, myself, Dawn, and Trina. We were in Melissa and Trina's dorm room after an Omega frat party."

"No men?"

"No, it was girls' night out. The entire night we were

hanging all over each other. All of us had too many daiquiris at the party, and we walked back to the dorm just laughing and falling all over each other. When we got to the room, Melissa put on music and we all started dancing and taking off our tops, arguing whose titties were bigger." Breck laughed and clapped her hands. "I stood in the middle of the floor and declared mine were bigger, and Melissa ripped off her shirt and stood in my face and exclaimed hers were bigger. So I reached out and cupped her left breast with my right hand, then cupped my own with my left hand, and by God, her breasts *were* bigger than mine."

Chi sat agape for several long seconds before she spoke again. "You, Ms. Straitlaced Businesswoman, touched a woman's breast?"

"Hey, I'm not dead," Breck said, taking her fist to the table. "I'm just focused on building my company and getting this damn contract. I can let loose too."

"That I haven't seen yet, and I've known you for two years," Chi asked, countering her. "Well, what happened after you grabbed her tit?" Chi asked, urging her on.

"We kissed, and I'm not talking about a peck on the cheek. I mean a head-turning, lip-locking *kiss*."

Chi's mouth hung open so wide it seemed it would drop to the floor. Breck went on to tell the entire story.

THE OMEGA psi phi annual house party was live, and the girls ended up dancing all night. It was Breck, her roommate, Dawn, and their friends Melissa and Trina, who had the room adjacent to theirs. The dorms were designed so that between two rooms was a bathroom, shared by four girls.

It was at least ten degrees hotter in the frat house than it was outside. To cool off, everyone had to step out onto the porch or front lawn. The fraternity boys kept the beverages coming: strawberry daiquiris for the women and beer for the men. Glasses were replenished as soon as they were emptied. Melissa's boyfriend, David, had pledged Omega, and he made sure her group was taken care of.

The girls lost count of how many times their glasses were refilled that night, but not before they realized that they needed to get the hell out of there before they ended up in the room of someone they didn't know. They left together and walked across campus back to the resident hall. They chose Melissa and Trina's room because they had the most current music.

Melissa put on some music—more of the same dance tunes they had just heard—and turned it up.

"You better turn that down before Robin comes knocking on the door," Melissa said, referring to their residence assistant, who followed all the rules and wouldn't let a thing like loud music on a Friday evening slip past her. Melissa turned the music down a little, and they danced around the small, cramped room, standing on beds and the sofa, showing their curves, sticking out their butts, and swinging their arms through the air.

"Damn, my shirt is wet," Trina said. "It was hot in there." She unbuttoned her shirt and swung it around like she was doing a striptease.

The girls whistled and cheered her on as she danced on the bed in her bra. Her small breasts barely jiggled.

"Girl, you need to sit down," Melissa teased. "You don't have any tits to bounce."

"My tits bounce," Trina countered. "See?" She pulled down the straps of her bra and unsnapped the hooks. Her A-cup breasts were firm but too small to sag.

"You don't need a bra," Breck said. "Why the hell do you wear a bra?" She stood up and took off her bra. "*These* are tits." Inheriting the genes from a lineage of full-figured and shapely women, Breck was well proportioned. She stood five-seven, weighed 130 pounds, and wore a perfect size eight, as she had since early high school. Her breasts were not the largest, but because she exercised they were firm and full. She kept her weight under control by jogging, which she continued to enjoy after competing on the cross-country team in high school.

"Those meatballs," Melissa exclaimed, and stood up in front of Breck and took off her bra. "*These* are breasts." Melissa stood inches from her and bounced, making her breasts wobble up and down. Breck reached out and grabbed her left breast, full in the palm of her hand, then grabbed her own.

"Yeah, your breasts are bigger than mine," she said, and everyone broke out in laughter. She and Melissa laughed the hardest. The fun was good-natured, and no one seemed overly concerned.

"Damn, y'all look like you're about to kiss," Trina burst out, sitting down after losing the battle of the breasts. Without hesitation, as if they had the same thought simultaneously, Breck and Melissa took a step forward and kissed. Their soft lips touched, blending together Breck's mauve lipstick and Melissa's hot red. Trina and Dawn hollered and cheered them on. It was the first time Breck's lips had touched a woman other than her mother, sister, or some other relative, and those kisses were always for a split second.

When they separated, they hugged each other, their bare breasts pressed together, and laughed hysterically. Then they joined the other girls on the floor as the music continued to play. They all sat around and talked. The conversation easily drifted from classes to their boyfriends.

"Mark and I have sex," Trina announced, then dropped her head as if waiting to be scolded, but the other girls just looked at her, waiting for Trina to announce something startling. Trina looked up again. "Are you having sex too?" she asked.

"Of course!" Melissa exclaimed. "I lost my virginity when I was seventeen."

"I was eighteen," Dawn announced.

"Eighteen for me too," Breck said, waving her hand.

"My mother would kill me if she knew I was having sex and not married," Trina said.

"Trina, you're a grown woman," Melissa said, standing up and putting on more music. "You don't need to be afraid of your mother anymore."

"You don't know my mother. She would take me to church and have the entire congregation pray over me."

"Oh, my God," Dawn said, covering her mouth in disbelief. "Are you serious?"

"Well, I can relate to that because my mother would probably do the same," Breck said. "So I just don't tell her shit like that."

"That's horrible," Dawn said. "My mother and I talk about everything. She knew when I was thinking about having sex, and she went with me to get birth control."

"Mine too," Melissa interceded. "And not only that, my mother talked to me about how to please myself if my man just don't do it for me. She said, 'You can have a good man, but he might be ill equipped or misinformed about what pleases you. Be prepared to tell him and show him what does.' "

Trina's eyes grew bigger. "Your mother said that?"

"Yes, and told me to know my body well enough to know what pleases me and what doesn't. I love it when David goes down on me. His tongue makes me wanna holler." She slapped her leg. "But if he tries to stick his cock in my ass, I'll turn around and slap him. That shit hurts."

Trina frowned. "Mark goes down, but I don't feel anything."

"That's because he's not licking the right place." Melissa stood up, unzipped her skirt, dropped it and her panties to the floor, and then, sitting back down, spread her legs to show Trina where she liked to be licked. "Now you do it," she said, pointing to Trina.

Trina shook her head vigorously.

"Why not? You're ashamed of your body? Shit, we all have the same thing. You won't be showing us anything we haven't seen before." Trina hesitated. "If you don't know what pleases you, how are you going to be able to show Mark? You better know what you like because if you don't, you'll settle for less. My mother taught me that too." Melissa closed her legs.

"I'll do it with you," Breck said. She stood up, dropped her blue-jeans skirt and panties to the floor, sat down, and spread her legs too. She touched herself and found her clitoris. "That's it, right there," she said, then closed her legs.

Trina sat frozen for a few seconds longer, took a deep breath, then stood up and unzipped her jeans. She dropped her jeans and panties to the floor and, like Melissa and Breck, sat down and spread her legs. She fumbled between her legs before she hit a spot that made her scream.

"What the hell are you screaming for?" Melissa said. "You don't have to be afraid of feeling good. Enjoy it."

Trina touched herself again, and her eyes grew wider in amazement. "I never felt that before," she said.

"What did you do before you had a boyfriend?" Dawn asked.

"Nothing. I thought about sex a lot. I wanted to touch it, but I couldn't. All the women at the church and my mother said that women didn't do that. Only nasty, dirty men."

"Your mother needs to take a lesson from my mother."

"wow." CHI looked wide-eyed at Breck when she'd finished telling the story. "It sounds like it was a great evening."

"It was a crazy evening, but nobody in the room freaked out. Everybody just started laughing, and afterward we all just sat around with no clothes on and listened to music, talked about our families, sex, and what we wanted to do when we graduated. It was total freedom."

"Whatever happened to Melissa?" Chi asked. She leaned forward, engrossed by the story and a side of Breck that she'd never seen.

"She graduated, went to Harvard Law School, and is now a law clerk for one of Georgia's supreme court justices. She and David got married and have two children. Trina is in her final year of the doctoral program in psychology at the university. She stays in touch with everyone and keeps me informed of how they're all doing. Dawn majored in political science and moved to Africa. She works at the United States embassy in Nigeria. Her parents were second-generation in this country, and she wanted to connect with her culture and her history, so she decided to spend a few years discovering who she is."

"Did you girls get closer after that night? I mean, my God. You were sitting in front of each other with your legs spread open for all to see. You can't get more intimate than that."

"I think we got closer to ourselves, not necessarily each other. Trina and Melissa were always close, but Dawn and I really were not. We were friendly but not sisterly. We just didn't make that connection. But it seemed after that night all of our lives became much clearer. We all seemed to let go of every fear that would keep us from exploring life and taking chances.

"Being in that room with those girls without feeling any defamation about my body, my thoughts, my actions, or my sexuality was probably the first time I'd ever experienced no boundaries in my life, and I loved that feeling. I'm addicted to it, which is probably why I live the way I do and why it is so hard for me to live within predetermined boundaries."

"What do you mean?"

"All around me people try to put me within boundaries. When I announced I wanted to be an architect all I heard was, You're a black woman, you'll never make it as an architect. When I wanted to start my own firm all I heard was, I should settle for working for the top architecture firms instead of starting my own. My mother warned me about making a lot of money because"—Breck mimicked her mother's tone and mannerisms—" 'No man wants a woman who makes more money than he does.' All boundaries and no freedom."

"Maybe that's why you're having problems moving forward with Quentin."

"Quentin is a wonderful man and I know he wants to get married one day, but when I think of marrying him I feel like someone is holding a plastic bag over my head."

"Yikes," Chi said, squinting.

"I know."

"Why don't you just dump him?"

"Because he hasn't given me any reason to, and he's a nice guy."

"And the sex is good," Chi added.

"That too." Breck grinned. "And getting some is better than getting none."

"Just like a dog," Chi said with a smirk. "Wants the cake and eat it too."

"Don't we all?"

TWO

"YES," BRECK said, as her hand landed on the speakerphone. It had been one of those damn days when it seemed nothing went right, and Chi had the nerve to leave her alone in the knotted mess. Breck couldn't blame Chi for not wanting to stay longer. The phone had rung incessantly throughout the day, the fax machine spilled papers continuously, and the copier got stuck on an incorrigible paper jam in the middle of a job. Chi placed the service call, then left.

"Excuse me," a deep, sexy voice said. "I'm calling for Ms. Breck Larson."

Breck's pencil stopped gliding across the drafting paper, and she looked at her watch. It was six o'clock, and no one called her to discuss business after hours, ever.

She turned and spoke directly into the speakerphone. "Speaking."

"Sorry to interrupt you, but this is Eric Warren from Warren and Peterson."

"Shit," Breck muttered, tossing the pencil onto the desk and straightening up in her chair as though the commander in chief had just entered the room.

"Hello, Mr. Warren," she said, and reached for the handset to take him off the speakerphone. "I apologize. I thought you were someone else."

"It's quite all right. I should have called during normal business hours, so I should be the one apologizing."

"Don't worry about it, Mr. Warren. I usually work late. How can I help you?"

"You can start by calling me Eric." He spoke in a quiet but intense voice with a trademark Bostonian accent.

Breck released the air she held in her chest. "Okay, how can I help you, Eric?"

"First of all, I need to apologize for taking so long to get back to you. I returned to Boston just a few days ago, but I did get a chance to go over your designs." Breck held her breath again. "Do you think you will have any problems working with Martin and Brian?"

Breck wanted to scream but contained herself. A wide smile appeared on her face as she stood up and paced the floor.

"I won't have any problems working with Martin or Brian. How soon do we start?"

"We need everything finalized before the new year. We want to begin preparing the ground by mid-February."

"Will the weather allow for that?"

"We'll do what we can, and we think we will be able to make some significant progress. We want this project complete before next Christmas. Can your office handle this?"

"Yes," Breck replied quickly. She realized that it would require her to devote damn near all of her days and nights only to this project, but she knew what it would mean to her business if she could pull it off.

"You were able to look over the paperwork Stephen gave you, correct?"

Breck nodded. "Yes, I was." She'd looked at the papers long enough to know that the convention center would be a one-story brick building with several meeting rooms and a small theater. It was a simple design idea, and if everything went smoothly and the weather cooperated, it wouldn't take long for an experienced builder to put it together in a few months. "I'll send you a blanket proposal."

"Not necessary. Just let me know how much this is going to cost me, and we can go from there. Sound good to you?"

"Sounds wonderful to me."

"Excellent. I look forward to working with you."

"I should be able to get you that contract in a few days," Breck added before he hung up.

"Let's talk beforehand. How does Friday evening look for you?"

Breck quickly slid the papers from her desk calendar, causing several of them to fall to the floor. She scanned the calendar until she found Friday. She had a date with Quentin.

"Friday looks good. What time?"

"I have meetings all day, then I'm out of town for a few days, so I'm looking at around nine o'clock eastern standard time, which would be eight o'clock for you. Is that too late?"

"No, not at all." She wasn't going to risk saying yes, then waiting until he got back into town to have that conversation with him. She needed to feel this deal was concrete, and she just didn't feel that yet. "I'll be waiting for your call."

"Wonderful. I'll talk with you then." The phone clicked.

Breck screamed, then stood up and danced around the room. Since leaving the architectural firm she'd been employed with after college, Breck had been able to get a few clients through word of mouth. Most of her designs were two-room office buildings and single-family homes. She loved working with newlyweds on designing their dream home, but the big money was in commercial real estate and it was hard to break in there. Contracts such as the one with Warren & Peterson went to well-known firms around the country who would have the money and clout to take a contract such as this whether her bid was higher or lower. But Warren & Peterson was not interested in a bidding war. They were offering her the contract outright.

After her celebration dance Breck picked up the phone and called Chi. As soon as she answered, Breck let out an ear-piercing wail.

"What's wrong?" Chi screamed back into the receiver.

"I got the contract! I got the contract!" she yelled.

Both women screamed. Breck took several quick breaths. "Eric called and told me to send him the contract so we can get to work. This is it, Chi. I'm in."

"You deserve it. You've worked hard, and it's about damned time you got a break."

Breck sat back in her chair and took a deep breath. The architectural world wasn't too kind to women, particularly attractive, headstrong, twenty-six-year-old African-American women. At her first job after college, all of her white male colleagues were given assignments and the most she could do was look over their shoulders. But she had been determined not to spend her entire career that way. When the next assignment came in she'd practically snatched it from her boss's hand and gone to work. He didn't stop her, but he spent the next few weeks looking over *her* shoulders. When she had completed it, she'd gained the respect of her boss and everyone else in the office.

"You want to go out and celebrate tonight?" Chi asked, breaking the short silence.

"I can't, I have work to do. If I'm going to take this on, I've got to get further along with the three projects I'm currently working on and give Larry a call so he can draft a contract for me."

"Always working. It's a wonder Quentin still puts up with you."

Breck gasped. "I have to call him and break our date Friday."

"Breck, he's going to get tired of your ass sooner or later."

"I know, I know," Breck said. "I'll talk to you in a bit." She hung up, and before she picked up the phone again to dial Quentin's number, she mentally rehearsed what she was going to say. Then she took a deep breath and dialed. She regretted doing this to him again. Too many times over the past few months she had called to cancel a date at the last minute. Chi was right: sooner or later Quentin was going to get tired of it.

"Hey, Quentin," Breck said, holding on to a breath longer than usual.

"Hi, honey. Stopping by when you leave the office?" As usual, Quentin's voice was exciting and cheerful. If he was ever in a bad mood, she'd never know it. It was one of the things that had attracted her to him initially.

"I think it's going to be an all-nighter," she said. "I got the call from Warren and Peterson." She smiled broadly when she said the name. She hoped Quentin would feel her excitement and would understand when she broke the date.

"That's wonderful!" he exclaimed. "This is your big chance."

"I know and I'm so excited. We're having a conference call on Friday evening to discuss the details."

He was silent while this sank in.

"I guess that means you won't be going to the concert?" Quentin asked.

"I'm sorry."

"I should have expected it. It's only the fifth date you've canceled in the past two months."

"No, it is not."

"Yes, it is, Breck. I'm beginning to wonder if you're using work as an excuse."

"Quentin, that is not true. You know I adore you."

"That's the problem, Breck. We've been going out for

eight months now, and all you can say is that you adore me."

Breck was quiet. She wasn't sure if she loved him, but he was a good man and she wanted to love him. It was almost as if she were trying to force herself to fall in love with him.

"Listen," Quentin said, "I know you have a lot of work to do and a lot on your mind, so I am not going to press you on this, okay? Just make sure you get some sleep tonight."

Breck smiled. "Thanks, Quentin." The phone clicked before she replaced her handset.

Quentin was one of the good ones and she knew it. She couldn't say anything bad about him. During a time when most of her friends complained about having good-for-nothing husbands or boyfriends, Breck couldn't complain one bit about Quentin. He was very attentive to her, got along great with her parents and friends, and was an excellent lover. She couldn't figure out what was missing in their relationship, and it bugged the shit out of her. She shrugged off the thought, took a deep breath, then stood up and walked back to her drafting board. She picked up the pencil, looked at the sketch, and sighed. At least she hadn't lied to him. It was going to be an all-nighter, for sure.

THREE

TODAY WAS Friday, and Breck was prepared for Eric Warren's phone call. She strolled into the office wearing one of her best pantsuits and carrying her work in her best portfolio case, instead of the used one with the worn leather bottom. In her other hand she carried her morning coffee.

"He's calling, Breck," Chi said. "He's not coming into the office."

"I know, but I want to feel this. I'm going to present myself to him like he's sitting in front of me." Breck danced across the floor as if Eric Warren had led her into a ballroom dance.

Chi shook her head. "Larry said to call him if there are any questions about the contracts," she said, handing her boss the morning mail.

"Wonderful." Breck flipped through it seeing nothing of major importance, just regular bills. Chi had already discarded the junk. "Looks good." She nodded and headed for her office.

"Quentin and your mother called this morning."

"Did Mom say what she wanted?" Breck asked, reaching for the doorknob.

"Nope," Chi said, not missing a keystroke. "Quentin said call him."

Breck walked into her office and closed the door. She picked up the phone and called her mother. "Hey, Mom, what's up?" she asked, fumbling through things on her desk.

"Nothing. Just called to see how you are. I don't hear from you much. How's Quentin?" Breck stopped moving things around on her desk and tried to focus on the conversation. She didn't talk to her mother much because she never knew what to say to her. She and her mother had never bonded. They'd never gone through a major crisis together, never talked about life issues. Breck didn't know how to bring her mother into her life without being judged by her. She sensed her mother didn't approve of her lifestyle. Her mother always accused her of working too hard and said she needed more of a social life, but Breck simply had too much to accomplish to feel that it was time to settle down and take it easy.

"Quentin is fine," Breck said.

"Why don't you and he come over for dinner tonight?"

Breck shrugged, then remembered her mother couldn't see her. "Can't, I have to work."

"You're always working. Don't give Quentin a reason to go meet someone else."

Breck sighed. Her mother was beginning to sound like Chi. "If he does, there's always someone else," Breck countered.

"Quentin is a good one, Breck."

"Mom, I have to go," Breck said, cutting her short. "Love you. Bye." She quickly hung up the phone and then picked it up again to return Quentin's call. Before she began dialing the number, she hung it up again.

Later, she thought, and got to work.

ALTHOUGH IT was difficult, Breck managed to concentrate on the project on her desk, one that did not involve the Warren & Peterson name. She was putting the finishing details on a three-story Victorian-style house for a prominent attorney and his wife. There weren't many uncommon details about the house, which made it easier. Victorian-style homes were her specialty, and she was sure that would be the type of home she would design for herself someday.

Chi wasn't waiting around for Eric Warren to call and said her good-byes at five o'clock, as usual. It was Friday night, which meant she had some date lined up. Not many weekends went by that Chi didn't have at least one date. Chi adamantly claimed to be looking for a permanent partner, but Breck had her doubts. Chi dated many good potential partners, but every time Breck met Chi's date, it was someone new.

By seven-thirty, Breck's stomach had begun to growl and she was in desperate need of caffeine. Chi had gone out to the nearby deli and picked up sandwiches for them for lunch. Breck's still sat in the wrapper on her desk. She had been too excited to eat it earlier. Now she picked it up, took a huge bite, and smiled. Chi had remembered the extra pickle this time.

The phone rang just as she was about to take another bite. It was not quite eight o'clock, so she answered before swallowing.

"Breck Arson." Her name came out as she held the food in her mouth.

"Hello, Ms. Larson. Eric Warren here." He was talking to her on a speakerphone, and his voice bounced around like a ball.

"Hello," she said as she swallowed.

"I'm a little early, so if this is not a good time I can call back."

Breck took notice of his politeness. "No, it's okay." She pushed the sandwich away and took a quick drink of ginger ale. Not the strong coffee she needed, but it had to do. "I was just eating a sandwich."

"Should I give you a few minutes?"

"No, it's fine." She took another sip and set the can aside. "I was just finishing up," she said.

"How's the weather there in Indiana?" he asked. Breck lowered the receiver from her ear and looked at it for a brief second, wondering if she was supposed to answer the question. She was sure Eric Warren wasn't the least bit interested in the weather in Indiana, but it was the second time during the short conversation where he came off as being a cordial human being, a character trait most of her clients with way too much money didn't have.

"Cold. We haven't had much snow, but it's been pretty cold." She grabbed the envelope Larry had left for her and spread the papers across her desk. "Did you receive the contract?" she asked.

"Yes, I did, and I have it in front of me," he said. She heard rustling over the speakers as he moved his fingers between the piles of paper on his desk.

"Do you have any questions? Any modifications that need to be made?" She grabbed her pencil and prepared to write. This was usually the phase when clients attempted to negotiate the price, room sizes, door locations, and the potential to reduce cost by eliminating rooms. It happened all the time.

"Everything appears to be in order to me."

Breck paused and stared at the receiver. Had he even looked at the contract and the designs? Did he not see how much she was charging him for this? "Hmm," she said, not quite knowing how to proceed. "Do you have any questions at all?"

"No. Everything looks great. We approved the contract. It's signed and you should be receiving the certified copy in the mail next week."

Breck placed the pencil down on her desk and scratched her head. "This is very unusual," she said finally.

"And why is that?"

"Because this has never happened before. People always want to change something. You do realize that if you want to change something, now is the time to do it." She hoped he would at least challenge her about the price.

"Ms. Larson, I understand all that. This isn't the first time I've had a building designed and built."

"I didn't mean it that way," she said. Perhaps it had come out like she was patronizing him, but that was not the case. The last thing she needed to do was to lose the account because she had offended him.

"I know you didn't, but I knew exactly what I wanted before I ever came to you, and you've given me that."

She paused for a moment and settled back into her chair. Was this really going to be this easy? Eric Warren was a powerful man, probably the most powerful man she had ever had to work with, and she had prepared herself to deal with him. These men usually exerted their power by making a change or two to the designs simply because they could and to see if they could get a rise out of her. She'd learned to recognize the game, keep her mouth shut, nod, and play along. When she first started out she'd lost a couple of clients by challenging them; now she knew to smile and wait until she was in the safety of her car to curse them out. Eric Warren appeared to be none of that.

"Are you still there?" he asked.

"Yes," she said quickly, then added, "Mr. Warren, I just want to make sure we have everything in check before the construction begins. It'll save you a lot of money and everyone a lot of time."

"I understand that, but I've looked over the designs and everything is exactly what we've wanted. Since we're going to be working together, please call me Eric."

She tossed the pencil on the desk and watched it bounce. "Are you always this way?"

"What way?"

"So easy to work with."

He laughed. "No."

She breathed deeply. For some reason that made her feel better.

"If it bothers you, you can continue to call me Mr. Warren."

She drew back, surprised. "Eric is fine," she said, then paused. "Why are you making this so easy?"

"Because I know what I want and I have it sitting on my desk."

Breck nodded. Now, that was the demeanor she was accustomed to, and something about the way he said it stirred her curiosity even more. There was something about Eric Warren that set him apart from her other clients. He was just as powerful and just as wealthy, but his way of dealing with people was in complete contrast.

Breck stood, took her jacket off, and draped it on the back of her chair. "You're very different," she said, sitting back down. "You're assertive, but in a way that isn't arrogant, which will make working with you very enjoyable." She felt strangely at ease with him, enough to speak openly.

"Thank you. I imagine you're very accustomed to dealing with difficult men."

"Yes, I am, but I handle myself fairly well."

"Is your husband the same as you are?"

Breck thought for a moment. Quentin was very assertive but lacked aggressiveness. She immensely disliked men who attempted to tell her what to do, but she was extremely turned on by the ones who took control without making her feel as if she'd signed away her freedom. "Contrary. My *boyfriend* is more passive."

"I suppose that's an even balance," he said. "Is that

the reason why he let you work this late on a Friday evening?"

"What do you mean, let me work?" she bellowed.

"Oh, don't tell me you're one of those types."

She damn near stood up from her chair. "What are you talking about?"

"You're one of those 'I don't need a man' types, aren't you?"

"Well, I don't." Robust laughter startled her. Why the hell was she having this type of conversation with him? He didn't know her or what type of person she was. All he knew about her was that she was a damned good designer. He had no right to assume anything else. She wondered if all men with money felt that once they'd reached a certain rung on the social ladder women became *things* that are seen and never, ever heard. Did that explain why most of the men she'd come across with a stash of money had beautiful trophy brides, whose opinions never left the bedroom, dangling on their arms? "Would you mind including me in on the joke?" she asked, frowning and growing increasingly annoyed. She hadn't decided yet if she liked Eric Warren.

"If it makes you feel better, my wife is like that too," he said. "She's one of those 'I don't need a man' types and she would never admit that she has me around because she *does* need me for some things."

"Like what, taking out the trash?" Breck added with a hint of sarcasm in her voice.

"Oh, that's hitting below the belt," he growled. "But I can take it. I sense that you can hold your own. That will be important, since we're working together."

Breck nodded at somehow getting his approval for standing up to him.

"I can be frank with you," he added. "That's important because I speak my mind."

"So do I, and I hope you're not offended by a woman challenging you."

"Bring it on."

Breck cleared her throat before she continued. "I don't agree that a woman needs a man. I can afford to buy my own car and my own house, and I have my own money in the bank. I don't need a man to support me." She pulled her shoulders back in pride. In contrast to what most men said about women with their excess baggage, she didn't come with any baggage at all. She didn't have any children or "baby-mommy" drama to speak of either. "I think it's the ultimate male ego that assumes a woman needs a man to be her protector, provider, and savior, when in reality many successful women in our era are not married, but a majority of successful men are."

"Oh, I agree with you. If I were to drop off the face of the earth tomorrow, my wife would be just fine, and I love that about her, but I think you've got me all wrong. Women like you and my wife need a certain kind of man, and money has nothing to do with it. My wife didn't need me to be a protector or to support her. She already had that going on, and you're the same way."

"You seem to know a lot about this," Breck said, settling easily into her chair. It intrigued her to be having this conversation with him. Was this the prologue to a friendship?

"I learned the hard way."

Breck snickered. "I can't believe we're talking about this. Aren't we supposed to be going over a contract?"

"I supposed so, but I get the feeling this is going to be a good working relationship."

Breck paused, and her mind went quickly to Quentin. She wondered about the appropriateness of discussing her personal relationship, but they had already crossed that line. "I believe that is the problem with my boyfriend," she said.

"What is?"

"He wants to do more for me than I need him to do. Most of what he wants to do involves money, and I don't need that from him, so he's lost as to what to do."

"How old are you?"

"Twenty-six," she answered.

"You're just getting started," he joked. "The things you need most from your boyfriend are the things money can't buy, including the reason you may have a little device in your dresser drawer."

Breck's mouth almost dropped to the floor. Did he just say what she thought he just said? He was bold. He had to be to make a comment like that and know that she wouldn't curse him out and hang up the phone. He had crossed the line of obnoxious, and her opinion of him nose-dived.

"I don't believe I like what you just said, Mr. Warren," she huffed. In fact, she more than didn't like what he had just said. If it weren't for the numbers on that contract, she would have cursed his ass out and then told him to go to hell. "And also, let me educate you on something," Breck said. Her voice rose an octave as she sat on the edge of her chair. She couldn't let him get away with making a statement like that even if it was risking their working relationship. The more she thought about it, the more pissed she got. He didn't have the right to make a blanket comment like that, and he needed to be corrected. "Women use those little devices whether they have a man in their life to please them or not. A woman who uses them knows exactly how to please herself and doesn't have to wait on a man or anyone to do it for her."

He was quiet, and Breck prepared for him to cancel everything and bid her good riddance. Working with an asshole was one thing, but she didn't have to put up with blatant disrespect. "I apologize if I offended you, and I stand corrected," he said. Breck folded her arms across her chest and took several deep breaths to calm down. "If you'll allow me to redeem myself, I would say, like my wife, it'll take a certain kind of man to satisfy you, and it won't be based upon how much money he makes because you don't need that. Let me put it this way." He paused and thought. "Do you bicycle?"

Breck squinted. Where was he going with this conversation? "Bicycle?"

"Yes. Do you ride a bike?"

"No."

"Do you do any form of exercise? You don't strike me as being a loafer."

She rolled her eyes. "I jog every morning," she answered.

"With your boyfriend?"

"No."

"Why not?"

"Because he doesn't live with me."

"What does that have to do with it? When you go to the movies, whom do you go with?"

"My boyfriend."

"But he doesn't live with you."

Breck threw her hands in the air, more confused now than ever. "I have no idea where you're going with this."

"The man you need in your life is one with whom you'll be able to do the things that don't involve money. If you jog, he should jog alongside you. If you bicycle, he should be riding with you. There must be something that will solidify the relationship other than financial security. The security you'll need from him is to just know that he's in your world and you're in his. Your passions will be mutual, and you will have happiness."

"Have you accomplished that with your wife?"

"Not entirely. I'm one hundred percent a part of her world, but she's still trying to figure out mine. A lot of it has to do with discovering who you are. She knows exactly who she is and what she wants, but I'm still learning."

Whoa. Breck flinched. That was a powerful statement, and one she never expected to hear from him. He was Eric Warren, one of the most successful African-American men in America. Of course he knew who he was. How could he become so successful not knowing who he was? And why would he tell her that? Breck shook her head, deciding that she would rather forget this conversation had ever happened. She didn't understand the meaning of it and couldn't explain why he felt compelled to lecture her on what type of man she needed. Even her mother didn't do that.

He chatted more, and Breck glanced at the clock again. They'd been talking for three hours. Breck blinked, then looked at her watch to make sure she was reading the time correctly. She was. Yet she settled back into her chair, switched the phone from one ear to the other, and let him keep talking. He spoke in great depth about how his wife didn't understand this philosophy either. Yet he spoke very favorably of his wife, which Breck appreciated. She hated talking negatively with her male friends about their girlfriends or wives, particularly if she was expected to entertain them one day. How could she sit in that woman's face knowing that her man had verbally slammed her a few days ago? Whenever any conversation threatened to go that way, she immediately changed the subject. But Eric wasn't doing that. He was obviously very much in love with his wife and their son.

Breck asked him about Boston and Mansfield, where the center would be built. Once he began talking about Mansfield, getting him to stop was damn near impossible. Breck immediately sensed Mansfield was his passion. She'd never heard anyone speak so fondly of a place before, and she herself had never felt zealous about any place. Breck liked Indianapolis, but she didn't know if she loved it. She had been born and raised there and had attended a local college for financial reasons, but she had demanded that she live on campus—she needed to at least feel like she was in college. There was nothing about Indianapolis that she felt so passionate about that it would prevent her from relocating. She had never made Indianapolis into her way of life. It was simply where she lived. But for Eric, Boston was a place of domicile, while Mansfield was where his heart was. "When I'm in Mansfield, I belong," he said.

Breck was intrigued. She settled into her chair and smiled at his stories. The more he talked, the more she wanted to know about him. He offered her a glimpse of his life that she had never expected to see and never thought she would be interested in. But she was. She longed to experience a connection to a place and call it home.

"If I'm boring you, just say so," he said, perhaps noticing that she had remained quiet for longer than a minute.

"I'm not bored," she said with a giggle. "I'm enjoying this conversation. I am a bit confused though. If you feel so passionately about Mansfield, why don't you live there?"

A deathly silence fell between them, and Breck knew she had hit a nerve.

"Do you always work on Friday night?" he asked.

Breck was startled. He'd completely blown her off. She cleared her throat, deciding not to revisit the question. "Well, I had plans, but *somebody* chose to have a conference call."

"You should have said something. I would have picked another day."

"Yeah, right," Breck said with a sarcastic tone.

"No, I'm serious. If I interfere with your family, let me know and I will reschedule. My family comes first with me, so I'll respect it if you have other plans."

"Thanks, but Quentin isn't exactly family, yet."

"If you think about what I said, he might be."

"I haven't decided if I want him to be," she countered.

"How long have you been dating? If you don't mind me asking."

He didn't answer her question, so why should she answer his? she thought, but she decided not to challenge him. "Eight months."

"And you don't know if you would want to marry him or not? If you don't know by now, then the answer is no."

"I resent that. My career is very important to me, and that's my priority. How long did it take you to know you wanted to marry your wife?"

"A month."

"A month!" Breck yelled. "And how long have you been married?"

"Four years."

Four years was a fair amount of time to be married to someone you knew for only a month, but Breck's rationale wouldn't allow her to accept it as ideal. "A month is not enough time. How did you meet her?" She was curious for some reason. She wanted to know if it was a whirlwind romance that had somehow persevered. She loved those types of stories. Quentin had been a blind date that went right.

"On a flight to Brazil," he answered. "I was going there on business to check out some property in Rio de Janeiro, and she was going to collect art for her gallery. We ended up at her family home."

"Wow, that was fast."

"It turned out that she's from Brazil, but her parents were living in New York and both worked for the

United Nations. She opened a gallery in Boston that sells exotic art, and she travels abroad quite frequently. She gave me an extensive tour of Rio while we were there, and we stayed at her parents' estate."

"So you married royalty."

Eric laughed. "In a sense, I guess you could say that."

"I suppose the boy from Mansfield, Massachusetts, was pretty overwhelmed by it all."

"Perhaps, but she's pretty incredible."

"I'm sure." Breck envisioned the tropical prize Eric Warren went home to every night. "I've always wanted to go to Brazil, but I haven't made it there yet," Breck said.

"Oh, you should." That opened another extensive monologue from Eric. When Breck looked at her watch again, she bolted straight up.

"Oh, shit!" she exclaimed.

"What is it?"

"It's past midnight."

A few seconds of silence followed as he drew in a deep breath. "It's after one here. I can't believe I let time slip away like that."

"You mean your wife let you work this late?" Breck asked, mimicking his earlier remark to her.

"Are you kidding? She yells like hell at me."

Breck laughed.

"Hey," he said. "I've kept you long enough. Please, be careful driving home, and we'll talk soon."

Breck smiled, pleased that he expressed concern. "Thank you. I look forward to talking to you again. Now, get home so your wife can stop using the devices she has in her dresser drawer."

"I deserved that," he admitted. "I'll talk to you later."

Breck hung up and stared at the telephone. What an unexpectedly pleasant and incredible conversation! She sighed. She had placed him on a proverbial pedestal based solely upon what she had read and heard about him from colleagues. A successful businessman with enormous clout in the business community who had the potential of providing her firm the type of breakout success she had longed for. Her thoughts about Eric Warren had been only of what he could do for her firm. She had never expected to find a friend in him, which is exactly what she had just found. Yes, Eric Warren was a successful businessman, but at this moment he was unlike any other man she had ever met. He was human, and she had never expected him to let her see that. She should never have put him on a pedestal to begin with.

As she drove home, she wondered what would happen at the Warren household when Eric walked through the door at two in the morning. Would his wife throw a hissy fit and start shouting obscenities and accuse him of having an affair, or would she lovingly accept that her hardworking husband had late nights at the office and it was just the nature of things? How would she handle it and what would she think if she and Quentin lived together and he came home at two in morning, saying he'd been stuck at the office? Tonight definitely proved that it could happen.

She suddenly felt a pang of envy toward Eric's wife but immediately shook it off. Quentin wasn't such a bad catch either. He wasn't a multimillionaire, but he showered her with sentimental gifts for no reason at all, took her to all the concerts and plays that came to town and to the best restaurants. He had a desk job, but he made sure he kept his gym membership active and he used it often. When he spent the night with her, she loved throwing her arms around him and feeling the hard muscles in his chest. Quentin pleased her sexually. Breck could never pinpoint what it was that was missing from their relationship, so she could never try to correct it.

She pulled up along the steel gate outside her building and fetched the pass card from the glove compartment.

She watched the gate slowly rise high enough for her Volkswagen to glide through. Once she was past, the gate quickly began to close again. She always kept an eye in her rearview mirror to make sure no one slipped in after her. It happened rarely, but often enough for her to pay attention.

Home for Breck was a stylish condo in a once-abandoned building in downtown Indianapolis. The building had been saved from the wrecking ball by an imaginative real estate developer not unlike Eric and Stephen. He'd converted the eyesore into a beautiful brick haven for people like her—professionals with no children who wanted a quick commute to a downtown office without having to battle the overpopulated highway. There were eight floors, each with two spacious units. Naturally, the top floor was the most expensive because of the view of downtown and access to the roof, on which the owner had installed a hot tub. For Independence Day and any other celebration that warranted fireworks, he always invited everyone in the building to a roof party. Breck and Chi had made it a part of their annual social calendars. Breck lived on the sixth floor. Her neighbor was a female physician who was always on call and seldom home.

Tonight she rode the freight elevator to her floor with thoughts of Quentin still heavy on her mind, remembering the last time she'd spent the night at his house.

She stepped into her unit and took her shoes off at the door, as usual. The old concrete floors had been replaced with expensive hardwood that she kept well buffed. She'd learned that no matter how carefully you walked, high heels always left some type of scratch on the glossy finish.

Although she loved the convenient location, she'd really bought the unit because of the space and lack of walls; the only walls in the unit separated the two bedrooms and one and a half baths from the rest of the unit. Walls were confining and Breck hated confinement. Along a far wall was an area she designated her home office, equipped with everything she had at the office. On any given morning she could choose to stay home and still be able to put in hours of work. Having a separate office served dual purposes: it gave her clients the sense of dealing with a real business and not just a person, and it gave her something to look forward to, a means for her to get out of the house. If she didn't have the office to go to, she doubted she would ever leave her condo.

She walked through the living area toward her office, leafing through a barrage of mail. Most of it was catalogs and other junk. The electric bill and credit card statement were the only two pieces worth opening. She looked at the bills, then dropped them on the desk and reached for the remote control for her CD player. Beginning her nightly ritual of relaxation to the sound of Mozart's *The Marriage of Figaro* over the speakers, she took an opened bottle of Chardonnay from the refrigerator and filled a single wineglass. She glanced at the telephone and saw the message light blinking. It was probably Quentin, calling to check up on her. She decided not to listen to the message until morning, then grabbed her glass and headed to the bedroom.

FOUR

THE ALARM went off at six o'clock as usual Saturday morning, but Breck turned over and slapped it off instead of hitting the snooze button. When she finally decided to crawl out of bed, it was well into the afternoon.

She staggered into the bathroom, where she splashed her face with water and brushed her teeth. With ideas for the convention center fresh in her mind, Breck quickly slipped into a pair of shorts and a T-shirt and changed the music from classical to jazz. She sat down at the drafting board and started working. The afternoon sun shone bright enough that she didn't need to turn on the lamp over the drafting board. As her pencil slid across the paper, she could still hear Eric's voice. She wondered if he had gotten into "trouble" for coming in so late. She fought the urge to call his office to see if he was such a hard worker that he went in on a Saturday morning, and to find out what excuse he had given his wife about his late arrival home.

But then she realized that there was no reason for him to make up an excuse. He was at the office, even though their conversation had drifted beyond that of work. Why was that, anyway? she wondered. He had been cordial with her, friendly even, and she had not expected either. Surely Eric Warren hadn't become a successful businessman by telling his female clients they needed a man who could be just as assertive as she. She grunted. He'd had a lot of nerve telling her that. How did she know she wouldn't take offense and tell him to go to hell? Then she really laughed. Of course he knew she wouldn't do that. The numbers on the contract told him so.

Breck's weekend continued the same way it began: with her sitting at her drafting board. Her only connection with civilization was on Sunday evening, when Chi and her date stopped by to bring her a dinner of lemon chicken Alfredo and garlic sticks. Breck opened another bottle of wine to share with her guests.

The moment Chi and Kris walked in the door Breck started talking about Eric and couldn't stop. She told Chi almost everything they had discussed, and not once did she mention the contract.

"He's married, Breck," Chi said as she placed her wineglass on the cocktail table.

Breck looked at her, puzzled. "What does that have to do with anything? I was just saying—"

"I hear what you're saying. Do *you* hear what she's saying?" she asked Kris, giving her a nudge.

"I hear her loud and clear," Kris said, sitting back against Chi's outstretched arm.

Breck settled into the soft upholstered chair with her legs crossed in front of her. "Well, you guys want to let me in on the secret?"

"You have a crush on him," Chi teased.

"Yup, I hear it too," Kris added.

"What?!" Nervously, Breck tossed her hair from her face.

"Oh, what a tangled web—" Chi sang until Breck cut her off.

"Don't you even think about going there!" Breck screamed. "You're both crazies. I do not have a crush on Eric Warren. I have a boyfriend, remember?"

"A boyfriend you don't love," Chi added.

"But a boyfriend nonetheless."

Chi pressed on. "Is Eric flirting with you too?"

"No one is flirting with anyone," Breck said, trying to sound annoyed. But a knot had developed in her stomach. "Eric and I had one conversation. That's all."

"And how long did you talk?"

"That's not important."

"How long?"

Breck pretended to count, but she knew how long they had talked because she was amazed by it herself. "Four hours," she said, and rolled her eyes.

"A four-hour conversation with a man you have no interest in?"

"It was a very interesting conversation, that's all," Breck said, her voice rising in annoyance.

"You're pretty sensitive about this. You do have a crush on him."

"Get off it." Breck stood and walked to the refrigerator for nothing in particular but grabbed another bottle of wine.

"It's okay to have a crush on him!" Chi yelled to her. "Just don't let it get out of control."

"I don't have a crush on him." She popped the cork and poured only herself a glass of wine.

"It is kind of exciting, isn't it?" Chi said, walking toward the kitchen. She got glasses for herself and Kris. "A powerful man flirting with you has got to turn you on. Maybe even empower you." She nudged Breck's arm.

"I wish you would just leave this alone." Breck was not at all comfortable with the idea of being turned on by a married man, no matter how powerful he was.

"Okay, I'll leave it alone," Chi said, pouring two glasses of wine. "But I'm not wrong. You do have a crush on him and nothing's wrong with it. Just leave it at that." She rejoined Kris on the sofa.

ALL WEEK Breck stared at the phone, resisting the urge to call Eric. She knew he was out of town, but she didn't know for how long. He could be back now, and she had a perfectly good reason to phone him. She could very well update him on her progress, but he would not be expecting her call. What if he felt she was coming on to him? He would fire her and cancel the contract.

Why would she even care about all that? She called other clients all the time, and it was never a problem. She asked questions and updated them on her progress. Eric Warren was no different. After all, she did get the contract today, certified mail, just as he promised. He would want to know that.

Oh, no, she thought. What if Chi and Kris were right? It couldn't be possible. She'd never even met the man. For all she knew he was five feet tall, 300 pounds, and flat-footed.

She giggled. If that were the case, Breck doubted he would have nabbed a Brazilian princess. Unless, of course, his wife was four-eleven and weighed 350. Breck laughed softly at her own warped humor.

"Breck, you have a call," Chi said, peeking into her office. "It's Eric."

Breck wiped the smile off her face and cleared her throat before answering. "This is Breck," she said with nervous excitement.

"Good afternoon, Ms. Larson." Breck loved his voice. She held her breath.

"Eric, I wasn't expecting your call today," she said, then felt guilty that she had thought so much about him.

"I've been thinking about you since our conversation last Friday," he said, and her heart pounded hard in her chest.

"Oh, really?" She wanted to sound aloof but doubted she had pulled it off. What about their conversation? she quickly wondered. Was he going to say it had been inappropriate and they should stick to business? Her pulse quickened in anticipation.

"I've never had a conversation like that with a business associate, so I hope I didn't say anything to offend you too much."

Breck released the breath she held in her chest and smiled, realizing that she had been in his thoughts as he had been in hers. "Not at all. Actually I've been giving some thought to some of what you said."

"Oh?"

"Besides the fact that I think you're full of shit . . ." His laughter widened her smile, and a warmth came over her that she had never felt with anyone, especially a client. "I think men have a certain insecurity about being with women who don't need men to take care of them."

"And you think that's my problem?" he asked.

"Along with most of the male species, yes, I do."

"Species?"

"Yes," she said. "Men are a totally different fucking species."

He laughed, then quickly added, "I'm really sorry I didn't get the chance to meet you when you were in Boston."

At that moment Breck wished she were standing face-to-face with him. She would love to see his expression, and a small part of her wanted to reach her hand out and touch him. She shrugged off that thought. "So am I. You left me with that partner of yours." She squeezed her eyes shut, realizing that she might have become too relaxed with Eric. It might not be quite time for her to bash the other half of the business entity that would sign her check. "I'm sorry," she apologized. "That was way out of line."

"It's quite all right. It's the reaction most people have to Stephen. He lives for this business. His focus is not people or socializing, unless it's to advance the business. This project does not satisfy that criteria."

·

Breck settled into her chair and kicked off her shoes. One of them hit the desk with a thump that resounded throughout the room.

"What was that?"

"My shoes. I hate shoes and I take them off at every opportunity."

"You walk around your office with your shoes off?"

"Well, I hate shoes and there's no one here but Chi and I."

"My secretary is such a straight arrow she would never dream of it. I kid you not, Breck. This woman wears two-inch heels every day for eight to ten hours."

He had said her name and there was a sweet tone to it that Breck hadn't heard before. She had always criticized her mother for giving her such a masculine name, but coming from Eric, it suddenly made her feel very feminine and sexy.

"I know. She wore them when she took me to the site." She settled into the conversation, switching hands when the hand she held the phone with began to sweat. "Chi is a supermodel in training, so she does the whole nine-to-five dress-up thing too. It really wouldn't matter because the woman could wear a bag over her head and she would still look good."

"I know what you mean. My wife is like that." His wife. Breck straightened up in her seat, realizing she had gotten too comfortable with the conversation again. Not only was he an important client, but he was also married and making no attempt to conceal it. The conversation was friendly, and she needed to keep it that way. He was not flirting with her. She imagined Eric's wife, a tropical goddess in flowery garb standing on the white beaches of Brazil, her golden, flowing hair swept up by the wind caressing her smooth, glistening skin. Eric was still talking when her attention returned to the conversation. "She wears the best clothes and shoes. I understand in her business she has to be very well dressed, but I couldn't begin to tell you how many suits and dresses she owns, and she has at least two pairs of shoes for each."

"Oh, but come now, Eric, you know how we women are when it comes to our shoes."

"Don't remind me."

"What about your son?"

"Darius?" he asked.

"Yes. What is he into?" she asked, eager to drink in information about Eric's life. The more he told her, the more she wanted to know.

"He's only three. The only thing that's important to him is whether or not I put enough jelly on his sandwich." Breck burst into a round of laughter that made her face hurt. "He says, 'Dadda, mo' jellry, mo' jellry.' "

Breck laughed even harder and pounded her hand across the table. "Okay, okay, okay. You're going to make me wet my pants." She wasn't sure if it was what he had said that was so funny or the fact that it was coming from him. His jokes were funny, but she doubted she'd be so tickled if they came from someone else. She was drawn to him and she couldn't explain why. Was it the fact that he was a successful man but still made a feeble attempt to amuse? Or that he spoke so eloquently of his family and his passion for the neighborhood he grew up in? Whatever it was, she was getting sucked in and she made no effort to pull back from it.

That's it, that's what's missing with Quentin, Breck thought. It's that indescribable feeling you get when you're with that person you really want to be with and you feel it in your stomach. Your stomach gets tight, your heart beats a little faster, and no matter how hard you try, you can't keep that smile off your face when you take that first look at them. That was what she didn't feel when she was with Quentin. Why was she feeling it now?

Tears streamed down her face and her stomach began to hurt because she couldn't stop laughing. Then she finally asked the burning question. "So tell me, what did your wife say when you walked in the house at two in the morning?" What was Eric's relationship with his wife that he didn't mind staying at the office until two in the morning instead of rushing home and crawling into bed beside his princess?

"She's okay with it," he replied. "She knows I love what I do."

"I love the way she decorated your office."

"You saw my office?"

"Yes, when I was in Boston. Your walls are adorned with what I assume are Darius's masterpieces."

"You're right, and I'm looking at them now. The paintings were my idea. She did Stephen's office as well."

Breck leaned forward and sighed. "You're pretty amazing, you know that?" she said, before she realized she had spoken aloud. She sat back in her chair and tried to think of some way out of the hole she had just dug. "I love the way you talk about your family." She was trying desperately to kill any thought that she was coming on to him. "I've never heard a man talk about his family the way you do. How old are you?"

"Thirty-six."

She gasped. "You're pretty young."

"What, you thought I was an old man?"

"No, but I thought you were older. What do you do when you're not working? If you're ever not working, that is." Eric chuckled, but she interrupted him before he could answer. "No, let me guess. You shoot a couple of rounds on the green with Stephen, your lawyer, and some political bigwig in Boston. All of this testosterone then sits around the clubhouse smoking cigars while talking about lucrative portfolios or the latest downturn in the market."

He snorted. "I don't think so."

"How close was I?"

"Far off, young lady! First of all, I hate golf. It's the most boring game I've ever played. I prefer the home-court advantage at the neighborhood playground where I meet Martin, Brian, and a couple of other regulars to shoot some hoop with my boys from the office."

"No way! You shoot hoop?"

"Breck, I'm six-five. I better be able to hold my own on the court."

Breck closed her eyes, letting the puzzle piece fall into place. An image of Eric Warren was being formed. The five-feet, three-hundred-pound stubby man was eradicated.

"You thought I was some stuffy office chicken shit," he taunted. "Admit it." Her mind had been far off the mark, putting together every inch of him, possibly making him into a much more formidable creature than he really was.

"Well—"

"Not!" he screamed.

Breck giggled. "Okay, you got me."

"Despite what I'm worth right now, I wasn't born with a silver spoon in my mouth, Breck. My mother raised three children alone in one of the worst parts of Massachusetts. I was the oldest. When my father left, I couldn't finish high school because I had to work to help my mother, my sister, and my brother. When I was eighteen, I got a general equivalency degree—as in GED."

"This was in Mansfield?" she asked, getting more and more sucked in by his story.

"Yes. Martin, Brian, and I hung out at the park shooting baskets until it was too late to see the ball. None of us were ever in a rush to go home because there wasn't anything waiting for us except a television depicting programs of how life should be outside of Mansfield. We would look at those shows and the white families sitting at dinner tables in beautiful suburban homes with both parents. Moms stayed at home, dads worked, big brother went off to college, little sister was captain of the cheerleading squad, and you're riding your bike to Little League practice or finishing up a paper route. Perfect American life, according to Hollywood, and our lives were far from it.

"In my family, I was the big brother who walked little sister home to keep the boys on the corner from turning her into the next neighborhood trick, and my little brother had to start bagging groceries because he didn't grow as fast as big brother and all the hand-me-downs were too big. The basketball court was the neighborhood refuge."

Breck sat speechless. What could she say? His life was nothing less than extraordinary, a story of perseverance and determination pushed to the maximum.

Her silence must have given him the incentive to continue. "Martin and Brian went to work for a local construction company after graduating high school," he said. "I studied for my GED, then went on to college and double-majored in business and finance. I met Stephen at the University of Massachusetts, and we basically stumbled into this business. That is my story, Breck Larson."

She definitely had misunderstood Eric Warren. He was just one of the guys, she realized, but instead of sitting back and griping about the hand that was dealt him, he had done something with it. She had always believed that there comes a time in your life when you have to make your own luck and decide your own destiny, and Eric was proof of that. She thought of how she had gotten her first assignment. It wasn't given to her—she took it. Sometimes you have to do that. "I'm speechless," she finally said. "I had no idea."

"Not many people do. Now you know why this center is very important to me. It's personal, and it doesn't matter what anyone else thinks."

"And what will the center bring to Mansfield?" she asked.

"Culture and a sense of being. When people go to conventions there, they'll see how far Mansfield has come. It's a great, rising community that doesn't deserve to be hidden away any longer."

A stirring inside her made Breck shiver. She paused for fear her voice would crack if she dared try to speak too soon. "You must think I'm awful." She spoke in a low voice, ashamed that she'd depicted him as self-centered, which clearly he was far from being.

"Why would I think that?"

"Because I had you tagged all wrong."

"It's not the first time. Most people think success means getting as far away from your roots as possible. A sign of arrival is to be able to buy the biggest house on the hill or drive the most expensive car on the market. But in reality you've really made it when you can go back to where you came from and make it better for those who are still there."

Breck thought about what she had done to give back to the community or to her parents for helping her "make it." Her mother had taken a job at a local private school, working in the kitchen so that Breck, her sister, and her brother could attend the school for free. If her family had to pay tuition, she wouldn't have been able to go, and she would never have met her art teacher and mentor, Mr. Bryant. It was Mr. Bryant who had discovered her creative abilities and pushed her to take classes at the community center and major in architecture in college. Breck wondered if she had ever thanked her mother or Mr. Bryant. "You sound like a saint," she said to Eric.

"I am far from a saint. We go out, dance, and probably have more beers than we should." He laughed, "My wife hates it when I hang out with those guys because the 'hood comes out in me."

"You dance?"

"Yes, I dance, and damn it, I am good," he boasted. Breck visualized him sticking his chest out.

"I know you can't outdance me on the dance floor."

"Hell, Breck, you're twenty-six years old. I'm not going to try."

This started a fresh round of laughter, and once again Breck was doubled over her desk holding her stomach. She had never met anyone who made her laugh so much.

"Listen, Breck, I have to get my ass home before Gaby has a fit."

Gaby. His wife's name was Gaby. How cute.

"Okay. Thanks, Eric, for the conversation. I really enjoyed it."

"Likewise. I think we can be friends, Breck," he said, then paused. "Well, if you're working late tomorrow night, give me a call. Gaby and Darius are visiting her parents on Long Island, so I'm coming in to work."

Breck's heart skipped. Eric wanted to talk with her. She didn't know how to respond or how she was supposed to feel about it. He was a married man and seemingly very happy. She knew he wasn't making a pass at her, but she was intrigued by the thought of talking with him again. Gaby will be away and he'll be lonely. There was nothing wrong with talking with a friend, she thought. So why was her heart beating so fast and a cloud of guilt hanging over her? These feelings she was having were not safe, and she knew it. She was thinking about him too much.

"Okay, I will do that," she said.

"Night, Breck. Be safe."

She smiled. "I will. Good night."

She couldn't sit at her desk any longer. She got into her car and let her mind wander from Eric to Quentin and back to Eric. All she thought about was his voice, his laughter, him on a basketball court going out for a layup or a dunk. Could he dunk? At six-five, he probably could. She thought about how his arms would look in his basketball jersey, strong biceps developed at a gym or by tossing a basketball in the air. What about his legs? Were they scrawny legs, or did he have developed quadriceps and hamstrings that bulged beneath his shorts?

Breck rested her head on the tan leather seat and took a deep breath. "Stop it, Breck, he's married," she said, pressing her palm against her forehead. "Don't think about him like that. He's a business associate." She put the key into the ignition and drove off.

The sound of Kenny G filled the car as she cruised down the road. The smoothness of the sweet saxophone was the perfect background to the drive and matched her mellowing mood. The window was down, and the warm air lifted her hair. She pressed the back of her head against the headrest and let the breeze cool the sticky moisture in her cleavage.

She reached over to the empty seat and picked up her cell phone. "Call Quentin," she said into the phone, and the voice-activated speed dial took over the job.

"Hello." His virile voice was exactly what she needed to hear.

"Hi, it's me," she said. "Are you busy?"

"No, just going over some papers for next week." By day, Quentin was a successful agent for several professional athletes and entertainers. He had graduated from law school, but instead of practicing, he used his skills to negotiate multimillion-dollar contracts.

"Feel like some company?" Breck cradled the phone in her hand as she carefully maneuvered in the traffic. When she left her office, her intention had been not to go home.

"Sure, come on over." Quentin had never turned her down in the past, and she hadn't thought he would this time either.

"I'll be there in fifteen minutes." Breck tossed the phone onto the seat. After picking up a bottle of their favorite wine, she rounded his circular drive, pulled up neatly beside his white Mercedes sedan, walked swiftly to the front door of his house, and rang the doorbell. Quentin had offered her a key many times, but each time she turned him down. Having a key to his home would force her to relinquish a set of keys to her place, and she feared that would thrust the relationship toward a serious commitment that she was not sure she wanted. The thought of it was suffocating.

Quentin rushed to the door, bare-chested and wearing a pair of worn jeans. Without giving him much of a chance to say anything, Breck walked into his arms, the bottle of wine still in her hand, and kissed him hard on the lips. She set the wine on his letter desk as they backed into the house with their lips still locked.

He lifted her skirt, and pulled the delicate lace panties from around her hips and dropped them to the floor, returning his fingers to the moisture between her legs. She wrapped one of her legs around his waist while he fumbled with the buttons on her shirt. Her shirt fell to the floor while he moved her bra aside and cupped one breast in his hand. She moaned while his tongue found her tongue and his lips covered hers. He freed the bra and it too fell to the floor. Then he lifted her in his arms, her legs wrapped around his waist, and carried her, holding her by her thighs, to the bedroom. The only clothing that remained on her was the skirt gathered at her waist. He planted her on the bed and she quickly wriggled out of it while he slipped out of his jeans.

When he entered her, she gasped, and for that moment, all thoughts of Eric disappeared.

FIVE

BRECK AWOKE the next morning and rolled over to find Quentin still fast asleep. After their first round of lovemaking, he had fetched the bottle of wine she had brought with her and they sat on his terrace and drank the entire bottle.

"Quite some mood you were in," he said, tipping the bottle to refill her glass for the second time.

"It's been a long week." Breck inhaled deeply, then tossed her head back and looked up at the stars sprinkled across the sky.

"How's the Boston deal coming?"

Her heart jolted while she returned her gaze to him and took a quick sip from her glass. "It's coming along very well. Eric Warren is a very nice man. Easy to work with." Thinking about Eric unnerved her. It would have been easy for her to tell Quentin that she and Eric had really hit it off, but she was afraid her enthusiasm would betray her and Quentin would see what Chi and Kris had seen.

"Good. I'm glad it worked out for you." Then he immediately began to fill her in on the deal he was pursuing with a college football player about to enter the NFL draft.

"Quentin, I've been thinking about joining your gym," she said, circling the rim of her glass with her finger. "I want to add some weight training to my exercise program. Perhaps I can go with you sometimes." She had been thinking a lot about what Eric had said. Besides their nights out and sex, she and Quentin didn't share much.

"I think that'll be great."

"Yeah?" she said, getting excited that he was receptive to the idea.

"I think it's great for you to join, but I have a pretty rigid workout, Breck."

"Well, I won't do what you're doing but maybe buddy up with you a few times so that you can show me what to do."

"Your body is fine. You don't need to build muscle."

"I have no strength at all. My endurance is great, but I want to be stronger." She flexed her biceps.

Quentin shook his head. "For what, lifting your pencils?" Breck dropped her arm and stared wide-eyed at him. "They have aerobics and yoga classes you could join," Quentin continued. "You don't need to lift weights."

"The idea, Quentin, is to work out with you."

"If you work out with me, it'll slow me down."

She rolled her eyes in frustration. "Never mind," she said, and tried to shake off her agitation. When the wine bottle was emptied, they returned to his bedroom for more lovemaking until they both passed out from exhaustion.

Now Quentin's hairy chest was exposed while the rest of his body was hidden underneath the sheets. She slid out of bed, grabbed his housecoat, draped it around her, and tiptoed out of the bedroom. She needed caffeine.

The love of strong, real coffee at the start of the day was one thing she and Quentin shared. It was probably their only common interest. She liked mornings, while Quentin was at his best at night. Her wind-down music was jazz and classical. Quentin turned up the volume whenever the latest hip-hop song came across the airwaves. He told her she needed to loosen up a little, but she felt she was loose enough. He never made her laugh so hard that her stomach ached, and she never gazed at the phone, anticipating his call. Being with him made her feel good for the moment. Their lovemaking was good, but when she was home she seldom missed him. With Quentin in her life, she was secured only against being alone.

While the coffee brewed, she slipped into the bathroom, took off the robe, and stepped into the shower. When she closed her eyes, her mind immediately went to Eric, and as she smoothed the soft, creamy lather over her body, she imagined Eric's hand circling her breasts while he planted small kisses on her neck. She quickly opened her eyes, the water beating heavily against her skin. Where had *that* thought come from?

Steam filled the bathroom before she turned the water off and stepped from the shower. She stood in front of the mirror and wiped the moisture from it so she could get a look at herself.

"You're falling for him," she mumbled, then dropped her head and inhaled deeply. She thought spending the night with Quentin would rid her mind of arousing thoughts of Eric, but it had failed. She pulled the robe off the hook behind the door and slipped it on.

The smell of coffee was in the air. "Ah, morning," she said, taking a deep breath. How could he sleep through that aroma? She inched around the room, grabbed an extra-large T-shirt from his dresser drawer, slipped it over her head, then returned to the kitchen to pour herself a cup of coffee. Breck grabbed a large, colorful ceramic mug from the cabinet and filled it, leaving enough room for sugar and cream. She took her first sip of the day standing in the kitchen with her eyes closed, then she sighed and walked through the living room to Quentin's office on the opposite side of the house. Careful not to make too much noise, she turned on the computer and sat down at his desk waiting for the machine to boot up. The loud-awakening sound of Windows coming to life echoed in the room. She'd forgotten to check the volume on his computer. She looked up to see if Quentin would emerge from the bedroom. He did not.

She accessed his Internet connection and typed in the URL of her online financial account. Checking the performance of her stock portfolio was a morning ritual. During the week she checked hot stories in *The Wall Street Journal* to see if she needed to place a sell order on anything she currently owned or a buy order from her watch list.

For a single woman her age, Breck had quite a hefty portfolio. She had first learned about investing from an old banker boyfriend. Once she had gotten over her initial fear of the stock market, she invested her first thousand dollars, which doubled within three months. After that she was hooked. To get a better understanding of when to buy, when to sell, and when to just watch market trends, she signed up for personal-investment seminars and listened to the men who sat around their lunch table at work watching CNBC. After a few months she was sitting at the table with them.

Twenty percent of her investments were in individual stocks, which she knew she had to watch most closely. Even though she didn't care much for mutual funds—she found them boring—she still kept the balance of her investments in one for safekeeping. She didn't watch it as frequently because she never saw enough gain or loss to warrant it. Most of her stock picks were in technology and biotechnology.

As she surfed through various accounts, she heard Quentin walking across the carpet toward the kitchen. She smiled. The smell of coffee was nature's only true alarm.

"Morning!" she yelled, and returned her attention to the computer.

"Morning," Quentin yelled back from the kitchen. "You're up early. Did you go running this morning?" He walked into the office with a mug in his hand.

"It's not that early but I didn't run this morning. I'll go if you go."

He snickered. "I don't think so."

Breck didn't think he would oblige. He never did. She continued to look at the computer screen and click the mouse.

"I guess you didn't need the exercise." He walked behind her and kissed her gently on the temple. "What are you working on?" he asked, looking over her shoulder.

"Checking my performance from Friday." She scribbled notes on a piece of paper as she read headline news about her stocks. Quentin lifted a lock of her hair and kissed the back of her neck as she wrote. Another thought of Eric flashed across her mind, and she tensed.

"That's your portfolio?" Quentin asked, edging away from her.

"Yeah."

"Impressive." He leaned into the computer. "Risky business."

"I know."

"Not good." He walked away from the computer and adjusted the blinds to allow the emerging sun to creep through the window.

"I'm aware of the risk." Breck had gone over this before with most of the men who sat at the lunchroom table. They swore she was insane to put her money into anything technology-driven. "I've created a dummy portfolio, and I've been watching some of these companies for months, waiting for the right time to get in," Breck said as she wrote feverishly on the notepad. "Like this one." She pointed to the computer, even though Quentin had opted to sit in the recliner and look at her rather than the computer screen. "The price is right and I'll be crazy not to get in right now."

"That may be true, but the market is extremely unstable. Everybody knows that. You should go into real estate or invest in mutual or government bonds." It was Breck's turn to snicker as she continued to point, click, and write. "I can help you get a safer portfolio and introduce you to a Realtor friend of mine," Quentin offered. Breck heard him but did not respond. "Breck."

She finally looked up.

"I can help you get your portfolio set up the way it should be."

Breck smiled. "Quentin, there's nothing wrong with my portfolio. It has been very profitable for me."

"But investments should be geared toward retirement. You shouldn't use them to try to get rich quick."

"Quentin, I've made money when most people have filed bankruptcy. I've made enough to put a nice down payment on my condo and pay off all of my student loans. I have debts only to maintain my credit rating, and I keep a separate retirement fund that I do not touch. I'm not looking to get rich quick, but why should I wait until I'm too old to move to benefit from my investments?"

Quentin stared at her before he spoke. "You're taking too big of a risk with your money," he said.

"It's the stock market, Quentin. Taking risks is what the market is all about. Besides, I'm twenty-six years old. I can afford to take some risks." She stopped writing and logged off the computer, then stood up and stretched. The hem of the T-shirt just barely covered her naked buttocks.

"What do you need me for?" Quentin said. "You seem to have it all worked out."

"I never said I didn't need you. I just may not need you for that."

"Yeah, only for when you're feeling horny at the end of the day."

"That's not true." She walked around the desk and sat on his lap, her bare behind against his legs. "So, what's on our agenda for today?" She wrapped her arms around him and leaned into him.

"I didn't have anything planned." He reached underneath the T-shirt and began to massage her erect nipples. "Any ideas?"

"Actually, I need to go to the mall." She jumped up from his lap and headed out of the office toward the bedroom. "I saw a beautiful chest that would look great in my living room."

"Sounds like a plan," he yelled back at her, then reached for the remote control and turned the television on to CNN.

Breck pulled on a pair of jeans and a shirt she had tossed in his closet on an earlier visit and waited until after Quentin had taken his shower and was ready to join her. They drove to a quaint breakfast restaurant tucked away in a suburban district of the city. Breck had happened upon it one afternoon after taking a wrong turn off the main road. Located on a side road, hidden from the busy streets heading into downtown, it was a huge, white house; the owners lived on the top floors, above the restaurant. It remained open only during the morning hours; the arrangement seemed profitable for the owners because there was rarely a seat vacant.

Breck did most of the talking during breakfast; for the first time since they'd begun dating, she talked about work, about the convention center and the ideas she had for it. She purposely refrained from mentioning Eric by first name, only referring to him as "they," meaning the entity of Warren & Peterson. Immediately after breakfast, they headed to the mall.

"If you're working late tomorrow night, give me

call," Eric had told her yesterday, and she couldn't keep the thought from reentering her mind no matter how much she tried. She glanced at her wristwatch so frequently that Quentin asked if she needed to be someplace.

"I'd thought about going into the office today," she answered. She knew that if she did, she would only stare at the phone and think about calling Eric.

"You talked about work at breakfast," Quentin said. "Let's talk about something else." But he didn't volunteer what that would be.

A rap song came over the car radio, and Quentin turned up the volume and bobbed his head to the beat. When they arrived at the mall, they walked to the furniture gallery where Breck had seen the chest while she was out shopping with Chi. Now the glossy red cedar chest was arranged elegantly beside a red leather chair, with an orange tag attached to it, meaning it had been put on sale since then. She beamed. "This is it," she said, bending down and lifting the top to peek at the tapestry that lined the inside.

"What do you need it for?" Quentin frowned.

"It's decorative. It'll go perfectly in my living room against the wall, where I have the bronze statue." She gestured to try to arrange a picture with her hands and hoped that he would see the image she saw. The blank expression on his face told her he didn't. "Just wait until we get it to my place, then you'll see."

He peered over and looked at the tag. "You're going to pay two hundred dollars for this?" The wrinkles on his forehead deepened.

"I would have, but it's on sale for thirty percent off." Breck reached for the chest. "I like it and I'm getting it."

"I think you're wasting your money, just like you're doing with your portfolio."

Clearly annoyed, Breck sighed heavily. "Are you going

to help me or just stand there and lecture me on how I should spend my money?"

"You seem to have everything under control," he said, and stepped back. "You don't need my help."

"What is your problem?" Breck put her hands on her hips and waited for him to explain his attitude.

"I don't have a problem."

Refusing to stand there and argue with him in the middle of a store, she lifted the chest and carried it to the counter. After the clerk rang it up, she took out her credit card and paid for it. When Quentin reached to take it off the counter, she slapped his hands away. They walked back to his car in silence, and she waited for him to unlock his trunk. He just stood there and looked at her.

"Will you open the goddamn trunk?" she screamed, trying desperately not the drop her delicate purchase. A crooked grin formed on the side of his mouth. He unlocked the trunk by remote, then got into the car.

"I was just trying to prove a point," he said as soon as she slid into the car beside him.

"And what is your point?" she screamed, and snapped her head around to glare at him.

"I am the man in this relationship, but I can't do shit for you except fuck you or lift a goddamn chest. There's something wrong with that. My opinions mean nothing to you."

"I don't need you to take over my finances. There are things I may need, but that's not one of them." She waited for a response, but he said nothing. Breck turned and stared out the window, watching cars pass.

How would Eric handle this? She wondered if he had ever tried to tell Gaby how to run her business or criticized the way she decorated their home.

"I really want to know where we're going with this relationship, Breck," Quentin said after a long silence. She shook her head at his ill timing. That's one hell of a question to ask her now, she thought, still staring out the window. "I think we need to talk about the next step we're going to take in our relationship."

"Steps like what?" she asked, turning to face him.

"How about moving in with me?"

Breck couldn't help but stare at him, speechless. Their relationship was in no way solid enough to make a commitment like that. Moving in together? She had never even told him she loved him. How could she take such a drastic step like moving in without even being sure if she loved him? They'd only been dating for eight months. Was that long enough? "I knew after a month," she recalled Eric saying.

"And if I moved in with you, how would we handle the finances?" she asked.

"I would handle the finances. I think what you're doing is risky, and I wouldn't trust our future with it."

He said exactly what she'd thought he would say. "What about my furniture?" she continued. "I have some nice stuff." Her furniture was durable, elegant, and comfortable, each piece carefully selected as a representative of her personality.

"So do I. You can keep a few items, like your chest, but I have everything at my house already. It's a big house, and if we decide to get married, it'll be a great place to raise kids. We won't have to move. You can't raise kids in your condo."

"I never said I wanted to have children."

"No, but you've said you wanted to get out of the city one day, and that usually goes with having kids." She didn't argue with him, but she thought about everything she would give up instead of what she would gain if she moved in with Quentin. She wouldn't be able to make decisions about her future any longer. She wouldn't even be able to keep her furniture. She would gain a constant companion, someone who would pay all of the bills and make sure she wouldn't want for anything. Hell, she could pay her own bills, and if she wanted something, she got it. Why give up her freedom just to have a constant companion who would give her no voice in running her own life? "I don't think that's a good idea," she said finally.

"And why not?"

"Because I don't think we're ready."

"So how exactly do we get ready?"

She shrugged. "I don't know."

"Do you have any intention of going further with this relationship, other than calling me up whenever you need a quick fix?" She closed her eyes and shook her head. This was not a conversation she was prepared to have today. "I suppose, since you have it all together, sex is the only reason you would need a man in your life," he said, turning the car onto his street. Breck eyed his big brick house as they approached. She was sure most women would be thrilled by the offer to live in it. It was a great-looking house with a well-manicured lawn, a circular drive, and a fenced backyard large enough to add a swimming pool and a hot tub one day.

"I'm sorry if your manhood is threatened by my success," she grumbled.

"My manhood is not the issue. If you weren't so hell-bent on proving you don't need a man, you just might have one." He paused. "Or perhaps Chi's already proved to you that you don't."

She whipped her head around and looked at him straight-on. Her heart thumped hard in her chest. That he was capable of stooping that low, against someone who had been his ally all along, infuriated her. "I can't believe you just said that," she said between gritted teeth.

He didn't bother to offer an apology. The tension between them grew so thick that the slightest word, no matter how trivial, would have caused her to snap. They sat in total silence until he pulled into his driveway. As soon as he put the car in park, Breck jumped out and slammed the car door behind her. With the remote control for her own car, she opened her trunk and walked to the rear of Quentin's, stepping in front of him before he had the chance to reach for the chest.

"I got it," she said, and lifted it from the trunk. Staggering to her car, she placed the chest inside while he stood and watched her. "I guess I don't need you for much," she said as she walked to the driver's side of her car and got in. Without hesitating, she started the engine and drove off, her tires screeching across the asphalt and leaving a permanent burn mark in his driveway.

"How dare he, how dare he, how dare he!" Breck screamed as she turned the corner and drove away, pounding on her steering wheel. As she attempted to calm herself, her mind went to past boyfriends. First there was Rodney in college, who had graduated from the engineering program two years ahead of her. It was after his graduation that things started to change. He got his first job and started making quite a bit of money. He became so sure of himself—cocky was more like it—and at every opportunity criticized Breck and her earning potential. "You have two vices against you, Breck," he had pounded into her head. "You're black and you're a woman. Think about going into interior design—at least that way you'll have a shot at making money."

"I'm going to get a job in my field."

"Breck, you are going into a profession that is dominated by white men. If you don't find a job, then you are not going to be able to pay back those loans and you are going to screw up your credit. If you and I get married, I don't want to be stuck paying back your student loans."

That was the end of Rodney. She had never asked him to pay back her student loans—hell, she had never even discussed marrying him!

The next significant boyfriend was Darrell, a branch manager at a local bank. She had dated Darrell until she decided to quit her job and open her own firm. She had never had any intention of working for other people for the rest of her life, and she went to Darrell at his bank first for a business loan. When she placed the immaculate business plan on his desk, all he could say was, "Are you crazy?"

"No, I'm not," she said. "This is something I really want to do, and I know that I will be successful."

"What happens if you don't get any clients?"

"I already have contacts. My business will need to grow and I admit it won't be easy, but I can do it. I've worked really hard on this plan." She pushed it toward him.

Without even glancing at his desk, Darrell shook his head. "Breck, you were lucky to get the job you have. I think you should stay where you are."

"Darrell, this is my dream and you know it."

"But I didn't think you were serious!"

Breck stared at him, dumbfounded. He went on to call her ideas sophomoric and refused to consider giving her a loan. That was the end of Darrell.

Every man in her life wanted her to lean on him, wanted to control her life in one way or another. She enjoyed her independence and took pride in the fact that she didn't need to rely on the earning power of a man to get approved for a mortgage, a credit card, or a car loan. She didn't come with financial baggage that needed to be carried. She'd listened to men talk about how they couldn't get with a certain woman because she didn't have her "shit" together. Well, Breck did, and she lost men because of it.

"Make up your damn minds!" Breck screamed at no one in particular but at men in general. While she sat at a traffic light, she looked over and saw the driver of a pickup truck staring at her. She stared back at him until the car behind her honked for her to move.

"Oh, whatever!" she yelled, and stepped on the accelerator. She pulled into the parking lot of her condo and parked close to her door. She walked inside the building and got the appliance dolly her building manager kept in the hall closet. She took the dolly to her car and lifted the chest from her trunk, secured it on the dolly, then rolled it to her unit. Once inside, she put the chest beside the bronze statue and stood back to admire it.

She nodded. She had known it would look great there. Satisfied, she returned the dolly and then hurried back to her condo to pour a glass of wine, hoping it would calm the fury boiling inside her. She downed the glass with one gulp and immediately poured another before she walked to her office area and sat behind her drafting board.

Her mind went to Eric. She looked at the clock on the wall—it was five o'clock—and wondered if he would still be in the office. He probably would be gone by now, she thought. Or maybe he's not there yet. She looked at the clock again as her leg began to shake. After five minutes she looked up again. Her leg was still shaking. Another five minutes, then another.

"Oh, hell." She reached for the telephone and called Chi.

". . . sorry, I'm not in right now. Please—"

Breck hung up. She glanced at the clock again and nibbled on her lower lip. It was five-twenty. Surely he's not there. Why would he be in the office after six o'clock on a Saturday evening? He's probably at home watching ESPN or hanging out in Mansfield with the boys.

She picked up the phone and dialed the first five numbers of Warren & Peterson, but she lost her nerve and hung up before finishing. What would she say if he picked up the phone? It was not a business call. She really wanted to talk to him. Her leg began to shake again.

Breck stood up, taking the wineglass with her, and walked to the window. The streets below were empty. There was nothing happening outside her window to take her mind off calling Eric. She sipped her wine.

"I'm going to call," she announced to no one. "If he's not there, fine, I'm not calling back." She walked back to the drafting board, picked up the phone, and pressed 1. She paused. Then she pressed the area code.

She paused.

Then she pressed all but the last number. Pause.

What if he answers? What if he wants to know why I'm calling him? What if his wife changed her mind, didn't go, and was there with him? What if he's not there? Do I leave a message?

Breck pressed the last button and the phone began to ring. She held on to the receiver tightly, fighting the temptation to hang it up. It rang several times, and she sighed heavily, disappointed that he wasn't there but also relieved that at least she didn't have to explain the call.

"Eric Warren." His deep voice suddenly interrupted her thoughts.

"Hello," she said, calming the nerves that flew all around her stomach.

"Hello?"

"Eric, hi. This is Breck Larson in Indiana." She wanted to smack herself in the head for sounding so ridiculous. Of course he knew where she lived. She didn't have to make that announcement.

"Hello, Breck. Are you at the office?"

Oh, damn, I should have called him from the office. What would he think now?

"No, I'm at home."

"Is everything okay?"

Breck paused. "Everything is fine, thank you."

"Are you sure?"

How did he know something was wrong?

"Well, no, everything is not okay. I really shouldn't have called you, but I needed to talk to someone. I may be totally out of line and I apologize."

"What's the problem?" he said, seeming unfazed by her rambling.

She heard rustling in the background on his end of the line. "Am I interrupting anything?"

"No, not at all. Talk to me."

She took a deep breath and held on to his words. Eric Warren was obviously accustomed to taking charge, and his tone revealed his comfort in that role. Breck settled against her chair and recounted the blowup with Quentin and her frustrations with all of the men she'd ever dated. The fury ran so deep that the pitch of her voice rose as she reached the climax of her story.

"I don't know what to tell you, Breck," he said when she stopped long enough to take a breath. She leaned forward on her desk and waited for him to say something meaningful. He was silent.

"That was not what I expected to hear," Breck said, breaking the silence. "I want some answers. You're a man, give me some answers."

"If I had the answer, I would give it to you, but I don't. It seems you want a relationship, but you also want your independence."

"So, are you trying to say that all this has been my fault?"

"No," he said quickly. "But you should question why every relationship ends up being a struggle against your independence."

Breck shook her head. "I disagree," she said, and began pacing the floor. "I've worked really hard to get where

I'm at, and I shouldn't have to be a damsel in distress or give up everything that makes me *me* in order to have a successful relationship."

"Then Quentin isn't the one for you, unless you are willing to step down a bit and let him feel like he's useful in places other than your bedroom."

"That's ridiculous," she huffed, and sat down again.

"It's the best I can offer."

Breck closed her eyes wearily and fought the burning sensation in her eyes. She wasn't going to cry. That would be so much like a typical woman and what most men would expect her to do. She took a deep breath and held it before exhaling.

"Are you going to be okay?" he asked.

"Eventually." She paused. "Thank you for talking to me. I promise not to call you again with my problems."

"Don't be silly. Call whenever you like. We've developed what I would like to consider a really nice friendship."

Breck smiled. "Yeah?"

"Yeah. And I was hoping you would call. It's getting lonely in here."

"Is Gaby in New York?"

"Yes. She and Darius flew out early this morning."

"You miss them?" She clinched the receiver harder.

"Very much. That house is much too big for one person. That's why I came to the office."

"You should go to Mansfield and hang out with Martin and Brian."

"Excellent idea. I may take you up on it." Breck realized that the conversation was coming to an end; she didn't know how to say good-bye to him, and she didn't want to. "I guess it's tough being single these days," Eric continued.

"I certainly don't think I'm very good at it."

"I bet you do fine. Just may not be meeting the right man."

"What do you think the right man for me would be?" She settled into her chair, glad the conversation wasn't finished.

"From what I know of you," Eric said, "I think you need a man who will find a way to balance your need for independence within the confinements of a relationship."

Breck nodded. "Does a relationship like that exist?"

"Hmm, good question." Breck tapped a pencil on her drafting board, thinking about the relationships of everyone around her. The only person she knew who was truly free was Chi, and that was because Chi committed herself to no one. "He's going to have to be very secure with his role in your life, and Quentin is not. That's why you guys are having problems."

"So, how do you manage it with your wife? You've said she and I are a lot alike."

"True. For starters, I don't try to run my wife's business. That's her thing. If she needs my help, I'll be there for her, but she never does. She's a fine businesswoman, and I don't try to take that away from her. Her money is hers. When it comes to household finances, that's my job, and she and I do not argue about it. She knows where our money goes, and she knows how much is in the bank. She sometimes sits in on board meetings because if something happens to me, this business is hers. She decorates our home and I try not to interfere, but I've had to intercept a few of her ideas." He laughed.

"Sounds like a plan that works."

"It works well."

"So where does the problem lie?" Breck asked unexpectedly.

"What do you mean?"

"It seems to me that the business plan of your relationship is working, but something else is not." Eric was silent. "Did I say something wrong?" Breck asked.

"No, not at all," he answered, but he didn't rush to say more.

"Are you going to answer, or am I treading dangerous waters?"

"My wife is very aristocratic. Mansfield doesn't fit that manner."

"You're very sensitive about that, aren't you?"

"Yes, I am. I find myself apologizing for her behavior or making excuses for her absence." He paused, and Breck looked down at the phone as if she was looking at him. "I must really trust you. I've never said that to anyone."

Her heart fluttered. "The feeling is mutual, but I worry about revealing too much of myself to you."

"Why?"

"Because I'm a businesswoman and I'm in a testosterone-laden field. I have to be tough and I have to be strong. I can't show weakness, especially not to a client."

"Well, I certainly hope by now you see me as more than a client."

"I'm beginning to."

"You can trust me, Breck. I'm not going to yank this contract from you just because you show emotions."

Breck wondered if Eric had told Gaby about her or their budding friendship. Would he mention this conversation? How would Gaby feel about another woman—a single woman—talking to her husband about relationship problems? If they met, would Gaby know in an instant that Breck had feelings for Eric?

"Eric, I have to run," she said suddenly. "I have some things to do. I hope I didn't keep you too long."

"No, not at all. What are you going to do for the rest of the evening?"

She wasn't expecting him to ask her that. "I think I'm going to visit my mother," she stammered. "She's been bugging me."

"That sounds like fun."

"Are you going to go to Mansfield?"

"I think I will."

"Well, let me know how it goes."

"I will do that."

"Night."

"Night, Breck. Thanks for calling."

Breck hung up the phone, stared at it, and smiled.

SIX

BRECK OPENED the office door on Monday morning and was greeted by an imposing glare from Chi.

"Good morning," Breck said as she walked in and picked up her messages.

"You are very popular today," Chi said.

"What do you mean?"

"Go into your office." Not missing a keystroke, Chi returned her attention to the computer screen in front of her.

Breck squinted toward her office, walked over, and turned the knob, expecting to see someone waiting for her. Instead, she saw two arrangements of flowers on her desk. One arrangement was a mixture of full-blossomed yellow, white, pink, and red roses accentuated with fresh baby's breath. The other really caught her attention; it was an abundant assortment of white and purple calla lilies. She'd received many floral arrangements over the years, but never calla lilies. "Wow," she said aloud. She tossed the message slips onto her desk and walked to the arrangement of calla lilies. Taking one of the delicate stems into her hand, she inhaled the fresh floral scent and held it in her lungs. She reached for the card placed on the plastic prongs and read it.

Thank you for a pleasant conversation
and wonderful suggestion.
I had a ball in Mansfield.

Your friend,
Eric

Breck read the card again, a huge smile stretching across her face. She reached for the card in the second arrangement and read it.

I'm sorry, call me.
Quentin

She tossed Quentin's card onto her desk and reread the one from Eric.

"Okay, what's the deal?" Breck looked up as Chi strolled into her office, plopped down in a chair, and crossed her legs.

"What do you mean?" Breck asked, walking behind her desk and pulling her chair out.

"Quentin sends you flowers, apologizing. Eric Warren sends you flowers, signing it 'your friend.' What's the deal?"

"Well, Quentin pissed me off, and Eric . . ." She placed the card on her desk but couldn't fight the smile illuminating her face.

"What is he like?"

Breck looked up at her. "Who, Eric?" Chi nodded. "He's great. He's not at all what I envisioned him to be. We have the best conversations, and he seems to understand me."

"How so?"

"We talk about problems I have with Quentin and other relationships in my past."

"You guys talk about personal things like that?" Chi stared at her wide-eyed.

"Yes," Breck said. "He has become a friend."

"He's a business associate, Breck, who happens to be very married."

"It's not like that. He's not coming on to me, and I'm

not flirting with him. He talks about his wife and son all the time. Even some of the problems they have."

"He should not be telling you about problems he's having with his wife."

"I think he just needs to talk and I'm the only one he can talk to. There's nothing wrong with that." Breck busied her hands by moving papers around on her desk.

"Have you thought that he may be leading you on and you may not be the first one?"

"That's absurd. He's not the type."

"How do you know what type he is? The only thing you know about Eric Warren is what he's told you over the phone."

"I don't feel that he's the type, okay? Please don't ask me how I know—I just know."

"Breck, you're falling for him."

"Don't you have work to do?" Breck asked.

Chi rose to leave. "Be careful," she said as she headed out the door.

"That's ridiculous," Breck said, ruffling the papers on her desk. "This is strictly a professional relationship. We just happen to have . . . clicked. That's all." She was shouting into the other room now. She picked up a charcoal pencil and turned toward her drafting board.

"Uh-huh," Chi grunted, but Breck chose not to argue.

Occasionally Breck looked up from her desk and glanced at the flowers. She thought about Quentin. She wasn't in love with Quentin in any way. She couldn't even get excited about his flowers. She stopped drawing and hid her face in the palm of her hand. "This is not good," she said. "This is not good."

The phone rang. The double ring signaled that the caller had the number to her direct line. It could be Quentin, and she was sure she didn't want to talk to him. Or it could be her mother. Usually Breck welcomed a brief conversation with her, but she wasn't in the mood to search for something concrete to talk about. She loved her mother dearly, but whenever she talked with her, Breck felt like she had to work too hard for material they could both relate to. Or it could be . . .

"Breck Larson," she said, gripping the handset and holding her breath.

"Hello, Breck. I'm calling to see if you received the flowers."

She exhaled. "Hi. Thank you. They are beautiful. I don't know what to say."

"I'm glad you like them."

"I'm glad you had fun in Mansfield."

"We went out for some beers, and I ended up drunk and dancing all night."

Breck laughed, envisioning Eric pouncing around the dance floor. "Sounds like you did have fun."

"Oh, it was a blast. I always have fun with those guys. Brian had to drive me home and ended up staying the night. We have season tickets for the New England Patriots, so we went to the football game Sunday and out for dinner Sunday night before I drove him back to his house in Mansfield. I haven't spent that much time with Brian in forever. It turned out to be a great weekend, and I owe it to you."

I could fall in love with you, she thought, then shook the words from her mind.

"I felt better after our conversation," she said, "but then I felt awful that I had to talk to you about my personal problems. I—"

"Breck, stop apologizing about that. I'm okay with it, really. If you ever need to talk, just give me a call. It's no big deal."

Please stop being so understanding. Please say something horrible.

"How was your weekend?" he asked.

"Not bad. I did go to my mother's house for dinner. She likes it when I do that."

"Are you and your mother close?"

"Probably not as close as we should be. What about you?"

"The same, I suppose. My mother lives in a small bungalow on Martha's Vineyard. She had enough of Mansfield, and I can't convince her to go back."

"Not even for a visit?"

"Nope. I've been telling her about the wonderful things we've done, but she's not having it."

"Perhaps you can convince her after the center is built."

"I doubt it. When my mother makes up her mind, it's hard to persuade her another way."

"Sounds like my mother." They laughed together.

"By the way," Breck said, "I'll have the rough sketches ready for the second floor by the end of the week. Is that okay?"

"That's exceptional. I forget that we're actually doing business together."

"Well, I can't forget."

"I'm glad you don't, and that reminds me of the other reason I'm calling. I'll be out of town the rest of the week, so if you need to reach me, feel free to call my cell phone. Business or just to say hello."

That was one hell of an offer, one she wasn't sure she should take advantage of. "Oh." She paused. "That's very thoughtful of you. Do you call all of your business associates to let them know that you'll be out of town?"

"No, just the ones who may have a crisis with their boyfriends and need to talk." He laughed.

"Very funny. I'll try not to take you up on the offer."

"It's going to be a boring trip, and I may need the conversation. Most of the people I do business with are very uptight and strictly business, no matter how much I try to convince them to relax."

"And you understand why, right?"

"No, I don't. I'm the most down-to-earth person you could ever meet."

"As well as intimidating as hell," Breck added.

"I beg your pardon?"

"Oh, come on, Eric." Breck leaned back in her chair. "Are you purposely being inane, or what?"

"I have no idea what you're talking about." The questioning tone in his voice told her he really had no clue.

"You are very intimidating. It doesn't matter that you happen to be six-five. Your name does the job well enough on its own."

"But it doesn't have to be that way. I'd prefer to talk business, seal the deal, go out and have a few beers, then shoot some hoop. That's the way I would love to conduct business, but it's never that easy."

"Dunk the basketball and the deal at the same time. Sounds ideal to me, but what about the man who tries to undercut one of your deals?"

"Then it really becomes a game, one that I very seldom lose."

Breck whistled. "Do you always get what you want?"

"Usually, but not always. I figure if I don't have it, it's not meant for me to have."

Breck felt a stirring that started in her stomach and stopped between her legs. "Are you talking about business?"

"I'm talking about everything."

"Have you ever made a wrong move?"

"Only when I don't move."

For the first time, it sounded like Eric Warren was flirting with her. The electricity that had built up could have jolted the receiver from her hand.

"You seem comfortable enough with me," Eric continued.

"I am now."

"And I am glad for that. I would hate it if you felt intimidated by me."

He was doing it again. Did he know how damned charming he was? What woman wouldn't be turned on? Breck definitely felt his spark.

"So, where are you going?" she asked, grounding the voltage from the conversation.

"California, to look at some property."

"That's a long way from home."

Breck heard Eric take a deep breath before he spoke. "Yes, it is, but apparently some prime real estate is about to go on the market, and if we want to take advantage of it we have to check it out before the end of the week when it's made public."

Breck chuckled.

"What's so funny?" he asked.

"You have knowledge of available real estate before it's made public?"

"Yes."

"And you wonder why people are intimidated by you. That's power, Eric." Breck threw back her head and laughed.

"No," he said. "That's paying the right people to be in the right place at the right time."

"Call it what you wish."

"Give me a call if you like, or I'll phone you when I return and we can go over the designs." Breck picked up a hint of sarcasm in his voice. "Smart-ass," he said beneath his breath.

"Oh, so now I'm a smart-ass?" She tried hard to keep the amusement from her voice.

"Yeah, you are."

"But I'm a good smart-ass."

"That you are. I'll talk with you soon," he said, then hung up.

Even after he had hung up, Breck couldn't keep from doubling over with laughter.

"What's so funny?" Chi asked, peering around the corner into her office.

"Eric just called me a smart-ass."

Chi squinted. "And you find humor in that?"

Breck waved her off and returned to her drawings.

SEVEN

THURSDAY-NIGHT HAPPY hour at the Martini Bar started slow. After sitting at the bar and snacking on chicken wings, Breck and Chi walked into the next room, closer to the musicians. Breck caught the eyes of the saxophonist following Chi to her seat.

They sat down at an empty table. Breck's glass was half full with Tanqueray gin, tonic, and a saturated lemon wedge. Chi sipped white Zinfandel.

"Have you made up with Quentin?" Chi asked. Breck shook her head. "Do you intend to?"

"I doubt it. What's the point?"

"Well, it keeps your mind off of Eric Warren, for starters."

Breck turned toward Chi. "Will you stop it about Eric? It's not like I'm meeting this man for a secret rendezvous. We talk on the phone. That's it."

"You talk to him almost every day," Chi pressed.

"What's wrong with that? You're my friend and I talk to you every day too."

"I'm not married. Don't you think something is wrong with a married man talking to a single woman every day?"

"Not if she's a friend."

"I think you're in denial. I wonder if he's told his wife he talks to you every day. Do you think he's told her about you?"

Annoyed, Breck shook her head. "I don't know. I'm

sure he's told her something about me. After all, I am the architect assigned to his project."

"Excuse me, ladies." Breck welcomed the interruption and turned toward the voice. The saxophonist from the band was leaning toward Chi. "May I?" He pointed a bony finger at the empty seat beside her. Chi nodded toward the chair, giving him permission to sit beside her.

"Are you ladies enjoying yourselves this evening?" His baritone voice was barely audible over the music that played while the band took a short break. He spoke to both of them, but his eyes revealed that his interest was in Chi.

"Yes, we are," Breck volunteered. "We always enjoy the music here. You gentlemen play very well." He nodded graciously and returned his attention to Chi. "Do you perform in other clubs around Indianapolis?" Breck asked, once again disrupting the man's stare and his feeble attempt at appearing suave.

"Yes, we do," he said, then immediately looked at Chi. "Perhaps you could give me your number and I'll call you and let you know where we'll be playing next." Breck leaned back in her chair and grinned. It was not an uncommon scene for her. Most men tripped over furniture to speak to Chi.

"I don't think that would be a good idea," Chi said with a smile.

"Why not?" He wasn't going to give up without a fight. Very noble of him, Breck thought, but she had seen it all too many times before. If Chi had to go so far as to announce her sexual preference, the embarrassed, jilted men sometimes shouted obscenities at her. Those times were few, but it did happen.

"Because I don't think your intentions are just to inform us of your tour, and I'm not interested. Do you have a web page that lists your performance dates?"

The man frowned. "No."

"Oh, well, perhaps we'll stumble upon your band again one day." Chi shifted in her seat and positioned her body far enough away from him that she didn't have to breathe in the alcohol from his breath.

"If you're married or got a man at home, that's all you have to say." His ego was bashed, and now he was going to make a complete ass of himself to recover it. Breck shook her head in disgust.

"I'm not married and I certainly don't have a man at home. I'm just not interested." Breck wondered if it would have been easier for Chi to just announce that she was a lesbian, but she shouldn't have to do that. No meant NO and that should have been good enough without explanation.

The man looked at her strangely. Obviously he was not accustomed to being turned down. "Are you one of those types that thinks she's too good for everybody? That's why most of y'all end up by your damn selves."

Chi ignored him and took a sip from her glass, accepting that his ego was bruised. Breck admired the way she handled most of these situations—better than she herself would have. If it were up to her, the man would be wearing her drink by now. When he saw that Chi was not going to give in to his advances or be fazed by his insults, he finally took the hint and walked away.

"Doesn't it bother you when they act like that?" Breck asked, watching the ridiculous spectacle as he crossed the room and began talking to another group of women, who seemed receptive and flattered by his presence.

"No, not really, because I don't go home with one. You do."

"Not when they act like that," Breck said, shaking her head.

Chi changed the subject. "My friend Ashley and her brother came over last night. He's so fine."

"I didn't know you were interested."

"I'm not, but you might be."

"I'm not interested."

"You haven't met him yet."

"I'm still not."

After two drinks, Breck and Chi left the bar and said good night. Thursday-evening drinks were an excellent way to wind down after a long week or to prepare for the weekend. They had braved the Friday-evening happy hour at the Martini Bar once and regretted it. Breck was sure the place violated the maximum-occupancy rule and posed a fire hazard, because they couldn't take a step without bumping into someone. The men who approached them that night were hilarious. They wore suits in vivid turquoise, red, or gold, with shirts unbuttoned to the abs, sheer or two sizes too small. The men at the Alley were by far better dressed, but unfortunately Chi was the only one who ever got lucky there. After that night, Breck and Chi decided to stick with Thursday-evening happy hour.

Breck walked into her condo, placed her keys on the kitchen counter, then reached up and pulled out the two hairpins that held up her hair. She shook her head and let her hair fall to her shoulders, then gently massaged her scalp. She pushed the button on her answering machine and listened to her messages.

"Breck, it's me, Quentin. I've been calling you all week. I just want to apologize for last Saturday. Give me a call." There was a beep as the recorder announced the time and day of the call. He'd called at 6:45 P.M.

Breck listened to the next message. "Breck, it's me, Quentin, again. I hope you got the flowers. Haven't heard from you all week. Give me a call." That call had been made an hour later. She glanced at the clock on her nightstand. It was nine o'clock.

Breck stepped into the bedroom and began to peel off her clothes. Cigarette smoke from the Martini Bar made her clothes and hair reek, and even staled the air around her. She brought a lock of her hair to her nose, took a whiff, then frowned. She wouldn't be able to sleep tonight if she didn't get that smell out of her hair. She walked barefoot across the hardwood floor to the bathroom and started to fill the tub, pouring in her favorite bath gel. As the water ran, Breck washed her hair in the kitchen sink and then added conditioner, which would sit in her hair while she took a bath. When she was done with her bath, she would shower the conditioner out. That was her usual routine. Afterward, she would braid her hair to get the crinkled look she loved, although it would only last for a day unless she washed her hair again. Usually she would have to straighten it to have it look decent again.

What an incredible week, she thought as her eyes closed and the bubbles began to caress her body.

Quentin. Her eyes tightened when she thought of him. Was she going to call him back? She didn't know what to say to him. This is your out, Breck. Take it. She sank deeper into the lather until her chin touched the bubbles.

Eric. She took a deep breath and moaned. Her mind went to Boston and eased into Eric's office. She saw him sitting at his desk with his legs stretched out and crossed at the ankles. He leaned against a high-back leather chair, his shirt loose and unbuttoned just enough for her to glimpse a hairless chest. A killer smile stretched wide across his face, revealing perfect white teeth. She heard his laugh and her body began to quiver. Then his eyes caught hers, and every piece of clothing melted from her body.

Breck opened her eyes and sat straight up, catching her breath. Steam had moistened her skin, and the mist dripped into the water. Her hand was cupped around her breast, and her thumb had begun to caress her nipple. She pushed her hair from her face and leaned back, knees bent, against the porcelain tub. Chi was right. She was in way too deep.

NO CALLS from Eric all day. With the office door opened, she could hear Chi tapping away on the computer out front. She wondered if he had made it home safely from his trip. He had called her twice while he was away, and she had gathered the nerve to call him once. She'd purposely chosen to call him while she drove home so that she could keep the call short, but he'd ended up calling her at home later that evening, and they'd talked for several hours.

He should be back in the office by now. Why hasn't he called? She stared at the phone.

"This is silly," she said, waving her hands through the air to try to shake off her anxiety. "Get to work." She turned her chair toward the drawing board and focused on the sketches. She was finishing up a house, one of the last of the remaining projects she'd had before getting the call from Eric. She heard the door open in the lobby and Chi's voice immediately afterward. A few seconds of silence followed.

"Hey."

Breck looked up and stared at Quentin standing in the doorway. "Hello," she said, and placed her pencil down on her desk.

"You haven't returned any of my calls." He walked into the office and sat down in the empty chair in front of her desk. "What's up?" She had not prepared a speech for this, even though she'd known Quentin wasn't going to just disappear.

Breck shook her head. "I don't have anything to say to you."

"You're going to be mad about this forever?" Quentin shrugged. "I said I was sorry."

"Apology accepted, but I still don't have anything to say to you."

"Is that it? You're breaking off with me and that's the only explanation you can give me?"

Breck felt bad that he had no idea what was happening inside her, but she couldn't tell him that she felt more about an invisible man than she did about him. She couldn't tell him that he had never made her feel the way she felt when she talked to Eric. She stared at him, and before she could speak the phone rang. "Hold on," she said, thankful for the intrusion. It bought her a little more time to think of what to say to Quentin. "Breck Larson."

"Breck, hello. It's Eric."

Her heart skipped, and although she was overjoyed to hear his voice, she fought like hell to keep it from showing on her face. "Hello, Eric, how are you?" Damn, why now? This was the voice she'd wanted to hear all day, but why now?

"Wonderful. How are you?" He sounded as cheerful as ever.

"I'm fine. How was California?"

"California was great, but let me tell you a joke I heard today." He began to recite the joke, and she didn't have the heart or the desire to stop him. Despite her direst effort, a smile sneaked onto her face.

Quentin shifted in his seat, growing more agitated the longer Breck held the phone against her ear. She put up a finger, signaling to him that she would be just another minute.

"Will I ever come first?" Quentin blurted, and Breck immediately put her hand over the receiver, hoping that Eric hadn't heard him, but he had.

"I'm sorry, am I interrupting?" Eric asked.

"No," Breck said quickly into the phone, but Quentin mistook her answer to Eric to be for him.

"Fine, good-bye." Quen... ...of the office, slamming her door b.. ...headed out

"Breck, is everything okay?" Eric ask... ...of concern. ...full

"No . . . yes. Let me call you back." She hung up and chased after Quentin, catching up with him in the parking lot.

"Damn it, Quentin! Why the hell did you just do that?" Breck screamed without realizing her hand had curled into a fist. "That was one of my most important clients. I would never have disrespected you like that at your place of business."

He stopped and turned toward her. "Disrespect?" he hurled at her. "You don't know the meaning of disrespect. That's all you've been doing to me since we met. Your most important client was on the phone, and the most important person in your life was sitting right in front of you, trying to work things out with you, and all you could do was hold the phone against your ear. I'm tired of it. I'm out." He walked the last few steps to his car and got in. He sat in the driver's seat and looked at her, but Breck didn't make a move toward him. She knew he was giving her a chance to come after him and apologize. He would have accepted her apology, but she couldn't move.

She didn't deserve Quentin and she knew it. She'd done nothing to advance the relationship and everything to pull back from it. Even if he was willing to work things out, she still wasn't going to give in to him. She wasn't going to give up her voice or her freedom, or compromise everything she had worked so hard to achieve in order to keep him. The best thing she could do for him was to let him find someone who would appreciate everything that he was.

This is your out, Breck, she told herself. Take it. She stood cemented to the sidewalk. Quentin started his car

...ned, frozen, and pulled out of th..._ing she had been holding her as his car cars ...wnen he was out of sight sh.. angry, confused, and sorry. Quentin bre.. deserve what she had tossed at him.

Was she doing this for Eric? She shook at that thought, but the moment Quentin's car disappeared from sight, Eric was the first thing she thought of. She couldn't possibly be breaking up with Quentin for a chance with Eric. She suddenly had the urge to hit something, anything, but the best she could do was kick the front of the brick building.

"Shit!" she yelped, and grabbed her foot when she was suddenly reminded how hard brick really was. She limped back inside and slumped against the door.

"Is everything okay?" Chi asked.

"No," she mumbled. "It's over." She walked into her office and closed the door, leaning against it and looking at her phone. She was sure Eric was waiting for her call, but she didn't want to call him back. She didn't want to tell him about this. Her personal life was a wreck. What if he saw that as a sign of instability and decided to cancel the contract until she got her life together? She couldn't risk that. She returned to her desk and continued to stare at the phone until she decided to pick it up. She had gotten herself into this; now she had to get herself out. She called his direct line, and he picked up after the first ring.

"I was just about to call you back," he said eagerly. "Is everything okay?" He sounded genuinely concerned. How could he care so much about someone he had never met? she thought.

Breck exhaled and slumped over her desk. "I'm so sorry about that," she said, and buried her head in her hands.

"What happened?"

"That was Quentin. It's over." She took a deep breath and closed her eyes. "Eric, I'm really sorry about all this. I didn't mean to bring my personal problems into this business arrangement. I can assure you that it will in no way affect the work that I do for Warren and Peterson—"

Eric interrupted her. "Breck, what the hell are you talking about? You're more than a business associate to me, and damn it, you should know that by now."

Her heart pounded in her chest. What had she become to him? She had never in her life been so torn about someone. She knew that Eric Warren was someone she would love to get to know, to hang out with and maybe even fall in love with, but she would never have the opportunity to do that. He was not available. "What have I become to you?" she asked. If he answered the question correctly, it would be enough to snap her out of this delirium. Against her better judgment, she continued talking, hoping that he would only stop her when she'd crossed the line. "I know I shouldn't ask this, but what have I become to you? I know what you've become to me."

"Breck, you're a dear friend and I'm concerned about you."

She wiped her face and straightened up in her chair. It wasn't exactly the answer she wanted to hear, but it was all she could ever hope for from him. "Thank you for your concern. I'll be fine," she said, attempting to pull herself back together.

"I hurt your feelings, didn't I?"

She paused. Why was he doing this? Was he toying with her?

"Breck, are you there?"

"Yes, I'm here."

"I'm sorry if I hurt your feelings."

"You didn't hurt my feelings," she snapped. "I'll be fine, so let's leave it at that." As the tears fell, she didn't know if it was because she was on the verge of blowing a multimillion-dollar contract or because Eric couldn't reciprocate her feelings. Several minutes passed and neither of them spoke. At first she thought the phone had gone dead, but then she heard his faint breathing.

Oh, she really had blown it. He was just trying to be a friend, and in her stupidity she had mistaken it for something more. He wasn't interested in her that way, and it was her frustration with Quentin that made her think that there was more to this than friendship. She'd been a complete idiot. She dropped her head in shame. "I feel like such a fool," she said aloud.

"Why?" Eric asked, but she didn't answer him. She didn't feel she needed to. "Breck, you're not a fool. I do have feelings for you." She wiped the tears from her eyes. "You were one of the few people I spoke to while I was in California, and I thought about you a lot. Probably more than I should have." Breck sat straight in her chair. Her breathing mellowed and her heart calmed. She was more relieved than anything else that this whole thing had not been merely the exaggeration of an overzealous imagination.

"I think about you a lot too, Eric. I know I think about you more than I should, but I . . ." She stopped. How could she tell him she was falling in love with him? How insane would it be for her to tell him that?

"I bought you a present while I was in California," Eric said, relieving her from having to finish her sentence.

She pulled her shoulders back, surprised. "You did?"

"Yes. I've never done that for anyone, other than my wife, and I don't know why it was important to me for you to have it."

Breck gasped. "I don't know what to say."

An awkward silence fell between them as they both tried to deal with the emotional tug-of-war. Everything she had ever been taught about right and wrong and good versus evil seemed to evaporate. The way she felt about Eric contradicted everything she had ever known to be true about love and relationships. Do we choose the one we love, or does love somehow choose us? She didn't choose to fall in love with Eric, but she was choosing how to deal with it—which, she concluded, wasn't very well.

"Eric," she said, then paused. "I could easily fall in love with you." It was the closest she could come to actually telling him she *was* in love with him. Her heart punched hard against her chest, but she had to come clean and there was a nervous excitement about telling the truth. If he rejected her, then so be it. At least she would not go through life with the burden of never telling him how she really felt about him.

She heard a click, then panicked; had he hung up on her? "Breck, I would be lying if I said I didn't feel the same way." She realized that he had been talking on his speakerphone and had just taken her off. Now their conversation was private, and his voice sounded as if he were standing right beside her. "I think about you all the time too. When I'm sitting in my office, my mind drifts to you, walking around with your shoes off, and I laugh. I asked my secretary if she'd ever taken her shoes off at work, and she looked at me like I was crazy." Breck smiled, feeling secure in the knowledge that he was comfortable about her feelings. "I'm not sure what I'm feeling, but I wouldn't dream of doing anything to jeopardize my marriage or hurt my wife. I hope I'm not leading you to believe this could be anything more than what it is."

"No, you're not, and I would never ask anything more of you."

"I know you wouldn't, and I love that about you."

"Do we have to stop being friends?" Breck asked.

"No, not at all. I look forward to this almost every night. Unless, of course, you think we should."

Breck pondered his question. Why was he making this her call? "I don't understand," she said. "I would like to keep talking with you. I don't have a problem accepting things the way they are."

"If it hurts you to keep talking to me knowing it would never be anything more than what it is, then maybe we shouldn't. I don't want to feel that I'm hurting you in any way."

"Eric, I'm a big girl. I can look after myself."

"I don't doubt that," he said, then paused. "Are you going to be okay? About Quentin?"

Breck sighed. "Yes. I think so."

"Are you sure you're doing the right thing?"

"Yes. I'm not in love with him, and he deserves that. He's a good man."

They talked for a few minutes longer before Breck needed to end the call to get back to work. After he had hung up she sat looking at the phone. Eric was her perfect man, Prince Charming, Mr. Right—whatever you want to call it, Eric was it. Their conversations were wonderful and kept her wanting more. Every night when she said good night to him, she couldn't wait until the next night so she could talk with him more. It seemed some cruel twist of nature that their feelings had grown for each other, knowing they could never know each other as lovers.

She returned her attention to the sketches on her drawing board and picked up her pencil. Her mind was far from the drawings.

Was this infatuation or something much more? Everyone knows that women fall for strong men in positions of power—presidents, ministers, heads of corporations—but she had never thought she would be one of them.

Whatever she felt for Eric, she wasn't ready to let it go completely, even if that meant just being his friend.

I'm a big girl, she thought. I can handle myself. She looked down again at her drawing board and let out a gasp. Absentmindedly, she had scribbled his name in big bold letters across her sketch.

EIGHT

THE GIFT from Eric was a vintage handwoven cashmere-and-silk afghan with a Native American motif of mauve, sea green, and earth tones. It arrived at her office the next Monday, delivered by messenger, packed in a matching box lined with soft black velvet. "Oh, my God!" Chi exclaimed. "He must have paid a fortune for this."

Breck could only stare at it as she lifted the delicate afghan from the box and wrapped it around her shoulders. She immediately felt its warmth, and the moment she pulled it tightly around herself Breck knew she was in love. There was no more claiming that she was falling for Eric, she had fallen for him, hard.

In the weeks that followed, she told Chi practically everything they talked about. It was still business as usual, but they always managed to talk on the phone for hours almost every night. She ecstatically shared with Chi the details of the evening Eric attended a monthly sleepover at the Boys and Girls Club in Mansfield. He had telephoned her at home from the club, and she'd talked with Eric's friends Martin and Brian. Both men shared stories with her about wild-man Eric. Breck knew the stories were highly exaggerated, but she laughed so hard she almost fell off the sofa. As she talked with Eric, she wrapped the afghan around her and felt so close to him it seemed he was in the room with her.

When he said good night to her that evening, he blew a kiss into the phone. She was stunned. Eric had kissed her. Granted, it wasn't a real kiss, but it meant the same thing. As soon as the line was disconnected, she called Chi. "He kissed me, he kissed me!" she screamed into the phone.

"Who kissed you?" Chi asked.

"Eric! He kissed me."

"Eric's there?"

"No, silly, he blew me a kiss over the phone!" Breck screamed again.

"Breck, honey, you're crazy as hell. Go to bed." Chi hung up, and Breck screamed again. Eric had kissed her!

She didn't sleep much that night. The classical music that would normally soothe her into a sound sleep now filled her head with thoughts of Eric lying beside her. She closed her eyes and felt his legs entwined with hers. Stroking the empty space beside her, she gently massaged the sheets with the palm of her hand. She turned on her side, imagining Eric's body, and positioned her legs to rest between his. Her arms stretched across the bed where his chest would be. Her head rested on the pillow so her breath could tickle his ear. She snuggled closer to him and fell asleep.

THE WEEK went by without any calls from Eric. After the evening they spent on the telephone at the sleepover, he seemed to disappear. Toward the weekend Breck began to worry. She called and left messages for him, but none of her calls were returned. If he had gone out of town, he didn't call to let her know like he usually did.

Thursday evening she and Chi went to the Martini Bar as usual, but to her surprise Chi had taken it upon herself to invite Ashley, and of course Ashley brought her handsome brother, Farrell.

Chi had not exaggerated. Farrell was princely. He strode into the bar, tall and fit, wearing a full-length leather jacket, crisp blue jeans that looked as if they had just come from the cleaners and had been heavily starched, and a brown silk shirt opened to expose a thick platinum necklace. He was light-skinned and wavy-haired. His presence commanded immediate attention, and all of the women turned to stare at him. He was simply beautiful. If it weren't for the faint beard, his face would appear as soft as a child's. When he walked across the floor, his jacket swayed with each step. His stylish, shiny loafers looked as if he had just taken them out of the box.

"Hello," he said when he reached their table and looked at Breck. Her eyes were glued to him. She had never seen a better-looking man.

"Hel-lo," she said, emphasizing each syllable of the word. He smiled, revealing perfect white teeth that glistened in the light. He and Ashley sat down. Ashley sat closer to Chi and put her hand on Chi's leg. Like her brother, she too was beautiful, except her complexion was a little more golden against soft black hair. Breck guessed their ethnicity was a mix of black and possibly Hispanic.

"I've heard a lot about you," Farrell said to Breck. "I'm thrilled to finally get to meet you." He pulled his chair closer to her, leaving Chi and Ashley to their own conversation.

"I've heard a bit about you too," Breck said.

Farrell talked and talked, mostly about himself and his playing career for the Indianapolis Colts. Turned out Farrell was a wide receiver for the Colts and quite popular.

"Who's your agent?" Breck asked.

"Quentin McGregor. Do you know him?"

"Oh, yeah," she said, and took a sip of her gin and tonic. He didn't bother asking her anything more about Quentin. It would have taken the attention from him.

"I hear you're a successful architect," he said finally, after they had been talking for an hour.

"I do fairly well."

"It's good to hear our sisters making their own way. I like women like that. Most of the women I meet want to ride my coattail, and I don't have time for that. Give me a woman who can hold her own any day."

"Well, that's me," Breck said, growing more bored with the conversation by the minute. There was nothing remotely interesting about Farrell other than how gorgeous he was. He was arrogant, self-serving, and now she had just learned that he had a selfish view of women.

"I make several million dollars a year, and most women know that when they go out with me. It's always in the papers. The last thing I need is to hook up with some woman and all she wants to do is have a baby and start collecting ridiculous amounts in child support."

"That's a very low opinion of women."

"I'm just telling you how it is. A woman like you isn't about that. I can get with a woman like you. You're beautiful, you're smart, and you got your own thing going on." He nodded. "Yeah, I can get with a woman like you."

"Why, because you feel you could fuck me and I won't ask a damn thing from you?"

Farrell's face was close enough that she felt his breath, but as soon as she said that, he pulled back.

"Nah, it isn't like that."

"You know, I have to go." She'd stomached enough. It was time for Breck to get the hell away from him before she really gave him a piece of her mind, but Farrell wasn't letting her go without trying to explain himself.

"I think you got me all wrong."

"I don't think I do. Let me give you some advice, Mr. Grant. No matter what type of woman you get with, pussy isn't free. Whether you're married to it or just having it for a night, you end up paying for it one way or the other. Just because I got my own thing going on doesn't mean mine is free, either." With that, she grabbed her coat and left while Chi and Ashley danced away on the floor.

She was screaming inside of her head as she drove around town, going no place in particular and far from home. What in the hell had gotten into her? She was frustrated with men, starting with Quentin and ending with Eric. Quentin wanted to dominate her, Farrell would let her be as free as she needed to be as long as she didn't ask him to do anything for her, and Eric just simply didn't want her. What did *she* want?

Breck pulled in to her parents' driveway and answered the question: she didn't know.

It was still relatively early when she rang the doorbell. She heard footsteps as she stood outside the door, wrapping her arms around herself and shivering slightly. It was a cold autumn in Indianapolis.

"Girl, where's your coat?" her mother asked, opening the screen door and stepping aside to let Breck slip through.

"I forgot it."

"Well, come on and I'll make some coffee. What you doing here this time of night?" To her mother, "this time of night" was any time after dinner.

"I just didn't feel like going home. Where's Dad?"

"You know he goes to bed as soon as he's finished eating. What's wrong? You and Quentin fighting again?"

"We broke up weeks ago." Her mother paused after pouring the water into the coffeemaker.

"What? Why?" She reached into the cabinet and pulled out a couple of coffee mugs.

"I wasn't in love with him."

"Quentin was a good man, Breck. Are you sure you're not one of those like Chi?" she asked, fanning her hand back and forth.

"Mom, no. I'm not a lesbian. I can't believe you asked

me that." When the coffee was made her mother poured each of them a cup. Breck wasn't crazy about coffee from a percolator, but it would have to do.

"Well, you've never had a boyfriend longer than a year."

"You ever think that it's them and not me?"

"All of them, Breck?"

Breck shrugged. "Well, I'll admit, the problem with Quentin was mostly me."

"Okay, enough of the babbling. What's bothering you?" Breck took a deep breath and placed her cup on the kitchen table. "Is it another man?" her mother pressed.

Breck nodded.

"Ah, should have known. So what's the problem?"

"What isn't a problem? He lives a thousand miles away, and I'm working for him, for starters." She didn't mention the most damaging detail, his marital status.

"Well, that's not good. Don't mix business with pleasure. Bad move."

"I haven't."

"Is it a relationship that has promise?" Breck shook her head. "If you know that, then what are you moping about? Get over it and move on, girl. You're too beautiful and smart to be sitting around the house with your head between your legs." With that, her mother dismissed the conversation, got up from the table, and headed into the living room. Breck joined her there. They watched the nightly news, and as soon as it was over, Breck kissed her mother good night and drove home.

SHE ARRIVED at her office the usual time the next morning and expected to be chewed out by Chi about her abrupt departure from the Martini Bar the night before, but surprisingly Chi didn't mention it. Either Chi didn't know what had happened or Farrell had told her. In that case, Breck decided to tell her version of the story. Before she even uttered the first word, the telephone rang in her office. She rushed to answer it in hopes that it might be Eric.

"Hello," she said, nearly diving over her desk to pick up the phone.

"Hello, Breck. This is Stephen Peterson. I'm returning your call for Eric."

"Oh? Is he ill?"

"No, not at all. He told me to tell you he's been very busy and unable to return your calls. Were you calling with a status report?"

"Um, yes . . ." Breck stammered. She grabbed a few notes and flipped through some of her papers. "Basically, I was calling to let Eric know that everything is on schedule. I will have the designs ready for final approval within the next month."

"Wonderful. I will make sure he gets the message."

"Thank you."

Breck hung up and almost fell to the floor. What the hell is going on? she wondered. This wasn't like Eric. Over the past six months they'd managed to talk almost every night. If he couldn't talk to her, he always left a message. Two weeks had gone by with not one word from him, and now Stephen was returning her calls.

"What's up?" Chi asked, walking into her office and sitting down in the chair opposite her.

Breck shook her head and slumped deep into the chair. "Nothing."

"Lie."

Breck bit down on her lip before she spoke. "Eric's not returning my calls."

"Maybe he realized he shouldn't be talking to you every night," Chi offered. "Have you thought of that?"

Breck shrugged. "It's still not like him." She picked up her pencil and began flipping it on her desk.

"Well, what are you going to do?"

Breck threw the pencil across the desk and shrugged. What could she do? She couldn't storm into his office and demand answers, and she couldn't telephone his home and masquerade the call as only business.

"Are you going to tell me what happened at the Martini Bar last night?"

Her mind was too convoluted to think about the Martini Bar or Farrell. Chi didn't seem concerned or alarmed that Eric had decided not to talk with her anymore, but Breck was devastated. No one would understand that she was hurting right now, possibly more than she had ever hurt. She shook her head. "I'll tell you later."

Chi stood up. "I'm ordering cookies. You want any?" At least once a month Chi and Breck ordered several dozen gourmet cookies off the Internet. Chi had discovered them at a party and brought some back for Breck. Since then, they'd been hooked and always ordered the cookies for parties, holiday and birthday gifts, or whenever they wanted to indulge themselves.

Breck turned to Chi. "You're ordering cookies?"

"Yes."

Breck smiled. "Send a dozen to Eric."

Chi looked squarely at her. "Not a good idea," she said. "Let it go."

"I can't let it go," Breck said. "Order the cookies and send a dozen to Eric," she repeated the command.

When the cookies arrived, Breck knew Eric should have received his as well. She remained in her office the entire day. She was so excited about the possibility of hearing Eric's voice again that she was able to block almost everything from her mind and get into a groove. For the first time in weeks, she managed to escape for a few hours without thoughts of Eric interrupting her flow. Since they had begun talking, he filled her thoughts in the morning when she woke up, all day at work, while she was stuck in traffic. When she finally looked up from the sketches, she marveled at her progress. She placed her pencil on the drafting board and exercised her fingers.

"Breck." Chi stood in her door, leaning against the frame. "Eric's on line two."

Breck's stomach dropped. She hadn't heard the phone ring. Then she realized that she had forwarded her calls to Chi.

"You're going to take the call?" Chi asked.

Breck glared at her. Of course she was going to take the call. She had been waiting for this call all day. She reached for the phone. "This is Breck," she said, then bit down on her lip.

"Hi, Breck. Eric." Her nerves jumped in her stomach as her leg began to shake. "Did I catch you at a bad time?" Breck noticed the melancholy tone in his voice. He lacked his usual chipper tone that she loved so much. He seemed a bit standoffish, and that immediately alarmed her. Then she felt insidious. He called because of the cookies, just as she had wanted, but that was it. It was only because of the cookies. She wanted him to call because he really wanted to and not as a result of something she had done to initiate it.

"No, not at all," she said. "I can afford a break. How are you?"

"I'm well, thanks. And thanks for the cookies. I passed them around the office, and everyone loved them."

He passed them around the office? Did he even eat one? Breck nodded. Mission accomplished, she'd gotten him to call, but she was unnerved by all the other questions she had and by the silence that had fallen between them. This was such a contrast to their earlier relationship that it seemed as if they had barely known each other. As she listened to the silence, tears filled her eyes.

At that moment she knew Eric's silence over the past week hadn't been because he was busy with the center or traveling. He had purposely ignored her. The awkwardness in his voice told her that. She picked up the pencil from her desk and began to flip it between her fingers. "What's going on, Eric?" she asked as she watched the eraser hit the desk and the pencil cartwheel off of it. She heard him take a hard breath.

"I had to leave this alone for a while." He paused. "But to not return your calls was wrong, and I'm sorry." A tear ran down her cheek, and she quickly wiped it away. "Breck," he said quietly.

"Yeah?" She tried without success to hide the sob in her voice. She heard him take another hard breath.

"Are you okay?"

"I'm fine," she said, and wiped the tears as soon as they fell from her eyes.

"You sure?"

"No," she said heavily. She couldn't sit anymore. She stood up and paced the floor, trying to collect her thoughts while calming the rush of nerves that jumped inside her. Then she stopped pacing and slumped down in her chair again. "The truth is, I'm in love with you and this hurts." The words spilled from her lips, and she couldn't help but feel exposed and vulnerable. She had put herself on a stage, and all she could do at this point was wait for him to throw an egg in her face. She dropped her head into her hands and cried until she could no longer breathe through her nose.

"I should have stopped this the moment I realized we were getting too involved," Eric said, and she heard him fumbling with something on his desk. "Breck, I'm not the type of man who cheats on his wife, but I didn't stop this when I should have and I'm sorry for hurting you."

"So am I." She held her head down close to the desk and began to doodle on a piece of paper. "How is it possible to fall in love with someone you've never met?" She chuckled softly, not expecting Eric to respond.

"I don't know, but I question if you're actually in love with me or the image."

Breck paused to give that some thought. She loved Eric because he seemed perfect in every way—the perfect husband, the perfect friend, the perfect father.

"I'm not perfect," he said, as if he'd read her mind. "I know that I have feelings for you that I shouldn't have, but I don't know if it's love or something else." He paused. "When I was at the sleepover and we talked, Martin told me I had fallen for you and I denied it. I swore to him that we were just good friends. But the more I thought about what he said, the more I realized he was right." Breck wiped her eyes again and sat up in her chair. "If things were different . . ." He paused, not able or not willing to say what he was thinking. If things were different, would he rush from Boston to be by her side? If things were different, would he pursue a relationship with her? What would happen if things were different?

But Breck understood. Things weren't different. He was married, and therefore they couldn't explore what they had stumbled upon.

"Have you finalized the contracts with the electricians and plumbers?" Breck asked, deliberately changing the subject.

A few seconds of silence went by before he answered. "Yes. Everything is set to go."

Breck patted her eyes as she walked to the drafting board. "Good, then everything is on schedule."

"When will you visit the site?"

"I should be there for the last month. In the meantime, I've picked up a couple of new contracts I'll be working on here in Indiana."

"Very busy lady."

"Well, I try to be. I don't have much of a personal life, but Chi did try to fix me up with the brother of a friend of hers."

"And?"

"He's arrogant and selfish and was just interested in meeting a woman who would demand the least from him."

"I'm sorry it didn't work out."

"Don't be. There will be other dates, I'm sure."

"I'm sorry."

"Please, don't pity me."

"I don't pity you, but if I were single, I would be at your doorstep tomorrow."

"But you're not single, so please let's leave it at that." She tried hard to disguise her bitterness, but it wasn't working.

"I'm sorry," he apologized again.

"Stop apologizing." She was silent for a moment but decided she had better get off the phone before she ended up crying a river. "I really need to go."

"Okay. Still friends?" he asked before she had the chance to replace the receiver.

Breck smiled. "Still friends."

BRECK STOPPED by her parents' house again before going home that evening. It was probably the most time she had spent with her mother since she moved out on her own, but for some reason she needed to be near her.

This time the door was open, and Breck walked right in. As usual, her parents sat in the living room in front of the television. Breck wondered if they ever did much else.

She thought about her parents, Rick and Camille, married for thirty years, and wondered if her father—or worse, her mother—had ever had an affair. Her father used to travel a lot when she was younger. He had been a regional manager at an automotive plant before retiring and had spent a lot of time attending conferences and trade shows around the country. Had he ever picked up a girlfriend along the way? She cringed. She couldn't imagine either one of her parents with anyone else.

"Hi, honey," her mother said, turning around. Breck walked into the living room and plunked herself down heavily on the sofa. "How was your day?"

Breck didn't answer, just laid her head on her mother's shoulder. She wanted so badly to tell her mother the truth about Eric, but she knew her mother wouldn't approve. Camille Larson was a churchgoing, God-fearing woman, and if Breck told her that she was in love with a married man, she'd probably have her minister on Breck's doorstep the next morning ready to rid her of some evil demon.

"Come help me with dinner." Her mother patted her on the leg, then rose to walk into the kitchen.

Breck rolled her eyes—she was not in the mood for cooking—but she followed her mother into the kitchen anyway and sat at the table. "Mom, I can go get some takeout."

"What for?" her mother asked. She reached into the refrigerator and pulled out a package of chicken she had taken out to thaw earlier. "So what's up with you?"

Breck took a long breath and leaned forward on her elbow. Should she tell her mother she had fallen for a married man? She might freak out. "Nothing," she finally said.

"Liar." Breck shot a quick look at her mother as she sat down beside her. "I don't know why you find it so hard to talk to me."

"Because you wouldn't understand."

"You've never given me a chance."

Breck thought for a minute. "It's work," Breck said, figuring that was safer. "I'm working with a difficult client in Boston." It wasn't a total lie. Breck couldn't stand Stephen Peterson.

"Oh?" her mother looked at her, puzzled. "I thought you had grown fond of him."

"Different client. Not mixing business with pleasure, I'm working with the partner, and he's an . . ." She stopped just short of cursing for the first time in her mother's presence. "A difficult man to work with."

"Well, tell him you want to work with the other partner."

"I can't."

"My goodness. You must really like that man."

Breck sighed. If she only knew.

"Quit."

Breck almost choked. "I can't quit."

"Sure you can. Just tell him you can't work with the other partner and you have to remove yourself from the project."

"I can't do that."

"Why not?"

"Because this project is important to Eric."

"Who is Eric?"

Breck thought quickly but decided to wave her off. "It doesn't matter. I can't quit."

"Then handle it," Camille said, annoyed. "Breck, you're a stronger woman than that. Don't lose your mind over some man." Camille busied herself with the dinner while she kept one eye on Breck. "You've never had a problem walking away before. Why is this so hard?"

"Because I love him," Breck mumbled, so low that her mother didn't hear her.

NINE

BRECK SHIVERED as she stepped onto the concrete walkway outside her condo. The air was chilly, and the branches were full of colorful autumn leaves. She breathed in the cool, damp air and thought twice about going for her morning run. The gray cotton-and-lycra pants hugged her thighs, and the matching sports jacket kept her warm. She tied an extra white cotton jacket around her waist and started her side bends. She stretched longer than usual this morning. She felt tired. She hadn't gotten much sleep last night. There were too many questions floating around in her head for her to get any comfort.

She'd lost her best friend. At least that was the way she felt. Of course, she still had Chi, but that was different. She'd lost the best male friend she had ever had. She'd never been able to talk to a man the way she had talked with Eric. They'd bonded. She didn't know how, but there was something about him that comforted her.

Despite her trying to make everything okay between them, he slipped farther and farther away from her and she couldn't stop him. She understood why he had to do it, but that didn't make her feel better. The fact that his absence upset her made her feel even worse.

Never had she thought she would be in this situation. Eric had a wife and child, and she was putting herself into their lives. Her mother was right; she'd never had a problem walking away before. But for some reason this was tearing her apart.

The characteristics that made her fall in love with Eric were the same traits that kept him away. She should not have been the least bit surprised that he chose to back off. In fact, that wasn't what bothered her. She was ticked off by the fact that he had totally dismissed her from his life, like she meant nothing to him at all.

Maybe he didn't trust her. Maybe he thought that if he continued talking with her, she would eventually knock on his door and demand that he choose between her and his wife. Breck shivered at that thought. She would never do something like that, and she hoped Eric thought more of her than to believe her capable of such an act. But she *was* capable of having an affair with him, and that was just as devious. She knew without a doubt that if they were in the same city, she would be in bed with him if he allowed it. She wanted to make love to him—there was no point in denying that. She fantasized about his body, his lovemaking, what it would be like waking up beside him, how his lips would feel against hers.

Breck stood and took in her surroundings. A few late-model cars were parked along the curb, and even fewer passed by on the almost deserted street. The silence was the thing she enjoyed most about her morning runs. All she heard were the ramblings in her mind. Finally she broke into a comfortable stride, taking her usual route around the block.

At first her conversations with Eric had dwindled down to a few short exchanges during the week about the convention center—nothing like the long chats she had fallen in love with. He no longer made nightly phone calls to her office, and when she tried to phone him, she usually ended up getting the corporate voice-messaging system. Then the conversations had stopped altogether and she missed them. She couldn't conceal that from anyone, especially not Chi, who had never been fooled about Breck's feelings. Chi saw it even when

Breck refused to see that she had gotten way too deep in this and the only way out was with a broken heart.

Breck smiled when she remembered the night she kept him on the phone, switching the conversation to the speakerphone so that each of them could work and listen to the same music. Eric had wanted to hear her new Diana Krall CD, which she had been boasting about. It was that sort of thing that had made their friendship so remarkable, so real, even when she still had yet to lay one eye on the man.

The past several months had been extremely difficult. The construction had begun on the center, and everything was progressing on schedule. She had finalized the plans with Stephen instead of Eric, which had made her more than a little pissed, and received weekly status reports from his secretary. But the heartbreak came when she was featured in two national magazines and she couldn't call Eric to tell him the news. In fact, she couldn't celebrate with anyone. Chi was there as always, but it wasn't the same. She felt alone, more alone than she'd ever felt. That was when it hit home with her that he would never be in her life the way she needed him to be.

Breck rounded the corner. She'd jogged this route so many times that she often joked that she could run it with her eyes closed. With her mind on Eric and the happenings hundreds of miles away in Boston, she was practically doing it. At the last moment she saw the crack but it was too late to avoid it. Her right foot dug into it and twisted. "Ouch!" she screamed as she leaped onto her left foot, lost her balance, and fell. She landed hard on the ground, using her hand to break her fall and ending up with tiny pebbles in her palm. She grabbed her ankle and squealed in pain.

"Damn it!" she wailed. The pain deepened, as though a pack of steel needles had just gone into the side of her foot. She made a tight fist as she fought the tears and tried to stand up. She attempted to apply pressure on her ankle but immediately relented. She managed to stand but realized there was no way she could finish the run. Getting home wasn't going to be easy. She untied the jacket from around her waist and put it on, zipping it up to her neck to shield her sweaty body from the cool air as she limped and cried the two miles home.

"YOU'RE LATE," Chi broadcasted when she opened the office door.

Breck hobbled across the floor, careful not to put too much pressure on her ankle. She had driven herself to see her doctor after she made it back home and got showered. Her ankle had swollen so large in that short time that she had to stop a mile from her house and take her shoe off or risk having it cut off. Luckily for her the ankle wasn't broken, but she needed to be careful for a few weeks anyway, which meant no more running for a while.

"What happened to you?" Chi asked, peering over the desk at Breck's neatly wrapped foot inside one of her house slippers.

"Stepped in a crack," Breck announced, and flipped through the messages. She stopped when she found one from Stephen. "What does he want?" She frowned.

"He wants you to call him." Chi walked around the desk and took Breck by the arm to help her into her office.

Breck hated talking to Stephen. He was so cold and abrupt. She doubted the man ever smiled a day in his life. How in the world had Eric and Stephen become friends?

It was protocol for Breck to visit a site during the last month of construction, just to make sure the builders were following the plans. She'd never had any problems with construction companies skimping on plans in order to save money or time, but she had known it to happen to other designers. She doubted Martin and Brian would ever dream of it. She was sure her visit to the center site was the purpose of Stephen's call, but now she wished she could get out of it.

Breck settled into her chair, and Chi fetched her a pillow from the storage room and placed it underneath her foot.

"Thanks," Breck said as she glanced at the pink "while you were out" slip with Stephen's name and telephone number scribbled across it. Besides the fact that she really didn't want to talk to Stephen Peterson, she couldn't dismiss that the only reason she was talking to him was because Eric refused to talk to her. Every time she had Stephen on the phone she couldn't erase the image of Eric sitting in his office less than fifty feet away. A few times she had come dangerously close to requesting that Stephen transfer her to Eric, but she quickly dismissed the thought. It would only add fuel to an already out-of-control fire.

Breck punched in the number.

"Warren and Peterson." It was Amy's friendly voice; Breck couldn't understand how the woman maintained such poise working for an impersonal man such as Stephen.

"Hello, Amy. This is Breck Larson. Is Stephen available?"

"Hi, Breck. Yes he is. I'll transfer you." Breck heard several clicks before the call went through. No doubt Amy had to go through the full formalities to get to Stephen. All of this could have been avoided if he had given her the number to his direct line in his office when they'd started working more closely together. That's what Eric had done.

Eric. She sighed heavily and waited on the phone, resenting the call even more.

"What an ass," Breck said as she listened to the hold music.

"Hello, Breck." Stephen interrupted a song she actually wanted to hear. That was so like him.

"Hello, Stephen. You left a message for me?"

"Yes, I did. Are you still planning to visit? We only have about a month of construction left. Eric and I discussed that now would be a good time for you to come and check things out."

Eric, Breck thought, and shook her head. The last thing Eric wanted was for her to visit Boston. She was certain that if he could reverse his decision to even have her on this project he would do that.

"I agree. Now would be an excellent time. Can I use someone in your office to help me select a place to stay that isn't far from the site?"

"We'll take care of that for you. There will be a car available for your use as well."

Breck nodded. "Thank you."

"When should we expect you?"

Breck looked at her calendar. Thanksgiving was the following week, and she planned on spending the day with her family in Indianapolis. "I'll arrive at the site one week from today, but I'll book a flight for Saturday. Is that reasonable?"

"That's reasonable. Will you be staying through the completion?"

"Yes."

"Wonderful. I'll inform Eric of your plans. Have a good day." With that, he hung up the phone without waiting for her to say good-bye as well. She heard the hum of the disconnected line.

"Ohhh, that bugs the shit out of me." Breck tensed as she slammed the receiver down on the phone. That man was so damned cold. No heart, no compassion, nothing. She positioned herself more comfortably in her chair, trying her best to alleviate the throbbing pain of her ankle.

"Chi!" she yelled into the outer office. She heard Chi's chair scratch across the linoleum floor and counted her footsteps as they inched closer to her office. It took Chi six steps to make it to her door. "I'm leaving for Boston next Saturday. I'll be gone for a month." Chi nodded. "I'll take a fax with me, and my board, so it'll be business as usual. Tell Jonathan that I'll overnight any designs I'm working on. Can you come on weekends?"

Chi leaned against the door. "Why?"

"Because I may need a friend. Hell, it's a business expense." She picked up the pencil, the closest thing to her hand, and hurled it across the room. "Stephen Peterson is a fucking asshole, and Eric doesn't want to talk to me." She buried her head in her hands and cried again. She'd been crying too much over this. For Christ's sake, she hadn't even met him. For all she knew she could be stressing out over the Elephant Man.

Chi walked over and leaned down to wrap her arms around Breck's shoulders. "I'm so sorry this is happening to you," she said as she rested her head on top of Breck's.

"Yeah, but you told me so. You tried to warn me that I was getting too deep, but did I listen?" Breck shook her head feverishly as the tears fell.

Chi didn't comment but Breck didn't think she would. Chi wasn't the type of friend who reveled in the "I told you so" opportunities. Ever since they'd become friends, Chi had been a wonderful ear and a great shoulder to lean on. Just like her, Chi had her difficulties with relationships, with her family, and with the world in general. Her mother, who was African-American, was very accepting of her coming out, but that was not the case with Chi's father, a Japanese-American. His alienation caused Chi tremendous grief and kept her from having the type of relationship with her mother they both longed for. Oftentimes they met for lunch in secrecy, only because it would cause her mother so much misery if her husband knew about it beforehand.

"What's going to happen when you get there?" Chi asked.

Breck placed her foot on the floor again. "Eric will probably ignore me."

BRECK LIMPED from the ramp onto the concourse. The ankle pain had subsided a bit, but she still couldn't walk without a limp. She looked around at the men standing nearby with signs and didn't see one with her name on it. Stephen had told her that someone would meet her at the airport. Her eyes stopped on a good-looking, brown-skinned man standing alone against a far wall with his hands buried deep inside his pants pockets. His eyes were fixed on her. She turned from him and glanced around the airport to see if anyone was walking in her direction, but she saw no one. She looked again at the man standing against the wall. He was dressed in a pair of jeans and a black T-shirt, tucked in. There was nothing extraordinary about him aside from the fact that he hadn't taken his eyes off her. That made her uneasy to be there alone.

Trying to dismiss him, Breck looked around again for someone approaching her, a driver or perhaps Stephen Peterson himself. She dreaded having to spend a car trip with the man, but he had told her that she would be taken to her hotel and she had no idea where her reservation was, how far it was from the airport, or how to get there.

Now the man had left his place against the wall and begun to walk toward her. Breck watched him very closely. He was very tall, his shoulders were broad, his chest full and deep. His dark skin seemed to glow in the airport light. He had a sure step, each stride confident and long. The closer he came to her, the more overpowering his presence became. Suddenly she felt a bolt inside her chest, and she almost fainted.

Eric.

The airport seemed to go deathly quiet, with no one but her and Eric there. She planted her eyes on him as he stepped closer. Her breath rose and fell in her chest, and she was thankful it didn't require a conscious effort on her part. He was upon her, and she inhaled his scent. Tuscany Forte, one of her favorites. Perhaps he knew that, but she didn't recall ever telling him. She took a deep breath before even attempting to look into his eyes. She had only seen them in her dreams. When she found the nerve to finally look up, she saw that his eyes were wide and brown and shiny, everything she could ever have imagined they would be. Her heart beat so hard and fast in her chest, she could swear everyone in the airport could hear it.

He reached to touch her face, and all she could do was close her eyes and catch her breath. "How did you know it was me?" he asked. He dropped his hand to his side. He stepped away from her, perhaps distrustful of the force that seemed to pull them together.

"I felt you," she said, her voice slightly above a whisper.

Eric fell silent, and suddenly a voice over the loudspeaker reminded them they were standing in the middle of a busy airport. Breck coughed to break the silence and glanced around to see if others had noticed the awkwardness. No one seemed to be looking at them.

"Stephen told me about your ankle. I came to help you with your bags."

"Bullshit," she said, unable to keep the words from escaping her lips. Eric stepped back and glared at her, but she was in no mood to apologize. It had been a long flight and her foot still hurt. She didn't need or want the confrontation, but the least he could do at this point was to be honest with her.

"Don't look at me like that," she said, beating down his stare. "You could have easily had someone meet me."

"I was trying to be helpful."

"Bullshit," she said again. "You wanted to see me. Can't you at least admit that much?"

Eric didn't say anything. He took the baggage-claim ticket from her hand and walked on, leaving her trailing behind him with a full view of his backside.

Yes, it was definitely a nice view. Still, she'd rather be walking beside him, but there was no way she was going to catch up. Well, her snappy mouth was the cause of that. You've got to calm down, Breck, she repeated in her mind as she limped after him. When they reached the luggage carousel, she pointed to her two bags as they circled around. Eric quickly grabbed them and headed toward the exit, still not uttering a word to her.

Oh, great, she thought as she headed out onto the concrete walkway. Is this the way this visit was going to be? She shook her head and stepped into the busy drive, causing a few cars to go around her. Eric took her hand firmly into his and pulled her with him.

"This can be pretty treacherous," he said, looking for the best time for them to cross the busy road into the street-level parking garage. His body had become a protective shield, and his strength pulled her quickly across the street. Once they were on the other side, she stopped to take in the pain. "You okay?" he asked.

She nodded and placed the foot easily on the ground again. He started walking again and stopped just a few spaces away from a black Range Rover.

"Nice car," Breck said, grimacing through the pain.

"Thanks," he said flatly as he opened the back and tossed her luggage inside. Breck stood outside the passenger door and waited for Eric to let her in. He walked to her side and opened the door for her, then he helped her up to the seat so she wouldn't have to put pressure on her ankle. Inside the truck, she saw a few kiddie toys and a car seat in back.

"I'm not going to apologize for being right, you know," she said as soon as they rode out of the airport traffic.

Eric remained silent as he looked straight ahead, only occasionally turning her way when he checked the side-view mirror. His obvious decision to take no notice of her only irritated her more. "I'm sitting right beside you and you're still shutting me out! Why the hell did you bother to pick me up?"

"What do you want from me?" Eric retorted, making it a fair shouting match.

"I want you to be honest with me and stop shutting me out."

Breck watched as he sucked breath into his lungs and held it, then forced it out through pursed lips.

"Why did you meet me at the airport?" she asked again.

"I can't avoid you for a month, so I might as well get it over with," he said. He rounded a sharp corner off the exit and headed down a tree-lined avenue.

"Oh. Well, thanks a lot." So much for chivalry.

"I didn't mean it like that," he said, and settled against his seat, one hand on the steering wheel and the other on the gear shift.

"I don't understand why you're avoiding me at all. You asked me if we could still be friends, and then you disappeared. Some friend."

"Breck, you have got to understand how I feel."

"Understand how you feel? What about how I feel? You and I had become so close. I could talk to you about anything, even things I wouldn't dream of telling Chi. I feel like I've lost one of my best friends."

He remained silent, staring straight ahead.

Seeing that he was not going to be a willing partici-
pant in any type of conversation, Breck followed his
lead and settled against her seat as well. She didn't know
where he was taking her, so she had no idea how much
longer she would have to be stuck in this uncomfortable
position. "I wish none of this had ever happened," she
said beneath her breath.

"What? Me or the contract?"

"What's the difference?" she mumbled, and rested her
head against the seat. She closed her eyes for the re-
mainder of the drive.

More than a half hour later, they turned down a remote road and drove until they reached a secluded lot
with some townhomes. The lone building was set in a
grove of trees, almost as if someone had placed it there
and forgotten about it. The land around it was completely undeveloped.

Breck looked around and pulled her sweater tight
around her body. The temperature in Boston had to be at
least ten degrees lower than in Indianapolis. She had arrived at the end of the foliage season. Brown and burnt-
red leaves littered the ground and drifted into piles
around the townhomes.

Eric took her luggage from the rear of the truck and
walked a few feet ahead of her to the building. There
were six units, each with a private entrance. Eric opened
the door, then handed her the keys. "I came earlier and
lit the fireplace for you. It's been chilly all week." He
carried her luggage into the bedroom.

The fire lit the dark room, so she could easily make
out where everything was, even though all of the blinds
were shut. When Eric returned, he walked around and
pulled them open, letting the sunlight in. She noticed the
assortment of wildflowers in a vase on the kitchen table.

"Was that your idea too?" she asked, nodding toward the flowers. He ignored her. "This is a very nice

building," she said, removing her sweater and tossing it across the cushioned sofa. "Is it one of yours?"

"Yes. You're about five miles from Mansfield. You won't be able to find a place like this in Boston."

"Why not?"

"Land is scarce and expensive in Boston." He walked to the sofa and sat down. At least he wasn't going to rush away, leaving her stranded in the middle of nowhere.

She hobbled to the sofa and sat down inches from him. She lifted her leg and rested it atop the coffee table, frowning.

"How on earth did you manage to sprain your ankle?" he asked, grabbing one of the sofa pillows and placing it underneath her foot.

Breck sighed. "Not paying attention."

"Are you going to be okay here by yourself, or do I need to hire a nurse for you?"

Breck chuckled. She was mad as hell at him, but he was still the sweetest and most considerate man she had ever met. *Met.* She could actually say that now. "I think I can manage."

Eric slid closer to her, took her leg from the coffee table, and placed it in his lap. He began to massage her calf, while she settled farther down on the sofa and enjoyed his touch.

"You're very beautiful, Breck," he said.

This took her by surprise. She hadn't noticed him looking at her long enough to form an opinion about her beauty. "Sorry to disappoint you. It probably would have made it easier for you if I wasn't attractive." She stared at him for what seemed like forever until he finally looked away.

"You don't let up, do you?" He dismissed the conversation. "Does that help?" he asked.

"Yes," she said softly. The awkwardness had returned, but not because of ill feelings. It was passion, love, and maybe even a little lust. Whatever it was between them, it was stronger than she'd ever imagined.

"Did you have a pleasant Thanksgiving?" he asked, still massaging her leg.

"Yes," she responded. Breck had once told him how much she loved her family Thanksgivings. Breck had a typical dysfunctional family. When she arrived at her parents' modest three-bedroom home in central Indiana, her older brother, Alex, and younger sister, Tamara, usually greeted her with the latest family gossip. Tamara lived in California, and no one really knew for sure if she would make the festivities until the last minute. There were times when she planned to come out but didn't make it because of bad weather or a canceled flight.

Alex's girlfriend had the only grandchild in the family so far, his fifteen-year-old son, Jeffery. Alex and his girlfriend, Celeste, had had Jeffery immediately after high school, but the relationship had ended not long after Alex left for college. Alex and his wife, Robyn, had been married for eight years now and had no plans to have any children of their own, despite a rapidly ticking biological clock, about which Breck's mother kept reminding Robyn.

Tamara was two years younger than Breck and still in the prime of her partying days. She gloated about the beach volleyball league she was in and the usual group of friends who took weekend excursions to Vegas, Mexico, or some other party scene around the globe. Tamara had finished college two years ago, majoring in computer programming, and made a good living at McDonnell Douglas. She usually brought home a gentleman guest, but the family had come to accept that that never meant he was a potential husband.

The Larsons sat for dinner in Sunday attire but soon afterward changed into oversized sweatshirts, turtlenecks, jeans, mittens, and hats for the annual game of touch football at the middle school. They would conclude the weekend by putting up the Christmas decorations and the Christmas tree. The angel was a simple black ceramic angel that Breck's mom had found after Christmas one year on clearance at a local African-American bookstore.

The food was the typical southern feast that included a golden-brown turkey, a honey-glazed ham topped with pineapples and cherries, yams mixed with sweet marshmallows, collard and mustard greens seasoned with ham hocks, green beans simmered with potatoes and ham bits, chitterlings and hog maws thoroughly cleaned and seasoned with red pepper, cole slaw, macaroni and cheese topped with bread crumbs, and dressing seasoned with turkey broth and cream-of-mushroom soup. The grand finale was all the homemade cakes and pies you could think of, but Breck's favorite was the triple-layer chocolate cake topped with pecan halves.

After she had described the meal to him, Eric practically fell to the floor. He would kill to have a meal like that again. He and his family had left to spend a week with Gaby's parents in upstate New York. Gabriela Aletor's family owned several homes, one of which was on several hundred acres of land in Syracuse. At Thanksgiving, she, Eric, and Darius, along with her two brothers, their wives, and their kids, all returned to the large ten-bedroom home for the week. Thanksgiving was a very formal, black-tie affair, complete with a gourmet dinner and printed menus at each place setting. There were always at least two other couples joining the Aletor family, usually a diplomat or some other political figure. The weekend following Thanksgiving, everyone participated in setting up the Christmas decorations. By Sunday night all the decorations would be hung, including the Christmas tree, topped with an African angel dressed in white and trimmed with fine gems and gold. Eric estimated the angel was worth over twenty thousand dollars, based on the emeralds, sapphires, rubies, and diamonds sewn onto the clothing and the golden halo that circled the head. The eyes of the angel were black onyx. It was a family heirloom, passed down from the oldest child of each generation. Gaby's oldest brother, Kofi, stood to inherit it.

"Not exactly something you would keep in a shoe box in the basement," Eric had said. The Aletors were a very nice family and very close, but he said he was always glad for the week to be over. "It's just too long of a time for a child to be in a museum." He always found it difficult to relax there because everything was incredibly expensive and all the children had to be closely supervised. He mimicked Gaby's mom walking behind them, saying in a tiny but pesky voice, "Mind the children."

"Every year when we return home, Darius and I are so tense from being in this museum. We walk into the kitchen and take a glass or a plate and just drop it." He laughed. "It feels great."

"And who cleans it up?"

"Oh, I clean it up. We do it because it's a great release." Breck could picture Eric urging little Darius into the kitchen to break something. She wondered if it was a great release for the both of them or just Eric.

"I should go," he announced, and rose from the sofa.

"You don't have to." She grabbed his arms, wanting desperately to fall into his embrace and kiss him. He took her fingers and their hands were joined. When he looked at her, Breck knew his thoughts were the same as hers. She knew that he couldn't deny how he felt about her any longer, because it was in his eyes. If he said anything contrary to the fact that he had fallen for her, he would be lying.

"I have to go," he repeated. He took a full step from the sofa and leaned safely against the wall on the opposite side of the room.

Breck covered her face. It wasn't the sense of defeat she was grappling with but the mixed signals and the heightened emotions. He was capable of taking her to a summit, only to drop her so hard it knocked the wind out of her. "Why are you doing this to me?" she asked.

"What am I doing to you?" he replied, almost sarcastically, as if it was the most ridiculous thing she could have asked.

"You're toying with me." Breck pulled herself up from the sofa and stood in front of him. "You came here to start a fire. You stopped to pick wildflowers for me and thought enough to put them in a vase. You picked me up from the airport, and then you massaged my leg—" Breck's voice reached a high pitch before she paused and took a quick, deep breath to settle herself. "You asked me what I want from you. I should be asking you, what do you want from me?"

"Breck, give me a break. I'm trying to do the right thing here. I knew I had gotten too deep with you. That's why I had to separate myself."

"Then why did you?"

"Why did I what?"

"Why did you get emotionally involved with me?"

He shrugged. "I honestly don't know."

"You have to do better than that." She leaned against the back of the sofa to take the pressure off her left leg, tired from carrying the extra weight.

"Breck," he said, "I'm in love with my wife." She felt a dagger through her heart. She nodded. She had that coming and she knew it, and all she could do was relent. Maybe that was what she needed to hear to just leave it alone.

"Okay," she said, holding back the tears.

"I'm sorry," he said, seeming to realize he had hurt her.

"Please, spare me the pity. I've reconciled how I feel about you, and I'm not going to apologize for it. Just stop playing me like a yo-yo. Either you want me or you don't. Don't play with my feelings, because it hurts like hell to want you and know I can never have you." She turned away from him and headed around the sofa to sit again.

"I never meant to hurt you—"

"I know," Breck interrupted him. "You've told me that many times already." She turned to face him, trying to control the sobs in her throat. "You can go now."

But he didn't move. He leaned against the door and looked at her. When she looked at him, his eyes were still on her.

"Please leave," she said. "I can't do this anymore. You've made your choice, now I can move on."

He nodded and left.

TEN

SETTING UP an office in the townhome was easy. The office equipment arrived early Sunday morning, and Breck made sure the fax machine and the computer were connected first. She hopped around searching for AC outlets and found one near the breakfast bar, where she placed the fax machine. When she found the telephone outlet, she discovered the townhome was equipped with two outside phone lines.

"Hmm," she said as she stood and scratched her head. She had no idea what the telephone numbers were. She made a mental note to ask Stephen or Eric. She didn't know who would be calling to check on her or visiting the site with her. Eric might very well go into hiding again and stay away from her for the next month.

The two-bedroom furnished townhome was huge compared with townhomes she had seen in Indiana. The bedroom fit a king-size bed, two dressers, an armoire, a desk, and a chair quite comfortably. When she opened the closet door, she was surprised to step into an area large enough to fit a twin-size bed. From the living room, French doors opened out onto a brick patio. When Breck stepped outside and looked around, she saw that her neighbor's patio area was hidden by a large cement wall at least twenty feet away from her area. The master bathroom came equipped with a black whirlpool bath large enough for two people, as well as a shower. There was also a half bath off the kitchen. The furniture looked as if it had never been used. She wondered if the firm reserved the space for business associates only and rented out the other units.

Breck set up her drawing board and chair in the bedroom, then changed her mind and placed them in the living room, across from the fireplace. When the blinds were pulled, there was more light than in the bedroom, and she worked better in a well-lit room. She stood in front of the doors with her arms folded across her body and stared out onto a wooded lot. The warm, comforting rays of the sun reached into the room and kissed her cheek.

It was peaceful here. She couldn't tell if anyone else was in the building or if she was its lone tenant. She heard nothing from outside of her unit, not even the cars on the road, quite a contrast to what she was accustomed to back home. She imagined the scenery during the winter months and wished she could stay longer to capture the essence of its snow-covered trees with her camera or a paintbrush. She shivered as a soft wind brushed against the door and crept between the thin door frames. The trees seemed to wave at her, welcoming her to the neighborhood. She smiled and took a long sip of coffee.

She was up the next morning at her usual hour even though she still was not able to jog—a five-year habit that wasn't so easy to break. Her ankle was not well enough for her to do any other form of cardiovascular exercise outside of riding a bike, and she didn't have one of those with her, so she sat on the living room floor and stretched, did her crunches, and exercised her arms with her dumbbells. Several times she squinted in pain from a sudden movement of her ankle. It seemed like it was never going to heal.

Halfway through her second set of crunches, the telephone rang. Carefully she rolled over on her stomach and pushed herself off the floor. She made it to the phone by the fourth ring. "Hello," she said, wheezing into the handset.

"Morning." She recognized his voice immediately, although she had not expected to hear it—at least not this soon. She switched the telephone to her other ear, mostly out of habit but also to steal a few seconds to collect her thoughts.

"Morning," she said. She couldn't think of anything else to say to him.

"I just called to make sure you were comfortable and to see if you needed anything. If you rather I not—"

"Eric, please stop," Breck huffed. "It's okay. Really." He remained on the line, even though words seemed to fail him. He was extremely uncomfortable around her. "I don't know the telephone numbers here," she said.

"They're in the drawer along with the number for the grocer. They'll deliver your groceries for you, so you won't have to worry about it."

Breck nodded. "Thanks, but I doubt if I'll use it. I wouldn't mind taking the opportunity to get out of here."

"The key to the car is also in the desk drawer. When you walk out your door, the door to the left leads to the garage. It's the black Mercedes."

"The company car is a Mercedes?"

"We make sure all our clients are well taken care of."

"I can see this. I have to admit, this place is incredible."

"You're going to be here for a month, and I didn't think you would want to be cooped up in some dingy hotel room."

Interesting, Breck thought. So it was Eric's idea for her to stay here. Then it occurred to her: the scenes around the townhome perfectly described the type of place she had mentioned to Eric as her ideal home on one of those nights when they'd talked on the phone for hours. Eric, of course, lived in *his* dream house, but Breck knew she was not there yet. She loved her condo but hoped to move one day to a house in an active community that was more isolated, with a lot less traffic.

"I wish I could jog," she said.

"I'm sure you'll be able to before you leave us."

"I hope so." She paused. "I need the directions to the construction site."

"I'll e-mail them to you. Did you bring your laptop?"

"Of course."

"Good. Well, I have to run. If you need anything today, give me a call at the house. Otherwise, I'll see you Monday morning."

"Okay. Have a good day." Breck hung up the phone and smiled. "He loves me," she declared.

MONDAY MORNING she did her exercises, unwrapped her foot, and took a long, hot bath. When she was done, she wrapped the foot again and headed to the site.

Eric was there when she arrived, along with Martin and Brian. She hadn't seen them since she first met them several months ago. When she pulled up, the three chums were standing around immersed in a private joke. She wondered if they would ever get much done if they had to work together every day.

"Welcome back, young lady," Martin said. He walked over and gave her a big hug. He was definitely not concerned about being slapped with a sexual-harassment suit. He hugged her like she was a part of their clique. And she liked it.

"Thanks. Hi, Brian." She turned to face the most quiet of the trio. Brian seemed to not speak unless he was spoken to.

"Hello. You getting around okay with that foot?" Brian asked.

Breck looked down and wished they didn't make such a big deal about her damn foot. "I'll live. How's it going here?" She sniffed in the cool air and started walking around. Martin handed her a hard hat and they began the tour of the building. Breck took the designs and began inspecting the building as diligently as possible. After several hours they stopped for lunch, deli sandwiches and sodas at a nearby café.

There was something euphoric about sitting in the company of three very powerful, handsome black men. It wasn't just their physical presence that captivated her; all had demonstrated a prowess that made her feel as if she were sitting among kings. She relaxed and drank it up. They were friends who loved one another much the way she loved Chi, and by the easiness between them she could tell they had shared good times and maybe a few tears as well. Eric, she could tell, was the jokester of the trio. Martin was the leader and, quite possibly, the authority figure, while Brian was the baby. Eric and Martin both seemed to feel they needed to take care of him, which she immediately picked up on by the questions they showered on him. Physically, Brian was in no way a baby. He stood just an inch under Eric's nose and eye to eye with Martin, so she wondered what had happened in his life that made Eric and Martin feel responsible for him.

After lunch, Breck parted company. She hated leaving them, but she needed to head back to the townhome and catch up on business in Indiana. When she arrived, she started a fire in the fireplace, then saw that she had several faxes and e-mails from Chi. Before answering the messages Breck stripped off her work clothes and slid comfortably into an oversized T-shirt, baggy sweatpants, and ankle socks. Once she was comfortable on the sofa, she picked up the phone and called Indiana. "Hey, Chi, what's up?" she said, tucking her feet underneath her, still conscious of the ailing foot.

"Business as usual. How is it going there?"

"Not bad," she said, unable to conceal the happiness in her voice.

"I take it you've seen Eric?"

"Yup. He met me at the airport."

Chi waited for her to offer more information, but she didn't. "And?" Chi finally urged.

"Nothing. Everything's cool." They spent the next forty-five minutes going over each fax and e-mail Chi had sent and the phone calls she'd taken at the office in Indiana. Breck wrote notes on the urgent matters and told Chi to handle the rest. When they had finished with business, Chi immediately wanted to know all of the details of her first meeting with Eric.

"So, what is he like?" Chi asked. "Is he as good-looking as he sounds on the telephone?"

"He's very good-looking and polite and we've kept it very professional."

"Good. I'm glad to hear that."

"Listen, I have to run. I have a lot of work to do," Breck said, cutting the conversation short. It was good that she and Eric had kept things on a professional level, but that was not by her choice. "Are you coming this weekend?"

"Yeah, I'll be there. Tell Eric to make sure he tells us where all of the hot spots are."

Breck grinned. "Yeah, right. Later." She replaced the phone and sat in front of the fireplace. Her condo back in Indiana didn't have a fireplace, and she now wished it did. She could get used to this place.

SHE HAD fallen asleep on the sofa. When she opened her eyes, the blazing fire had been reduced to smoldering ashes. She was wiping the sleep from her eyes when the doorbell rang.

She leapt up and limped to the door. She looked out the peephole to see Eric standing on the other side. She threw the door open and stared blankly at him.

"Did I wake you?" he asked. It must be obvious, she realized.

"I fell asleep. Come on in." She stepped aside and let him walk through. "What's up?" she asked, and hopped back to the sofa.

"I stopped by to get your report on the progress. We didn't get a chance to talk after lunch."

"Oh." She sat down on the sofa again and fluffed the pillow in front of her. She took a deep breath to get her bearings. She wasn't fully awake yet. She had rarely taken an afternoon nap before, and it seemed to immobilize her. "Well, so far I'm impressed with everything. They are excellent builders."

"Yes, they are. We use them every time we have a project in Boston." Eric sat down in the chair opposite her.

"Can I get you anything?" she said, sliding forward on the sofa. "Coffee?"

"No, I'm fine," Eric said, settling into his seat.

"I think I'm going to have a cup," she said, easing up off of the sofa and limping into the kitchen to start the brew. "Chi will be in town this weekend, and she wants you to hook us up with all the hot spots!" she yelled from the kitchen.

Eric laughed. "I can arrange that. I can ask Brian to show you around. I'm kind of out of touch in that area. He's the only single man left. Maybe you can hook him up with Chi."

Breck chuckled. "I don't think so. She's gay." She returned to the living room to wait for the water to boil.

"Oh."

"You mean you're not going to be our personal tour guide?" Breck joked.

"No, not this weekend. It's Gaby's birthday."

"Ah," Breck said, embarrassed that she had asked. "So how are Stephen and Gaby reacting to the center?"

"They still don't get it, but they're tolerating it. This

project is very low on Stephen's list of priorities, and Gaby just can't wait until it's over."

"Is that why you've been so involved lately, because Stephen doesn't want to do it anymore?"

Eric snarled.

"I'm sorry. Don't mean to be an annoyance. I know this project means a lot to you."

"Yes, it does, and it's not that Stephen wouldn't look after it. He's just overlooked too many details, so I had to step in. Like I said when I hired you"—he leaned forward—"this project is very personal, and I want it done just right."

Breck looked at Eric and saw that he was troubled. She knew he wanted Gaby to understand why this center meant so much to him, but she had been raised in an upper-class family in Brazil. She'd been educated at private schools and had earned undergraduate and graduate degrees from Columbia. She'd lived the perfect life, grown up and married Prince Charming, who happened to be from a blue-collar neighborhood in Massachusetts. Gaby had no way of understanding his need to give back to his old hometown and his effort to uplift it. The fact that she made no attempt distressed him the most.

"Is there anything I can do to help?" Breck asked.

"Yeah." Eric smiled and rubbed his forehead. "You can stop giving me a hard time."

Breck dropped her head and chuckled. "Deal," she said.

"What's with the getup?" he asked, pointing to her clothes.

"Hey." Breck stood up and modeled her baggy clothes. "This is my everyday after-work attire. If you don't like it, you can leave," she said, pointing to the door.

Eric waved her off. "No comment."

The smell of coffee sent her scrambling back into the kitchen.

"Does your ankle feel any better at all?" Eric asked, joining her there.

"It's still very sore. The doctor said it would be for at least three weeks."

"I'll leave you the name and number of the doctor who helped me with my shoulder injury."

"You mean after you discovered you couldn't fly like the eagles?" She giggled while she poured out a mug of coffee.

"You're such a smart-ass," he said, leaning against the doorway.

"Yeah, I know."

He smiled at her, which was a pleasure to see. She had often imagined his smile while they talked on the phone, but this was the first time he had actually smiled at her. She drank it in. "I have to go, but I'll see you at the site tomorrow," he announced, then leaned forward and kissed her on the cheek. It was a simple, spontaneous kiss, and she knew it would be a mistake to make it more than that.

"Okay," she said, making no attempt to stop him or give him a hard time.

Before he opened the door to leave, he turned once again to face her. "Are you really sorry that you met me?" he asked.

Breck had totally forgotten she had made that comment to him. She wondered how long he had wanted to ask her that.

"Does it bother you that I said that?" she asked, still standing in the kitchen doorway and taking a small sip from her mug.

"Yes, it does," he said without hesitating.

At least he was honest about this, Breck reasoned. She shook her head. "No, I'm not sorry I met you. I was angry and I shouldn't have said it."

He stared at her for a second longer, patted the wall, then left, closing the door softly behind him.

Breck returned to the sofa and pondered lighting another fire. The room was slightly chilly, but not cold. Winter was definitely on its way.

ELEVEN

THE INVITATION to the grand-opening gala was spectacular. Breck was lucky enough to have hers personally delivered by the man himself. It was printed on a scroll, and Breck unrolled it and read. She was impressed by the artistic and elegant touch of the keepsake, and she knew immediately the idea had to be Gaby's.

"I would have settled on the standard card invitation," Eric admitted after she commented on the presentation.

"Will anyone I know be there?"

"Martin and Brian, of course. You'll be able to meet Martin's wife, Alyce, and about a hundred other people from Boston and the area, including the mayor of Mansfield and his wife."

"Wow," she said. "Sounds like fun." Breck was walking much better now. When the pain had still persisted after several more days, she had finally taken Eric up on his offer and visited his doctor. It turned out that her ankle was a lot worse than she had realized but not incurable. He wrote her a prescription to reduce the swelling and also gave her three treatments of cortisone shots to alleviate the pain and help with the healing. The shots hurt like hell, but after the first week she was glad she had taken them. It took no time at all for the inflammation to subside, and in two weeks she felt good enough to jog again. However, instead of rushing back into her jogging routine, she began with five-mile brisk walks along the country roads near the townhomes. The cool air was crisp and clean, and she almost dreaded the time when her walks came to an end. But she also looked forward to the drive into Mansfield to work with Martin and Brian—and Eric, whenever he could escape the office to hang out with them. He usually managed to visit at least three days a week.

In the evenings she often sat out on the patio to enjoy a steaming cup of after-dinner coffee, snuggled in the quilted afghan Eric had sent her. She had grown very attached to the patchwork masterpiece. Although the night air was cool, the coffee and the afghan managed to keep her warm. After the second night of her new ritual, she had started writing in her journal while listening to her usual selection of classical or jazz. The stereo equipment at the townhome was just as elaborate as hers at home. She wasn't one of those people who had to have the latest in electronic gadgetry, but she did enjoy the sound of good music. It seemed Eric shared that sentiment.

"Care to join me for a cup of coffee?" Breck asked tonight as she filled her mug. The music she was playing was from a *Best of Beethoven* CD.

"Sure." Eric joined her in the kitchen and watched as she poured the fresh brew into a new mug. "Nice mugs," he commented.

Breck smiled. "I'm very particular about what I drink my coffee from," she said, handing him his mug. "I don't want to taste paper and I don't want to taste Styrofoam. I just want a good cup of coffee. It doesn't have to be fancy. It just has to be good."

"You should do a commercial," he teased.

They walked through the slightly opened patio doors. Breck sat down on the cushioned wooden chaise, while

Eric chose an iron chair and placed his mug on the matching table. Breck had grabbed her afghan before she headed out, and wrapped her feet in it.

"Glad you like it," Eric said, pointing to the afghan.

"Love it, actually," she said. "You have excellent taste."

"Nah. I just knew you would like it."

"And you were right." She looked across at him as she sipped from her mug. "Are you comfortable?"

"It's a little chilly out here."

"It's just the way I like it. I call it snuggle weather." Breck scooted her butt as far against the side of the chaise as possible and motioned for him. "Join me," she said.

He shook his head.

She grinned. "Are you afraid of me? I promise I don't bite." She patted the empty space beside her.

He gave her a look that suggested he was at least entertaining the thought, but he didn't move toward her.

"Are you afraid to sit next to me?"

He rolled his eyes. "I'm not afraid of you, Breck."

"We're friends, right? I'm not going to seduce you."

After a short pause he relented and accepted the offer. Once he was comfortably beside her, she wrapped the afghan around him too.

"It is very warm," he agreed, then leaned against the chaise and wrapped his arms around her.

Breck settled next to him and rested her head gently on his shoulder. They talked for a while, then she closed her eyes and listened to the wind whistling through the trees. The cool, peaceful night soothed and gladdened her.

"I noticed you're packed and ready to leave us," Eric said, disturbing the hush that had fallen between them.

"Yes," she said, and shifted sideways to be more comfortable. She pulled her knees up and crossed her legs until they rested on top of his. "My work is done here, and I need to get home and get ready for Christmas." She took a deep breath and snuggled closer to him; he wrapped his arms around her and pulled her into his chest. Breck inhaled his cologne and felt his heartbeat.

"Are you comfortable?" he asked.

"Yes," she said in a lowered voice. "Are you?"

"Yes. Maybe a bit too much."

Breck pushed off him and looked into his face. Her lips were inches from his, and his breath was at her nose.

She knew he cared for her—she saw it in his eyes and in the simple things he did for her. She had been snotty to him most of the time for rejecting her, but how could she condemn him for holding fast to his principles? She should respect his choice and simply walk away from him and Boston and let her feelings subside with time. Breck knew in her heart that was the right thing to do, but whenever she was near him, like this, she was reminded of how much she loved him. That wonderful, comforting feeling she had when she was with him was addictive, and she didn't want to lose it.

All she had to do was lean forward and she could steal a kiss.

Instead Eric pulled back and took her hand. "Have you ventured beyond the woods?" he asked.

She shook her head. The spell had been broken. He walked inside, grabbed a wool blanket, then came back out.

"Bring your afghan," he said, guiding her away from the patio and into the woods.

"Where are you taking me?" It had been years since she'd wandered into the woods at night. The moon lit their way through the trees and farther away from the townhome.

"You'll see." They walked a careful maze through the dense woods, crumbling crackling leaves with each step. Just beyond the trees was a small clearing of grass shining in the moonlight.

Eric spread his blanket on the ground, then motioned for her to join him. Once they were on the ground, he wrapped her afghan around them. Breck lay in his arms, her head resting on his chest. She closed her eyes and took a deep breath, enjoying the serenity that enveloped them. They lay there for several minutes, getting closer to each other. She should have been cold but she wasn't. The heat from Eric's body and the excitement of being so close to him was enough to warm her completely. When the cool air nipped at her nose, she only got closer.

"This only happens in the movies," Breck said, gazing up at the bright stars in the sky. "'It was a dark and starry night,'" she recited, and they both laughed.

DRESSED FOR the party but wishing she could cancel, Breck waited until the limousine came to pick her up. The idea of finally seeing Eric with his wife did not excite her. She had known this day was coming, and there was nothing she could do to prevent it. She would get to see firsthand the happy couple, holding hands, loving each other. She knew she'd wish it could be her.

Chi could not make it to Boston for the gala, so Breck was alone, with no shoulder to lean on, and she was sure she was going to need it tonight. "Lets get this over with," she said aloud, and stepped over the packed boxes and luggage. She was scheduled to leave Massachusetts first thing Sunday morning, and after tonight it wouldn't be too soon.

But she was going to miss Mansfield. She had actually grown to love the area, particularly Boston. Although Mansfield was at least forty-five minutes away, she had spent quite a bit of time at Boston restaurants, savoring the New England clam chowder. Other than the time she had spent with Eric, one of the highlights of her trip came when she, Chi, and Brian had taken an excursion to the observation deck of the Prudential Tower in Back Bay. They had arrived just before sundown, and although they had thought it would be too late to get a full glimpse of the city, it was just the right time to see the sun brush a magnificent shade of orange across the sky. Breck leaned against the protective glass and knew she had fallen in love with Boston. Leaving it would be like leaving her heart behind.

Then there were Martin and Brian. They had welcomed her into their world. She was more than just the designer; she had become one of the guys, experiencing a sense of belonging she had not shared with anyone other than Chi.

Dressed in fashionable black, Breck slid a red pashmina shawl with fur trim over her bare shoulders. She'd purchased the tight-fitting strapless dress in New York a year ago during one of her shopping adventures with Chi. Chi had first spotted the dress and urged Breck to buy it. After looking at the price, Breck had declined, but now she was glad she'd been such a pushover. She checked herself in the mirror again before she opened the door for her driver. He was dressed equally impressively in a black tuxedo, and courteously helped her step down the flight of stairs onto the pavement. Once they reached the car, he opened the door for her and stood aside for her to get in. Inside, Breck helped herself to a glass of chilled champagne, courtesy of Warren & Peterson. She had to hand it to Eric and his gang; they sure did know how to throw a party.

Ten minutes later, they pulled up to the Eric D. Warren Convention Center. Eric had intended for the center to be named after the community, but he lost that vote by a huge margin. The building stood gallantly on a prospering street. On either side were newly renovated buildings and some still undergoing changes. These projects had started within the last month of Breck's stay. Warren & Peterson had owned most of them but had sold them off, as usual, below market value. One of the buildings would become the community's new and improved library. Not far away, several homes that were once prime candidates for the wrecking ball were now under massive renovation.

With the aid of her elegant chauffeur, Breck stepped from the limousine and stared at the center. Born in her mind, the structure stood noble and proud in a community that well deserved it. She finally strolled into the center along with a rush of other invited guests. Once inside, she blended in well with the slew of women wearing evening gowns and shimmering after-five attire, while the men were splendidly dressed in tailored tuxedos. Breck joined the line moving toward the flowing champagne fountain and grabbed a flute.

"Breck, over here!" She turned and saw Martin motioning for her to join them. He stood with a group on the other side of fountain.

"Hello, Martin," she said, approaching the handsome group.

"To the woman of the hour," he said, lifting his flute to salute her.

"Hardly. Has Eric arrived?" The image of Eric parading around the center with his Brazilian princess on his arm flooded her mind.

"Not yet. You know he's going to have to make a grand entrance."

Was that his idea or his wife's? she wondered. She would never voice such a thought aloud or risk being branded as a jealous lover. But hell, she wasn't even a lover, so she should be able to say what she pleased about a woman she'd never met.

"Breck, I want you to meet my wife, Alyce," Martin said, saving her from her own deranged thoughts. He stepped aside to offer her a full view of the petite woman beside him. Breck turned and shook her hand, amused by the sight of Alyce, no more than five feet tall, dwarfed by her husband.

"It's wonderful to finally meet you," Alyce said. "Martin has said some wonderful things about you." Her voice was very soft and gentle.

"Breck is responsible for this magnificent building," Martin added.

"It was Eric's vision," Breck protested. "I just put it on paper for him." She'd never learned to accept compliments. "And besides, you guys built it," she said, motioning to Brian and Martin.

"You're too humble. Let me introduce you to some important people. Eric told me to make sure I took care of you until he got here." Martin seemed bemused.

Breck found it flattering that Eric felt it was his responsibility to look after her, even in his absence. It was things like that that convinced her that his feelings for her went deeper than he'd ever reveal. Breck wondered if Martin suspected anything and if he could sense the tension whenever she and Eric were together. But what did it matter? In two days she would be gone and the rest would be closed text. Life in Mansfield would continue, and she would become a distant memory, if not a ghost.

Eric had indeed invited the elite of Boston, and each of them complimented her on a job well done. She also managed to give out a few business cards and collect a few, which she made a mental note to have Chi follow up on.

"You are looking very delicious tonight, Ms. Larson." Breck turned around, and a middle-aged man dressed impeccably in a well-tailored suit maneuvered closer to her and slid his hand around her waist. "Eric tells me that you're single. I have to ask why a beautiful and re-markable woman such as yourself hasn't been snatched up yet?" A crooked smile crept across his face while his eyes roamed the full length of her body.

"Oh, it just hasn't happened yet," Breck said, stepping back from his grasp. "I don't believe we've met." She held out her hand, which he gingerly accepted and held on to. Looking down at his soft brown hand, she saw that his nails were neatly manicured and brushed with a thin coat of clear fingernail polish. His hand felt cold even though the room was warm and comfortable.

"Roger Bracken, president of Mutual Bank. Eric banks with me, as do most of the men here tonight." He waved his finger toward the crowd.

"Pleased to meet you, Mr. Bracken." He had the at-tributes of a man who was used to having his way.

"Call me Roger. I'm someone you should know, Ms. Larson. Give me a call. We can make things happen for you." He reached into a side pocket and extracted a gold case carrying carefully engraved cards. Then he took a pen and wrote on the back of one. "This is my private line. Not everyone gets that number." He winked.

"I'm honored," Breck said, trying to smile as gra-ciously as she could.

He chuckled through closed lips and carefully slid his hand down her back to the curve of her ass before he walked away.

"I need a drink," she said beneath her breath, and strolled to the flowing fountain. She eyed Brian standing beside it.

"No date tonight?" She rubbed his shoulder as she stood beside him.

"She dumped me."

Breck laughed. "What did you do?"

"More what I *wouldn't* do."

"Would you be my date?" she asked, turning to face

him. "I'm not in the mood to fend off these sticky-fingered little old men." She looked around her and spotted Roger standing off with another group of impeccably dressed men. She shivered.

Brian laughed. "Who's coming on to you?"

"Roger Bracken." She frowned.

"Ah, now that's interesting. He happens to be married to the mayor's sister, who happens to be standing over there." He pointed to an elegantly dressed young blonde.

"What does she see in him?"

"Money," Brian whispered, and entwined his arm with hers. "In any case"—he handed her a glass filled with champagne, then filled another for himself—"I would love to be your date." They clicked glasses and drank. "Now, let's dance," he said, taking her glass from her hand and placing both glasses on a nearby table before waltzing with her to the dance floor.

Brian turned out to be better company than Breck had imagined. She didn't mind clinging to his arms, and he wasn't a bad dancer either. What was the deal with him and his girlfriend, and why had she dumped him? Definitely her loss, Breck thought.

Suddenly, as they moved together during another dance, the room filled with applause and cheers. They turned around to witness the grand entrance of the man of the hour and his very lovely wife.

Gaby was unlike any image Breck had conceived of her. She was not the amber-skinned beauty with flowing golden hair that could blow in the wind. Small curls were chopped close to her scalp, and her skin was lustrous, beautiful, and dark—she was the darkest woman Breck had ever laid eyes on. She was indeed a princess, but of visible African descent. As she strolled through the entrance holding Eric's arm, her strapless, white chiffon gown hugged her hourglass figure and sparkled against her flawless jet skin. Breck nudged Brian's arm. "I thought she was from Brazil," she whispered between her teeth.

"She is. Her father's descendants are from Nigeria, and her mother is native Brazilian," Brian answered.

"What's native Brazilian?"

"Indian. Brazil is not a Spanish-speaking country," Brian offered. "The three common ethnicities of Brazil are Portuguese, Indian, and African. The official language is Portuguese."

Interesting. Breck had been under the false impression that the majority of Brazilians had common Hispanic characteristics and spoke Spanish. She'd pictured Gaby like Mexicans and South Americans. Gaby had inherited high cheekbones and full lips, possibly from her African roots, while her glow and her jet-black hair passed down from her mother. When she walked, she graced the floor like a model on a runway, taking command of the audience simply by her presence.

No wonder Eric had fallen hard for her. The woman was, without argument, stunning. Breck felt like a viper.

She needed another drink. She withdrew from the round of applause and practically ran to the fountain to drown herself in the river of flowing champagne. If the room had been empty, she would have just lay down and allowed the bubbly liquid to fall into her mouth.

Someone handed the couple full champagne flutes, and the evening's festivities officially began with toasts by Eric. He first dedicated a toast to Breck, which took her by surprise, but she accepted by raising her glass amid a round of applause. An even louder round followed when he made toasts to both Martin and Brian. They, too, declined to speak. Eric then turned to his wife and clicked her glass, then gave her a passionate kiss. The crowd roared. Breck downed her champagne and immediately stuck her glass under the stream for a refill.

Gaby took the floor and congratulated her husband on his vision, mentioning the political figures in attendance who had also made this night possible. At that Brian and Martin coughed, obviously in some protest that only they would understand. Gaby then turned to introduce the mayor of Mansfield, who according to Martin and Brian hadn't cared about the city's rehabilitation until the prestigious Warren & Peterson firm stepped in and purchased most of the commercial and rental properties available. Once that happened, all of a sudden the commercialization of Mansfield became the city's top priority.

". . . such a commendable effort by a once-struggling community to achieve prosperity, success, and the American dream . . ." the mayor was saying. Brian and Martin let out a few more annoyed coughs.

Next on the program was the evening's entertainment. To start it off was a highly charged African dance troupe who used all of the reception room as their stage. Breck eyes remained fixed on Eric and Gaby as they watched the dancers. Smiling brilliant white smiles, they stood gallant and beautiful with Gaby's arms entwined with her husband's. Breck watched as they looked at each other and shared a tender kiss. That was all she could stomach, and she headed back toward the flowing fountain.

She maneuvered between people watching the dancers as they tried unsuccessfully to solicit volunteers from the audience to join in their stomps, but most of the women were in dresses that didn't permit much movement. Once the dancers had finished, the entertainment was turned over to a jazz quartet and the evening began to mellow.

"Good thing you're not driving," Brian said, walking up behind her and whispering into her ear as she downed another glass of champagne. "Are you enjoying your-self?" She nodded. "Are you sure?"

She gave Brian a long, hard look. She had to be care-ful. She had enough alcohol in her to really open up and tell him everything, and he was cute enough that she could forget Eric for one night and spend it in bed with Brian. Seeing Eric and Gaby holding each other, laugh-ing together, and kissing made her feel ridiculous for ever approaching him about her insidious crush.

"I need it to get through the night," she said, not both-ering him with details.

"And why is that?" he asked, standing inches from her face.

She didn't get the chance to answer him. They were in-terrupted, for which she was thankful; she was sure the alcohol would have taken away her ability to lie.

"Breck." She turned and saw Eric walking toward her, her royal highness on his arm. "Breck, I would like you to meet my wife, Gabriela." Gaby detached her arm long enough to offer a handshake. When Breck touched Gaby's skin, she envisioned it turning to slime.

"Nice to meet you," she said, and bit back the chuckle in her throat. Okay, no more champagne for you, she warned herself.

"Breck is the true mastermind behind this building," Eric announced. Nothing inside of her would allow her to accept the compliment and share in the glory. How could she feel good about herself when all she thought about day and night was being in his bed? Yet here he stood with the most beautiful woman she had ever seen.

She needed to get away from them, and quickly, be-fore she threw up all over herself.

"You are so talented," Gaby added, and replaced her arm around Eric. Why was she holding on so tight? Breck thought. Maybe she sensed something. Women do have a sixth sense about things like this. Gaby's thick

Portuguese accent, untouched by her years in the States, added to her sexiness.

As they stood in the company of friends, a thought exploded in Breck's mind: she was standing in Eric's perfect life. He had started rough but had managed to excel against immeasurable obstacles. He plotted his path, he did all the right things, met all the right people, married the perfect woman, and made all the right choices—and this was his reward. Breck looked around at the people in the room, important people you just didn't stumble across in a sports bar. The boy from Mansfield had made it, pulled himself up by his bootstraps and made it. If he got involved with her, she would quite possibly become his first mistake, and Eric wasn't about to let that happen, no matter how he felt about her.

"I've seen your work as well," Breck said. "You've done an excellent job in Stephen's office."

"I just collect works of art; I don't create them, like you do. You shouldn't be so modest. Take a bow. You've earned it."

Damn it, and she's nice too. Why did she have to be nice? I have to get the hell out of here, Breck thought, and looked toward the floor.

"Eric speaks very highly of you," Gaby added.

"It's all a lie." Breck tried to voice a nervous laugh. She wondered exactly what Eric had told Gaby about her. Did he share all of their conversations with Gaby? Did Gaby know she and Eric used to talk almost every night? Did she know she had lain in Eric's arms last night under the stars and a full moon?

"You're cute" Gaby said with a girlish snicker.

Suddenly Gaby was sounding more condescending and less nice. *Cute?* What the hell did she mean by that? Breck gasped inwardly. She knows I'm in love with her husband.

"Will you excuse us?" Gaby asked, and pulled Eric away without waiting for them to reply.

"What did she mean by *cute*?" Breck asked Brian the second Gaby and Eric were out of earshot. Was Gaby trying to ridicule her? Well, if she was, I can tell her a thing or two, Breck thought. She was arguing with the woman in her thoughts, a clear sign that she'd probably had enough alcohol for the night.

"Don't worry about it," Brian said. "Trust me." He took her hand and led her away from the fountain. It was probably a good thing that he did because alcohol always gave her the courage to say and do the things she wished she had the nerve to do sober.

She really needed to get the hell out of there and away from Eric and his perfect life.

"So, what are the plans for the rest of the evening?" she asked Brian.

"We're all meeting at Frankie's in about an hour."

"What's Frankie's?"

"It's a club a couple of blocks from here. Small but nice. Would you like to go?"

"Love to, but I need to change. Did you drive?"

"No, I came with Martin."

"You're in luck." She took his arm and walked with him toward the door. "I have a limo."

Brian smiled wickedly. "Oh, yeah . . ."

"Don't even think about it," Breck said, immediately shooting down any thought he entertained of their evening being a lot more exciting than he'd planned.

Brian hadn't thought to bring extra clothes, so he was stuck wearing his tuxedo to Frankie's, but they stopped at the townhome so that Breck could change. She put on a pair of black straight-legged jeans and a turquoise long-sleeved side-tie shirt. Brian took off his jacket and loosened the bow tie until it dangled loosely around his neck, and he left the cummerbund in the limousine. They walked together into Frankie's, Breck still hanging on to his arm. She felt safe there.

As soon as Brian opened the door for her, they were engulfed by the sound of Marvin Gaye's "Let's Get It On." Looking around the room, they spotted Martin and Alyce waving at them from a far table where they sat with another couple.

"Hello again," Breck said as soon as she and Brian had joined them.

"I told you we should have gone home to change," Alyce said, nudging Martin's arm.

"Woman, as long as it takes you to change, we would never have gotten here," he said, sliding his chair closer to his wife to allow Breck and Brian to sit down. "Did you enjoy your stay in Massachusetts?" Martin asked Breck, and everyone else at the table turned to stare at her.

"Loved it," Breck yelled over the music blaring from the speakers. The song had changed from Marvin Gaye to Chic's "Le Freak." Breck patted her hands against her thighs and began to move in her seat. She hadn't danced in over a month, and she hadn't heard music like this for even longer. Tonight was the perfect night to listen to the old classics. "You want to dance?" she asked Brian.

He took her hand and led her onto the tiny dance floor. They careened around, Breck swinging her arms in the air and snapping her fingers, enjoying the music and her dance partner. For the first time that night, she managed to forget about Eric and Gaby.

They kept dancing even when the music slowed down to Al Green's "Let's Stay Together." Walking into his arms, Breck rested her head comfortably on his chest. He was a smooth dancer and a courteous partner. He allowed her to get close to him without taking the opportunity to exploit the moment by feeling her up. She was still feeling the effects of drinking more glasses of champagne than she could remember, and the fact that he wasn't taking advantage of her drew her closer to him. When the song ended, they walked off the dance floor together, her fingers entwined with his.

Back at the table she saw an addition to the party. Eric had slipped past them and sat down with Martin and Alyce.

"Didn't see you walk in," Breck said, and took the seat opposite him. She sat next to Brian, and their legs touched flirtatiously.

"You were preoccupied," he said. He took a long swig from his beer.

"Brian's a great dancer," she said, cozying up to Brian.

"I didn't realize you guys were that close," Eric said, watching her rub arms with Brian. Breck noticed the solemn look on his face, and it puzzled her. Was he jealous? She dismissed the thought as ridiculous almost as soon as it came into her mind. Eric had no reason to be jealous of a budding relationship with Brian. If anything, he should celebrate it. It would get her off his back, and Brian was exactly the type of man she would gladly introduce to a good single female friend. As far as she was concerned, that was exactly what she was to Eric.

"Where's Gaby?" she asked, and the others at the table immediately burst into laughter. The joke was centered on Eric, and he apparently didn't think it was funny. All he could do was look down at his beer and take another drink. "Did I say something wrong?" she asked.

"You won't find Mrs. Gaby in a place like this," Martin volunteered. "She's much too refined." That started another round of laughter that they tried unsuccessfully to keep to themselves. Eric rolled his eyes but didn't bother coming to the defense of his lovely wife.

"Is that true?" Breck lowered her voice and stared straight at him, but the fact that he didn't meet her eyes told her it probably was. She watched Eric's expression change dramatically from exhilarated and in charge at the convention center to dull and introverted. She was beginning to think that Gaby's refusal to share 100 percent in his life might be the cause of it. How embarrassing it must be for him to have to come here alone because his wife thought less of this world. Could she not make the connection that if it had not been for this world, he would not have been driven to work his ass off so hard that it landed him among Boston's elite and therefore in her bed?

It seemed that Eric was the perfect husband for Gaby as long as he was a partner of Warren & Peterson and dined with the mayor. Gaby didn't want any part of the making of Eric Warren, just the finished product. That obviously created enough of a rift between them that Eric sought refuge elsewhere. Was that the missing link? Breck wondered. She couldn't turn her gaze from him, from his somber expression as he drank his beer and tried to chat with the others. His eyes were transparent.

"Breck, is Brian going back to Indiana with you?" Martin interrupted her mental ramblings, and she turned away from Eric long enough to notice that the others, including Brian, had turned to stare at her. Martin had just put her on the spot, but she deserved it. After all, she had been hanging on Brian all night. They had a right to wonder what her intentions were with him. But Breck also wondered if it had something to do with the caretaker role Martin and Eric had toward Brian. She wished she could stick around long enough to find out what that was all about.

"He might get an invitation," Breck said, leaning her body into Brian and satisfying Martin's well-meaning meddling.

"Be careful, Brian," Eric said. "Breck is married to her work." He signaled for the waitress to bring him another beer. "You want a drink?" he asked, looking only at Breck.

He was still doing it. He couldn't bring himself to stop looking out for her. Why did he feel she was his responsibility? She had come with another man, who happened to be sitting right beside her and was more than capable of buying her a drink. How would he have felt if she had asked him a similar question while his wife stood with them?

Breck shook her head. "I've had enough for tonight."

"Yeah, she set up camp beside the champagne fountain," Brian teased.

"I felt like celebrating," Breck said, and stood up. Her shirt had peeled open and exposed her black bra, so she pulled it down—but not before sensing Eric staring at her. "Well, Eric. I believe you owe me a dance," she said, leaning on the table and staring across at him. She had captured his attention, and he took his eyes off of her breasts and back to her face.

"How so?"

"I remember a certain phone conversation we had about how well you can dance. Are you ready to show your stuff?"

"I don't think so." He shifted in his seat.

"Why not? You said you could hold your own on the dance floor, so let's see it." Even as she urged him on, for some reason she suddenly felt sorry for the man— though she was sure Eric D. Warren did not need her pity concerning his marital squabbles.

Eric finally accepted her challenge and dutifully stood to join her. They walked out onto the floor, not holding hands as she and Brian had done earlier. She tried extra hard to maintain a comfortable distance.

And the man didn't lie, Breck discovered. Eric had some good moves on the dance floor. Even though he was a little out of touch for the hip-hop era, his moves were just fine for Carl Douglas's "Kung Fu Fighting."

"Not bad," Breck teased, snapping her fingers as she moved about the floor.

"Compared with what?" he retorted. The smile on her face couldn't be erased. She delighted to see him smile, and his spirits lifted again. The roles had been reversed, and she had become the sympathizer and rescuer. They danced closer with each step. She couldn't help but keep her eyes glued to his torso. Eric had the body of a Greek god—athletic, muscular, and wrapped in a milk-chocolate package. Looking at him made her mouth water. She swallowed hard.

"Kung Fu Fighting" faded out, and as Breck began to walk off the floor the mighty O'Jays came across the speakers belting "Stairway to Heaven." Eric grabbed her hand to stop her. He careened her around to face him and wrapped her in his arms. Her breasts pressed against his chest as she rested her head on his chest. She closed her eyes and her mind to everything and everyone around them and just enjoyed being in his arms. She'd never been one to live for a single moment—she was always preparing for what was to happen next. But now she didn't think beyond the end of the song.

"So, what's up with you and Brian?" he whispered.

She didn't want to open her eyes, but she suddenly became conscious of the fact that Brian and the others at the table may be watching them. "Just getting to know each other. He's not a bad guy."

"I am aware of that."

"You have anything to warn me about?" She inched far enough from him to look up into his face. If there was a devil underneath, she was sure Eric would warn her.

"No. He's a good man." His voice remained steady and low.

"Then I should be happy with him," she replied. She closed her eyes again, returning her head to his chest.

BRECK MANAGED to make it back into the townhome without dropping to her knees and crawling in. The two-inch heels had finally taken their toll on her pedicured feet. Sure, they looked good on her, but she paid a hefty price for the glamour.

She left Brian at the door, having decided against inviting him in. She hadn't awakened in a man's arms since she broke up with Quentin, and Brian wouldn't have been a bad choice, with or without the influence of the alcohol. The fact that he was Eric's friend made it difficult. She was in love with Eric, and being in his arms on the dance floor filled her with so many dangerous emotions that the best thing for her to do was to take a shower and sleep alone.

As soon as she stepped from the bath, she threw herself atop the bed naked. She debated whether or not she had the energy to at least put on her pajamas, but she'd found a comfortable spot on the bed and she didn't want to move.

The telephone's ringing exploded in the room.

"Ohh," she fussed, agitated that she would have to turn over on her stomach to reach the phone. "Who the hell is this?" It was a little past three o'clock, so whoever it was had better make it worth her effort. "Hello," she said into the phone, not bothering to disguise her annoyance. It was probably Chi calling for details about the night. Chi sometimes couldn't wait till morning.

"Breck, it's me."

She bolted upright and sat on the edge of the bed. "Eric?"

"Are you alone?"

She hesitated. What if she wasn't alone? Would it matter to him? "Why?"

"Please don't give me a hard time, Breck. I just asked if you're alone."

"I'm alone. What's up? Where are you?"

There was a sudden hush over the phone. She heard only his breathing and the sound of an occasional car passing in the background.

"Eric."

"Breck, I'm not as perfect as you think," he said. She drew back and squinted. Where had that come from? She quickly tried to remember how much beer he'd had at Frankie's.

"What are you talking about?" she asked.

Eric took a deep breath, then continued. "I've never had a problem walking away from things I knew were wrong for me or not good business decisions . . ." His voice trailed off. "I can't walk away from you."

"Am I a bad decision?" she asked, cupping the handset so tightly she was in jeopardy of cutting off the circulation to her hand.

"You're one of the best decisions I've ever made."

She listened to his breathing while her heart beat fast in her chest. Eric wasn't calling her at this hour to tell her she'd done a great job on the convention center. There had to be more, but she wasn't going to push it out of him. To do that would be to push him away. Maybe finally he was ready to come clean.

"Eric, I don't understand why you're calling."

"I'm in love with you."

Her breath caught in her chest and she closed her eyes. "Eric, please tell me you're not drunk."

"Breck, I'm not drunk," he said, and she sat quietly on the bed and listened to him. "I watched you tonight. I walked around that center and no matter where I walked my eyes found you. All I could do was introduce you as the woman who designed this magnificent building. I couldn't say what I wanted to say. I wanted to tell them about how you could answer any trivia question about jazz and classical music. I wanted to say that you prefer your coffee in one of your special mugs . . ." His voice trailed off as he took a deep breath and exhaled into the phone. "Seeing you with Brian tonight nearly ripped my heart out."

"What?" How could he be jealous about seeing her with Brian when she had to endure an entire evening of watching him parade around with his wife on his arm knowing that she could not justify the overwhelming rage and jealousy that boiled inside of her? He had a lot of nerve, when all she could do was hold on to Brian's arm and fondle him on the dance floor.

"I know it sounds ridiculous and selfish and absurd, and you have every right to hang up on me, but seeing you in another man's arms made me realize exactly how important you are to me."

Breck was speechless. This was Eric on the phone, saying things to her she wanted to hear months ago. But telling her this now meant what? What was she supposed to do with this information? She was flying back to Indianapolis Sunday morning, and he would never have to set eyes on her again if that was what he wanted.

Before she could say anything to him, she heard a soft knock at the door.

Damn, she thought. The only person she could think of who would come to the house was Brian. He could have come back after the driver dropped him off at home. How was she going to get rid of him without losing Eric? If Eric knew Brian was at the door, he would feel obligated to hang up and let her have a chance with him. There were too many things going on at once, and she didn't know how to juggle them.

"Hold on. Don't hang up." She threw the phone onto the bed and then grabbed her housecoat to cover her naked body. At the door she quickly glanced through the peephole, and when she saw the face, she held her breath. She stepped back, pulled the door open, and stared at Eric as he stood in the chilly early-morning air. A brush of wind gathered between them and lifted her hair from her shoulders.

"I've been sitting in my car," he said, closing his cell phone and disconnecting the call.

Breck stepped aside and let him in. When she closed the door, he put his arms gingerly around her waist and pulled her body into his.

Her breathing became shallow as she anticipated what it would be like to kiss him. She'd dreamt about this moment so many times, but she had given up hope that it would actually happen. She was in his arms now, her body touching his, her eyes closed against his chest. He lifted her face to his, and she stood utterly still, not even moving her eyes. She watched as he leaned closer, parted his lips, and touched them to hers. His lips lingered there, softly at first. Then he pressed them hard against hers. She closed her eyes. As they kissed, she felt his hand inside her housecoat touching her bare skin. He pulled the robe away from her shoulders while Breck dropped her arms to let it fall around her ankles. She stepped out of it, then walked into his embrace again. She wrapped her arms around him, kissing all the while.

His chest rose with each breath as he stepped from her and looked at her nakedness. With the tips of his fingers he traced the outline of her face and down past her shoulders. He stopped when he reached her breasts.

Breck unfastened the buttons on his shirt one by one, then reached inside and touched his plain white T-shirt. The shirt fell to the floor. He dug the hem of the T-shirt from his pants and lifted it over his head until he stood bare-chested in front of her. He pulled her body to him again, pressing her breasts against his chest. Effortlessly, he lifted her and, while kissing her lips, walked with her into the bedroom, shutting the door with his foot.

He carried her to the bed. The sheets were still ruffled from when she had lain on them after her shower. His lips pressed hard against hers as he lowered her naked body onto the bed and slipped off his pants.

He leaned over her as he separated her legs and pulled her hips toward his face. He kissed her between her legs. His tongue touched her clitoris, and her body jolted from the powerful sensation. He held her down while she squirmed. He sucked on her clitoris and entered her with his finger, pushing it deep inside of her and hitting *that spot,* almost sending her body leaping from the bed. She moaned and grabbed hold of the headboard to keep from crawling along the wall. The sheets beneath her were saturated from her moisture.

His head moved toward hers, kissing every inch of her body—her abdomen, her nipples, the softness between her breasts, her neck, her chin. When he reached her lips he paused, then looked at her. His body stretched full on top of her. Breck opened her eyes and met his, and he brought his lips to hers. When he did, he lifted her hips in the palms of his hands and slid inside of her, so smoothly, so gently. They moaned.

His body was a perfect fit for hers. With every thrust it seemed she felt her blood warm and flow through her vessels, igniting every nerve inside of her. She wrapped her arms around him and pulled him closer, feeling him breathe against the side of her face while he moved inside of her, taking her higher than she'd ever gone before. Her clit continued to throb, heightening the pleasure of Eric thrusting inside of her.

Within the first hour they performed every position she knew, including her favorite of sitting on him with his back pressed against the headboard and his arms at her back pulling her deeper into him. She tossed her head back while he flicked her nipples with his tongue. Whenever she straddled him, he went so deep inside of her she felt he would go straight through. Every position they moved into, she climaxed. Chanting his name, louder each time, she wondered if the people next door heard her. Every time when she felt there was no way she could climax again, she did. Her pussy was so moist, Eric easily slid in and out of her, without resistance. He entered her from behind while holding her ass in his hands. He climaxed too this time, but instead of pulling out and lying beside her, he continued to move inside of her until he had achieved another erection.

She was drained. That was new for her. No man she'd ever been with was able to do that. His tempo never slowed, even after she felt she could no longer move her hips in sync with his. He was moving to his own beat but definitely with the goal of taking her higher. Breck felt her body floating away. She closed her eyes and relinquished herself totally to him. Her arms went limp. When she thought of lifting them, her body felt paralyzed, no longer responding to her will. Her legs relaxed, her head fell upon the sheet—she was free.

"I'm yours," she whispered in a husky voice. "Oh, God, I'm going to float away." As soon as she said that, he climaxed again. This time he went limp on top of her, breathing heavily, squeezing her breasts against his chest. Breck still couldn't move. She couldn't lift her arms and wrap them around his body. She couldn't do anything.

Eric finally rolled off of her, lay beside her, and placed her head on his chest.

Breck inhaled deeply, breathing in the cologne he had splashed on a few hours ago before stepping into his splendid tuxedo. As soon as her lungs emptied, she fell asleep.

TWELVE

BRECK OPENED her eyes and met Eric's gaze. He was lying beside her, gently stroking the side of her face, brushing away every strand of hair that had fallen there. He kissed her gently on the lips, a gesture she took to mean everything would be okay.

He pulled her body closer to him, and she rested her head against his chest. "You floated away," he said.

Breck smiled. She had indeed. "How long have I been asleep?"

"Just a few minutes. Are you okay?" he whispered and kissed the side of her face.

Breck nodded. "I'm in love with you too," she said.

He sighed heavily and squeezed her again. "I know."

"This is like a dream," she said, sliding her hands across his chest. "Almost too perfect," she said.

"How so?"

She shrugged.

"I know that you think I'm perfect," he said, taking a lock of her hair and caressing it between his fingers. "I have faults, and I'm certainly not perfect."

"I know, but being here with you, like this, is like a dream."

He drew in a deep breath before he spoke again. "What happens when you wake up?"

She closed her eyes and rested comfortably against him.

"I have to go," he whispered in her ear. She had known

this moment was coming. She didn't want to look at the clock beside the bed, because she knew it was late, too late for him to excuse as time spent at the office. She briefly wondered how he would explain his lateness, knowing it would involve some sort of lie. The most incredible night of her life would have to be dismissed by a lie. Breck nodded and accepted the inevitable.

"I'll be back later," Eric said. "I promise."

"If you can't make it . . ."

"I'll be back." He kissed the back of her head and slid from the bed. Breck pulled the blanket to her shoulder and watched him slip into his pants. Before he walked out of the bedroom, he leaned over and kissed her hard on the lips. "See you in a few hours," he said, then walked into the living room to retrieve his shirt.

She heard the door close behind him. A few seconds later the car started, then pulled off down the road. She stayed fixed on every sound he made until she couldn't hear him anymore.

She curled up under the wrinkled sheets and pressed her head against the pillow. The sun had started to come through the blinds, promising yet another beautiful day. Breck rolled over and stared up at the ceiling until she could finally brave a look at the clock. It was six-thirty.

She growled. She'd gotten no sleep last night except the few minutes she'd dozed off. They'd both known they couldn't get too comfortable. She sat up in the bed. The room smelled like sex and love. She lit a scented candle on the nightstand and decided it would be better for her to go for a light run than to fight through conflicting thoughts and emotions.

The thin white sheet gathered at her ankles as she rolled out of bed and stretched high to the ceiling. Her body was relaxed and appeased but fatigued.

So what happens next? she wondered as she walked

into the bathroom and quickly washed up. Brushing her teeth in front of the mirror, she saw the images of the morning still fresh in her mind.

She would be happier if she were certain she would see Eric later, but she just wasn't sure. He had struggled for months, knowing he had fallen in love with her, and now he had acted on it. Would he run, scared by loving her and betraying Gaby?

It was too soon to say good-bye.

WHEN SHE returned from her run, she stood under hot water in the shower while the steam filled the bathroom. She used her favorite lavender bath gel, hoping the calming scent would settle her mind. When her shower was over, the fatigue had finally turned to sleepiness, and all she had the strength to do was to fall upon the bed.

She slept for hours. When she finally awoke, it was two o'clock in the afternoon. It would have been so easy for her to stay in bed and replay the night in her mind, but she didn't want to spend her last night in Massachusetts curled under the sheets. She pulled herself out of bed for the second time that day and staggered to the kitchen for a faithful cup of coffee.

Everything was packed, including her drafting board, so she decided to watch the TV that sat inconspicuously in the corner of the living room; this was the first time she had thought to turn it on. When the phone rang she rushed to it, excited.

"Hi, Breck." Her enthusiasm waned as soon as she heard Brian's voice. She felt guilty—Brian was oblivious to what had happened between her and Eric earlier. She would like to think she hadn't used Brian to creep into Eric's heart, but she couldn't deny that being in Brian's arms resulted in Eric spending the morning making love to her.

"Hi, Brian. Did you have fun last night?"

"I had a great time. So what are your plans for your last day in Massachusetts?"

Eric said he would be back, she thought. "I don't have any. I'm just watching television."

"You can't stay inside on your last day. How about if I treat you to dinner and an evening on the town?"

I can't leave, she thought. If there was even a slight chance that she could see Eric, there was no way she was going to leave this house.

She settled against the wall, conscious that she was taking too long to answer him. "That's really sweet of you, but actually I'm a little tired and I just want to stay in today and get some rest. I'm sorry." And she genuinely was sorry. If this morning with Eric had not happened, she would have taken Brian up on the offer—but last night did happen, and that changed everything. Even if Eric didn't come back today, her sexual involvement with him eliminated any likelihood that she would have a relationship with Brian.

"I understand." She heard the disappointment in his voice and sank deeper into sorrow. She had given him hope last night and had even kissed him good night—not a passionate kiss, but it was on the lips and it was longer than a few seconds—and now she had just ripped those hopes into shreds.

"I'm really sorry," she said earnestly. She was sorry that she'd led him onto a ledge, only to drop him without a parachute.

"It's okay. I hope you visit us again. Have a safe trip back." They said their good-byes and she replaced the handset. She snuggled on the sofa and prepared to wait for Eric. He had said he would be back, but Breck wondered how he would justify coming to see her after spending the entire night away. Was Gaby that understanding, or did she even care? Perhaps this was normal for him. After all, he did once talk to her until two in the morning. How would she feel if she was married to him and he pranced into the house after two in the morning? She was certain she wouldn't like it and that she would have voiced her opposition to it loud and clear.

What if he can't get away? What if Gaby puts her foot down and demands that he stay home with them today? Breck could certainly understand, but she'd just turned down an invitation to at least get out of the house, which meant one of two things was likely to happen: either she'd waste her day by waiting for Eric only to have him not show up, or he would show up sometime today—only she didn't know when.

Was this a preview of what life would be like if she chose to continue having an affair with Eric? Would she spend her days waiting for him, not knowing if he'd ever show up? Would her schedule be suddenly planned around his?

Ramblings. That's what all this was, unnecessary ramblings. She stood up to fetch another cup of coffee.

The clock ticked. Another hour had passed and still no word from Eric. She'd drunk so much coffee that even she was sick of it. When she'd almost given up, the phone rang again. She ran to answer it, sending a statuette placed on the end table toppling to the floor.

"Hello." Breck grimaced, looking at the delicate wooden minimasterpiece, thankful it hadn't broken.

"Have you eaten?" Eric said quickly into the phone. A smile suddenly brightened her face. He was already in his car—she could hear the noisy traffic in the background.

"No."

"Chinese sound good?" he asked.

"Sounds great."

"Okay, light a fire and I'll be there in forty minutes. Love you," he said, and just like that, he was gone.

She lit up like a schoolgirl whose boyfriend has defied his parents, climbed out of his bedroom window, and risked life and limb to see her.

When Eric arrived with a ready kiss and food in hand, it made the wait worthwhile. They sat in front of the fire and ate, talked, and laughed. It was the way she always knew it would be with Eric. And he stayed long enough to make love to her right there in front of the fireplace.

"I missed you," she said between kisses, while they lay on the floor and stared into the fire. It had started to dwindle down until Eric threw another log onto it, and once again it became a magnificent blaze framed by the beautiful wood mantelpiece.

"I thought about you all day too." He kissed the nape of her neck. "Sorry it took me so long."

"I didn't think you were going to make it," she said, and licked the dryness from her lips.

Eric pushed himself up from the floor and stared at her. "I said I would be back."

"I know, but I didn't think you could get away."

"Breck, if I say I'll be back, I will. I wouldn't do that to you."

She nodded and rested her chin on her hand. "So what now?" She didn't want to look at him but felt the situation warranted it. If he smashed her feelings against the wall, then it would be no worse than she deserved, she supposed. "The convention center is done. I don't have an excuse to call you anymore."

"I've never been in this situation before."

"Neither have I," she said, and began to pick imaginary lint from the carpet. "Do we get together from time to time when you're in town or when I'm in town? Do we meet a weekend a year until one of us gets tired or we get caught—whichever comes first? Or do we pretend that this never happened?" She stopped picking and looked at him.

Eric slid down on the carpet and propped his head on his hand until he was eye to eye with her. "You believe me when I say I love you?"

She stared directly into his eyes. She imagined the next thing out of his mouth: *I love you, but you know we don't have a future together* or some other careful letdown that would slap her back into reality. He was not about to risk everything to continue a fling. He had never made a bad business decision before in his life, so why would he start now?

"What I feel for you goes beyond what happened this morning and tonight," he said. "I really do care a great deal about you."

Breck nodded. She knew that, but it didn't change the obvious. How far was he willing to take his feelings for her? "I know that too."

"How did you like Boston?" he asked, and she looked down at the carpet again, figuring this was his way out of an uncomfortable predicament.

"Loved it."

"Enough to move here?"

Breck's eyes widened as she caught her breath. "I hadn't thought about it," she said with a shrug.

"I think you'd like it here."

"How do you figure?"

"Well, you have friends here now. There's Alyce and Martin."

"And Brian," she added, only to have Eric drop his eyes toward the floor. "Sorry," she apologized. Obviously he hadn't thought that far in advance yet.

"And I need to keep an eye on you," he said.

Breck snorted. "You don't need to keep an eye on me."

"Maybe not, but I do want to spend time with you."

Breck rolled over on her back and looked up at the

ceiling. It hadn't quite sunk in yet. He was asking her to move everything she owned to Massachusetts. Her family was in Indiana, and although she didn't see them often, she'd never been that far from them. Moving to Massachusetts would mean she would see even less of them. But there was always the other side to this, and that was Eric. She couldn't lie and say she didn't want him in her life, because if that were true, this trip wouldn't have been as hard as it was.

"What are you thinking?" he asked, stroking the side of her face.

"All this is happening so fast."

He lay on the floor beside her and joined her in looking into space. "So what do you want to do about this?" he asked, breaking the silence.

Breck shrugged. "Eric, we're having an affair."

"Thank you, Breck, for bringing that to the forefront, but that wasn't the answer I was expecting."

"But that's what it is without sugarcoating it. Before I came here I struggled with the right and wrong of loving you. I didn't have too many rights except that you make me feel like no other man ever has. But the wrong involves people getting hurt. Why are we doing this?"

"I'm in love with you. I haven't figured out why I haven't been able to let this go."

"I'm in love with you too, but you have a lot more to lose than I do. I don't want to be that one mistake that destroys your life."

"Then should we say good-bye at the airport tomorrow?" Eric asked, staring straight at her. Breck felt like he had just ripped into her chest and pulled out her heart.

"That's not what I want," she said, holding on to his arm.

"Then what do you want?"

"I want to be with you. I don't want things to go back to the way they were. I want to be near you and I want to see you and touch you and make love to you."

"Then let's do it," he said, and leaned forward and kissed her. She still had a somber look on her face. "Is there something more?"

Breck gave the question serious thought before she answered. "I like the idea of being closer to you and making love. I just don't know how I feel about having my life revolve around yours."

"I don't understand." His voice was flat.

"Brian called today and asked me to go out with him."

"Oh," he said, apparently unnerved.

"I turned him down," she said quickly. "But I really didn't know if you were going to be able to show up or not. My day consisted of waiting for the phone to ring or for you to appear at the door. I don't know if I can live like that."

"What if I promise to let you know what's going on with me so that that won't happen?"

"Can you make that promise and keep it?"

He shrugged. "All I can do is try. I can also give you some space to build an independent life."

"And you'll be okay with that?"

"Breck, you are a woman who needs her independence. I'm okay with it as long as it doesn't involve you sleeping with another man."

Breck looked at him, amused. "But you'll be sleeping with another woman."

He rolled over on his back again and growled. "Please don't give me a hard time about this. It's hypocritical and it makes me very selfish, but that's how I feel. I can admit that. Nothing about this is normal. It's a paradox of everything we've ever been taught or thought that love and relationships are supposed to be." Breck looked at him strangely. He seemed to be picking words from the air and having a conversation with himself. "Do you think I'm a horrible person for feeling this way?" he asked.

Breck shook her head. "No. Do you think I'm a horrible person for being involved with you?"

"No," he said, and she kissed him hard on the lips. She loved the feel of his lips against hers. Right or wrong, she felt good being in his arms.

"Does this mean you're moving to Massachusetts?"

She grinned. "I think this means I'm moving to Massachusetts."

CHI GREETED Breck at the airport with flowers in hand. Breck ran into her arms and hugged her tight. They walked together to the baggage claim, picked up her luggage, and headed to the parking garage, to Chi's cherry-red Mustang convertible. It was much too cold to put the top down. Before long, Chi would have to park the sporty car in the garage and drive the older, unattractive but reliable four-wheel drive.

Breck rambled on about her trip and the party without hinting at the very latest development. She knew Chi's response would be less than gracious, so she bought herself a little more time. "I'm hungry," she said. "You feel like getting some lunch?"

"Didn't they feed you on the plane?" Chi merged onto the highway and headed toward Breck's condo downtown.

"I couldn't eat. My treat."

"Can't turn down free food. You have any place in mind?"

"The Marriott has a nice brunch. Let's go there."

After they were seated near a window at the hotel restaurant, out of direct earshot of other diners, Chi filled Breck in on the happenings at the office—mostly who'd called and whom she needed to call back right away. It seemed some of the connections she'd made in Massachusetts had serious potential.

"Looks like you're going to be a busy lady," Chi said cheerfully.

Breck had ordered smoked salmon on a slice of Asiago-cheese bread, salad, and a glass of Bardolino. Chi had opted for the classic chicken Caesar salad and white Zinfandel.

"Share a slice of cheesecake with you later?" Breck offered.

"Deal," Chi said. "So how did things finish with Eric? Did he finally snap out of his childishness?"

Breck kept from choking on her mouthful of food and quickly took a sip of the wine. "You can say that," she said. "He asked me to move to Massachusetts."

It was Chi's turn to cough. "What?!" she screamed after drinking from her glass of wine. Other diners turned to stare at her.

"We're having an affair," Breck said, and rushed some salad into her mouth, trying not to lose her composure.

Chi stared at her. "You're shitting me, right?"

Breck shook her head and continued to chew her food as casually as she could.

"When did this happen?"

"Saturday morning after the party," Breck replied.

"What?!" Chi screamed, once again capturing the attention of those nearby. "Wasn't his wife there?" she asked, quieting her voice to a whisper.

"She was at the party, but he came by the house afterward."

"What?!"

"Will you please lower your voice?" Breck said.

Chi leaned toward her. "Have you lost your damn mind?"

"I'm in love with him."

"Breck, he's married, or have you forgotten that?" Breck sighed heavily and settled back against the chair. She sipped her wine. "You're not seriously considering moving to Massachusetts, are you?" Chi continued.

Breck didn't answer her but continued to drink her wine until the glass was empty. The waiter was right on cue. "Would you ladies like another glass of wine?" he asked.

"Yes, please," Breck said.

"Make mine a rum and Coke," Chi said. He nodded and walked away. "You're moving to Massachusetts, aren't you?" Chi asked, slamming her hand down on the table. Breck nodded. "Oh, my God," Chi said, and straightened up.

"I can't believe that I'm doing this—but I can't imagine not being with him. You saw how I was before I left for Massachusetts. I was a wreck."

"And you would have eventually gotten over it. You can't seriously think there's a future with Eric. What happens if his wife finds out, or has he promised to leave her?"

Breck shook her head. "No, no promises."

"Breck, come on." Chi buried her head in her hands to ward off her frustration. "You know I've always supported you and I'll go to the end of the world with you—"

"Good, because I want you to move to Massachusetts with me," Breck rushed in before Chi had the chance to finish her sentence.

Not giving a damn about who was watching her, Chi dropped her head and started banging it on the table. Breck just watched as she carried out her tantrum. "You've lost your damn mind," Chi said, just when the waiter returned to their table. She grabbed her glass and quickly gulped half of it down, then leaned back in her chair. "You're going to move to Massachusetts so that you can continue this affair. That's fucking crazy."

"I know, but I love him and he's in love with me."

"No, he's not," Chi said with a sneer. "He's just sleeping with you."

Breck knew that would be Chi's opinion of the relationship. If a friend had come to Breck with the same scenario, she would have drawn the same conclusion. But Breck was in it now; she had walked into it knowingly, devoid of expectations, and that was her choice. She didn't have to apologize or try to justify it to anyone, not even Chi.

"He's not going to leave his wife for you," Chi continued.

"I never asked him to."

"Then what do you want from him?"

"Right now, nothing. I'm happy." Breck sat up again. "No man has made me feel the way Eric has made me feel. I can't walk away from that. Not even with the knowledge that he has a ring on his finger."

"You can walk away from it—you just choose not to," Chi countered.

"You're right. I choose not to. People always tell me that I'm a strong, independent woman. They're right, I am a strong, independent woman, and I've made my choice. I'm strong enough to deal with the consequences."

"I've always supported and respected your decisions about your business even when I didn't agree with them, because it's your business. But I can't support this."

They sat uncomfortably quiet, leaning against their chairs. Was Eric worth her losing her best friend over?

Breck heaved deeply, trying in vain to fight the tears that burned her eyes. She reached across the table and held her hand out to Chi. Her heart was heavy, and she fought to keep from sobbing.

Chi squeezed her hand. "I love you, girl," she said, and forced a smile.

"I know," Breck said, wiping a tear from her eye. "And I'm scared and I need you."

"I don't want to see you hurt, but you're about to rearrange your entire life for a man who belongs to someone else. I think it's wrong, and as a friend, I have to tell you that."

"I know," Breck said.

"But you're right, it's your choice. You're going to do it regardless of how anyone else feels about it, aren't you?" Breck nodded. "Have you told your mother?"

Breck shook her head. "Hell, no. She'll freak. I'm going to tell her I'm moving to Massachusetts of course, but I'm not going to tell her about Eric."

After a long pause, Chi asked, "So when are you leaving?"

"After the New Year."

"That soon," she said, shaking her head.

Breck smiled. "It won't take much for me to move. All I have to do is put my condo on the market and pack."

"And the business?"

"Change-of-address cards," Breck said lightly.

"You're serious about this, aren't you?" Chi said, letting go of Breck's hand and taking another forkful of salad.

Breck nodded. "Will you come with me?"

Chi stopped chewing, then spoke with her mouth full. "To Massachusetts? What will I do in Massachusetts?"

"Well, you'll have a job, for starters, with a huge raise." Breck took a sip of her wine and leaned forward to finish her sandwich.

Chi shook her head. "You're crazy."

"I know, but it'll be one hell of an adventure. So

please, please, please say you'll come." She dropped her
fork again and folded her hands together to beg.

"Damn you, Breck," Chi said, shaking her head but
obviously warming up to the idea. "It better be a damn
good raise."

THIRTEEN

BRECK SMELLED the food as soon as she stepped onto the front porch, and when she walked into the house her mouth began to water. She tiptoed past her mother, who was busy dicing onions on the cutting board. Breck lifted the lid off an iron pot to peek inside. The intense stench of the chitterlings rushed to her face, and she replaced the lid.

"How could something that stinks so bad taste so good?" Breck asked, getting her mother's attention. The tempertaure outside was in the midteens, but there was no need to have the heat on in the house. The stove generated enough heat to keep the house warm. She reached for another lid and dipped her fingers into the pot, pulling up several strings of mustard and collard greens.

"What are you doin', girl?" Her mother caught her as she dropped the greens into her mouth.

"Hi, Mom," Breck said. She walked up to her mother, squeezed her, and kissed her on the cheek. "Smells good in here."

"I could use some help too." Her mother scooped up the diced onions and placed them in the pot with the greens.

"What do you want me to do?" Breck grabbed an apron, slipped it over her head, and tied it in the back.

"Cut me up a few more onions and those celery sticks there," her mother said, pointing to the long celery stalks.

Breck got busy dicing while her mother tended to other matters in the kitchen, preparing for Christmas dinner.

"How was Boston?" her mother asked, dipping her hands in a sink filled with water and suds. "I haven't really seen you since you've been back."

Breck took a long time in answering. It was time to break the news. "Great," she said first. "I've decided to move there." She kept dicing, deciding not to look up.

"What did you say?"

"I'm moving to Boston." She finally looked at her mother, who stood in the middle of the kitchen floor just staring at her.

"What's his name?"

"What do you mean?"

"Breck, I'm not stupid. There are only one or two reasons why you would pack up and move to Boston on such short notice. Either you are in trouble with the law or you met a man. I don't think you are in trouble with the law, so obviously you've met a man."

Breck was quiet. How was she going to tell her mother that she was involved with a married man?

"Why the secrecy?" Her mother continued to probe.

"There is someone," Breck said simply. "What do you want me to do with these?" she asked, hoping to distract her mother from this line of questioning.

It didn't work.

Camille took her by the hand, led her down the hall to her bedroom, and closed the door.

"What's going on, Breck?" she demanded. Breck and her mother had never had the type of relationship where they went shopping together and became best buddies, but there was always a genuine respect for each other, and Breck knew if she ever needed anything, her mother would be there.

"I am involved with someone," Breck finally confirmed.

"Why the secrecy?" Camille asked again.

"It's Eric."

"Eric," her mother interrupted, recognizing the name. "Isn't that the rich black man you designed the building for?"

"Yes."

Her mother looked toward the ceiling as if the pieces of an imaginary puzzle had suddenly fallen into place and everything was starting to make sense.

"Oh, Breck," her mother said, shaking her head and sitting down on the bed.

"Mom, I really don't want to argue. I've gone through this so many times, with myself, Chi, and Eric—"

"Breck, I hope you know what you're doing."

"Mom, I love him and I'm tired of defending how I feel."

"Breck, it's wrong."

"I knew you would feel this way. That's why I didn't want to tell you. I'm not a little girl anymore, Mom. I don't need your approval on this."

"Sit your ass down!" Camille commanded, pointing to the bed. Breck dared not protest. She sat down with her arms folded across her chest, waiting to be scolded by her mother. "I'm not going to insult you and tell you what you feel is not real. You're a grown woman. You know what love is and you know the difference between right and wrong."

Breck stared at her mother. That was not the comment she had expected. Was there a hint of understanding here?

"I didn't raise you to be a fool or to settle for less than what you're worth."

Breck gave her mother her full attention as she sat back on the bed.

"You're hurting people and you're hurting yourself, and you're a selfish fool if you don't see it."

"We're not hurting anyone."

"Get your head out of your ass, girl. Ain't no good end is going to come of this." Camille started pacing the floor. "You're about to move across the damn country for this man! Girl, have you lost your mind?"

"I love him and he loves me."

"Then ask him to leave his wife."

"I'm not going to do that," Breck shot at her.

"Why not? He loves you so much."

"You don't understand," Breck said, getting up and walking to the opposite side of the room.

"What is there to understand? Help me to understand, then, Breck." Her mother folded her hands across her chest and waited for an explanation Breck couldn't give her.

"This is why I didn't tell you."

"You didn't tell me because you didn't want anyone to tell you what you're doing is wrong even when you know damn well it's wrong. This is not the way I raised you."

"No, you raised me to be judgmental and afraid of everything," Breck said, standing far enough from her mother so that she couldn't reach out and slap her for talking back. "If I question you or Dad, then I'm damned to hell. You wanted me to go to college and become successful only to make me feel inferior when I did. Limitations are all you've ever taught me. Don't make too much money. Don't work too hard. Don't wear that, it's too short. I have a nice body that I've worked hard for, and I want to show it off sometimes!"

The two women just stared at each other without saying a word. Breck had never intended to go off on her mother that way, but she couldn't take it anymore. "Why did you sacrifice so much for us to get good educations only to drill into me that I should be less?" Breck said in almost a whisper.

"That's not true."

"Yes, it is. You never said you were proud of any of my accomplishments."

"I want you to have it all, Breck. I want you to be happy. You had the career, but I didn't want you to sacrifice having a family for it. I knew you were struggling with men. You're a smart and beautiful woman. I just wanted to show you what it took to keep a man, so you wouldn't have to work so hard."

"Mom, I'm happy."

Camille shook her head. "You can't be happy with this man."

"Mom, I'm happy," Breck repeated.

Her mother sat down slowly beside her and stared straight ahead.

"Your father had an affair many years ago when you kids were young," Camille began. Breck turned to look at her, stunned. Her parents had been married for over thirty-five years. Growing up, she remembered a few arguments but never anything major. She always remembered her parents together, never apart.

Her mother continued before Breck had a chance to comment. "I found out about it after your sister was born, and we went through the usual hell of trying to piece our family back together. He straddled the line for a long time, not knowing what he wanted. Sure, I told him to stop, but it didn't just go away just because I found out. I sincerely believe that he had feelings for this woman, or at least a strong sense of obligation, I don't know." She shrugged. "But my point is, he came back home. Infidelity doesn't always break up a marriage. Sometimes it makes it stronger, but as the other woman, you are the one who will end up hurt the most."

Breck sat quietly. What could she say? She couldn't say, "No, that would never happen to me," because it could and she knew it. She lived every day with the possibility of Gaby finding out about them and demanding that Eric stop seeing her. Breck knew what kind of man Eric was, and she knew what he would do if that happened.

"You have to think through the consequences, Breck, and they could be losing your business, losing him as a friend and a lover. Not to mention if his wife goes berserk and decides to come after both of you with a gun."

Breck really hadn't thought about that happening, but once again, her mother wasn't telling her anything that hadn't happened before. Crimes of passion filled the newspaper every day.

"Believe me. I even thought about killing your father." She pulled her dress down as she sat up straighter on the bed. Breck doubted her mother was capable of committing murder, but Breck had never known the pain of betrayal, so she didn't know if, in an instant, her mother could have been driven to commit such a heinous crime.

Breck took a deep breath. "It bothers me sometimes when I think about it, but when we were apart I felt so alone that it was unbearable."

"She's going to find out. You know that, right?" Her mother looked at her with the firmest expression Breck had ever seen. "You do realize that this will not go on forever." Her mother was testing her, making sure she had really thought through everything. "You don't need to do this to yourself."

"I'm not doing anything to myself. I made a choice. I'm with Eric because I want to be. I know I don't have to be, but I love him and I want to be with him."

"Even though you have to share him?"

That stung. "Even though I have to share him."

"It won't last," her mother said, shaking her head.

Breck shrugged. "Maybe not, but we're happy right now. If things change, then I'll deal with it. Right now I'm happy. He's a wonderful man, he makes me happy, and I haven't had to relinquish any freedom."

"But, baby, it comes at a price, and eventually you will learn what that price is. One day you'll be older and you're going to want more from him than he's willing or able to give you. This is pretty serious, and you need to think about your future. Don't tell me you and Eric are just exploring each other and having fun, because that's bullshit. You wouldn't move to Massachusetts to be close to him if you were just exploring each other. He's living a double life, and you're his second wife. You need to think about what is going to happen when the real wife finds out."

"She may never find out," Breck said, getting frustrated with the conversation.

"Oh, she'll find out. If you ever become a wife, you'll understand what I'm saying." Her mother waved a finger at her. "I guarantee you that if you ever become a wife, you will know when your husband is seeing another woman," Camille said, then left Breck staring after her as she stormed out of the room and returned to the kitchen.

Breck seriously considered skipping Christmas dinner and returning to her condo. She didn't want to be sitting at the same table with her mother only to have her glaring down at her or, worse yet, tell everyone in the family and then have them ridicule her at the dinner table.

She decided to endure dinner and risk the possible ridicule, and nothing happened other than her mother glaring at her from time to time and shaking her head. Breck knew she'd better make the move quickly, otherwise her mother would have Pastor Banker and the entire New Hope Baptist Church on her doorstep. After spending a few hours with her family, Breck met Chi and some of their friends at her condo for drinks and gift exchange, and to start saying good-bye to everyone.

BRECK SHOT across the floor when she heard the doorbell, stepping over furniture, boxes, and everything else that happened to be in her way. She flung the door open and threw herself into Eric's arms.

It had been weeks since she'd seen him. Christmas and New Year's had passed. They managed to talk briefly every day, but there was nothing like being in his arms. They backed into the room, locked in each other's arms with their lips joined together like they had been born that way. Breck dangled from his neck. His weekend bag was in his hand. Once inside he dropped the bag by the door.

"Hello, Eric," Chi said, folding her arms across her chest and leaning against the wall.

The week she returned from Massachusetts, Breck had sent out letters to all her clients, notifying them of her move. Eric offered her the townhome, and she took him up on it until she could find a permanent home. He had extended the same invitation for Chi to stay in one of the other units, but the idea of being trapped forty minutes from the city didn't appeal to her. She wanted to be downtown, and with the help of a Realtor, she had found a place in the South End.

Breck had also offered a job to Jonathan, but relocating to Massachusetts was not feasible for him, with or without a raise. He took the six months' severance pay. A week later, he called Breck to tell her he had found another job and wished her luck in her new home.

Breck found someone to take over the office lease only days after she had posted an ad in the newspaper. It was true, location was everything, and her office and home were in prime locales. At the same time, she listed her condo, a Realtor's dream. It sold rather quickly, to a young broker, and Breck walked away with five thousand dollars more than she had asked for.

Eric backed away from Breck when he heard Chi's voice. "Hello, Chi." He extended his hand, which Chi accepted after a moment's hesitation.

"I just want you to know that I think this is wrong," she said, undaunted by his presence. Before he had the chance to respond, she returned to the bedroom to finish packing the box she had started.

"Ouch," Eric said, staring into the empty doorway. "You want to take that dagger out of my back?" He stretched behind him as though he were reaching for something rammed into his body.

"Well, I warned you," she said, hugging him.

"Yes, you did." Eric returned his attention to Breck. "And how are you?" Breck had called him after the incident with her mother on Christmas and he was concerned about her.

Breck smiled. "Happy," she said, and wrapped her arms around him and kissed him. "Are you ready to get to work?" She maneuvered him among stacks of boxes to reach the sofa.

"Well, I told you I would help you pack, so let's get to work," he said, clasping his hands together. "This is a really nice place," he said, finally getting a chance to look around.

"Gee, thanks," she said, walking beside him to the window.

"A place like this in Boston would cost a half million dollars."

"Well, let's lift it up and carry it to Boston," she joked.

Eric took her hand as he stared down onto the street below. "Are you okay with this?" he asked. "You're giving up a lot."

"I'm not giving up anything. I'm just changing my surroundings." At least, that was the way she wanted to view it. It made things easier.

"I love you," he said, and kissed her. It always amazed her how he said that with so much ease. She had never been able to submit to someone that deeply so quickly, but once he accepted his feelings, he had no problems expressing them. She loved that about him the most.

"Is Chi spending the night?" he asked, inches from her lips.

Breck grinned. "Not if I can help it."

THE MOVERS arrived the next morning. Three bulky men in tan baggy overalls moved all the boxes and furniture into two large trucks. After everyone had cleared out of the condo, Breck stole a moment and looked out the window one last time before she joined Eric and Chi for the drive. Breck and Eric took her car, and Chi followed in her Mustang. The night before, the three had stayed up, sitting on the floor, sharing a pizza, and mapping out the drive to Boston.

"I say we drive straight through to New Jersey, stay the night in Fort Lee, and finish the drive Friday afternoon. It's about four hours from New Jersey to Boston. How does that sound?" he asked, taking a bite of his pizza.

"Sounds good," Breck said. "The movers are not scheduled to arrive until Saturday morning, so that'll give us some time to relax."

The drive to Fort Lee, although twelve hours long, went by entirely too fast. As usual when they were together, she and Eric never ran out of things to talk about. Chi followed close behind, looking dynamic in her sports car. Occasionally, she pulled up alongside them to make a funny face or stick her tongue out at them. The resentment Chi had expressed the first day had vanished, and Breck could almost guess that Chi approved of Eric, or at least his personality and good looks. Chi would never approve of the relationship, and she made that point very clear.

The drive from Fort Lee to Massachusetts was as uneventful as the previous day. Once they reached Connecticut, they were only a short distance from Mansfield. Eric pulled off the road to refill Breck's fuel tank and to stretch. "Are you ladies hungry?" he asked as Breck and Chi stretched their legs.

"Don't you have to go home?" Chi asked.

Breck gave her a sharp, disapproving glare. Leave it to Chi to say something that no one else would dare say, even though it would be exactly what everyone was thinking. The thought had come to Breck's mind as well, but unlike Chi, she would never have questioned him.

"I will get there," he countered. "Don't worry."

Chi shrugged.

"Yes, we're hungry," Breck interceded, and pinched Chi's arm when Eric had turned his back.

As they neared Mansfield, Eric took them to a small and intimate bed and breakfast on the Connecticut/Massachusetts border. They sat at a window table that overlooked a deserted garden Breck assumed would be filled with a colorful assortment of flowers during the blooming season.

A waitress made her way to their table, filled the crystal water glasses, and handed each of them a menu. There were three entrees to choose from.

"What happens if I don't want anything on this menu?" Chi griped, flipping the menu card over to stare at a small passage describing the history of the bed and breakfast.

"Then you don't eat," Eric said matter-of-factly. His manner took Breck completely by surprise, and she heard firsthand the tone he must use during difficult business meetings. She sipped some water and left Chi to fight her own battles with Eric if she dared.

"This is a charming place," Breck said, slicing the tension between Eric and Chi. "How do you know of it?"

"I've stayed here a few times."

"With your wife?" Chi asked, picking up her glass and eyeing him over the rim.

"No, not with my wife. That would be a little tacky, wouldn't you agree?" He would fight her wit with wit. He had given up being charming with Chi a long time ago.

"Can you two knock it off?" Breck said, almost slamming her glass on the table. "Especially you, Chi. I love you both, but don't make me have to choose—and don't make me separate you two."

"She started it," Eric said, pushing his glass forward.

"No, I didn't," Chi shot back at him. They were bickering like a couple of five-year-olds. Apparently they must have realized it too, because the next thing to happen Breck could only describe as miraculous. Chi and Eric stared each other down until both of them started laughing. They sealed their truce by clicking glasses. Breck looked first at Chi and then at Eric. She didn't know what had happened to melt the tension, but she wasn't going to challenge it.

The drive through Massachusetts soothed Breck, who rode cuddled under Eric's arm. They arrived at the townhome and parked outside. Chi pulled up beside them, and the three walked in together. Chi was eager to see her rented brownstone apartment in the South End, forty miles away, so she stayed long enough to get detailed instructions from Eric, then headed out.

"See you Monday," she said, jumping into her car and peeling off.

"That is quite some friend you have there," Eric said while they stood in the doorway and stared after her car.

"She loves you. She doesn't want to see you hurt."

Breck turned to face him and wrapped her arms around him. "I know."

Most of Breck's belongings went into a rented storage facility not far from the townhome. The only things she needed were her office supplies, clothes, and a few sentimental belongings. After spending the night at the townhome, she and Eric met the movers at the storage facility, where she separated her things.

Eric stayed with her the entire time. He excused himself once when his cell phone rang and he had to take the call from Gaby. He stepped far enough away from Breck so that eavesdropping was virtually impossible.

"Everything's okay?" she asked.

Eric nodded. "Darius wanted to talk to me."

"Cute."

"I told him I'll be home in time to tuck him in tomorrow night."

Breck nodded. That gave her another night with him, and she liked that. She could get used to playing house with Eric, making love nightly and taking a shower together every morning after several rounds of playful lovemaking.

He knelt beside her and Breck tilted her head to get a full look at him. Without a doubt, he was the handsomest man she had ever laid eyes on, but she knew she was biased.

"Why are you looking at me like that?" he asked, carefully placing the glassware she had picked out to go with her in a padded box.

"I love you."

He turned his head and met her lips. He touched the side of her face so gently that she thought he was afraid of hurting her. He didn't speak—and he didn't have to for her to know that he felt the same way.

After an hour of sorting, they headed back to Mansfield, stopping to get some takeout before they reached the townhome. Once all the boxes were inside, Eric handed her the small metallic key ring with two sets of keys for the front and back doors. Breck kept one of each and handed the other set to Eric.

"Do you want to give them to Chi instead?" he asked before closing his palm.

Breck shook her head. "No. You can keep them. I'll have another set made for Chi, just in case." She walked into the bedroom to change.

"You want me to start a fire?" he yelled after her.

"Yes. That'll be great." When she stepped back into the living room, Eric had the fire going and all of the lights turned off. She cuddled beside him on the sofa. She had slipped into a pair of loose sweats and a tank top. Her nipples stood erect underneath the fabric, and as she snuggled against him, he began to toy with them.

"Can I ask you a question?" she asked, gazing into the fire as her nipples hardened even more and she felt a stirring between her legs.

"You just did," he joked.

"A more specific question."

"Okay." He relaxed his hand and braced himself.

"How does this make you feel?" she asked, turning to face him. "Being here with me?"

He took a deep breath and stared into the fire before he answered her. She saw the light in his eyes, but the look on his face was one of despair. "I've never cheated on my wife before and I never thought I would," he began. "I couldn't imagine wanting anyone other than Gaby. She's beautiful, smart, and a terrific mother to my son." He dropped his hand and leaned his head against the sofa, struggling with his feelings.

"But?" Breck said.

He shook his head. "I don't know. I didn't know there was a but."

"If you love Gaby as much as you say you do, then why are you here?" she asked, puzzled. There had to be a but. Any man who loved his wife as much as Eric claimed to would not be sleeping with another woman. Breck was sure of it.

"Other than the fact that I love you, I don't know. I know that I love her, but I also know that I love you, and I didn't think that was possible." He closed his eyes and shook his head, confused.

"You love us both, equally?" she asked. She was just as confused about the situation as he was. She adored him, but her desire was not for him to leave his family. She would never be able to live with herself knowing that she'd denied a little boy the right to grow up with a father who praised him. But fighting through the guilt of loving a married man, she couldn't deny the emptiness she felt being away from him. It was almost as if a very necessary part of her life was missing.

"Differently, but equally," he said. "I love sharing Mansfield and my friends with you. I can't do that with Gaby, but the life I have with her is pleasant as well. It's a very different world, but it's good. Gaby and I do not argue excessively or violently. We have disagreements, like most couples, but nothing so extravagant that I feel smothered by her. It's nothing like that."

Breck didn't know what to say, so she just sat quietly on the sofa with her arms folded across her chest.

"What were you hoping to hear?" he asked.

She shrugged. "I don't know. I didn't expect to hear you say that you hated her and you have a rotten marriage. I wouldn't believe you did."

"Breck, I'm not on the verge of getting a divorce," he said.

Breck shot a look at him. "Why would you say that?"

"Because I don't want to mislead you."

"I'm not some naïve kid. If I was unsure of anything, I would not have made this move."

Eric nodded, took her into his arms again, and settled with her against the sofa. "Will you be happy with me knowing that I'm not planning to leave my wife and that I have no answers about our future?"

"Right now, yes." She bit down on her lower lip before continuing. "Five or ten years from now, I don't know." She shrugged.

He kissed her temple and pulled her to his chest. Breck rested her head against him as they stared into the fire. They ended up falling asleep in each other's arms. The following afternoon, Eric left and returned home.

FOURTEEN

LOCATION WAS everything, Eric reminded her while she searched for the new home of Breck Larson Designs. She was looking for an office in downtown Boston, but nothing fit quite right. Then, while driving through Mansfield with Alyce, she stumbled upon the perfect building. It was just five blocks from the convention center, and it was owned by Warren & Peterson.

It took no effort at all to convince Eric to sell it to her. Jokingly, she told Chi it was the price of a blow job. She was only kidding, but Eric did sell it for less than the price of a modest car because of the amount of work that needed to be done to rehabilitate it. Most of the work was cosmetic. The structure of the building was in perfect condition. It was a deal she couldn't walk away from. She even paid cash for it. While the interior of the gutted warehouse was being renovated to house Breck Larson Designs, Breck began interviewing prospective architects to join her firm. She and Chi worked from her townhome.

Just as Breck had predicted, she'd become a prime candidate to design some of the new buildings going up around the Big Dig in Boston and major projects around the country. She received business calls directly from the city manager's office and from prominent businesspeople in the private sector whenever there were needs for distinguished architects. The work was coming in faster than Breck could keep up. Most of her new clients came to her as a result of her work with Warren & Peterson.

The check Breck received for completing the convention center had made her very comfortable financially, but she wasn't quite ready to consider herself independently wealthy. She reinvested the money into her business by hiring two more designers, gave Chi a raise, and in the process propelled Breck Larson Designs into a principal architectural firm. Chi's raise also came with a new title of project coordinator. When Breck told Chi how much she would be making, Chi nearly fainted.

The warehouse was a spacious two-story building with wide columns, high ceilings, and a lot of broken windows. According to the design plan Breck put together, there would be two rooms in the corner—one, her office, and the other, a conference room. Four other rooms would be added, one for Chi, two for the new hires, and one for storage and a copier. She hired Martin and Brian to do the construction. The bathrooms needed to be redone as well as the plumbing, electricity, and painting. Martin and Brian would lay hardwood floors over the ugly, cold concrete.

During Breck's first week in Mansfield she tried very diligently to stay away from Brian. She assumed her sudden move there would encourage him to pick up where they had left off the night of the grand opening. When Brian discovered she had moved, he was thrilled and immediately asked her out. Breck of course declined, saying she was just too busy. Instead of coming out and telling him she was dating someone else, she kept up the ridiculous farce of being busy until he stopped asking. Two months after the rehabbing started, she and Chi moved in. All of the work wasn't complete but they could work around it.

When it was finished, Breck's office was remarkable. The wall immediately behind her cherrywood desk and bookcase was three-fourths glass. She had thick gray curtains hung to block the sun, but she knew they would remain open most of the time. When she looked out the window she stared onto a wooded lot and small parking area. True, it was no panoramic harbor view, but she fell in love with it nonetheless. A sucker for bronze sculptures, she placed two in her office and another two in the reception area.

Besides being dull and dirty, the outside of the building was in good condition. The brick had to be cleaned and some of the wood trim replaced and painted. The first floor, Eric told her, was once used as the neighborhood candy store. Breck smiled when she stepped inside and immediately knew what she would use it for.

The BL Coffeehouse grand opening would coincide with Breck moving her business operation out of the townhome and into her new office building. The main attraction, besides its intimate appeal, would be interesting and exotic mugs Breck had shipped from various parts of the world.

When the construction began, Breck was too excited to stay away. She, Alyce, and Chi often lunched with Martin and Brian. Whenever Eric could slip away from Boston, he joined them. They managed to keep their distance and their hands off each other whenever anyone was around them, but they often wondered if the charade fooled their insightful friends.

"If they suspect anything, Martin hasn't let me in on it yet," Eric confided to her on one of his many visits to the townhome.

After an afternoon shopping with the interior decorators, buying new furniture, Breck drove back to the townhome exuberant. There was nothing more satisfying than shopping and knowing that you had the money to buy just about anything you wanted. When she pulled into the drive, she spotted Eric's Range Rover. Surprised, she rushed from the car and ran up the few stairs into the townhome. She stepped inside to encounter a delicious aroma and a romantic setting. Candles were lit throughout the room, and he had placed black china on the coffee table in front of the fireplace. Several pillows from the sofa were arranged on the floor for them to sit on while they ate.

Breck slipped off her shoes and strolled into the kitchen. She leaned against the open doorway as she watched Eric reaching for the champagne flutes. "Hello," she said, folding her arms in front of her. "This is a pleasant surprise."

He took a single step and kissed her before he returned his attention to the champagne bottle.

"We haven't had a chance to celebrate your new office and coffeehouse." The loud pop of the cork reverberated through the room while Eric rushed the flowing champagne over to the sink.

"What's for dinner?" Breck asked, walking into the kitchen and peeking into a huge pot. "Lobster." She immediately replaced the top.

"Didn't know I had it in me, did you?" he said, walking up behind her and rocking with her while he nibbled on her neck.

"That feels good," she said, turning to kiss him. He patted her on the behind and pulled away.

"Go relax while I get the food."

"Need help?" she asked, not one to relent so easily, especially when it involved being with Eric.

"Nope. I have this under control," he said, nudging her into the living room.

Breck sat down on the floor and folded her legs in front of her while Eric filled their glasses with the bubbling champagne. The fire warmed her while she sipped from the glass and waited for Eric to return with the food.

"So, how did it go today?" he asked, sitting down opposite her and spooning some rice pilaf onto her plate.

"Great. The place has gone through such a wonderful transformation." She cracked the lobster and pulled the meat from the tail, dipping it in the melted butter before shoving it into her mouth. "You should see the columns. They're fabulous. And the floors . . ." She took another bite. "The floors are so shiny I'm almost afraid to step on them."

"Slow down. You're going to choke."

"I can't help it. I'm so excited. I'm having so much fun with this."

"Better than your old office?"

"Much better. The other office was just rental office space. This building is coming alive right before my eyes." She ate some salad Eric had placed on her plate.

Eric grinned at her.

"Are you okay with all this?" she asked.

Stunned by her question, he squinted. "Why wouldn't I be?"

"Because I've done everything on my own. I haven't consulted with you on anything." Breck thought about the women in her life, from her mother to her friends. Almost all of them couldn't make a major purchase or a business decision without first consulting their husbands. Breck knew she wouldn't be able to survive a relationship like that.

"I'm okay with it. You know what you're doing, and I'm staying out of your way. If you need me, you know where to find me."

"Okay, but if you and I were in a relationship, I would have to consult with you first, right?"

Eric frowned. "We *are* in a relationship."

"What I mean is, if we were living together, would things be different?"

"No. You are a businesswoman. You know what's best for you and your business. I don't consult with you before I purchase a lot, so why would I expect you to consult with me? Handle your business. If you need me, you know where to find me."

Breck beamed as she sipped the champagne. "I like that," she said. "I like that a lot."

THE INTERVIEWING process was grueling. Breck received over a hundred résumés. Together she and Chi sorted through them. It was easy separating the "not a chance" résumés from the "possibles," but harder separating those from the ones for serious consideration. She also had to decide what to do with the out-of-town applicants—would she be willing to pay relocation expenses? Many of the applicants were from Boston and were recent graduates from one of Boston's excellent universities.

Eventually she narrowed it down to five candidates. After a two-month process, she finally hired two designers: David, a young African-American who had just graduated from Boston University, and Marla, a young white woman who had two years of previous experience and was returning to the workforce after having a child. Breck also hired two CAD specialists. She now had a buzzing architectural firm.

Everyone settled in well at the new building and their jobs. The dress code was kept casual when clients were not expected in the office; when clients were expected, it was business casual. It didn't take Breck long to slip into her old habit of prancing around the office barefooted.

Most days after work Breck and Chi stopped downstairs at the coffeehouse for a cup of coffee and a slice of cheesecake before heading home. Breck hired four area college students to run the shop, each working part-time.

Occasionally Alyce joined them for coffee. The twosome had expanded into a threesome, but neither Chi nor Breck complained. Alyce was in many ways a lot like them. She longed for a night out, away from Martin, the house, and their children, to hang with the girls.

"Hell, they do it all the time," she reasoned. "It's about time I did it too." She insisted that she and Martin "had a good thing" but admitted he could be a bit overbearing at times. "When he gets with Eric and Brian, honey, please," she said, shifting in her seat. "They all just get plain stupid."

She had known Martin, Brian, and Eric as teenagers and confessed to having been sweet on Eric back then, although her parents forbade her to date him. "When he dropped out of school, they said he would end up on the streets selling drugs and they wouldn't let me have anything to do with him. They're slapping themselves now," she said with a sneer. "My mother says, 'That boy turned out all right.' 'All right,' my ass! He practically owns Mansfield."

Today Chi had the day off, so Breck sat alone in the cushioned booth at the coffeehouse and flipped through a current edition of *Architectural Digest*. She was in no particular hurry to get home. Eric had made no plans for them this weekend, and she doubted she would see him at all. She heard the door chime ring, announcing a customer, but she didn't bother looking up. The coffeehouse stayed pretty busy and had become a hangout for older high school kids after school. Breck had been forced to enact a no-smoking rule to deter the crowd from smoking cigarettes most of them were too young to purchase. For the most part, the teenagers who took advantage of the coffeehouse came to study or meet with friends and drink a smoothie or iced-coffee drink. Most of them had not yet become hard coffee drinkers.

"Hey," Chi said as she walked closer to Breck. She took the straps of her shoulder bag from her arm and placed the bag on the table.

Breck looked up from her magazine, surprised to see her. "What are you doing on this side of town?"

"I stopped by the house, but you weren't there, so I figured you would be here or still in the office."

Breck moved her bag to the floor and placed her magazine down on the table.

"What are you drinking?" Chi asked, sitting back in her chair and taking a deep breath.

"Regular coffee."

"I'm in the mood for a smoothie." Chi flipped through her purse and pulled out her wallet, then got up and walked to the counter to order a fruit smoothie with whipped cream.

"What up?" Breck asked, eyeing Chi when she returned to the booth.

"I miss you. We haven't been able to hang out in a while."

"Yeah, I know. It's my fault."

Chi shook her head. "You don't have to apologize. I know you've been busy with the office." Chi took a sip of her drink before continuing. "How are things going with Eric?"

"Fine . . ." Breck hesitated. Chi's overall opinion of the situation remained unchanged, but her displeasure with Eric had vanished. Breck was grateful for that, but judging from Chi's subtle expression, she doubted this conversation had anything to do with Eric.

"Good." Chi nodded. "What are you doing tonight?"

"Nothing. Just going home and maybe read a book. Why?" Breck grew more suspicious. It was not Chi's nature to stall.

"Is Eric coming over?"

"I don't know. What is this about?" Breck asked, tired of the suspense.

Chi grinned. "Mind if I bring a friend over?"

Breck's mouth dropped open. "A friend?"

"I've met someone."

Breck screamed. "What?! Why didn't you say something?" She slapped Chi's hand resting on the table. She was excited because it meant Chi was settling into her new life in Boston and wouldn't announce she was returning to Indiana.

"Well, Breck, you've been so busy getting the office together," she said, rubbing Breck's hand. "You did a wonderful job, by the way. I knew you and Eric needed time to get things settled between you two, so I just wanted to give you some space."

"Well, give me details. What's her name? What does she do? How did you meet her? Tell, tell." Breck sat up in her chair and eagerly leaned over the table, waiting for Chi to fill in the blanks.

"Her name is Gena, and I met her at a park not far from my apartment. I walk through there every morning before coming to the office, and we kept seeing each other, so one day we walked together." Chi beamed. "She's an attorney, she works downtown, and she's pretty terrific."

Breck shook her head. She had never worried about Chi fitting in in Boston. Boston was perfect for Chi. She was young and she had a terrific income and no children. She fit the demographic of the South End, which was made up primarily of young professionals living in overpriced row houses and driving expensive late-model cars. Breck had figured that while she was getting things settled around the office and with Eric, Chi had ventured out and started making friends, which had never been difficult for her to do.

"Oh, my. How long has this been going on?"

"About a month. She took me to a great jazz club in Back Bay, and now we go about twice a week. I'm going to have to take you there. We also stopped in Gaby's gallery." She peered over her cup and stared directly at

Breck. "She has some great stuff. Gena bought a painting. Have you ever been in there?"

Breck shook her head. "No, and I don't think I ever will."

"Aren't you the least bit curious?"

"No, I'm not. I have no desire to laugh and socialize with this woman. Even *I* have some principles."

"It's a very nice gallery."

"I don't doubt that it is. But tell me more about Gena," she said, happy to shift the course of the conversation.

"Can I just bring her over for dinner tonight?"

"Of course you can. What time?"

"Couple of hours?"

"Wonderful. Let me run home and get things set. What does she like?"

"Everything."

"Okay, I'll stop at the store and grab some salmon, a bottle of wine . . ." Breck said, thinking aloud. She slid from the booth and grabbed her bags and her purse. "Ohh, I'm so happy for you." She gave Chi a quick hug. "Okay, see you in a couple of hours."

Chi and Gena arrived at the townhome precisely two hours later. From past experience, Breck was not surprised when she saw Gena. She was beautiful, caramel-skinned, and slender, like most of the women Chi dated. At a good five-ten, she dwarfed Chi. Even dressed down in a pair of neatly pressed jeans and a bulky sweater with her light-brown hair pulled into a ponytail, she was obviously sophisticated.

The budding lovers sat together on the sofa. Occasionally one stroked the other's leg. Breck could tell that Chi was completely smitten. She demonstrated a seriousness that Breck had never observed before—Breck had never seen Chi in love, and she smiled to witness it now.

It was well into the morning before Chi and Gena said good night. Dinner and the conversation had been wonderful. Breck hugged them both at the door and gave Chi a thumbs-up as soon as Gena turned her back.

BRECK TOOK her time getting out of bed Saturday morning. When she rolled over and looked at the clock on the nightstand, it was almost eleven. She growled as she buried her head in her pillow.

What was she going to do today? She stepped out of bed. She had plenty of work to do, but the idea of going into the office or pulling out any of the designs from her bag didn't appeal to her.

She quickly brushed her teeth and slipped into her jogging gear before she could talk herself out of going for a run. The hardest decision she made every day was to jog, but once she was outdoors, she always wondered why it was so hard for her to get out. Stepping out of the house as the mercury dipped further down the thermometer was also difficult, and she made a mental note to check out some of the fitness facilities in the area. She started out on her usual route and began to clear her mind. The morning run was more than for physical fitness; it served as her meditation hour as well.

When she returned to the house, panting, she looked at the answering machine. There were no messages.

She peeled off her sweaty clothes and headed straight to the bathroom to begin her morning beauty routine. While her face mask was tightening, she draped a towel around herself and walked into the kitchen. She started the coffee brewing and then returned to the bedroom to select a pair of jeans and a sweater. She took a quick shower, dressed, and then poured some coffee into a travel mug and headed out the door.

She decided to drive around. She just wasn't in the mood to sit around the townhome, even if it meant driving into Boston to get away. She had been consciously looking for a permanent house, but nothing had jumped out at her. She knew she could always stay at the townhome and Eric would never charge her any rent, but it didn't feel like home, and she needed that. She also missed her furniture and paintings, and she desperately wanted a place she could call her own.

She drove toward the heart of Mansfield. Mansfield was a small, forgotten community south of Boston that greatly resembled the neighborhoods she was accustomed to in Indianapolis. It didn't have Boston's splendor and energy, but she liked it. It was developing into the type of community where the young professionals in Boston would move once they'd settled into their careers and decided to start families.

Like any other city experiencing a renaissance, those who happened to get in on the ground level stood to make a lot of money. Eric had done well by buying up vacant properties and starting the process. It was quite feasible that in a few years the property values in Mansfield would equal those of neighborhoods immediately surrounding Boston. It would be good for the economy of Mansfield, but not so good for the people Eric was hoping to help, who couldn't afford quarter-million-dollar homes. That was the reason he'd bought up most of the properties and sometimes sold them cheaply. Either way, he came out a winner.

Breck drove around Mansfield absentmindedly. She always ended up here, because that was the area with which she was the most familiar. She thought about stopping at the coffeehouse but decided not to. As she rounded a corner a few blocks from the office, she pulled the car to the side of the road and shut off the engine. She stared across the street at a large Victorian house that had a FOR SALE sign dangling on chains, tossed back and forth by the wind.

Breck got out of the car and walked across the street. The gray house was in desperate need of a fresh coat of paint, but she quickly regarded that as minor. Most of the shrubs and trees surrounding the house had grown tall and wild for lack of care. Old fallen leaves that hadn't been raked in years provided a cover over the lawn. She would have to spend a significant amount of time and money to get a plush green should she decide to buy the house. The house looked like it had been deserted for some time and was waiting for someone to notice it among the other grand Victorians on the street. There were five wooden steps up to the porch, and Breck took the first step carefully, not sure if any of the planks would break beneath her weight. The steps held, and she walked toward the swinging screen door.

She peered through the uncovered bay window into the dark house. She could see a wooden staircase leading to the second floor. Dull wooden floorboards spotted with black patches of dirt were laid throughout the first floor and as far back as the kitchen. She had a clear view of the living room and a brick fireplace that made up a far wall. She could see that in some cases the walls needed not only paint but drywall and plaster.

Breck peeled her face from the glass and walked around the length of the front porch. Two hooks overhead must have held a porch swing. Perhaps parents had sat there and kept a watchful eye on the little ones as they played in the yard with other children. Breck leaned against a wooden brace and looked out onto the street, feeling very at ease in her surroundings. The wind lifted her hair and chilled her face just enough to make her shiver. If this were her house, she would definitely replace the missing swing. It seemed to belong there.

She walked off the porch and rounded the house, taking a path made of brick blocks to the back. Surrounding half of the house was a high wooden fence with tri-angular tips. She touched the black lever on the gate, careful that it didn't break off in her hand, and pushed the gate open. The old hinges squeaked loudly as she stepped through, and the gate slammed shut when she released the lever.

She was surprised to see that the back of the house was plain, almost neglected. It looked as if the designer had forgotten to add any detail. A wooden deck could easily be placed there. Stepping on the hard lawn, Breck walked toward a cement patio to a glass-paned door. She peeked inside and had a full view of the kitchen. It was large but old. All the fixtures were white porcelain with some peeled and rusty areas. The cabinet doors were slightly opened on rusty, weak-looking hinges. Breck imagined an island in the center of the kitchen and new cabinetry and appliances. She looked straight through the house but couldn't see any other rooms.

She looked out over the lot, guessing it to be at least three-fourths of an acre, enough space to hold a flower garden and a decent-sized deck with a hot tub. Satisfied, Breck walked back to her car, picked up her cell phone, and pressed a number in her speed dial.

"Fisher Realtors, Morgan Fisher speaking." Breck used Fisher Realtors when she purchased the building from Eric and had kept the number just for this purpose. This house was also listed with Fisher.

"Hello, Morgan, this is Breck Larson. Do you remember me?" Breck assumed the woman would remember her, since she had handled the deal with the office building.

"Of course, Breck. How are you?"

"I'm well, thank you."

"Wonderful. How can I help you?"

"You have a listing for a wonderful Victorian house

for sale on Arbor Drive in Mansfield, and I would love to see the inside of it."

"What's the exact address? I should be able to get some information on it for you." Breck gave her the street address and waited while Morgan typed it into her computer.

"Well, it looks like the house is still available, no sale pending, and it's listed for two hundred fifty thousand dollars. Are you interested?"

"Yes. Will you be able to show it to me this afternoon?"

"I most certainly can. Give me your cell number and I'll call you back." After Breck gave her the telephone number and hung up, she sat and stared at the house a little longer. The house was three blocks from Alyce and Martin, so she drove by to see if their cars were in the drive. Alyce's navy Camry was there, but there was no sign of Martin's huge black F-350 Ford truck. He was probably at a site.

Breck parked her car alongside the curb and walked to their house, a beautiful two-story brick home. Martin and Alyce had returned to Mansfield five years ago after living in Norwood, Massachusetts, for the first ten years of their marriage. They were both thirty-seven and had married immediately after college. Alyce had taught second grade until their first child, Londrick, was born. A year later she gave birth to a girl, Madison. Londrick and Madison were now four and three, and Alyce had her hands full trying to keep the precocious toddlers from destroying the house and killing each other.

Breck knocked on the door and waited patiently. Chances were Alyce was in the kitchen preparing the kids' lunch and had to drop everything to come to the door.

"Breck, hi," Alyce said, swinging the screen door open and stepping aside. Breck walked in, stepping over a couple of toys in the process.

"I'm sorry to come by without calling first, but I was in the area. I hope it's okay."

"Oh, don't be silly. Of course it's okay. I'm making sandwiches. Want one?"

"Sure," Breck said, slipping off her sweater and following Alyce into the kitchen. Martin and Alyce kept their furniture to a minimum—after all, they had two toddlers around who were prone to jump and spill. Although Breck was sure they could afford more expensive furnishings, they didn't have anything of great value that could get easily broken.

She joined Alyce in the kitchen and sat on one of the breakfast-bar stools.

"What brings you this way?" Alyce asked, taking out two additional slices of bread.

"I was driving around and I stumbled upon a house for sale on Arbor Drive. I'm waiting for my Realtor to call me back."

"Arbor Drive? That's just a couple of blocks away."

"I know."

"We'd be neighbors. That would be wonderful."

"Don't get too excited just yet. I haven't seen the inside." Alyce made peanut butter and jelly sandwiches for the kids and turkey and Swiss on dill rye for Breck and herself. While the kids sat at the kitchen table to eat their lunch, Alyce joined Breck at the breakfast bar. Immediately after lunch, Breck helped her put the kids to bed for a nap. It didn't take them long to fall asleep, and Alyce and Breck returned downstairs to sit in the family room.

"You have your hands full," Breck said, moving aside another toy as they sat on the sofa.

"Tell me about it."

"Are you going to have another?"

"I'm done. As soon as Madison is in school all day, I'm going back to work. I have to get out of this house." She kicked her feet up and rested them on an ottoman.

"So, when are you and Brian going to start dating seriously?" she asked, hitting Breck on the leg.

Breck's heart thumped hard in her chest, and for a minute, she couldn't bring herself to even look at Alyce. Of course they would assume that she would pick up with Brian once she moved to Massachusetts, especially considering the way she had left it. Brian had probably thought the same thing. But she had been in Massachusetts for months now and had made no advances toward him. Likewise, Brian hadn't asked her out since that first week and had never hinted at wanting to pick things up where they'd left off. She had thought that maybe Eric had confided in his Mansfield friends about their relationship. But if that were the case, Alyce wouldn't be asking her this question.

"Oh, I'm not ready to date anyone seriously." She squirmed uneasily in her seat and tried to think of something to hide behind but could think of nothing to change the conversation to.

"I understand. You're busy getting your business going and looking for a house to get you out of that townhome Eric has you holed up in. He's a good friend though, isn't he?"

"Yes, he is. I enjoyed working with him and meeting you guys."

"Seems like you guys have gotten pretty close," Alyce said.

Breck paused. She knows something and wants me to confide in her, Breck thought. She knew she could trust Alyce, but she couldn't compromise Eric's trust to fill Alyce in on the details of their relationship.

"Eric's a charmer. Does he ever bring Darius by to play with Londrick?" A safety net, Breck thought.

"Oh, no. Mrs. Gaby would never allow that. Darius will be one of those kids who will go to private school his entire life, head off to Harvard, and become a diplomat, if Gaby has her way—and I'm sure she will." Alyce sneered.

"How does Eric feel about it?'

"Eric always tries to do the right thing, so he doesn't argue with her or her family. He reasons that she only wants what's best for Darius, but she's making that boy into a little snob."

"So you've met Darius?"

"Yes, when we go to Eric's house for Christmas Eve. We go every year. Did he tell you about it?"

Breck almost gagged but maintained her composure. "No, he didn't."

"Well, I'll make sure he invites you. They have a big, beautiful house in Back Bay. The damn thing is three times the size of this house." There was no way she would get that invitation, and if she did, she would politely excuse herself. She didn't want to see Eric's house, and she definitely didn't want to see him with his family. Even thinking about it made her feel like she was on the outside of his life looking in. She wished that instead of visiting Eric and Gaby's home, everyone would come to a home she shared with Eric.

She tried hard to keep such thoughts to a minimum, because she knew it would never happen. Before she could continue the conversation, her cell phone rang and she quickly answered it.

"Breck, Morgan here. I was able to get some information on the house, and I can meet you there in one hour. Sound doable?"

"Sounds great to me."

"Wonderful. See you then."

Breck flipped her phone closed. Alyce did not return to the conversation of Eric or Gaby, so Breck filled her in on Chi's new girlfriend. They made a mental note to try to get together at the coffeehouse one day the following week. Alyce began to pick up some of the toys from the living room and foyer, and Breck headed back to the house to wait for Morgan.

BRECK GOT the word that she was not alone in wanting the old Victorian. Although the house had been on the market for a while, several people saw it almost simultaneously, Breck being one of them. Two bids had been placed on the house, and the price reached $280,000 by that evening. Breck took a deep breath and made a counterbid of $290,000, as high as she was willing to go. With the amount of work that needed to be done, she couldn't justify spending more on an old house.

Monday morning Breck received the bad news. Someone had topped her bid. She plopped down at her desk, unable to believe the bidding had gone so high.

"I can't do it, Morgan," Breck said, shaking her head. "It's just too high." The disappointment was evident in her voice. She could have done so much to the place.

"I understand, Breck," Morgan said. "If I come across a similar house, I'll be sure to let you know."

"Thanks." Breck was stunned. The bidding on the house had exceeded the initial asking price by fifty thousand dollars. Since she's been in Massachusetts, nothing had captivated her as much as this house. She had loved watching her office come to life, transforming the formerly run-down rag to the lively building it now was, and she wanted to do the same to the house. In fact, she had looked forward to doing some of the work herself. But three hundred thousand dollars plus the cost of renovations was just too much for the old house. She had the responsibility of paying the salary of five employees at the firm, four part-time employees at the coffeehouse, insurance premiums, taxes, and other expenses associated with the businesses. She estimated that finishing the work she wanted to do on the house would add close to another hundred thousand dollars.

She tried to stop thinking about the house, to no avail. She especially loved the fireplace; she imagined sitting in front of it with Eric, talking and making love.

In the middle of her daydream, her phone rang, startling her back to the present.

"Breck Larson," she said.

"Hey, baby, how's your day going?" Eric said. His timing was impeccable. She always loved hearing his voice, and he always seemed to know when she needed him.

"Hi," she said heavily.

"Oh, that didn't sound good. What's up?"

"I didn't get the house."

"What house?"

Breck thought for a minute and realized she hadn't told him about the house. She quickly filled him in.

"So what happened? Why didn't you get it?"

"Bidding went too high. Too much for an old house that needs a lot of work."

"How much is it?"

"It's at three hundred thousand."

"Breck, you can buy a lot and design your own house."

"The character of this house cannot be duplicated. I can truly say that homes like this are not built anymore. But it needs a new kitchen, a new bath, electric work. It needs too much work for a three-hundred-thousand-dollar house." She tapped on the desk with her fingernails.

"Who's your Realtor?"

"Morgan, but it doesn't matter. I'm not going higher. It's going to take at least another hundred thousand dollars to bring it up to date. I'm just going to keep looking. Are you coming over tonight?"

"How about dinner at the bed and breakfast?" Since her move, she and Eric had gone back there for weekend lunches and occasional dinners. It was far enough away from Boston and Mansfield that they never worried about bumping into anyone they knew.

"Sounds good. I miss you." And she did. She hadn't seen him at all over the weekend, but she never questioned him when he couldn't make it. She had so many projects going on in her life that she could only squeeze in a few hours a week with him anyway. Eric never let a full week go by without coming to the townhome to hold her, kiss her, or make love.

"I miss you too. I'll pick you up around seven." He blew her a kiss before he hung up the phone. Breck settled back into her chair, her mind drifting back to the house, the first thing that hadn't gone her way since she'd moved to Massachusetts.

FIFTEEN

BRECK SAT at her high drafting chair, going over some graphics one of the CAD specialists had put into the computer. Everyone else had gone home. She hadn't planned to work late this Thursday evening. In fact, she was supposed to meet Chi and Gena at a Boston jazz club. It took forty minutes to get there, and she had promised Alyce she'd pick her up on the way. When she looked at the clock, she realized she would never have enough time to go home to change first.

The design she was working on was for a middle school in a Boston suburb. The community had expanded so much that the current school was simply not big enough to hold all the students. Breck divided the firm's projects so that she and David handled all of the commercial property, while Marla was responsible for private homes.

The phone rang, and Breck reached for it without turning her eyes away from the printouts.

"Hello, Breck. This is Morgan."

"Oh, hi, Morgan. How are you?" Breck wasn't sure if she was ready to look at another house; she hadn't gotten over the disappointment of losing the house on Arbor Drive yet.

"I'm well, thank you. I'm calling to see when you can come into my office so we can get the paperwork started and schedule the closing. I would like to schedule it for the twenty-ninth if you have that date free."

"What are you talking about?" Breck asked, the creases around her eyes tightening.

"Your house. We need to get the contract and sales agreement signed, among others." Morgan sounded so enthusiastic that Breck hated telling her that she had made a mistake.

"Morgan, you've called the wrong person. I didn't get the house on Arbor Drive. I pulled out."

"I know you did, but I got another call with another bid on your behalf, and it went through. All we need to do is get the paperwork in order, then it's your house."

Breck was quiet. That was not possible. She hadn't made another call. She wondered if someone was playing a very mean practical joke.

"Morgan, I'm telling you. I never called you back with another bid."

"I know you didn't, but Eric Warren did on your behalf. He made an offer for three hundred fifty thousand dollars. Is there a problem?" Morgan asked.

"I need to call you back." Breck replaced the receiver, stunned. Eric definitely had the resources to write a check for that much money and not think twice about it. But why would he do that? When it came to her finances and business, he had always kept his distance, and he'd promised to give her space to build an independent life.

This would change things. He would want a key to the house, like he had a key to the townhome. What if she angered him and he demanded that she leave? She stood to lose everything.

"Oh, no." Breck jumped down from her chair. "This just isn't going to work." She stormed out of the office.

She drove the forty-five minutes to Boston, replaying the conversation with Morgan in her mind and rehearsing her speech to Eric. She called Alyce before reaching Eric's office and canceled for the evening.

The office building was empty except for the janitorial staff busying themselves emptying trash cans and vacuuming the carpet. She waited for the elevator, tapping her feet on the floor, arms folded across her chest. The elevator opened and Breck stepped inside and pushed the button for Eric's floor. Once she stepped out, she quickly rounded the corner and stormed passed Gloria's empty desk into Eric's office.

Eric never left before seven o'clock, so she was not surprised to hear his voice as she approached his office. But then she stopped. It hadn't occurred to her that he might not be alone. She couldn't hear another voice, so he must be on the phone. She inched closer and peered through his partially opened office door. He sat straight at his desk, fanning through papers while he talked. He wore a casual collarless shirt with matching slacks. A suit jacket hung on a coatrack to the right of the desk, easily accessible if unexpected clients were to drop by.

Breck pushed the door open with her fingertips. It squeaked and caught his attention. He stopped talking long enough to look up and wave her in. She walked in but didn't sit down.

"Breck," he said, after abruptly ending his call and standing up. His black pressed pants were as neat as when he'd put them on that morning. He walked over to her and quickly kissed her cheek.

"What the hell do you think you're doing?" she demanded.

Eric backed away from her. "What do you mean?"

"The house. Why did you do that?"

Eric didn't say anything at first. He leaned against his desk and folded his arms in front of him as if he had expected this conversation.

"Are you buying me? Does this officially make me your mistress?"

"Breck, you needed my help."

"No I didn't. I'd moved on. I certainly didn't ask you to buy me a damn house." She shivered with anger.

"No, you didn't and you wouldn't. We are in a relationship and I felt that it was my place."

Breck frowned at him. "Your place?"

"I did nothing less than what I would have done if we were living together. I pay all the bills in my household, and you should be allowed some of those privileges."

"Oh," Breck said, exasperated. "So I *am* a mistress now. Does that mean that I sit at home and wait for you to call and I don't have a life unless it's with you?"

"Don't be silly."

"Well, you seem to be making all the rules here. Exactly what are the rules now, Mr. Warren?" Breck folded her arms and slumped in the chair, waiting for him to speak.

"We've never had any rules, Breck, and that's the problem."

"Why should there be rules?"

"Every relationship has rules."

"Especially relationships like ours, right? Do you want to keep me in line and tucked away? I am not going to become so absorbed in you that I don't have anything of my own. I can't do that."

"I'm not asking you to do that, and I know why you keep your distance. You don't ask much of me, and sometimes I'm not okay with that. I want to do more. I really do."

"But you can't, Eric, and I can't dwell on that, because if I did, that is all I would focus on. I cherish the times we're together because I'm not holding on to promises that you can't keep."

"Have I broken any promises?"

"No, because you haven't made any. You buying me

this house means that you are committing to our relationship, and that's a big-ass promise."

"I don't think I'm the problem," Eric countered. "I think you're the problem." He stood up.

"What?" How had he just turned the entire conversation against her? He was the one who had screwed up.

"I know what my responsibilities are in this relationship and in my marriage. I know my limitations with you, and I try to make it up to you as much as I can. I'm not denying what type of relationship this is and my role in it, but I think you are very much in denial about why you are involved with me."

Breck shrugged. "I don't know what you mean."

"I think you do. Why are you involved with me, Breck?"

"Because I'm in love with you."

"I don't question that, but what is the underlying reason? You certainly don't need to put up with my shit."

"I don't know what the hell you're talking about."

"Breck, you're with me because I am not a threat to your independence."

"This is absurd," she said, and began pacing the floor.

"I don't think it is."

She looked at him and realized there was some truth to what he said. She didn't want him fully in her life. "I just don't want you to do this for me," she said.

"Why not?"

She stood up, but her leg began to shake and all she could do to keep from swaying was pace the floor.

But Eric wasn't backing down. He waited for her to answer, refusing to dismiss or continue the conversation until she did. Breck stopped and turned to face him again. "I have all night," he said.

"Because it makes me vulnerable, and I do not like how that feels." She exhaled. Tears had welled up in her eyes, but she refused to let them fall.

"Breck, I'm married. There isn't a more vulnerable relationship than that, and that is not why you don't want me to buy you the house."

"You're wrong."

"You've made two references to the nature of our relationship being like we have only a partial commitment to each other. I'm as committed to you as I can be. You know more about me than my wife does, and I'm very certain that I talk to you more. However, you've never pressured me about my marriage or questioned whether or not I'm getting a divorce. Why is that?"

"Because I don't want to pressure you."

"Why not?"

"This is a ridiculous conversation," Breck huffed, and started pacing the floor again. She stopped when she realized that it *was* true. She loved Eric—she was sure of that—but she enjoyed the freedom of being involved with him. She didn't have to answer to anyone or explain her actions or account for every moment she was not with him. She loved that and she didn't want it to change. At least not right now.

"What if I choose to end this relationship and date someone else?" she continued. "I can't do that while I'm living in a house that you bought for me." As wonderful a gesture as it was on Eric's part, she couldn't bring herself to appreciate it. "I would be totally dependent upon you and making sure I don't anger you in any way, otherwise you'd take the house back. What happens if the relationship goes sour, or worse, your wife finds out? Either way, I'm out in the cold."

Eric was quiet. She could tell by the stillness of his eyes that he had not considered the possibility that she would want to date someone else. The mere suggestion stunned him.

"I can't stop you from dating someone else, but arrangements have been made that the house is yours, no matter if you piss me off or if Gaby finds out about us. You can dump me tomorrow and the house would still be yours. So keep trying."

"This is not funny, Eric." Breck fell silent. This was an argument she didn't want to lose, but she was running out of reasons why it wasn't a good idea. It would be so much easier if she'd rushed in and thrown herself into his arms and kissed him and thanked him repeatedly for buying the house. But instead of feeling elated, she'd felt like he was putting a plastic bag over her head, the same as she had felt with Quentin. "How would it make you feel if I started dating someone else?" she asked. She just couldn't give in to him.

"I don't like it and I would be pretty mad if you did. If that makes me an awful person, then I'm sorry." He threw his hands up.

"No more awful than I would feel if I asked you to leave your wife and come live with me. We can do neither of those things and still feel good about ourselves. You buying me this house puts our relationship on a level that I'm not comfortable with."

"Why? Because you feel someone else may have a say in your life? I would feel less than a man if I were in the position to help you get something that you really wanted but stood back and did nothing. If I did that, you shouldn't want *me*." He returned to his desk and took his seat. "So to me, by not letting me do this, you're telling me that you're willing to accept *less* from me. Is that the way you want me to feel about you? Isn't that the very reason why you *wouldn't* go out with that man Chi tried to fix you up with? Why would you want to be with a man who wouldn't help you if he could?" He was drilling her, and suddenly Breck felt like she'd stepped onto the witness stand to be cross-examined.

"But I'm not yours to take care of."

"Then what the fuck are you doing here?" he said,

raising his arms above his head. Breck stepped back, stunned. He had never spoken to her like that before. "If all I am to you is a convenient screw so that you can keep doing what the hell you want to do without any interference from a man, then you should not be here, because that is not how I feel about you."

Breck was dumbfounded. This was not the type of conversation she expected to have with him. One of the best advantages of their relationship was its convenience, and now he was taking it to a level she'd never allowed herself to go to with any other man in her life. Should she take a chance on it, or walk away like she'd done in the past? Vulnerability was not a favorable trait to her. "So what are my options?" she asked. He looked up at her.

"Without some commitment we're fuck buddies, and I'm not risking my marriage for a fuck. Breck, I can find someone to fuck if that's all I want. You mean more to me than that." He paused and leaned back in his seat. "I'm not Quentin and I'm not going to play this game with you. You're going to have to make a commitment, otherwise we end this now." His face was stern and his voice clear.

So this is what it was like to be on the opposite end of the table staring down Eric Warren. He hadn't reached his level of success by sitting back and going soft. He didn't do it in his business, and he wasn't going to do it with her.

"You're asking me to do something you're not even capable of doing," she said, challenging him.

"It's not like you didn't know about my wife before we started this. I've committed myself to this as much as I can, but if you are going to use that to keep from committing to me, then I'm not the married man you should be with." He held her stare. No man had ever stood up to her the way Eric just did, and it shook her.

"Okay," she said, "but it goes both ways. I need to see

you more, I need to be involved more in your life, and I need more of your time. I can't give you more if you don't do the same." She was a businesswoman. She knew how to negotiate. Now was the time for her to show Eric exactly what she was made of too.

Eric paused while he considered this. Then he nodded. "Okay, and we can start now. How about spending the weekend with me on Cape Cod?"

A smile crept onto her face. She tried hard to keep her stern composure, but she couldn't. "I would like that a lot."

He motioned her to him, and she came, walking slowly into his embrace as he stood and kissed her hard on the lips.

"You've never given yourself completely to anyone before, have you?" he asked, planting small kisses on her lips.

"No, and if you hurt me, I'll kill you," she said jokingly, yet making it clear she wouldn't take it lightly.

"You'd probably hurt me before I'd ever hurt you." He buried his tongue deep inside her mouth before she had a chance to speak again and pressed his lips harder against hers. She backed up against a wall, the nerves in her stomach clenched in a ball, the tingling between her legs telling her she wanted to feel a powerful thrust inside her.

His strong hand caressed the inside of her thigh, then between her legs and inside her panties. She softened and moaned, practically sliding from the wall to the carpet. The only thing that held her up was his hand, and his tongue had its way with hers.

"Eric, can you take a look—"

They heard the soft tap at the door, but it was partially ajar and Stephen burst through without thinking to wait for an invitation. Eric stepped back quickly, but it was too late to hide their embrace.

"I'm sorry." Stephen had a manila folder opened in his hand. "I didn't realize you had company." He looked at Breck but didn't even give her the courtesy of speaking to her.

"That's okay." Eric licked his lips and wiped his face with an open palm, trying to diminish the wine-colored lipstick and the embarrassment smeared all over his face. "What's up?" He walked away from her and toward his desk. All Breck could do was hold her head down. She didn't know if she should gracefully exit or attempt to play it off and make Stephen second-guess what he had just walked in on.

"I'll wait in my office." Stephen turned and left, closing the door behind him.

Eric slumped down in his chair and covered his mouth. Breck's heart raced as she looked at him. He was visibly shaken. She didn't know what to say. They had taken a stupid risk and got caught. She couldn't apologize for it, nor could she try to dismiss it. Eric just sat there and stared, his hand still over his mouth. For five minutes he didn't move. She needed him to say something, to reassure her that everything would be okay, that he would talk to Stephen and everything would be just fine.

They'd made weekend plans. Was he going to keep them? They'd made a deal, and she'd gotten a house and a boyfriend out of it. Did she still have a house and a boyfriend?

She couldn't stick around and wait for him to pull himself together. She grabbed her purse and left without even saying good-bye.

SIXTEEN

STUPID, BRECK, just plain stupid, she screamed at herself as she drove home. You should never have gone there. What the hell were you thinking? He was going to end it now for sure. They had gotten caught. Damn. How could they have gotten caught?

He didn't call that night. The next day, Friday, Breck took her first day off. She didn't know if they were still on for the weekend, or if it was over, just like that, over without explanation or anything. Would he do that to her?

He's such a damn coward! she screamed in her head. She'd packed up everything and moved to Massachusetts, and now she was going to be stuck here without a boyfriend.

"That's what the hell you get for moving your life for a damn man," she said aloud. She went back and forth, blaming first Eric and then herself for the situation they were in. She hated not knowing what was going on. Would Stephen blackmail Eric? Would he tell Gaby?

Shit. Why the hell hadn't he called?

Breck lay in bed that night, staring at the wall, the ceiling, and occasionally the clock, expecting the phone to ring at any moment with Eric canceling their plans because Stephen had threatened to tell Gaby—or gone ahead and told Gaby. The phone never rang, but when the alarm sounded at five o'clock that morning she had never fallen asleep.

Eric showed up at the townhome around seven o'clock that evening. She waited for him to fill her in on what had happened, but he walked in and proceeded as if everything was normal. When she stood in front of him with her hands on her hips, he just waved her off. "Don't worry about it," he said, and he picked up her bag and took it to the truck. Just like that, he dismissed it.

That's it? She frowned. She lay awake all night for that?

"What the hell happened after I left?" She joined him outside by the truck. She was not going to let this lie without some explanation.

"Nothing. I went into his office and we talked about business."

"Business?"

He nodded, closed the trunk, and went back to lock the house door. He had moved on and obviously didn't want to talk about it. Breck decided the best thing to do was to let it alone. She jumped into the truck and didn't say another word about it.

The midspring weather was chilly but tolerable. The constant rain kept the air damp. At night it sometimes got pretty cold. Breck had packed accordingly, filling her bag with jeans, long sleeves, a jacket, a hat, hiking boots, and a bulky sweater.

Breck talked about the house as they started the two-hour drive toward Chatham. Eric had not seen the house yet, and she vividly described it for him. She made a mental note to call Martin when they returned on Sunday to see if he could visit the house and give her an estimate on the remodeling.

"Martin could live off of me alone as much as I've used him in the last few months," Breck joked. She took advantage of the fact that Warren & Peterson contracted Martin exclusively. Now that she was in the clique, Martin wasn't going to turn her down.

"I just think he has a crush on you," Eric joked.

"No, but I think he knows that *you* have a crush on me," she said.

"Speaking of crushes, Brian asked me about you the other day."

Breck turned to look at him. This was the first time Eric had mentioned Brian to her since she'd moved to Massachusetts.

"Don't be surprised if he stops by your office next week."

Breck drew back in surprise. "Why?"

"He asked me if I knew if you were dating anyone yet, and I told him that I didn't think you were. So he took that as encouragement to ask you out."

"Oh," she said, and looked straight ahead. "Why did you do that?"

"What could I do?" He turned briefly to look at her before returning his eyes to the road.

He did have a point, Breck admitted. Eric couldn't very well tell Brian she had a boyfriend when she never brought one around them. She hung out with them all the time. It was one thing to live a lie, but it was another thing to have to admit it to other people. Maybe that was why he didn't want to talk about what had happened with Stephen.

"So what am I supposed to do?" Breck asked.

"Tell him you have a boyfriend," Eric snorted.

"Thanks a lot. You could have done that for me." She slumped in her seat and rubbed her head, trying to think of a plausible excuse to let down Brian without alienating him. "Why do you guys baby him?" she asked. She assumed this had something to do with Eric's inability to tell Brian she had a boyfriend.

"We don't baby him, but we do look out for him. Just always been that way since his parents were killed in a car accident when we were kids."

Breck drew in her breath and turned toward him. "That's horrible. Who raised him?"

"His aunt moved into his parents' house and raised him and a younger brother. She had two boys too, so life got pretty bumpy for them. He was about twelve when it happened."

"Does he talk about it?"

"Not anymore," Eric said. They drove off the main road and traveled for another twenty minutes through less populated areas of Chatham. They pulled up to a small wooden one-story cottage less than a hundred yards from the beach. Breck looked around and saw another one like it about a quarter of a mile away. Someone had been there ahead of them. She saw shadows of a dim lamp through thin white curtains.

She waited while Eric took their bags out of the rear of the Range Rover. The air blowing in from the ocean was a cool relief from the sticky heat. Breck looked up and stared straight into the sun as they hurried to the cottage, where Eric dropped the bags and fumbled for the keys on his key ring. It took him a few seconds to find the right key, then he unlocked the door and stepped inside, holding the door for Breck with his foot.

As soon as the door opened, the blast from the air conditioner fanned her face and cooled the trickles of perspiration already developing below her hairline. While Eric put the bags away, she walked around, soaking in the place. The cottage was modestly decorated, with a sofa and an armchair and pine accent tables. A matching entertainment center stood against a wall and held a reasonably sized television and stereo. A few inexpensive paintings hung from the wall.

"What's this place?" she asked, walking toward the bedroom.

"It's a weekend house. We come here a few times a year to get away from the city and to impress our clients," Eric answered as he returned from the bedroom.

That explained the absence of family pictures, Breck thought.

When he returned to the living room, he wrestled her to the sofa. She laughed and kissed him.

"I'm very proud of you," Eric said, looking down at her.

Breck looked up into his brown eyes. "Why?"

"You've done a wonderful job with your business, your building, and the coffeehouse in your first six months here. That's impressive. And you've done it all yourself and I'm very proud of you." He kissed her.

"But you got the house," she made sure to point out.

"It's the least I could do, and, to be honest, I probably should do more." He kissed her softly on the lips.

Later that evening, they snuggled in front of the unlit fireplace, covered only in the sheepskin blanket Eric pulled down from the closet. Whenever they were together, they made up for the time apart. They slept locked in each other's arms.

Breck was the first to rise the next morning. Wrapping herself in a thick, white terry-cloth robe and slipping on a pair of her wool socks, she walked into the kitchen to start the morning brew. She opened the refrigerator to see if there was anything that could be used for breakfast and found it fully stocked with eggs, sausage, bread, milk, bottled water, orange juice, grapefruit juice, butter, jams, cheese, and wine. Breck smiled. How lucky can you be to find someone who truly thinks of everything? She made a mental note of what she would prepare later for breakfast. She dressed in a pair of gray shorts and a T-shirt, then slipped into her jogging shoes. She stepped out the door in time to see the spectacular sunrise. Her first instinct was to head back in and wake Eric so he could enjoy it with her, but one look at him changed her mind. He was sound asleep. She decided to tackle the sand instead. She breathed in the cool morning air and exhaled to create a wisp of vapor in front of her face. She bent down and touched her toes, then stretched full to each side before taking off in a comfortable jog down the beach. The cool, clean air chilled her lungs and her feet burrowed into the sand as she ran the beach, scaring off a few seagulls.

Several people greeted her as she ran her course, avoiding a few puddles. She was delighted to know that she was not the only one enjoying the sunrise. She passed only a few obscure cottages before turning around. Once she was back at Eric's cottage, she stood outside for a short while to catch her breath. The humidity had already started to rise and beads of sweat formed on her forehead.

She leaned against a wooden post and stared off into the distance. The run had warmed her up, and now a different warmth spread inside her, the comfort of knowing Eric was on the other side of the door and that when she walked in, he would smile at her and kiss her. Knowing Eric loved her gave her a peace that she had never felt with Quentin or any other man. She'd always had questions nagging her—whether the man loved her and she loved him, wholeheartedly and unconditionally. She'd never experienced unconditional, unselfish love, until now.

When she finally walked into the cottage, she heard the water running in the shower. She tapped on the bathroom door before she went in.

"Come on in," Eric said. He was scrubbing himself with a washcloth. "How was your run?"

"Great," Breck said, slipping out of her shorts. "You should join me one morning." She slid open the partition and stepped into the shower with him. He stood with his back to the water. Breck took the soap and lathered it between her hands, then smoothed her hands along the hair on his chest, down the muscular lines around his magnificent body.

When she raised her eyes to him, he lowered his face toward hers and kissed her. His tongue slid easily between her parted lips and touched hers. She felt a trickle of water on the side of her face and then a sudden rush of water hit her full-force.

She gasped and blew the water out of her mouth, and he laughed and then smacked her on the behind as he stepped from the shower. "I'll get breakfast started," he said, and walked out of the bathroom without waiting for her to respond.

Breck showered quickly and wrapped herself in her robe before joining him in the kitchen. Eric smiled at her as he whisked the eggs in a large mixing bowl.

"I was going to make breakfast this morning," she said, standing behind him.

"You can help. You can put the sausage on." He nodded toward the counter where he'd placed the rest of the food.

"You cook a lot at home?" she asked, tearing the plastic from the package of sausage links.

"No. Gaby insisted we have a cook and a part-time housekeeper. I don't lift a finger at my house."

"Oh." She placed the skillet on top of the stove. It took them twenty minutes to prepare a breakfast of sausage, cheese omelets, and toast. When everything was done, Breck set up the tiny table in the breakfast room. She would have loved to eat outside, but all the furniture was wet. She opened the back door and saw that the caretaker had forgotten to toss the stack of newspapers that had accumulated on the porch—*The Wall Street Journal* and *The Boston Globe*—and most were wet. She found the current and dry copy of the *Globe* and tossed the others in the recycling bin on the side of the house. She looked up at the sky as the sun disappeared briefly behind a cloud. She tightened the robe around her and joined Eric in the breakfast room. She placed the newspaper on the table in front of him.

"Why do you get the newspaper every day if no one is here to read it?" she asked, picking up her coffee mug and sipping from it quickly while it was still piping hot. She liked it that way.

"Because we never know when someone will be here," he said, taking a bite of his toast. "We have someone come once a week to dust, look after the place, and prepare it for guests."

"People around here are a lot friendlier than I expected," she said, sitting down opposite him. "Everyone smiled and waved." She noticed a half grin on Eric's face as he bit into his food. "What?" Breck asked. She felt like there was some inside joke she was missing out on.

"This cottage and all of the other cottages along this coastline cost over a half million dollars. They know Warren and Peterson owns this cottage. They also know whoever stays here has money. People with money have a tendency to treat other people with money a little different. It really doesn't matter what color they are. Money is still green."

"A half million dollars?" Breck almost gagged. She looked around the cottage but couldn't see what was so special about the place that made it worth a half million dollars. It certainly wasn't the décor. "A half million dollars for this?"

"Location, location, location," Eric said, and sipped from his glass of orange juice.

"Okay, I see your point, but that's a lot of money for a place that sits empty most of the time."

"Trust me, Breck, one client can stay here one weekend, and as a result, this cottage is paid for three times over." Breck nodded, fully understanding the concept. "A lot of major corporations have regional offices around the coun-

try," Eric continued. "Those regional offices are in one-
to three-story office buildings that are either leased or
bought—nothing extravagant, just office space. That's
where Warren and Peterson comes in with a little place
like this. We invite the regional manager and the wife up
for a paid vacation. We provide them with a personal tour
guide. They visit the lighthouses and enjoy an evening at
the marina in Hyannis. They go home and brag that they
visited the same town where the Kennedys live—you
know how people are about that. And just like that"—he
snapped his fingers—"we get the business and this place is
paid for."

Breck had never given much thought to how much
Eric was worth, but she was beginning to suspect it was
a lot more than she'd realized. There was a quiet arro-
gance about him that came naturally to anyone who had
achieved his level of success, but he was one who could
back up everything he said with actions. He wasn't
ashamed of his success. He'd told Breck many times that
people used to come up to him and ask him "who he
thought he was." After all, he'd never graduated from
high school. Those people were no longer involved in his
life. He surrounded himself with things that money
could buy and didn't apologize for it. If he didn't feel
like driving to a party, he hired a limousine. If he felt like
going on vacation, he did.

"So, are you on a business trip now?" she asked suddenly after a brief silence.

Eric stopped chewing, looked at her, and then began
chewing again. He swallowed his food before he answered
her. "Yes."

"What if she needs to get ahold of you?"

"Cell phone," he answered.

"How does that make you feel?" she asked finally.
The nerves in her stomach went awry, and she squirmed
in her seat.

"How should it make me feel?" Breck shrugged. "How does it make you feel?"

"I try not to feel," she said, then put a forkful of omelet in her mouth.

"Don't internalize this, Breck," he said. "My relationship with Gaby and whatever happens in my marriage has very little to do with you."

She swallowed. "How can you say that? I'm involved in an affair with you."

"But you have absolutely nothing to do with how I feel about Gaby or my marriage. If I decide to stay with Gaby, that is something I have to work through. If I decide to leave my marriage, that is also something I have to work through. Either decision doesn't influence how I feel about you. You can choose to go on this journey with me or not. If you don't, it doesn't mean you don't care about me. I would be disappointed, but I couldn't hold it against you."

Breck blinked, trying to digest Eric's words. It was the first time he'd ever hinted that he considered leaving Gaby, and Breck didn't know what that meant. Did it mean that he wasn't as happily married as he let on or did it mean that he was falling deeper in love with her?

"I didn't know you ever thought about leaving Gaby," she finally said.

"It has crossed my mind once or twice."

"Because of your feelings for me?"

"That has something to do with it. Also, I can't deny that I wish Gaby was more involved with the things that are important to me. But I can't say that I'm not in love with her."

"Which one of the two reasons would you leave for?"

"I don't know. Both are very important to me. My feelings for you are something I have to deal with," he continued. "It took me a long time to accept that those feelings were there and would remain whether I got involved with you romantically or not. I've accepted that I'm in love with you. I want to have a relationship with you, and I've made the decision to be here with you. Even if I choose not to explore this, it has absolutely nothing to do with you. You'll still be a wonderful, vibrant woman whether I'm in your life or not. But we're here, right now, so let's just live it."

Breck took a small sip of her coffee. She'd listened to him and she'd wondered if what he was saying was that even though he was in love with her, she would not be the reason he would leave his marriage. Was she okay with that? For the moment, Breck rationalized, she was. But she also wondered silently how long she would be okay with it. "I don't mind living these moments with you because there's an ache when I'm not with you, even though most people feel that what we're doing is wrong."

"Do you feel strongly that what we're doing is wrong?"

She paused for a moment before she answered him. "Based upon what I've been taught, yes, there is a wrongness in this." She paused again. "But nothing I've been taught would explain the ache I feel when you are not in my life. There is no rationale for that. Is it lust? Is it learning not to give in to my desires? How do you explain why I love you despite the wrongness of it? Surely you must feel the same way, and probably even more so."

"I do," he answered. "So, do we follow what we've been taught about right and wrong and give up these moments we share?"

"I don't know, but I do know that if I'd done everything in my life exactly as I'd been taught, there would've been so much I'd missed."

"So is this different?"

"Yes, it's very different, because my not following everyone else's rules and expectations never impacted anyone but me. So this is very different."

"If Gaby discovered our relationship, it would be a problem I would have to deal with."

Breck shook her head vigorously. "Not true, because I may suffer repercussions as well. So it is not just your problem."

"If we focus solely on the consequences and repercussions of our union, then why are we here?" Breck shrugged. "I mean, I've always thought that there was one woman for me and as soon as I found her we would live happily ever after and I would have no desire for another woman."

"Do you not think that's true?"

"I don't know. I thought Gaby was that woman, but here I am with you."

"Then maybe Gaby isn't that woman. Like you once told me, I needed to find someone who shared in my life in ways that were different from money or financial stability. Perhaps you're in need of something similar. I'm not saying that Gaby isn't the woman to give you that, but maybe that's why you're here with me, because something is obviously absent from your relationship with her."

He shrugged. "I don't know. It's all very confusing to me. Let's just accept this as a wonderful journey. I don't want to spend all of my energy rationalizing why I feel the way I do about you. I don't know what's going to happen next week, next month, or tomorrow for that matter. I just know that I love you and I'm here with you, right now, and I can't think of anyplace else I'd rather be."

Breck nodded, took a sip of her coffee, and finished eating the breakfast he had so carefully prepared for her.

"I almost forgot," Eric said, standing up and reaching into his duffel bag to extract a nicely wrapped present. He handed it to her.

"Thank you," she said.

He laughed softly. "You better open it before you thank me."

Breck frowned and unraveled the purple silk ribbon, then ripped the wrapping paper. She opened the square box and gasped when she saw the vibrator. Then she burst into laughter.

"I figured we could do some exploring together this weekend," he said.

SEVENTEEN

ON MOVING day, the weather couldn't have been any more perfect. The sun was bright, the temperature was comfortably in the seventies, and most importantly, there wasn't a cloud in the sky. The movers picked up the few boxes from the townhome, then drove to the storage facility and carefully removed more boxes and furniture to transport to Breck's new house. They came dressed in baggy orange overalls, work boots, and dark, heavy-duty gloves. Breck stood in the doorway of the Victorian house, and directed the movers to the appropriate rooms. Her leather furniture was directed to the sitting room. The formal living room would remain empty until she found the right furniture for it. The bedroom furniture was directed to the master bedroom on the third floor. The three bedrooms on the second level would remain empty until she decided what to do with them. The office furniture went to the sunny corner room on the first level, beside the formal dining room. That too would remain empty until she went shopping for a formal dinner table. The pine dinette table and six matching chairs went into the breakfast room just off the kitchen.

Anything that didn't have an immediate home stayed in the sitting room until Breck had a chance to sort it all out. After only two hours the movers left, but not before they assembled her bed. They plugged in the refrigerator and then went to the basement to do the same with the washer and dryer. She complimented them on a job well done and then walked around the large house alone.

"Home sweet home," she said to herself as she stood in the kitchen looking out over the backyard. Then she heard her cell phone ringing. She hurried over to the kitchen counter and looked at the caller ID. It was Eric.

"Hey," she said, pressing the talk button.

"How's it going there?" he asked softly. Breck figured he must be at home, with Gaby somewhere nearby. He only talked this formally with her when it was not an appropriate time to talk.

"Great. The movers just left."

"I won't be able to make it over tonight."

Her first night in her new home would have to be spent alone. She had bought a bottle of champagne specifically for this occasion. "That's okay, I understand."

There were several long seconds of silence before Eric whispered into the phone, "Next weekend is the sleepover at the Boys and Girls Club. You want to go?"

Breck didn't say anything at first. What would it be like spending the night with Eric with other people around? Would the affair be more obvious once people saw them together? "Are you sure about that?" she finally asked.

"Yeah, it'll be fun. I have to go. I'll talk with you more about it next week. Love you, bye." He quickly hung up.

Breck delayed before she closed the flip phone. In an odd way she couldn't explain, she felt lucky to be with him. Of course there were times when she wished things were different—like now—but she never allowed herself to dwell on those times because she would miss out on the good times they did share. Sure, she could argue with him about celebrating her first night alone in her new home, but that would overshadow the wonderful horseplay they'd had a few days ago when she showed him the house for the first time. When they returned to the apartment, they could barely wait until they were finally inside before they stripped and made love on the living room floor. Hardly a week went by when she did not see him. If she really needed to talk to him, he was usually a phone call away. There were many times when she was tempted to call him during the evening, but she never did. She didn't want to push her luck.

Breck smiled as she walked toward the sitting room. Now would be a good time to start sorting through the boxes. She heard the doorbell and stopped, peering around the corner to see who it was.

"Chi!" she squealed, and dashed for the door. She swung the door open and hugged Chi and Gena as hard as she could. The two were inseparable these days. "I'm so glad to see you guys," she said, closing the door behind them. Breck had shown Chi and Gena the house before she closed on it, and they loved it.

"You just saw me yesterday," Chi said as they stood in the foyer. "We brought dinner." Chi held up a plastic bag filled with Chinese carry-out.

"And dessert," Gena said, holding up a gourmet cheesecake.

"What would I do without you guys?" Breck hugged them again and led the way to the kitchen.

"Okay, Breck, why all the sentimentality?" Chi asked, walking to the breakfast room and setting the bags on the table. "Gosh, I love this room," she added, looking out the high windows into the backyard.

"It's my first night in my new house, and I didn't feel like being alone." Breck rummaged through two of the boxes to pull out three plates and forks.

"Eric can't make it?"

"Nope." Breck set the dishes on the table and found three champagne flutes.

"We didn't bring champagne," Chi said, looking at the glasses.

Breck opened the back door and retrieved the champagne from the cooler. They laughed.

After dinner, they sat on the floor in the sitting room and Breck started a fire in one of the house's two fireplaces. The other was in her bedroom. She fetched the other bottle of champagne from the cooler while they talked and laughed and ate cheesecake.

"Well, Gena and I have something to tell you," Chi said, looking at Gena, then at Breck.

"You're pregnant!" Breck exclaimed.

"Very funny," Chi sneered. "I'm not pregnant, but we've decided to live together. I'm moving in with Gena."

Breck's mouth dropped open. "Wow," she said. "That's a pretty big commitment."

"Yes, it is." Gena took Chi's hand and kissed it. "But I think we're ready. We love each other." Gena and Chi looked tenderly at each other and kissed.

Breck was quiet as she watched the loving exchange. In the years she had known Chi, she had never seen her this serious about anyone. There was a spark in Chi's life that had never been there before.

"I'm so happy for you two." Breck crawled over to each of them and hugged them. "This is my best friend. You have to treat her right or you'll have to answer to me." She pointed a finger at Gena and smiled broadly. The three embraced again.

Breck wasn't worried about Gena. She knew she had just inherited a new good friend.

AUTUMN IN New England was something Breck had always dreamed of. Several weekends, she and Eric had gone on splendid day trips to catch the foliage at its peak. They'd picked spots from New Haven, Connecticut, to

Portland, Maine, spending a day or a weekend in each spot. Breck knew the approaching winter would bring more of the same. Despite the promise of cold weather, Breck relished that she lived near some of the most picturesque parts of the country, and during the fall and winter was when the splendors of New England were at their best.

However, this would be only her second winter in New England. The winters in Massachusetts were something Breck still had yet to get accustomed to. Being from Indiana, she was used to snow and the weather blown south from Chicago and Lake Michigan, but the arctic blast directly from the Atlantic Ocean was a different story. The first thing she did after she moved from Indianapolis was go shopping for more sweaters, a heavier coat, and lots of firewood. Last winter had taught her she was ill prepared for Massachusetts winters.

Now that she was an official Mansfield resident, she joined the "gang" and volunteered her time at the Boys and Girls Club. One weekend a month she and Eric, Martin, Alyce, Brian, and a few other adults from the neighborhood participated in the sleepover. To Breck's surprise, Chi and Gena occasionally volunteered their time as well. The sleepovers, a community-mentoring effort, were supposed to benefit the kids, keeping them thinking positively, giving them a chance to associate with professional and successful adults and, of course, to have fun. The more Breck volunteered, the more she thought the adults had more fun than the kids.

The young people usually arrived around seven o'clock Saturday morning. After everyone was checked in and sleeping arrangements were made, it was nine o'clock and breakfast time. After breakfast they broke into several groups. In each group, one or two adults who specialized in a given area would conduct classes. They offered karate, photography, cooking, crafts, art, painting, basketball, weight lifting, and many other choices. It depended on who was volunteering that weekend. One volunteer was a licensed psychologist and provided counseling for anyone who wanted it. Breck taught drafting. Eric and Martin coached basketball, and when Chi visited, she and Gena led a class on how to apply makeup and gave beauty tips to the girls.

Lunch followed morning classes, and the afternoons were set aside for a group activity, usually a team sport, such as kickball, soccer, basketball, or some type of obstacle course. Dinner was usually a grand pizza party, sponsored by the local pizza parlor, and then the kids were on their own to do their thing until later that night, when a G or PG movie was shown while the kids snuggled in sleeping bags on the gym floor. Eric and others donated sleeping bags to the kids who couldn't afford them.

The volunteers took turns supplying drinks and dessert. Making ice cream sundaes was the favorite. Lights-out was at nine o'clock, but by that time everyone was so worn out that only the older kids and the adults were still awake.

After making sure everyone was settled in, most of the volunteers usually escaped into the recreation room for a game of cards, Ping-Pong, or pool. Afterward everyone usually retreated to the gym and fell fast asleep beside their kids. Breck would sleep near Eric, but they tried to keep a comfortable distance.

Tonight Breck and Eric teamed up at the Ping-Pong table to challenge anyone who dared. It came down to Martin and Alyce attempting to dethrone them, but it just couldn't be done: Breck and Eric were unbeatable. The game was over after Martin dove and missed a killer spike that slammed off Eric's paddle.

After Ping-Pong, with the kids asleep, Breck, Eric, and Martin sat at the table drinking what remained of the soda. Martin stopped laughing and pointed at both of them. "I hope you two know what you're doing," he said. He didn't take his eyes off Eric.

Their laughter tapered off as Breck stared down into her cup.

"What are you talking about?" Eric said, trying to be playful—but he knew full well what Martin was referring to.

"Come on, man, I've known you a long time. Don't play me like that." Martin placed his drink on the table and leaned back in his chair. Eric twirled the soda can on the table. "It's not like you two are doing a very good job of hiding it when you're here," Martin continued. "Let me tell you, if Gaby ever sees you together, it's going to be hell." He waved a pointed finger at Eric that reminded Breck of the many lectures her father had given her as a child.

Breck sat quietly, glued to her chair, and Eric wasn't speaking either. She was sure he was just as shocked as she was. They had thought they were coming across as just good friends.

Eric cleared his throat. "Anyone talking?" he finally asked.

"Everyone's talking, but nothing that would get back home, if you know what I mean." Eric nodded. "Just be careful, that's all I have to say. The rest is none of my business," Martin said just as Alyce and Valerie, another one of the wives and a volunteer, joined them. Alyce took a comfortable seat on Martin's lap while Valerie sat beside Eric.

"Thanks for the invitation, Eric. Mark and I will definitely be there. We had so much fun last year. Are you going, Breck?"

Breck looked directly at Eric, waiting for him to explain what invitation Valerie was referring to. Eric had a blank look on his face, not his usual cheerful expression.

She then looked at Martin and Alyce as they stared coldly at Valerie. Breck was suddenly aware that either she was not supposed to know about this or, at the very least, it wasn't supposed to be mentioned.

"What invitation?" Breck asked.

"To Eric and his wife's annual Christmas Eve party. Eric, didn't you give Breck her invitation?"

Breck watched Martin slump in his chair and Alyce briefly close her eyes. "I have plans for Christmas," she said quickly. She wasn't sure if Valerie was trying to patronize her or if she really was unaware that she and Eric were involved and that she was more than likely not going to his house. But even still, Eric hadn't told her anything about the party, and she had forgotten about the annual event Alyce mentioned to her when she first saw the house in Mansfield.

"Well, if you can make it, you should. They have such a beautiful home and they really go out of their way for the Christmas Eve party. Gaby is an absolutely wonderful hostess, and they really do it up with servers and everything. I've never seen anything like it," Valerie boasted. "I don't know why she never comes to the sleepovers. If I was her, I would."

At that moment Breck knew that Valerie didn't like her and didn't trust her and that she could never consider Valerie a friend. "I'll keep that in mind," Breck said, and rose from her chair. "I'm going to sleep now," she announced, and quickly left the room. How could she stay in there and continue to talk with them and hide the hurt she was feeling? Of course she knew that she shouldn't go to Eric's house, but the fact that he hadn't even bothered to tell her about it hurt her more. She was sliding into her sleeping bag when Eric joined her.

"I guess you're mad."

"You should have told me so that I would have been

prepared for that," she said, and pulled the bag up so far it almost covered her head.

"I was going to. Gaby just mailed the invitations this week and I just hadn't had time to tell you about it yet."

"Does Gaby know I moved here?"

"No."

"You'd better tell her before someone else does. Everyone realizes that you and I are having an affair. How do you think they feel about me?"

"Everyone likes you, Breck."

"Everyone? Why do you think Valerie just told me about the party?"

"I don't know."

"She knows we're seeing each other. She knows I'm not going to your house. I never had any intentions of going to your house, even if you would have given me an invitation. Valerie was simply reminding me that there's a place I belong and there's a place I will never belong."

"I doubt that."

"Think about it. Maybe they think I'm going to sleep with their husbands too."

"That's ridiculous."

"Is it?" she asked. "Am I not the threat of most wives? The single woman who willingly has an affair with a married man. Have you ever stopped to think that maybe out of allegiance one of them would tell Gaby about us simply because she feels someone ought to?" Eric said nothing as he slid into his sleeping bag close to her.

Breck couldn't sleep that night. For the first time since becoming involved with Eric, she wondered what people thought of her. Did they think she was a vixen or, worse yet, a whore? She wanted to wake them all up and tell them personally that it wasn't like that. Her relationship with Eric was different. They loved each other. She was not a home wrecker, or a whore, or a bitch, or any of those things. She was just a woman who had fallen in love with a married man.

She rolled over on her back and stared at the ceiling. Why suddenly did she feel cheap?

The next morning she and Eric said good-bye, and for the first time they were totally conscious of their interaction. Eric didn't whisper in her ear that he would follow her home. She was sure this was going to change their relationship. They had to be careful. They had relaxed too much and started taking too many risks.

How much risk was Eric willing take? Now that all of his friends, including Brian, were mindful of their affair, would he ease back into his previous image? After all, he was Eric Warren, and Eric Warren made no mistakes.

Breck sat in her car outside her house, unable to gather the strength to get out. When she finally pulled it together, she stared at her house and her street and wondered how she had gotten home and what route she had taken. She got out of her car, walked into the house, and changed into her jogging apparel. No snow had fallen yet this season but the air was cold. She had hired a painter to repaint the outside of the house, but she wasn't changing the color from its deep gray with white trim. All the interior improvements had been made, and the house was slowly becoming home.

After she tied her running shoes tightly, she took off like she was sprinting from demons. Her arms pumped, her breath was short, and her legs carried her farther and farther. She was running and running, but she just couldn't reach whatever it was she was trying to catch.

What would she do if Eric told her it was over? He had become an integral part of her life. It would take her months, if not years, to fall into a lifestyle that didn't include him. And what about the Boys and Girls Club? She would most definitely have to stop volunteering there, even though she loved it. It wasn't fair, but it was a part of the consequences her mother had warned her about.

I don't want to lose him, she heard a soft voice say in the mush that was once her brain. She couldn't completely ignore the ethical dilemma of loving Eric. She was reminded of it every time she looked at his hand and saw his wedding band. Every time she sat in his car, she saw Darius's car seat. Every time Eric mentioned Gaby's name, it struck her like a blazing iron poker. It was a psychological hell to live with the constant reminders tossed at her like water balloons—each time she was expected to catch it without getting wet.

Breck had learned to let those emotions go through her. She didn't want to be trapped by the notion that she would be better for Eric than Gaby was. If that were the case, she would be his wife—she was certain of it. There was a reason Eric was married to Gaby, and it wasn't her place to judge it. So she avoided places where Eric and Gaby might be. She even fought through the urge to drive down his street to peek at his house. How would she explain her actions if he happened to be outdoors washing his car or playing with Darius?

There were many times when she wondered how he lived and what his house might look like. But it would be worse to see his house and his bed and then wish that it was she who was on the inside and not just the one passing by looking through the window. There were nights when she lay in bed and wondered if he was making love to Gaby at that moment. But she quickly banished those thoughts and held on to the trust that in his way he loved her. The way Eric felt about her went deeper than words. Anyone could say "I love you," but not everyone could make you feel it. No words could describe how she felt when she was with Eric. The best she could do was to say it felt like being thrown from a boat into the ocean: you're kicking and swimming, struggling to get to the surface, and once you do, you take that first breath and hang on to it as long as you can, because you know it means you are alive. Yes, he's married, she'd say in her mind whenever she was chased by those little demons. Yes, I'm in love with a married man. No excuses.

Her cushioned insoles did little to absorb the shock that shot up her calves as she hit the concrete pavement, but she kept running. Her heart pumped harder, and she took short, quick breaths through her parched lips. She could hear the words of her old track coach echoing somewhere in her mind: "Pump those arms, pull them knees up." She reached the end of the road and stood on the sidewalk, her hands clasped to her side as she struggled to catch her breath. She'd never run so far so fast before in her life. Her heart pounded so rapidly in her chest that she wondered if it would explode. She must have done a five-minute mile—a miraculous feat for her—but it had damn near killed her. She looked at the landmarks and noticed that she had run a mile and a half. Her usual run was five miles, but she had never run so fast before. Fighting to keep from keeling over, she bent forward, resting her hands on her knees, and held her head down, gasping for air.

"Don't sit down, don't sit down," she said to herself, trying to control her breathing. She knew that if she hit the pavement, she wouldn't get back up. "Keep walking, keep walking," she repeated, remembering the words of her coach. She shook her hands while she paced back and forth on the sidewalk. "Okay," she said between pants. "Okay. It's time to go back." She turned and walked toward her house, but her hamstrings tightened and her legs were barely able to carry her. Her calves and heels stung each time she placed her feet down.

She saw Eric's truck pull up as soon as she rounded Arbor Drive. She waved him down, and he pulled the truck toward her, reached and opened the door. "Want to go for a ride?"

Breck's legs hurt so badly she didn't question the offer. She put her hand on the edge of the door frame and lifted herself into the truck. As soon as she closed the door, he pulled off.

"How was your run?" he asked, rounding the corner and heading toward the highway.

"Sore." She flinched as she pulled her knee up to her chest, trying to relieve the pulling in her quadriceps. Sitting down left her powerless to do anything for her hamstrings, which grew tighter by the second. "Where are we going?" she asked.

"I just needed to get away," he said.

Breck looked at him and noticed something strange. His face was tight, almost as if he had clammed up. Her first thought was that something had happened either at home or at the club. She turned and looked out the window, trying to find some way to brace herself for whatever he had to say. First Stephen had walked in on them, and now the mumblings around the club. It had to be too much for him. His image was being destroyed, and he simply couldn't do it anymore. "What's up?" she asked, her voice cracking.

"I'm just so tired of going through crap every time I return home. I can spend a week in California and she says nothing, but if I spend one night at the club, I get hell as soon as I step in the door." He turned onto Interstate 95 and headed toward Boston.

Breck frowned. Was Gaby giving him hell because she suspected he was seeing another woman? "Does this have anything at all to do with me?" she asked.

"No," he said, looking in the rearview mirror and switching lanes. "I'm talking about the bullshit I go through every time I go to Mansfield. This was going on long before you came into the picture."

Breck scratched her head. Eric didn't come over to break up with her—and for that she should be glad—

but he had come over to vent about his wife, and that pissed her off. She didn't want to hear it. If he wasn't going to leave Gaby, then why was he using her as his therapist?

"Are you trying to tell me that you and Gaby had a fight?"

"Yes, another one."

Breck shook her head and leaned forward in her seat. "Eric, what the hell am I supposed to do about that?"

He threw a quick at her look and then returned his eyes to the road.

"You're gone all the damn time," Breck said. "If you're not at work, then you're with me. Of course she's going to bitch. But I don't want to hear about it."

He looked at her again. She turned and looked at the busy highway. "Excuse me?" he asked.

"After the conversation with Martin and Valerie, I was so worried you would come over and end our relationship," she said, now staring directly at him. "I freaked out. But seeing that you didn't come over to end things with us, I don't want to be put in the position where I even begin to think that I'd be a better wife for you than Gaby and you should leave her because she's no good for you. No. I'm not going to do it. You're married and I've accepted that, but I'll be damned if I'm going to be the one you run to when the two of you have a fight. You don't come and tell me when you've made love, and trust me, I don't want to know that either." She threw herself back against the seat and stared out the window.

"Shit!" Eric exclaimed. Then he slammed on the brakes, almost bringing them to a stop in the middle of the highway. He drove slowly and let several cars pass him, then switched lanes, but now the other cars slowed down as well. He swore again, then switched lanes. This time a few cars passed them.

"What are you doing?" she asked, watching car after

car pass them. She looked over at his speedometer; he had reduced his speed from sixty-five miles per hour to almost forty-five.

He hesitated, then said beneath his breath, "That's Kofi. Gaby's brother."

Breck felt a strong bolt go through her, and her heart dropped into her bowel. Suddenly she didn't feel so brave anymore. She wasn't sure if she should duck or act dignified and businesslike. "Did he see us?"

"I don't know." Eric looked in his rearview mirror and switched lanes again. The best he could do was try to avoid Kofi's car because the next exit was at least a mile up the road.

"Which car?"

"Black Mercedes." He kept his eyes glued to the road while she looked in front of them and immediately spotted the immaculate car only four cars ahead in the left lane. "He was directly beside us when I saw him."

"On my side?" Eric nodded. "Why is he in Boston?" Breck yelled, frustrated by everything that had happened that day.

"Well, he does have a sister and a nephew who live here. But since that involves my family, you probably don't want to hear about it," Eric snapped.

Breck looked sharply at him and for the first time had to bite back words to keep from really going off on him. He continued his highway maneuvering, letting several cars pass them while he got as far to the right as he could in order to take the next exit off the highway. Her heart had slowed, but she felt uneasy and dirty. She hated this, the secrecy, the dodging, and the pretending. Sometimes it just welled up in her and she wanted to scream and let it all be over. She understood why he had to keep her out of view of Gaby's brother, but it still hurt her that she had to be a secret at all. There was still a part of her that wished she could share every aspect of his life. The best she could do was share him in Mansfield, in his "second life," separate and definitely not equal to his life with Gaby.

"Could you take me home, please?" she asked, leaning her head against the leather seat and rubbing her temples. She couldn't believe what had just happened. Should she be satisfied with being an embarrassment, or should she be a prize? Her nostrils flared and the muscles in her temples tensed. I'm a prize, goddamn it! I shouldn't have to be hidden! She landed a hard fist against the side of the passenger door, getting Eric's immediate attention.

He didn't speak until after he had turned the corner and headed back onto the highway toward her house. "I'm—"

She quickly put her hand up to stop him from speaking. "Don't apologize to me. Just get me the hell out of this car." She closed her eyes and kept them closed until he came to a stop outside her house.

EIGHTEEN

BRECK WANTED to scream, but the sound was stuck in her throat. All she could do was slump over on the bathroom sink and douse her face with cold water to keep from throwing up. She looked at the long white tube again. Ninety-eight percent accuracy, the words on the test kit had read. That was the reason she had purchased the most expensive kit in the store: she needed to know that she was getting the most accurate product.

Positive. The test result came back with a big red plus, which meant she was pregnant.

She felt like she was going to vomit again. She rushed to the toilet, lifted the lid, and stuck her head almost into the water as she retched the yellow bile. She had been stuck in the bathroom all morning. She didn't know if she was sick from the realization that she was pregnant or from morning sickness.

Morning sickness. Pregnant. She retched again until her stomach hurt so much that all she could do was lie down on the bathroom floor. She pulled her legs to her chest and cried.

She heard the phone ringing, and she crawled from the bathroom to her nightstand.

"Hello," she said, pushing her hair from her face.

"Breck, are you coming into the office today?" It was Chi, and as soon as Breck heard her voice she started crying harder. "Breck, what's wrong?"

Breck couldn't speak. All she could do was cry. She

held the phone in her hand and dropped her head onto the bed. She didn't even bother trying to hang up.

It wasn't ten minutes later when she heard banging on the front door. She knew it was Chi. It couldn't have been anyone else. She dropped the phone on the cradle and stood up. Her legs were numb. She couldn't even feel her feet touch the floor, let alone hold her weight. She grabbed hold of the wall and felt her way to the top of the stairway.

What would happen if I fell down the stairs? The thought entered her mind and stuck as she held on to the banister tightly, struggling with an internal fiend who wanted her to throw herself down the wooden stairs. She'd never had to fight herself before, and it made for a hard battle.

Chi didn't wait for her to reach the door but used her extra key to let herself in. "Breck, where are you?" she yelled out.

Her voice stuck, Breck cleared her throat and swallowed. "I'm here," she croaked feebly. She sat down on the stairs and dropped her head between her legs. Chi ran to her and touched her shoulders.

"My God, girl. What's wrong with you?" Chi knelt down and lifted Breck's head to see her eyes, puffy and swollen.

Breck shook her head. She lifted herself from the stairs and returned to the bathroom with Chi following closely behind. She picked up the white indicator and gave it to Chi. Chi had no doubt seen enough television commercials to know what it was without even having to ask.

"Oh, my God" was all she could say before she slapped her hand to her mouth. "I thought you were on the pill!"

"I am."

"And you take them every day?"

"Mostly."

"Breck!" Chi screamed. "They don't work if you don't take them every day!"

"Don't lecture me about this right now." Breck walked out of the bathroom, flopped down on her bed, and buried her head in the pillow.

"Does Eric know?"

"No," she said, and that started a fresh round of tears. "What am I going to tell him? Things have been so strained between us lately that now is not the best time to be pregnant."

"What do you mean?"

"I don't even know if we're going to be together in nine months," Breck shouted, realizing that it would be less than nine months before the baby was born.

"I didn't realize you guys were having problems."

Breck shook her head. "Things have been a little weird the past month. I went home for Thanksgiving, and I talked to him while I was there, but I could tell things still were not right."

"Have you talked with him about what's been going on?"

Breck shook her head. "No, because I know what's going on. All of his friends know about us, and he's scared to death his wife is going to find out. I think he wants out." Breck sat down and hid her head in her hands. Chi sat down with her and put her arms around her.

"I'm so sorry," Chi said, and pulled Breck closer to her.

Breck wiped the tears from her eyes and lifted her head. "What am I going to do?" She dropped her head into her palms and covered her face.

"You have to tell Eric."

"I can't," she shot back. "What if he thinks I'm trying to trap him?" She couldn't stop the tears from falling harder and harder until she could no longer breathe through her nose. She sniffed but couldn't stop the mucus from running to the top of her lip.

Chi stepped into the bathroom and came out with a wad of tissue. "Well, are you?"

"What?!"

"You've just said things between you and Eric have been strained, and having his child would definitely put him permanently in your life."

Breck stood, mouth agape. "I can't believe you would think that of me."

"I don't, and Eric wouldn't either. I just needed you to hear how ludicrous it sounds and how selfish and ridiculous you sound to want to withhold this from him. Eric loves you and this is his baby and he has the right to know and I think he would want to know."

"What if we're wrong? What if he's been playing all of us and he doesn't want this baby or me? How the hell do you think I'm going to feel if, after I tell him I'm pregnant"—she stopped, and the sobs came even harder—"the first thing he says is 'You have to have an abortion'?" Chi took her into her arms and rocked with her. "I know I can't have this child. I just don't want to hear him say it."

Chi quietly kept rocking her, and after several minutes Breck seemed calm enough to wipe her face. "How far along do you think you are?" Chi asked.

"About a month, maybe." Breck shrugged. "I don't know."

"What are you going to do?"

"I'm going to have an abortion, and I'm not going to tell him." She felt a stab in her heart as she said that most dreaded word. Breck had never thought about being pregnant, and she most certainly never thought she would abort her first child. Tears began to burn her eyes again.

Chi shot up from the bed. "You've got to talk to Eric first."

IN SPITE of Chi's urging, Breck couldn't bring herself to tell Eric. When he called her later that day, she made up an awful lie that she was sick and couldn't see him. The next day the tears had stopped, but she still couldn't eat much. She managed to munch on some crackers without vomiting.

Pregnancy didn't agree with her. Chi came over again and sat with her most of the day. Marla and David kept things going at the office until Chi could make it back. Again Chi pressed her to tell Eric about the pregnancy before she made any decision, but again Breck refused. Too many things had happened already and she didn't want to add another problem. It seemed lately they were always dodging someone, putting a wedge in their perfect relationship. Even at their favorite bed and breakfast in Connecticut they'd had to make a quick exit one afternoon when Eric spotted one of Gaby's close friends.

Without Eric or Chi, she made an appointment at the Planned Parenthood clinic and had another pregnancy test and a pelvic sizing. She didn't want her regular doctor to know because he would ask questions she didn't want to answer. She learned she was at six weeks' gestation. The confirmation made her cry on the nurse's shoulders. She was pregnant with her first child, and instead of being joyous with her husband by her side, she was sitting at Planned Parenthood alone, scared, and in tears. The nurse let her cry and handed her a tissue to dry her eyes and clear her nose, then escorted her to talk with one of their counselors about options.

She cried in the counselor's office and told the woman that there wasn't any alternative but to have an abortion. She didn't go into details. How could she tell the woman that she was pregnant by a married man?

Before she left the clinic she made an appointment for the two-day procedure the following week. On the first day she would get more counseling and take a pill to start the dilation of the cervix. Once she took the pill, there would be no turning back. She would have to bring someone with her on the second day because she would not be able to drive herself home. The only person Breck could think of was Chi, even though she was adamantly against the idea of not telling Eric.

The vomiting continued and Breck knew the baby was purposely torturing her; it knew what she was going to do, so it was making her suffer. She tried not to talk to it. If she talked to it, it would be real, and she couldn't let it become real. It's not a baby yet, it's a fetus, she kept telling herself, but she knew that if things were different, she would have been thrilled.

She made every excuse she could think of to keep Eric away from her for a week. Regardless of her protest, he came over one night, and Breck went out of her way to annoy him until he finally left. She stayed away from the office too, leaving Chi to keep things together there while she worked from home. She was not in any mental state to deal with people, not even Alyce, but Alyce had talked her into coming over for dinner. Breck wasn't sure if she was going to be able to keep the food down, but what bothered her more was how she would feel being around Londrick and Madison.

"Are you feeling well?" Alyce asked the moment Breck stepped in the door.

Breck's heart jolted. How did she know? "Yes, I'm fine. Why?"

"Your skin looks a little flushed. You might be coming down with a cold." Alyce rushed to the bathroom while Breck settled in the family room with Londrick and Madison. "Here, take a couple of these." Alyce handed her two gel capsules, and Breck stared at them. She immediately wondered if taking them would harm the baby. She knew pregnant women should not take some medications, and for the first time in her life, she had someone else's health to think about other than her own. Then she remembered it didn't matter. She wasn't keeping the baby anyway. Tears began to burn her eyes, but she couldn't break down and cry right now.

"I'm fine, really," she said, pushing the capsules back to Alyce.

"Well, hang on to them just in case you need them tonight."

"Will Martin be joining us?"

"Yes. He's on his way."

Breck watched the children as they played. Already they had developed into their own personalities. Madison, exhibiting characteristics similar to her father's, played with the toy logs and was in the process of building a very nice miniature log house. Londrick chose to work on his 350-piece *Star Wars* puzzle.

"Do you regret quitting your job?" Breck asked Alyce suddenly.

"What do you mean?"

"You've chosen family over career. Do you regret that?"

"Oh, no," Alyce said, picking up Madison and giving her a big hug and kiss on the cheek. Madison beamed and it made Breck smile as well. "My children are very precious to me. Every little creation they make is just a wonder. Even though they are still so young, I marvel at how they have grown up already." She kissed Madison again and then put her back on the floor. "Why do you ask?"

"I was just curious. My mother didn't work until I was old enough to attend middle school, and then she went to work at the school so that we could attend for free."

"Was she a teacher?"

"No, she worked in the cafeteria. My mother always loved to cook."

"Her strategy paid off. I'm sure that's where you get your business savvy from."

"What does that have to do with business-savvy?"

"Breck, what your mother did was make a business

arrangement so that her children could get a great education."

"I've never looked at it that way," Breck admitted.

"Perhaps you should," Alyce said. "You may be more like your mother than you think." She headed into the kitchen, leaving Breck flinching at the thought. Breck had always thought of her mother as having a simple life. She'd never seen her as savvy in anything that didn't involve cooking. "She must be very proud of you," Alyce continued.

Breck shrugged. "I don't know. She's never said."

"Whether she's said it or not, I'm sure she is," Alyce said, returning to the family room with two glasses of water. "Do you want to have children one day?"

The question caught Breck off guard, but she tried not to reveal too much with her eyes. "Yes, I would, but not soon," she said, and quickly sipped from the glass.

"I think you would make a great mother."

"Oh, I don't know about that," Breck said. She certainly wasn't feeling like a great mother now. "I'm the typical hard-ass career woman who will always put the biological clock on snooze." She said it, but even she didn't believe it. She was career-minded, but under the right circumstances Breck was sure she'd make a great mother.

"I think there's a fallacy about having children. Your life doesn't stop. Granted, it does change, but you don't roll over and stop being an individual just because you have children."

"But you stopped teaching," Breck quickly reminded her.

"I'm not standing in front of a classroom anymore, but I'm teaching every day. I teach my children. I'm still teaching, whether it's to one hundred kids or two. My job didn't make me a teacher, and a teacher isn't the only thing I am. I also write, which I still do. I enjoy mentoring and I love pottery. I've created all of the vases you see in this room." She pointed to several. "There is so much more to me than just being a teacher. You're an architect, but is that all that you are?"

Breck thought. No one had ever put it so eloquently before. "Being an architect is very much a part of who I am."

"You're also a wonderful artist and businesswoman. If you weren't designing buildings, you'd be designing something else. You would be successful no matter what business you were in because that is what you are. Having a child isn't going to change that. Architecture is what you do for a living, but it's not what you live for."

Breck thought a lot about what Alyce said, but it didn't help her out of the dilemma she was in. She was in a relationship that had limits. Would it be fair to bring a child into that? As it stood, if Eric decided to end their relationship, she would be the only one hurt, and she could live with that because being with Eric was a choice she'd made a long time ago. However, the child could not choose its parents. If she had the baby, then he could leave them both, and she would have to explain that to her child.

The week crawled by while she holed herself up in the house. Chi volunteered to go with her both days. She slept over the night before the procedure, and they stayed up talking about everything except what was to happen the next day. Breck didn't ask her to stay, but she knew Chi was worried about her and didn't want to leave her alone. She had also thought Chi would make one last pitch to get her to tell Eric, but Chi didn't even mention Eric's name. Perhaps she'd finally realized this was for the best. Having a baby by a married man was not a good idea.

The information packet had told her not to eat or drink after midnight. It also said she could resume her normal activities within twenty-four hours, but she doubted she would have the stamina to do that. She'd planned to take another day or two off work.

They arrived at the clinic on schedule, at eight o'clock the next morning. She checked in and took a seat in the waiting area. Breck tried not to look around at the other women, but she couldn't help it. There wasn't a particular type of woman there. There were black and white women. Some were young girls sitting with older women. Others looked like professionals sitting with either a boyfriend or a husband. After a half hour they sat with a counselor who asked her again if she was comfortable with her decision and verified that she had brought someone with her. Shedding yet more tears while Chi held her hand, Breck confirmed her decision. They returned to the waiting area, where they took their seats again.

Her heart made one hard thump against her chest when the nurse called her name. She took a deep breath before she dropped the magazine she was holding onto the table. She and Chi stood up together.

"I love you," Chi said, hugging her tight. "I'll be here for you." Chi let her go, and Breck saw a tear in the corner of her eye.

Oh, please don't do this me. Don't cry, she thought. As she followed the nurse, she eyed Chi turning her back and wiping the tear.

They entered an empty exam room, where the nurse handed her a standard hospital gown and instructed her to remove everything and place it in a locker. Breck looked around the room. There was still time for her to change her mind, but she didn't see how she could. She slipped out of her jeans, sweater, bra, and panties and stood naked in the room before she slid into the gown. She touched her belly. It hadn't started to poke out yet. The only evidence that she was pregnant at all was the morning sickness. She took a deep breath and fought the tears that burned her eyes. She didn't want to start crying again.

It has to be this way, she reasoned as she sat on the inclined exam table and kicked her feet. Her hands clutched the edge of the table, and she held her head down, thankful there were no mirrors in the room. Time inched along slowly as she waited for her turn. A half hour later she was still waiting.

Her heart fluttered when she finally heard the door open. It was time, she thought. She looked up, expecting to see a white-coated doctor come into the room. Instead it was one of the nurses and Chi. Breck looked at them, puzzled.

"Eric is here," Chi said.

Breck slumped. "What?"

"I called him," Chi quickly added. "He wants to see you." Breck sat, shaking her head in disbelief.

"Is it okay for him to come back?" the nursed asked. Breck nodded, and the nurse disappeared back into the corridor, with Chi following close behind. The next time the door opened, it was Eric.

He rushed into the room, the door handle hitting the gray rubber protector attached to the wall. The loud thump sent two nurses scurrying toward her room.

"Why didn't you tell me?" he yelled.

Breck was numb. Her mouth remained opened while he grabbed her off the table and pulled her toward him.

"Damn it, Breck," he yelled again. She stood stiff, nervous about what else he might do. He held her so hard his nails were buried in her skin. "Chi called me and told me you were here. Why the hell didn't you tell me?" he asked again. Breck was voiceless. "Damn it, don't you know I love you? I would never desert you." His voice shook as his grip loosened. He slid down and his knees hit the floor.

He was crying, bellowing louder than she had ever heard a man cry. He wrapped his arms around her, resting his head on her stomach. Tears welled up in her eyes, becoming so heavy that she couldn't keep them in any longer. They rolled down her cheek and fell into his hair. She looked at the nurses as they stood in the hall. One had covered her mouth, and tears rolled down her face as well. The other reached for the door and closed it.

"I didn't think you would want this," Breck said between sobs. "I didn't do it on purpose. I promise." Eric didn't speak as he buried his face in her hospital gown. Breck wiped the rush of tears from her eyes.

"All I thought about the whole way here was being too late," he said, wiping his face on her gown. "I've never been so scared before in my life. I was so scared." He pulled her to the floor with him. She sat on her knees, unable to look up at him. When he lifted her face to him she cried harder.

"I love you," he said, wiping her tears. "I would never have wanted an abortion." He pulled her to his chest and held her so tightly her head tilted back. "I want you to have this baby. We'll raise it together. I won't desert you. I promise." He fought to talk between sobs that cracked his voice. "Please say you'll have the baby," he said, stroking her face.

Breck nodded. He sat on the cold, hard linoleum floor and cried until he lost his breath. He pulled Breck with him and they leaned against the exam table. They sat there while he gathered his energy.

Breck heard a tap on the door and cleared her throat to speak. "Come in," she said, trying to neaten her gown.

This time it was the white coats, two of them. A male and a female doctor and one of the nurses from the hall had walked in and closed the door behind them. The woman doctor took a seat on the exam stool and twirled it around to face them, while the male doctor leaned against the sink counter. The nurse stayed out of the way and rested against a far wall.

"Is everything okay in here?" the woman doctor asked, holding Breck's chart in her hand. Both she and Eric nodded. "I'm Dr. Levin, and this is the anesthesiologist, Dr. Bradford." Dr. Bradford nodded at them but didn't speak. "Your friend asked us to wait because she thought things might change. Did things change?" she asked, looking at Breck.

Breck nodded and lowered her head. Eric put his arm around her shoulder and pulled her head to his chest.

The doctor smacked her lips and clapped her hand on the clipboard one time. "You have a good friend," she said, and stood up. The doctors left them alone.

NINETEEN

BRECK SCREAMED when Chi told her. Breck had spent Christmas with Chi, Gena, and Gena's great-niece, Sierra. Being with Chi on Christmas Eve and Christmas had helped Breck not to think too much about the party going on at Eric's home that she was not invited to and couldn't attend even if she were. Now Christmas and New Year's had come and gone. Breck couldn't believe how quickly the year had passed and everything that had happened within that year. She'd moved to Massachusetts, opened a new office and coffeehouse, bought a home, was going to have a baby, and now, Chi had just announced that she and Gena had decided to adopt Sierra. Apparently, the nights at the Boys and Girls Club and Breck's pregnancy had made Chi think more deeply about becoming a mother and having a family of her own.

"We're going to be mommies together!" Breck screamed, and reached across the coffeehouse booth and hugged Chi. "But what about you being lesbians?" Breck asked. "Are they making an issue out of that?"

"No, not really, because the little girl is Gena's great-niece. Her mother is nineteen years old and pregnant with her third child. She approached Gena and me about adopting Sierra, and Gena's brother is taking the oldest boy, but he's not adopting yet. He's not sure if he wants to take on that responsibility."

"Why is she giving the children up?"

"Because her new boyfriend doesn't want them. He's

nineteen and doesn't want three kids, and she doesn't want to raise three kids by herself."

"Then why did she get pregnant?"

Chi shrugged. "It's either us or foster care for these kids."

Breck shook her head. "That's horrible."

"No. It would be horrible if we were not able to take these children and they ended up either in an abusive situation or shuffled from foster home to foster home."

"But she's going to keep his child?"

Chi nodded. "Yup, and they're moving to North Carolina."

Breck sat quietly and stared, teary-eyed, at her friend. Chi had evolved into such a different person. She had settled down into her life with Gena almost effortlessly, like the two of them had known each other forever. For the first time since Breck met her, Chi had relinquished the diva mentality, and Breck was tremendously proud of the way she had grown. Chi and Gena were more than lovers; they'd become family. And Breck loved Gena too.

"The adoption will be somewhat expedited, because it's a relative," Chi explained. "We still have to go through a lot of evaluations and counseling. I guess they do this to see if people are really serious about what they're doing."

"And are you sure about what you're doing?" Breck leaned forward, her hands wrapped around her mug to keep them warm. "You've never expressed an interest in having a child before. This is very sudden."

Chi sighed. "I know, but with Gena it seems right. We should be a family—a full family. We've talked about a sperm donor, but when Gena's sister approached us, it just seemed right."

Breck smiled, but it wasn't her usual happy grin that stretched wide across her face. She was glad for Chi, but she was envious as well, and Chi recognized it. Chi knew her better than most people, and she knew that this was not Breck's usual enthusiastic reaction. "Are you okay with this?" she asked.

"I think you guys are doing a wonderful thing and this little girl will have two terrific mothers." Breck paused, rubbing her hands around the cup. "I wish that Eric and I could be a full family, but I know that just won't happen." She dropped her eyes, feeling embarrassed that she had let that come out. "I'm sorry. This isn't a time for my self-pity. This is your moment."

"Don't be silly." Chi placed her hand on top of Breck's, trying unsuccessfully to console her. "You can still have that type of relationship, you know."

Breck shook her head. "Eric would never stand for that. He wants to be involved in this child's life." She rubbed her belly, protruding now, but only enough that people might just assume she'd gained a little weight.

She had gone out of her way to make things right with Eric so that he could trust her again. She told him about every appointment she'd had, only two so far. She'd also bought a few baby items—teddy bears and crib toys, neutral things like that, since neither of them wanted to know the sex beforehand. It had taken a few weeks before he was able to speak to her in more than a couple of sentences.

"Are you ever going to talk to me again?" she had asked one evening as they sat on her sofa.

"I'm talking to you."

"No, you're not. You speak to me but we haven't really talked since that day. You're still angry, aren't you?" she asked.

"I'm still very angry. Every time I look at you, I think about—"

"Eric, please," she said, taking his hand and pulling it to her heart. "I've apologized so many times, I've lost count."

"What the hell were you thinking?!" he yelled, then dropped her hand and stood up. He walked to the opposite side of the room and grabbed hold of the mantel.

"I was thinking how devastated I would have been if you'd told me to get an abortion."

"I would never have done that."

"I know that now. If you don't forgive me and allow me to show you how sorry I am and how much I really do want this baby, then you've just broken your first promise."

He quickly turned to face her. "What?!"

"You promised I would not have to raise this baby alone, and you're starting to make me feel like I will be." He just looked at her, not saying anything. Breck stood up and joined him at the mantel, taking his hand and placing it on her abdomen. "I need you," she said.

He let out a huge sigh and pulled her into his arms. He hugged her tight, tighter than he'd ever held her before. "I love you so much." He kissed her for the first time since he'd stormed into the clinic. He kept kissing her until she went limp in his arms. "We're having a baby," he said.

Breck smiled. "I know."

"Promise me you'll tell me everything. No matter if you think it'll hurt me. Even if you think it's silly, I want to know everything. Promise me."

"I promise," she said, and he kissed her again.

"I want to know when you feel the baby move for the first time. I want to know when he starts kicking."

"He?"

"He or she, it doesn't matter," he said, and kissed her again. "Although a little girl would be great."

"She would be spoiled rotten."

"As little girls should be," he said, and rubbed her abdomen. They talked freely about the baby from that day on, and soon Breck started talking *to* the baby as well. She even read to it at night and picked out special classical music for it. Every day she grew more and more excited about the baby and being a mother.

"SO HAVE things mellowed with you and Eric?" Chi asked. "He's not punishing you anymore?" Breck nodded. "To what extent is he going to be involved with the baby?"

Breck shrugged. "I don't know. I wish things could be normal. I know he wants the baby, and I do too now, but I can't help feeling like this." She took a deep breath.

"You need to tell him how you feel. Have you ever thought that maybe Eric hasn't done more because you haven't asked more of him?"

Breck shrugged. "What am I supposed to say to him? I've never pressured him about our relationship or given him an ultimatum," she said, biting her lower lip.

"You're not giving him an ultimatum. You're not saying, 'Leave your wife or else.' What you're telling him is, 'Hey. I have a child to think about now, and I want what is best, not only for my child but also for me.' You're finally growing up." Chi grinned.

"Where will I start?"

"Start with the truth."

BRECK DIDN'T immediately act on Chi's advice, not because she was too afraid but because she just didn't want to cause any more ripples between her and Eric. A few weeks later Chi and Gena brought home three-year-old Sierra Leoni Tanaka-Price, but the adoption was far from complete. In her role as godmother, Breck sat in on a few counseling sessions with Chi and Gena. Before Sierra moved in with Gena and Chi, they hired a nurse to visit and help them childproof everyone's home. Sierra was allowed several weekend visits, including sleepovers at "Auntie" Breck's house, during the adoption process.

When the adoption was approved and final, Chi's mother and sister flew in from Indianapolis. Gena's parents, who lived in Boston, came with Gena's two sisters, her brother, and his children. Eric also attended the welcoming party, as did Martin, Alyce, and their children, and several of the Boys and Girls Club counselors and their children.

Chi and Gena went overboard with the decorations and the entertainment, spending hundreds of dollars to make sure it was the best party a little girl could ask for. They had moved to Jamaica Plains, a suburb just outside of Boston, and had purchased a beautiful two-story home. They invited several neighborhood children, and Breck soon realized why Chi and Gena had chosen Jamaica Plains. Many of the couples who visited with their children were same-sex parents with adopted children. They even formed a small network of support for one another. At least five knee-high toddlers ran about the house and the fenced-in yard the entire afternoon.

Sierra received countless presents from her grandparents, all of her new aunts, uncles, and friends, and her moms. Her room was a little girl's delight, pink with white-and-lavender trim and a white canopy bed with guardrails. While Gena and the hired clown kept the children entertained, Chi filled in Breck and Alyce on Sierra's history and explained why she was so small for her age.

Sierra's biological mother chose not to attend the party; she and her boyfriend were now married and moved to North Carolina. Chi fondly remembered the day she first met Sierra at Gena's mother's house. Whoever had combed her hair that day hadn't parted it straight down the middle, and her little pigtails were crooked. Her denim overalls were slightly worn, and the T-shirt she was wearing had a permanent ketchup stain on the front. Chi couldn't take her eyes off the little girl and her crooked pigtails as she played in the yard with the other children. She searched through her purse for a comb and took Sierra by the hand, led her to a corner chair, and combed her hair right.

"Somebody has got to start caring about that little girl," Chi had said to Breck that day at the office. Breck remembered that day well—it was when Chi decided that that somebody would be her. She and Gena talked about it and they decided to say yes.

THE PARTY lasted three hours. Sierra laughed and played so hard that she fell asleep in Chi's arms. Most of the guests had gone, leaving Breck, Eric, and Chi, and Gena's relatives. Breck tried to help with the cleanup, but Chi's mom urged her out.

"You get out of here and go be with that handsome young man over there. We can take care of this."

"But—" Breck began to protest.

"Go on now," Chi's mother said, and pushed her out of the kitchen. "You'll have plenty of time to spend with that little girl. Probably more time than you want. G'on, get." She scooted Breck out.

Throwing her arms up in defeat, Breck hugged Chi and Gena before she and Eric left. She wrapped her arms around Eric as he led her to the car. Once they were in, Breck was quiet.

"They seem very happy," Eric said as they merged onto the highway heading back to Mansfield.

"Yes, they are. I'm so proud of Chi. She's going to be a terrific mother."

"So are you," Eric said, reaching over and rubbing her now plump and hard belly.

Breck touched his hand as a huge grin appeared on her face. "That was a wonderful party," she said.

"Yes, it was," Eric agreed with a grunt. "A lot of kids."

"Yes." She sighed. "How are Darius's birthday parties?"

Breck surprised herself. She hardly ever mentioned Darius.

"Pretty much the same," Eric said.

"You haven't talked about Darius in a long time."

"It makes you uncomfortable, so I don't do it."

"No, it makes me feel inferior and left out because I cannot share in that part of your world. I don't have any intentions of making you choose families." He reached across the seat and squeezed her hand. "Tell me about Darius," she said, and Eric began to talk. Darius was five years old now and, according to his father, quite a looker. He and Darius had many men's nights out, as Eric called them. They would usually go to a movie and then out for pizza afterward.

"Was he a good baby?" Breck asked. She smiled when she saw how much he loved talking about his son. It was very much a part of who he was, and she had denied it to him for a long time.

"He was a great baby. Didn't cry much and still doesn't." He paused long enough to check his position on the road. "When we brought him home from the hospital, there were so many flowers and gifts, we couldn't get them into the house." He laughed. "My mother bought him this huge panda that is at least five feet tall. For two years Darius was petrified of the damn thing. We had to put it in the attic."

Breck laughed with him.

"He's okay with it now, but it broke my mother's heart that she scared my child half to death."

"Does he have a lot of cousins that he plays with?"

"No. My sister, Karmen, lives in Washington, D.C., and we see her and her family about four times a year. My brother, Christopher, and his wife live in Atlanta with their two boys. We visit with them about twice a year. Darius's friends are the children of local politicians and professionals in Back Bay and Beacon Hill. He has quite a few friends."

"I wish I could meet him."

"So do I," he said, and squeezed her hand again.

Breck swallowed before she asked the next question. "Are you and Gaby planning to have more children?" She dropped her eyes and looked at her hands.

He took a deep breath before he answered her. "Gaby had a hysterectomy a year after Darius was born."

"Oh." Breck was very surprised to hear that. Eric had never mentioned that he and Gaby couldn't have more children. "Is she okay?"

"She's fine. She had a lot of scar tissue on her uterus, and whenever she menstruated she bled for a month instead of the usual five days. She had a bunch of surgeries, but the bleeding and cramping continued. There were times she'd be in too much pain to even walk. They wanted to do a hysterectomy before she ever got pregnant, but she waited. Once Darius was born she had it done."

"Hmm," Breck mumbled. "What about adoption?"

Eric shook his head. "Not an option. Gaby's family is very much into ancestral bloodlines and heritage. An adopted child would never be accepted into their family because it would not be a part of the bloodline."

"That's very callous."

"Yes, it is, but that's how they are. They're nice enough people and they're great to me and Darius, but if Darius was not Gaby's son, they would not have accepted him, so it was imperative for her to have a child that was her own."

"What if Darius was a girl?"

"That wouldn't make a difference. They're not concerned with gender, just the bloodline."

"Interesting," Breck said, then turned to face forward again. "How do they treat you?"

"Great. I don't have a problem with them and never did."

"What if you didn't have any money?" Breck asked.

Eric laughed. "That would be an entirely different story, I'm sure." They held hands as they pulled up in front of Breck's house. She climbed out of the car while Eric sought a small gym bag in the trunk, which meant only one thing.

"You're spending the night?" she asked, a smile creeping across her face.

"Yes. If that's okay with you."

"So, where are you supposed to be tonight?" she asked.

"They're in New York at her parents' house, and I told her that I was going to be hanging out. It's no big deal."

They walked into the sitting room. Eric placed his duffel bag on the floor and picked up the remote control to the satellite dish. "You want to go see a movie tonight?" he asked, flipping through the stations.

After a few minutes Breck tossed her clothes over the couch and covered his head. When Eric turned around, Breck stood in the doorway completely naked.

"Not exactly what I had in mind," she said, and began walking upstairs. Before she reached the second landing, he had caught up to her, and they walked up the remaining flight with her wrapped in his arms.

TWENTY

A M I supposed to be gaining so much weight so fast?" Breck asked the ob/gyn as she stood on the scale during her monthly visit. She'd gained ten pounds already.

"You're gaining at the right rate. Nothing unusual at all."

"And you're sure there's only one in there, aren't you?"

"Well, I only heard one heartbeat, but we won't know for sure until we have the ultrasound next month."

That made Breck slightly worried.

"I wouldn't worry if I were you," the doctor said as she wrote some quick notes on Breck's chart. "There are no indications that you're carrying more than one." She put the stethoscope to Breck's protruded belly. After the exam the doctor gave her a few exercise suggestions, but the thought of gaining a hundred pounds during the pregnancy and being unable to take the weight off unnerved Breck. As soon as she was home, she called her mother.

Breck had waited until after New Year's to tell her mother about the pregnancy for a couple of reasons. One was that she knew her mother would go into a psychotic rage, and second, she wanted to be certain that she and Eric were comfortable about having the baby before she let her family in on the news.

Breck was right. Her mother did have a fit when she told her, but it didn't take long for the excitement of having another grandchild to win over her rage. Her mother became excessively excited and started calling

Breck almost every day to check on her and immediately started sending baby gifts. Breck was sure her mother was more excited about her having a baby than she was.

"I'm going to be an awful mother," Breck said, sobbing into the phone. She couldn't stop crying. She hadn't been able to wear any of her clothes after the fourth month, and she had known women who wore their regular clothes up until the last trimester. Breck resorted to wearing baggy clothes and unzipped pants. Arriving at the office close to noon one day with an armload of new clothes to show Chi and Marla, Breck practically cried holding up the oversized wares while Chi and Marla laughed at her.

"My goodness, girl, those hormones are really getting to you," her mother joked.

"Mom, this isn't funny. Everybody laughs at me. Why does everybody laugh at me?" Again she broke into an uncontrollable sob.

"Breck, honey, I'm not laughing at you." The explanation did nothing to stem her tears. "Breck, is anyone there with you?"

"No," she said.

"What about Eric? Do you see a lot of him?"

"The usual," Breck replied, wiping the tears from her eyes with the back of her hand.

"This is the time when you really need him, and he can't be there for you."

Breck imagined her mother back in Indianapolis, fussing and pointing at an invisible image of her. "Mom, I can't argue about this with you right now."

"You should have thought about this before you decided to have a baby by a married man."

"I did think about this!" Breck screamed back her. "That's why I almost didn't!"

"I don't even want to talk about that," her mother said, dismissing mention of the close-call abortion.

When Breck had told her mother about that, Camille had screamed at her for even considering an abortion without telling anyone, including Eric, and then she screamed at her for getting pregnant in the first place. "Honey, I tell you what. I'll come and stay with you for a little while. Will that make you feel better?"

"Not if you're going to come out here and lecture me."

"I will keep my opinions to myself as much as I can."

"You promise?" Breck sniffled. She felt like she had entered a time warp, becoming a whiny teen again.

"Yes, I promise. I'll make the arrangements and I'll call you. Is that okay?"

"Yes," she said, then started on another round of tears.

"What are you crying for now?" her mother asked.

"I don't know."

BRECK'S MOTHER arrived a week later to keep her company. The moment Breck saw her on the concourse she began to feel better. Her mother made her go to bed early and sleep late. "You need your rest," she said firmly. When Breck prepared for her morning runs, her mother insisted that she walk instead.

"You still need to take care of yourself at this stage," Camille said. "You need nutrients and a little exercise." Some mornings her mother walked with her. When Eric came over, her mother always stared at him and didn't talk to him much.

"I have no idea why you two are doing this," she commented during dinner one evening when Eric had joined them.

"Mom, you promised," Breck said, and dropped her fork on the table.

"Well, I've kept my peace since I've been here, and this is my grandchild you are having, so I'm going to speak my mind." She turned to Eric. "If you can't be here for my daughter, how are you going to be here for my grandchild?"

"I'm here as much as I can be, and I'll be here for my child as well," Eric quickly answered.

"Do you have any idea how this is going to make your wife feel when she finds out? Or do you care?"

"I care," Eric answered.

"I don't think you do. My daughter thinks you are the best thing to ever walk the face of this earth, but I see a very cold-hearted man for what you are doing to your other family."

Breck threw her napkin across the table; it stopped just short of her mother's plate.

"I'm sorry that you feel that way," Eric said, taking Breck's hand to reassure her that he could hold his own. "I love Breck very much."

"Do you love your wife?"

"Yes, I do, and I don't want to hurt anyone, but this is the situation I'm in and I'm trying to live it as best as I can."

"This is going to destroy so many lives. I find it hard to believe that you two cannot see that and choose to walk away from each other."

"We tried that, but it didn't change the fact that we love each other."

"You cannot be in love with two different women!" her mother shouted.

"I'm sorry, but I can and I do, and there isn't anyone who can tell me otherwise. Until I met Breck, I would never have believed it myself. I love Breck. I love my wife as well, and it pains me that I can't give both of them one hundred percent of me, and it pains me even more that someone will probably get hurt from this. But this is how I feel, and please don't tell me that I can't feel this way." He paused. "I don't think the problem is that I can't love two women. The problem is that I can't have two women. Society doesn't accept it, so that makes me an awful person."

"You cannot have two families," Breck's mother reiterated.

"Maybe not, but it doesn't stop me from loving them both."

"The children are innocent, but they'll end up being the ones who will suffer the most."

"Well, Mom, what do you propose we do?" Breck said, angry that her mother had picked this time to confront them. She had known this moment was bound to happen, that her mother wasn't going to let this visit go by without bashing Eric and their relationship. "Do you suggest we abort the baby now and say good riddance to each other? Will that make everything okay?"

Looking from Breck to Eric, Camille said quietly, "There's an order to things. Things happen for a reason. Sometimes we don't understand what it is, but the good Lord will reveal it in time." She stood and walked upstairs to her room.

Breck shook her head and stared down at the table. "Ugh," she growled. "I'm sorry." But she knew her apologies wouldn't make things better.

"Breck, how do you feel about me?" Eric asked.

Breck turned to face him. "What do you mean?"

"How do you feel about me? Do you think I'm a cold-hearted monster?"

Breck wasn't sure what answer he was fishing for, but he should know how she felt about him. "I think you're wonderful. I don't think you are a monster. I see how you are with the children at the Boys and Girls Club, and not many men I know would devote their free time to those kids the way you do. You've donated millions of dollars to rebuild a lost community. We have no secrets in our relationship. I know how you feel about Gaby and Darius, and I know how you feel about me, and I'm comfortable with that. I've never trusted any man as much as I trust you, and I've never loved anyone, unconditionally, until I met you."

Eric put his elbows on the table and rubbed his face with the inside of his hands. "Do you remember the first night I called you from the sleepover?"

How could she forget? "You kissed me." She smiled as the memory came to her.

"When I hung up the phone that night, I knew I was in trouble. I knew that I was in love with you. When I left the club that weekend, I went home and made love to my wife." One minute he lifted her up, and then the next second he slammed her down again. Breck looked at the table and let the sting wear off. "Loving you scared the shit out of me," he continued. "You stayed with me and you were right there with me as I slept beside my wife that night. I wanted so much to pick up the phone and call you or fly to Indiana to hold you. Every night when I lay down beside my wife, I felt ashamed." He paused. "I struggle with this, Breck. No one sees it and I cannot talk to anyone about it, but I know how I feel." He clutched his hand to his heart. "It goes beyond just wanting to sleep around. Call me selfish, monster, cheater, or a liar, whatever, I don't care. But I know that I am a good husband to my wife, a good companion to you, a good father to Darius, and I will be a good father to our child. Your mother makes it sound so easy that I could have let you go and life would have been better. I couldn't." He shook his head. "I did try, but the emptiness persisted. My breath is gone when you're not with me. I feel as if I'm sinking or drowning, and I don't like that feeling."

Breck sat speechless.

"I have come to accept that no one will understand how I feel about you," Eric continued. "Maybe not even you. Before you, I would have debated anyone who claimed he loved two women."

Breck took his hand and entwined his fingers with hers. She loved the feel of his large hand that dwarfed hers. She felt safe with him. "I don't question your feelings for me. Like you once said, we can spend our lives questioning why we feel this way, or we can just live it. A lot of people will feel as my mother."

"You could have any man you want. You're beautiful, successful." He licked his lips. "Why do you love me?" He leaned forward and they touched, forehead to forehead.

Breck smiled. "Because you're Eric Warren."

BRECK'S MOTHER returned to Indiana when Breck was well into her second trimester, promising to come back when Breck was closer to delivery. Even though her mother resented Breck's relationship, she was thrilled with the idea of having another grandchild. Alex and his wife remained adamant about not having children, and Tamara was having too much fun being single.

The pregnancy progressed smoothly, and Breck took in all the charity that was doled out to her. People were always eager to help pregnant women. Breck didn't have to lift a finger to do anything. Almost every night someone was at her house to either prepare dinner or clean. They seemed to alternate with Eric: one night it would be Chi, Gena, and Sierra; other nights it would be Alyce. Breck had never been waited on or taken care of the way she was now. Now she understood why some women loved being pregnant. She could definitely get used to feeling special and doted on.

Neither Alyce, Martin, nor Brian asked about the father of Breck's baby. Breck figured that by now they all knew. It was probably best that way, some sort of secret-agent code: don't ask and you won't have to lie if someone questions you.

Eric and Breck's lives had changed so much since the day she first arrived in Massachusetts. Chi had to rush to the day care to pick up Sierra, so Breck stayed alone at the coffeehouse, drank juice, and snacked on a brownie. She wrote in her journal and then pushed it aside to thumb through a magazine.

The door chime went off pretty regularly, which was always a good thing to hear. The coffeehouse did very good business, better than she had thought it would, although she didn't own it for the money. It was the only coffeehouse in the tiny community and a great place to escape to, read a book, or meet friends. When Breck sat alone there she never worried about anyone bothering her, but now she felt a presence nearby and looked up.

She immediately recognized the face—how on earth could she ever forget it? The woman had smooth, silken, deep ebony skin, without a single wrinkle. Why was Gaby here, in Mansfield, at her coffeehouse?

"Hello, Breck," Gaby said, her Portuguese accent strong and prominent even with such a short phrase. She clutched her Louis Vuitton handbag under her arm as she stood looking down at Breck. Breck's voice was lost in her throat, and she couldn't think fast enough to come up with a greeting. "I'm sorry, you may not remember me. I'm Eric's wife, Gaby." She forced a smile and then shoved her hand across the table and in Breck's face. When Breck touched her hand, Gaby immediately pulled it away, so the shake was more of a quick tap.

"Of course I remember you. Please, have a seat." Breck moved her journal aside and made room for Gaby to sit opposite her. She tried to keep her hands from trembling. "What brings you to Mansfield?"

"I should be asking you that question," Gaby said, placing her handbag on the table. "Eric didn't tell me that you moved to Massachusetts. And to Mansfield of all places." She forced a laugh, but Breck could tell that Gaby was far from being in a giddy mood. "How long have you lived here?"

"Just over a year."

"Over a year?" she said with a raised voice. "Eric hasn't said a word to me. We could have all gotten together for dinner or had you over to the house." She and Breck kept their gaze on each other, Breck knowing the last thing she needed to do was to overreact or appear nervous. She doubted that this meeting was coincidental. She remembered what Martin had said about Gaby never coming to Mansfield, and Breck could see it in the way Gaby looked at the coffeehouse and wiped the table off with her bare hand, as if she assumed it was dusty.

"I'm sure Eric has more on his mind than me," Breck said, trying to throw her off.

"He was quite fond of you. Talked about you a lot, which is why I'm very surprised he didn't mention that you moved here or invite you to our home for Christmas." Gaby realized she was slouching and straightened her posture in the booth. "We Bostonians must have made quite an impression on you."

"I like it here."

"So what's going on with you and Eric?"

Breck's heart pounded hard in her chest, and she inhaled deeply. "What do you mean?"

"Have you two started a new project?" Gaby asked, leaning forward.

Breck was thrown off. She shook her head. "No. Why do you ask?"

"Because a lot of my friends that were at the grand opening have seen you two together, so I naturally assumed that you have another project in the works. Even though Eric failed to tell me that you moved to Massachusetts. But then again, Eric doesn't tell me everything about his work," Gaby added beneath her breath.

Breck searched her memory for any time she and Eric could have been seen. They had always tried to be careful, choosing out-of-the-way restaurants or staying at her house to avoid running into anyone who knew them. But she couldn't guess which friend or circumstance had tipped Gaby off.

There was the chance that Gaby was bluffing, but that wouldn't explain her visit. Gaby could have easily picked up the phone and called her. She didn't have to visit a place she so openly despised unless she had a solid reason to do so. Gaby knew something, or she wanted to see Breck's reaction to her in order to confirm or deny her suspicious.

Act normal, Breck told herself, but how the hell do you act normal without appearing to be acting? Her heart pumped hard and she felt as if her blood had developed icicles. "Eric and I have met to discuss a couple of projects, but nothing has materialized yet," Breck answered. It was the best response she could come up with to attempt to satisfy Gaby's questioning.

Please don't ask me if I'm having an affair with your husband, Breck thought. Would you lie, Breck? Would you? Her mind raced while she struggled to stay focused on being calm and acting normal. "Why are you asking me questions about Eric? Is everything okay?" Good question, Breck, she thought, congratulating herself. A woman as proud as Gaby would never admit that something might be troubling her marriage. Particularly not to a woman who lived in Mansfield.

"Oh, everything's fine," Gaby said in a proud and confident voice. "I was just surprised to learn that you were in Massachusetts and that you've been here for over a year without Eric inviting you to our home. That's not like him."

Breck shrugged. "I really don't know why Eric hasn't mentioned me. Perhaps I'm just not important enough to bring up at home," she said, sacrificing her ego in an attempt to bolster Gaby's.

"You know, I thought it was something like that,"

Gaby said, leaning back in the booth, and at that moment Breck thought about her swollen belly. She slid to the edge of her seat until her breasts touched the table.

Gaby leaned forward and whispered, "Why on earth would you want to move to Mansfield?" She shivered as the name rolled off her tongue.

"I like it here," Breck said again. "It's a wonderful community that is very involved, and the people care about each other. People speak to you here, no matter how much money you have."

"Or don't have," Gaby said, her eyes roving the coffeehouse.

Breck sipped from her mug, causing her gold bracelet to slide down her wrist and clang against its side.

"Nice bracelet," Gaby said, noticing the almost musical chime the bracelet sent off when it touched the mug. "Eric has one similar to it."

Breck's heart gave one solid pound in her chest, and her face heated up in an instant. The bracelet had been a Christmas gift from Eric. Eric had one just like it because they were a matching set. Eric had each of their initials engraved on the thick gold latch, and if Gaby asked to see it, she would immediately know that none of this was coincidental. Breck held her breath, hoping Gaby wouldn't ask to see. She was stuck. She couldn't get up to walk away, and she couldn't continue the conversation.

Instead Gaby changed the subject completely. "I have a wonderful personal trainer," she said, and Breck released her breath. "I can give you his name if you like."

Breck sulked. "That's okay, but thanks for the offer."

"Not a problem," Gaby said. "I gained a few pounds too when I first moved here. So many wonderful restaurants, and all of the food is fattening and delicious." She looked around the place again. "This is a nice coffee shop. I wonder why the owner chose to open it here." She squinted.

"Thank you. I own it." Gaby shot a look at her that screamed "I feel so sorry for you."

"You should ask Eric about renting one of his places in Back Bay. I have a gallery on Newbury Street, and there's a nice shop next door to me that's vacant. We don't own that building, but I know the owner and can talk to him for you if you'd like."

Breck shook her head. "No. I'm happy here and I don't want to expand."

"But you'd probably make much more money, and instead of high school kids ordering soda you'll get professionals having business meetings."

"I'll keep that in mind," Breck said. "Would you like a cappuccino?" She didn't want to be social with Gaby, but she didn't want to rush the woman out, either, even though her presence annoyed the hell out of her. How could Eric tolerate such a pesky woman?

"Oh, no. Coffee upsets my stomach."

"Tea?"

Gaby waved her off as she dramatically slid from the booth and wiped the seat of her slacks as if she had sat in crumbs. "Oh, your journal," Gaby said, picking up her journal as she stood up. Breck refrained from snatching it out of her hand. Luckily it was the kind that had an elastic band to hold it together. She couldn't risk the journal opening to even the first page. Eric's name was everywhere. "The advantage of being single," Gaby added. "You don't have to worry about a husband finding it and reading it."

"Look for trouble, you'll usually find it," Breck said. "Let me get that out of your way." She reached for the journal and placed it back on the table. "By the way, how did you find me?"

"You're in the book," Gaby said, securing her purse underneath her arm. "Sorry I have to run, but I must pick up Darius. He's at Eric mother's house, and God only knows where this woman takes my child. Call me sometime so that we can have lunch. Are you dating?" Such a conspicuous way of asking that question, Breck thought.

"I date," Breck answered. She slid even further toward the edge of the booth, hoping Gaby wouldn't think to look hard enough to notice that her weight gain was the result of a pregnancy and not New England clam chowder.

"Well, if you need a date, I happen to know some very influential, good-looking single men." Gaby winked and stood momentarily in front of her, perhaps waiting for Breck to stand and walk her out. But Breck couldn't do that, nor did she want to. "And Eric has some single friends. I'll be sure to talk to him about introducing you to one, and we'll have a dinner party. It may help to lose a few pounds first."

Breck cringed and felt her neck tightening. "Thanks, I'll keep that in mind. It was nice seeing you again," she lied.

"Not a problem. I'll call you," Gaby said before she strolled out onto the sidewalk. As soon as Breck saw Gaby's Jaguar head off down the street, she relaxed, leaned back on her seat, and tossed her arms up in the air.

"What the hell was that?" she said aloud. She slumped forward and banged her head on the table, then reached for her cell phone and called Eric. He answered after the third ring.

"Where are you?" she asked without saying hello.

"I'm on my way home. Why?" Cars whistled past and horns blared in the background.

"Your wife just left the coffeehouse."

"Gaby?"

"Do you have another wife I don't know about?" she yelled. "Of course, Gaby!"

"Why was she there?"

"Questioning me about us. Apparently people have been seeing us together. Do you know who or what may have tipped her off?"

Eric was silent before he answered. "I don't know. Did she say anything about you-know-what?"

That would have been a real kicker, Breck thought. "She thinks I got fat and offered me the name of her personal trainer."

"Well, don't worry about it," he said. "I'll take care of it." Breck had often wondered if Gaby ever suspected Eric of having an affair. She and Eric spent many nights together, and not all of them were over the weekends. Because of his business he could do that. His unpredictable travel schedule was a lifeline to their relationship.

"But I am worried, Eric. She suspects that we're having an affair."

"Breck, calm down. I'll handle it."

"YOU'RE INVITED to my house for dinner," Eric said to her two days later while they sat on her sofa listening to music. He waited until after dinner to drop the news on her while she relaxed in his arms.

"Excuse me?"

"Gaby insisted that I introduce you to someone and have you over for dinner. So I'm inviting you."

"Is this how you handled it?"

He shrugged.

Breck shook her head, feverishly. "I'm not going to your house."

"If you don't, she may get suspicious."

"Hell, she's already suspicious." Breck pulled herself from the sofa and stood near the mantel with her arms folded across her chest. "I'm not going to your house and parading around your wife, knowing I'm carrying your baby. That's fucked up." She turned from him. She'd broken every moral rule ever written while having this affair, she thought. She'd stepped beyond boundaries she'd never thought she would. When was it going to stop?

"I'm just telling you that she's going to call you and she's going to ask you to come over for dinner. It's your choice if you want to say no."

"Does Gaby always get what she wants?" Breck asked, throwing her arms up in the air.

"Pretty much, yes." He nodded. "But mostly, I think she just wants to see you with someone else."

"You were supposed to arrange my date. Who would be my date?"

"Brian."

"Brian!" she exclaimed. "He's already been tossed around this damn relationship. Why would he even want to do this?"

"Because I asked him to."

"Do you always get what *you* want?"

"Pretty much, yes."

"This shit isn't right," she said, starting to pace the room.

"I'm afraid that if you don't go, you'll see Gaby around more often. If you do go, she will see whatever she wants to see and it'll be over with."

"What if she sees that I'm pregnant and seeing us together reveals to her that we're having an affair?"

"Just act normal and it'll be okay."

"Act normal?" There were those words again, and she had yet to learn how to do it. "I can't believe you're asking me to do this."

"I don't want this situation any more than you do, but Gaby will not go away unless she gets what she wants." Eric stood up and walked over to her. "I know my wife. If you tell her you're already dating someone, she'll persist until you and that someone are at my house."

"And you've already talked to Brian about this?"

"Yes."

"He's okay with it?"

"Yes."

Breck shook her head. "You have a damn good friend."

"I know."

THE NEXT day Gaby called the office and invited Breck over for dinner the upcoming Friday evening. Breck told Chi about the debacle, and Chi didn't react well to the idea either.

"Just tell her you're a lesbian," Chi offered as an alternative, and for five seconds Breck considered it. "Why is Gaby doing this?"

"If I were Gaby, I would do the same damn thing. If I thought my husband was sleeping with some woman, I would want her right where I could see her—right in my face—and that would tell her, hey, I'm watching you."

Chi shrugged. "I think all of you are playing a dangerous game."

BRECK DRESSED in a stylish but oversized black dress. To anyone who didn't see her every day, she just had the look of picking up more than a few pounds. To those who knew her, she was obviously pregnant.

Breck followed the directions to Eric's house, on a narrow road off a main street. She had to come alone because her meeting with Brian was set up as a blind date. Gaby knew Breck had met Brian at the grand opening, but Eric had presented a picture that that was the extent of their meeting. Gaby didn't busy herself with details about Eric's friends, so she couldn't question it. Gaby wasn't even aware that Brian and Breck lived just a few blocks from each other. Stepping out of her car, Breck took in the immaculate brownstone. The entrance was one of three on the entire block, which led Breck to believe that once inside, she would enter into a world of royalty. She spotted Brian's truck a short distance from where she parked, so she knew her "date" had already arrived.

A knot had formed in her stomach before she even left her house, and the closer she drove to Eric's home, the tighter it got. Now it seemed to pull so tightly from opposite ends that she felt like at any moment she would rip at the seams. She walked across the street, clutching her handbag to her side. Before ringing the buzzer, she took a deep breath and released it.

She had expected to see Gaby or Eric answer the door, but instead, a plump woman neatly dressed in a plain black dress and white apron opened the grand wooden doors.

"Hello," she said. "Come in. Everyone is in the reception area." Breck noticed her strong Hispanic accent. She followed the woman, walking on shiny wooden floors. She was led just past the majestic living room to a smaller, more personal reception room, where Brian, Eric, and Gaby sat waiting for her arrival.

"Breck, welcome to our home," Gaby said, rushing to greet her and giving her a quick brush on the cheek with her own. Gaby's body never touched hers—in fact, it was the most impersonal hug Breck had ever received. Breck believed hugs involved the full body, and those were the types of hugs she gave. "I'll let Eric introduce you to his friend." She took Breck by the forearm and led her just a few steps farther into the room. Breck stood awkwardly in front of Eric while their eyes met.

"Hello, Breck," Eric said. "Always good to see you." He leaned forward and kissed her gently on the cheek.

"Likewise," Breck said. The knot moved from her stomach to her throat, and she coughed.

"I know you've met my friend Brian, but I would like

to introduce you again." Breck turned to face Brian and fought to keep from rolling her eyes at the charade they were performing. Why had Brian agreed to go along with such a terrible game?

"Hello, Breck," he said, stepping forward and extending his hand. "It's good to see you again. You should have called me the moment you arrived in Boston. I would have been more than happy to show you around our wonderful city."

"I've been busy," Breck said. Brian seemed to be enjoying his acting debut. The maid appeared with a tray of four flutes, each half full with bubbling champagne.

"Breck has been here more than a year, and she hasn't nabbed anyone yet," Gaby said. "We need to make sure she gets out more instead of wasting away in Mansfield in some coffee shop." Then she brought the flute to her mouth and took a large sip. If she was proposing a toast, they all missed it. Everyone followed her lead and drank. Breck put the glass to her mouth with Eric's eyes beaming on her, asking if she was actually going to drink it. She tilted the glass and appeared to take a sip, only none passed through her closed lips. She would only be able to get away with that a few times before Gaby noticed her drink not disappearing.

"What brought you to Massachusetts?" Brian asked. He appeared to be interested in her, playing along by asking her questions he already knew the answers to.

"Business," Breck said. "After the open house, a tremendous opportunity became available to me and I couldn't pass on it."

"And you couldn't do it from Indianapolis?" he asked, then took a quick look at Eric.

Breck took a deep breath while Eric downed his champagne. "It would have been a bit difficult."

"I see." Just then the maid brought out a tray of smoked salmon and hard crackers. She took the tray around to each of them before placing it on a small table.

"Must have been an excellent opportunity. Why didn't you move to town?"

"I'm happy where I am. It provides everything I need."

Everyone grew quiet before the conversation drifted on to other things. Several minutes later they began walking toward the formal dining room, and it was then that Breck whispered to Eric while Brian walked ahead with Gaby. "Give me your glass," she said. Eric slipped his empty glass behind his back where she grabbed it and put her full one into his hand. He quickly drank the now warm bubbly liquid and took a deep breath to hold down a belch. That brought a soft chuckle from Breck and got the attention of Gaby, who turned around to look at them.

"Would you like another drink, Breck?" Gaby asked, eyeing the empty glass in her hand.

"Perhaps after dinner," she answered. They walked into the grand dining room and sat at a wooden table large enough to seat twenty people with relative ease. The four of them sat at one corner, with Breck next to Brian and directly across from Eric.

The dinner turned out to be pleasant, mostly because Breck and Brian got along splendidly, as they had the night of the grand opening. She avoided making eye contact with Eric the entire night, and with Brian beside her most of the time, it wasn't difficult. Brian made her feel that he was interested, but on a different level. He wasn't trying to get into her bed, and that was the way he always came across, and Breck liked it. If anything, Gaby seemed as if her concerns were allayed, but Eric's increased at how comfortable Breck was with Brian. They even made a date to visit the art museum together, and this was done in front of Eric and Gaby. Gaby smiled but Eric's face went blank. By the end of the dinner Gaby seemed pleased and made one last attempt to give Breck the number of her personal trainer.

Breck now understood why Eric's friends didn't take to Gaby, which probably explained their silence about the affair. She found Gaby extremely difficult to like, and she suspected the best way to do it was to be like her. No one in Mansfield was like Gaby. But Breck did have one thing to thank Eric's flamboyant wife for: she and Brian indeed went to the art museum, and after that night they became closer friends.

TWENTY-ONE

BRECK'S WATER broke at precisely 8:14 on the morning of August 16, on her way to the office. Her back had been nagging her all morning, but she'd thought it was because of the way she had slept. For the past two months, sleeping had been difficult. No matter which way she turned, the baby didn't like it and kicked the hell out of her. Even if she tried to sleep sitting in a chair, the baby still kicked her. The tiny feet pressed up against her stretched belly, and Breck always smiled when she saw the ball pushing from her stomach. When Chi first saw it she was freaked out and thrilled all at the same time. "There's a little person in there!" she said with a giggle.

When Breck felt the wetness in her pants, she quickly reached for the cell phone on the seat beside her and activated her phone. "Chi," she said, and the phone immediately began to dial.

"Breck Larson Designs," Chi answered.

"Chi, my water broke!" Breck screamed into the phone.

"Where are you?" Chi screamed back.

"I'm in my car. I'll head over to the hospital."

"Where is your bag?"

"At the house with my mother."

"Okay. I'll go to the house and pick up your bag and your mother. You go straight to the hospital. I'll meet you. Have you called Eric?"

"Not yet. I'm about to."

"Do you want me to call him?"

"No, I'm fine. I can call him."

"Okay. I'll meet you at the hospital." Chi hung up. Breck said Eric's name and was connected to his office.

"Eric Warren." No matter how many times she heard his voice, it still gave her goose bumps.

"My water broke," she said.

"Where are you?

"In my car. I'm on my way to the hospital."

"How far are you from the hospital?"

"About ten minutes."

"Have you called the doctor?"

"Not yet."

"I'll call the doctor; you go straight to the hospital."

"Okay." He took charge but she didn't mind.

"Love you," he said. "I'll meet you at the hospital."

"Love you too." Breck hung up and touched her cramping stomach. It was time.

JORDAN WARREN Larson was delivered vaginally six hours later, with no complications. Eric stayed with her through the entire birth, holding her hand while Chi videotaped it. Breck stayed in the hospital for two days. Eric filled her room with flowers and stuffed animals.

The first time Breck held Jordan, he clasped his little fingers around her finger and tears trickled from her eyes. She wondered if she would ever tell him how close he came to not being born. Despite that, he was born healthy, with all his fingers and toes and a perfect face. She couldn't say that he looked like Eric or her, because at that moment he looked like every other baby in the nursery—simply beautiful.

The first few days after returning home, Breck struggled to regain enough energy to keep up with Jordan's appetite. He was a hungry baby. The hospital had adopted a routine with him and she tried to stick with it—he normally woke up twice during the night for nursing. Her mother was a godsend. Whenever she slept through Jordan's small cries, her mother would come and wake her.

"The baby's hungry," her mother would say, and nudge her arm. Breck had wanted to pump the breast milk into a bottle, but her mother wouldn't hear of it. "He needs to hear your heartbeat right now, honey. In time."

Eric stopped by every morning before going into the office. He would kiss Jordan and comment how much he looked like Darius as a baby. He showed Breck a picture of Darius when he first arrived home and a current one. Jordan had a remarkable resemblance to Darius. It was difficult to fathom that they had different mothers. Eric made a list of all his relatives and listed every known illness in his family so that Breck would have a medical history for Jordan.

"I also want to make sure he doesn't end up dating a first cousin." He said it in a joking manner, but they knew it could happen if Jordan grew up not knowing his extended family.

Breck loved holding Jordan and almost hated when he fell asleep because it meant she had to put him down. She'd stand over his crib and watch his chest rise and fall with every breath, and she'd place his tiny finger in her hand, amazed that something so precious and so perfect had come from her.

Marla and David held things together at the office as much as they could, but after a month of giving Jordan all of her attention, Breck had to go back. She arranged to work part-time out of the office and part-time out of her home her first month back. Breck's mom stayed for two months and was the perfect caregiver. When Eric managed to spend the night, he and her mother fought over who would hold Jordan when he cried. Eric usually won, which Breck's mother resented.

By the time Camille left, she and Eric seemed to have forged an unspoken truce. They spoke casually to each other and actually had pleasant conversations. Her mother even complimented Eric one evening after he read Jordan his nightly story. Whenever he was there, Eric insisted on reading the story while Breck sat back and watched the two most important men in her life bond.

After Breck's mother returned to Indianapolis, Alyce offered to look after Jordan while Breck worked, and the arrangement couldn't have suited Breck better. Alyce had at least a couple of more years at home with Londrick and Madison, so she became the parenting expert and Breck and Chi both ran to her for advice. Alyce gladly accepted the role, and the three of them, along with Gena, formed a support group. They often did things together with the kids and even left the babies with the guys while they continued their girls' nights out. Usually it was Martin who was stuck baby-sitting, but he never seemed to mind.

"WHAT HAPPENS to Jordan if something happens to you?" Eric asked. Jordan was just a few months old when Breck had gotten sick with a bad cold.

Breck sneezed. "What do you mean?" she asked, blowing her nose for the umpteenth time that day. She had caught a nasty head-and-chest cold that seemed to linger, and she tried to stay as far away from Jordan as she could. She hated not being able to kiss him and hold him as much as she wanted to. Instead, Alyce and Chi took turns taking care of him.

"We need to decide who takes Jordan if something tragic were to happen to you."

"I have a cold, Eric. I'm not dying." She blew her nose again.

"I know, but this is still something we should think about."

Breck sniffled, wiped her nose, and stared at him. "What do you have in mind?"

"I would like to take Jordan if something happens to you."

"Absolutely not," Breck said. She got up and walked to the kitchen to pour something to drink. She stood for a few seconds, deciding between a cup of hot tea to help alleviate her clogged nose and a glass of orange juice to load up on vitamin C. She took a tea bag from the pantry and poured some hot water she'd boiled earlier into a teacup.

"And may I ask why not?"

"Your wife," Breck said, taking the honey from the cupboard and squeezing a teaspoonful into the cup.

"I don't think it would be an issue. I want Jordan and Darius to know each other, and I would welcome the opportunity to raise them together."

"You're dreaming." Breck took her cup to the living room and sat Indian-style on the sofa.

"I'm Jordan's father, and I should have a right to care for him if something happens to his mother."

"Under normal circumstances I would agree, but this is far from a normal circumstance and I'm not going to jeopardize my son's mental health for some unrealistic wishful thinking."

"What do you mean?"

"Gaby is not going to accept Jordan, and I will not give her the opportunity to mistreat him. I will not tolerate it, dead or alive."

"Gaby would never do anything to hurt Jordan," he huffed.

"Yeah, right. You told me yourself how her family feels about bloodlines, and my son is not her child—and worse yet, he was the result of an adulterous affair. There is no way she's going accept him."

The discussion turned into a heated argument that continued for months and created enough tension between them that they had to leave it until they had the chance to discuss it with a third party.

"WE HAVE something very important to talk with you about," Breck said as she and Eric sat with Chi and Gena at a quiet restaurant on Boston Harbor. It wouldn't matter if anyone saw them together because they were a group—it could easily have been a business dinner. Martin and Alyce had agreed to baby-sit Sierra and Jordan for the few hours they needed to talk.

"Is something wrong?" Chi asked, leaning forward.

"No, nothing is wrong," Eric said quickly. "What Breck and I would like to discuss with you is who should care for Jordan if something were to happen to Breck."

"Are you sick?" Chi screamed.

"No, I'm not sick," Breck assured her, "but we need to ask you and Gena a very important question."

Chi gasped. "Are you asking us to be Jordan's guardians?" She crossed her fingers.

"We're getting to that," Breck said.

Chi raised her arms and celebrated, reaching over and kissing Gena on the lips.

"We would be honored to," Gena said, speaking up and taking Chi's hand.

"But . . ." Chi settled down and then asked the question that had been burning a hole in Breck and Eric's relationship. "If something happened to Breck, wouldn't you want your son?" She looked directly at Eric, and the look on his face told everyone she had hit a nerve.

Eric looked away as he spoke. "Yes, I would, but Breck doesn't seem to think that would be a good idea."

To keep her name from becoming mud again, Breck jumped in. "This was my idea, because I don't think Gaby will appreciate raising my son."

"Our son," Eric quickly added.

Breck shot him a frustrated glance. "You can't expect to walk into the house and announce that you have a child and have Gaby say, 'Oh, okay.'" She addressed Eric but refused to look at him. "I don't want Jordan to be in a hostile environment, and I certainly do not want him to feel inferior."

"Okay, but what if Gaby does accept it?" Gena interjected. "Would you want Eric to have custody? We need to know this, and it needs to be included in any papers we draw up," she added, bringing her legal prowess into the conversation.

"If it is proven that Jordan will be in a healthy environment, it would be fine with me. I trust your judgment," Breck said, looking at both Chi and Gena.

"Trusting our judgment is one thing, but precise instructions need to be included as to what is considered a healthy environment, because it could vary from person to person," Gena replied.

"Basically, if the woman locks my child in the basement whenever Eric is away, that does not constitute a healthy environment," Breck quickly countered.

"Give me a break." Eric slammed his hand on the table, shaking the glasses. "No one is going to lock Jordan in the basement. That is absurd."

"No one would have ever thought that you would have an affair either, but it happened. Things happen," Breck snapped, and immediately regretted it.

There was a sudden hush over the table. Eric leaned back in his chair and said nothing.

"I'm sorry," Breck apologized. "That was uncalled for."

"No, it was necessary, because facing the unthinkable now prevents distress later on." Gena was an ingenious mediator, and Breck was grateful to have her there. "These are real feelings and real situations. Eric . . ." She turned to face him. "You may want to take Jordan. It is the right thing to do, but it may not be the best thing to do. Gaby may not accept him." Then she turned to face Breck. "Breck, how do you really feel about Jordan living with Eric and Gaby if she does accept him?"

"Frightened." She paused and took a deep breath. "Frightened that Jordan would be made into a stepchild and displaced. With you guys, I know that will not happen." She turned to face Eric. "I'm sorry, but that's how I feel." Eric stood up, shoved his chair violently aside, and walked out of the restaurant, leaving everyone staring at the back of his head.

"Shit," Breck said as she dropped her head into her hand. After a few minutes she walked outside to join him. When she reached the parking lot, she saw him sitting in the car, his seat reclined as he stared out the window. She knocked on the glass, getting his attention. When she heard the doors unlock, she opened the door and got in.

They sat in the car, Breck trying to think of something to say to cut the tension. She couldn't, so she did the next best thing. She took his hand and squeezed it.

"I have two sons who I love very much," Eric said, breaking the silence. He was always braver than she was. "I would like very much for them to grow up knowing each other."

"That can't happen, Eric."

"I know it can't happen, but it doesn't mean I can't want it." He turned to face her. "As much as it hurts me to say it, you're right."

Breck looked into his eyes and saw a tear. He loved Jordan as much as any father could love his son, and he was trying hard to live up to his promise of helping her to raise him. She couldn't possibly ask more of him.

TWENTY-TWO

AFTER JORDAN'S first birthday, Eric took him for the first of many overnight weekend trips.

"Men Only," Eric called these trips, and Jordan stepped around the house reciting, "Me Onny." The first Men Only was a simple visit to the zoo, followed by a dinner of chicken nuggets, French fries, and chocolate ice cream. They spent the night in a suite in Boston, watching the Cartoon Network until Jordan fell asleep. Eric called Breck to give a status report and to recap highlights of the day's adventure. Breck loved to listen to these stories and didn't feel at all left out. Whenever there was a Men Only, she spent the weekend with Chi, Gena, and Sierra, or she stayed home alone and enjoyed a luxury she used to take for granted—silence.

From the start, Jordan accompanied Breck to the monthly sleepovers at the Boys and Girls Club, and Eric always seemed to take over from there. He seemed completely unconcerned with what anyone thought of him fathering Jordan or of his relationship with Breck. Jordan went wherever he went, and when he was old enough to sit up on his own he rolled the basketball along the gym floor while his father played. At lights-out Jordan slept in his own sleeping bag between Breck and Eric.

One night, while the two most important men in her life slept close to her, Breck looked at both of them. Their three bodies formed a triangle. Breck giggled softly. It was such an appropriate symbol for them.

The resemblance between Eric and Jordan was unmistakable, so it would have been useless for them to deny it. Breck often wondered why Gaby never "just appeared" at the club. She could so easily show up unannounced, like she did at the coffeehouse, and all she would have to do was take one look at Jordan and her curiosity would be satisfied. But Gaby never showed. Did she really hate Mansfield that much? Or did she not want to seek the truth for fear of finding it? Some women were like that. Some women knew when their men had affairs but decided to handle it by ignoring it and hoping that it would go away, like a cold. Breck wondered if she would have done the same thing.

"Hey." She was startled out of her thoughts. Eric was looking across at her. "You're not asleep."

Breck smiled. "I was just thinking." She snuggled in the sleeping bag.

"About what?"

After giving it a private thought, she decided to give him a glimpse of what was on her mind. "Do you think you will ever be able to bring Darius?"

Eric blinked several times before he answered her. "I've tried."

Breck was surprised. She hadn't realized that he still wanted to.

"She refused to accept this world, this part of me. According to her, it's not cultured enough, so she doesn't want Darius to be influenced by it."

"But you can be very persuasive if you want to be."

"In the past I could have, but now I will not. I don't want to hurt him. Darius is seven years old and very bright. He will see the resemblance in Jordan and question it. I will not flat-out lie to one son about another."

"Does he ever ask to come?" Breck asked.

"Gaby has pretty much convinced him that it's a part of my work, so he thinks I'm going to work."

Breck shifted in her sleeping bag. "It doesn't seem fair," she said. "You love this place and he would love it too."

"I know, but don't worry. Darius and I have special things we do together. He's my buddy." Eric smiled, seeing it comforted but also puzzled her.

"I don't worry, but I know your heart is here. You've managed to live two independent lives. I think I know you well enough to doubt that you approach the friends you share with Gaby the same way you approach Martin and Brian. If you are the same with them as you are here, then you are a hell of a lot better than I give you credit for."

Eric stared at her until she closed her eyes and fell asleep.

ERIC'S ROUTINE had always remained the same: one dinner a week and two overnight stays a month. One of those nights was reserved for male bonding. Most if not all of the telephone calls were made from his office before he left for the day. When he could, he called to say good night to Jordan, but those calls were sporadic because he couldn't always get free before Jordan went to sleep. If he couldn't call before Breck put Jordan to bed, he called much later, when everyone in his house had fallen asleep. He would tell Breck, "Makes sure he knows I love him."

With the house to herself when Eric had Jordan, she took advantage of the break and strolled with her dust rag in one hand and a can of Old English furniture polish in the other. With her schedule, she managed to keep the house surface-cleaned, but once a month she took it a step farther. She put on her favorite work shirt and old sweatpants and began cleaning corners, dusting ceiling fans, shining the hardwood floors, and spot-cleaning the carpet. The old, white, oversized button-down shirt used to be her father's. Breck had helped herself to it before she left for college and it became her most comfortable attire for studying and cleaning.

The now dirty rag accumulated dust like a magnet. Breck stood on top of a small stepladder in the family room and dusted the ceiling fan. When the phone rang she contemplated stepping off to answer it, then waved it off and let it go to voice mail.

After three rings the phone stopped. Breck knew whoever called was speaking to her voice mail, but within seconds the phone rang again. This time she was alarmed. It could be Eric trying to reach her, or Chi.

She stepped off the ladder and rushed to the phone. "Hello," she said hurriedly.

"Hello?" It was a soft, questioning voice, a woman's. Breck didn't recognize it as Chi or Alyce. Gena hardly ever called her.

"Yes?" Breck asked, annoyed that she'd stopped cleaning for a wrong number or a telemarketer.

"To whom am I speaking?" the woman asked.

Annoyed, Breck sighed deeply. "Who did you call?"

Without saying anything further, the woman slammed down the phone. Breck stared at the phone as the disconnected line buzzed in her ear.

"Ugh," she huffed, then threw the phone back on the table. She looked at the fan and adjusted her scarf to make sure dust couldn't get into her hair.

Four times throughout the weekend she rushed to the phone, only to have it slammed in her ear afterward. She wished whoever it was would get the correct number and leave her alone. Breck suspected it was the same confused woman. She eliminated Gaby from her suspicions because the woman did not seem to have an accent.

Eric and Jordan returned home Sunday afternoon, and Eric was in no hurry to leave, which pleased her.

After an hour of playtime in the family room, Jordan lay down for a nap. The moment his head touched the pillow, Breck and Eric rushed into her room and fell onto the bed. He wriggled her out of her jeans and laughed when they gathered at her ankles and wouldn't get free.

She had lost all of the thirty pounds she'd gained during pregnancy, thanks to her running. She couldn't run in the mornings any longer, so she and Chi gave up lunch and took to the Mansfield streets in their jogging shoes and shorts. The stretch marks remained, as well as more rounded breasts, which Eric liked a lot.

They finally managed to free her legs, and Eric tossed the jeans to the other side of the room and then did the same with his. He lowered himself onto the bed and slid between her open legs. They rolled together on the bed, loving each other until they were both short of breath. Eric kept her close to him.

"Oh, I missed you," he said, and pulled her to his lips and kissed her forehead.

"I missed you too." Breck took a deep breath as she buried her face in his chest. She closed her eyes as she listened to his heartbeat. She remained there, content, until the phone rang .

"Ugh," Breck grumbled. "Damn phone."

"Do you want to answer it?"

"No, some idiot keeps calling and hanging up," she said, making herself comfortable again.

"They'll eventually stop." They lay in the bed and talked for a few minutes longer before Eric pushed her gently to the side and went into the bathroom to wash up.

"You're not staying?" she asked, pulling the thin sheet over her as she watched his reflection in the mirror.

"No, not today. I have some work I have to get to." He walked back into the bedroom and began to dress.

"Oh." She looked down at the mattress to hide her disappointment.

"Are you okay?" He sat down on the bed in front of her and touched her arm.

Breck nodded. "Yeah, I'm fine. I just thought you were staying the night."

"I would, but I have to get home."

Breck rose from the bed and slipped into her housecoat. He took her by the hand and walked her downstairs. He stopped at Jordan's room and kissed him softly on the cheek. Breck stood in the doorway and watched him.

"Will he sleep all night?" He reached for the shoes he had left in the sitting room and slipped them on his feet.

"I'm going to wake him for dinner in a few minutes." Breck walked him to the door with her arms wrapped around him; they stopped and kissed before he opened it. This was always the hardest part of his visits.

"I'll call you tomorrow, okay?" Breck nodded, accepting that he had to leave but still not liking it. She pouted. "Love you," he said. He kissed her forehead and left.

Breck walked back into the house to prepare dinner. She wasn't ready for him to leave. She wanted more adult company tonight. After a weekend of solitude, she looked forward to curling up with Eric on the floor in front of the fireplace and falling asleep in his arms. She stopped at the refrigerator, but nothing looked appealing. She walked to the wall phone near the back door and pressed the speed dial for Chi.

"Hello." It was Gena.

"Hi, Gena," she said. She knew her voice had to sound pathetic—it sounded that way even to her.

"Oh, hi, Breck. What's up?"

"What are you guys doing tonight?" she asked, twisting the cord around her fingers.

"Hmm, we really didn't have any plans. Just bumming around the house."

"Mind if Jordan and I come over? I feel like getting out."

"Of course we don't mind. We can throw something on the grill and let the kids play in the backyard."

"Cool. I'll bring something. We'll be there in about an hour." Breck hung up and then rushed to her room to take a shower.

Chi met her and Jordan at the door. While Breck opened the back hatch of her car to get the food, Chi opened the back door and took Jordan from his car seat. Holding his tiny hand, she led him into the house.

"What's up with you?" Chi asked as they walked inside.

"What do you mean?" They followed Jordan to the kitchen and watched him slide the door open and step onto the deck, where Gena helped him down the stairs. Breck opened the plastic grocery bag full of hot dogs, chips, pork chops, salmon fillets, and broccoli. "You have any wine?" she asked, transferring the food from the bag to the counter.

Chi nodded and took a bottle of white wine from the refrigerator. "I know you," Chi said. "Something's up."

"I just didn't feel like being alone tonight, that's all," Breck said. She peeked out the glass doors and watched as Gena stirred the hot coals in the grill. Chi handed Breck a glass of wine. They both stood at the glass and watched the kids play. Gena waved at her. She waved back and sipped some wine.

"Is it different?" Breck asked, her arms folded across her chest as she leaned against the wall, looking out. "Is it different being in a lesbian relationship?"

Chi drew back and squinted at her. "Different how?"

Breck shrugged, unsure why she had asked. "Have you ever dated a man seriously?"

"My one and only true boyfriend was when I was in high school. I thought I liked him a lot and he was really excited that his sister and I had become such close friends. I ended up spending a lot of time with his sister, Jaqi."

"And?"

"Needless to say," Chi went on, "Jaqi and I discovered at the same time that we were attracted to each other more than we probably should have been. She was the first woman I was with and when we broke the news to her brother, it damn near killed him. He hated Jaqi and me for a long time. I couldn't see her anymore after that, but I knew it wasn't just a phase I was going through. I never truly wanted to be with a man."

"Have you ever felt lonely?"

"I used to feel lonely a lot. I was searching for something and not sure I could get it from a woman. I used to date a lot, as you very well know." She looked toward Gena. "I don't feel that way anymore."

Breck concluded that the feeling was mutual. She walked over to the stool at the island and put down her glass. "I get lonely." She sighed.

"I figured you would." Chi sat on the stool opposite her. "Have you talked to Eric yet?"

Breck shook her head. "When we're together everything is fine and I don't think about it. When we're apart, I miss him tremendously."

"That's natural. I would think something was wrong with you if you didn't feel that way."

Thinking this way always made Breck feel selfish and ungrateful because Eric did more than most absent fathers.

"Do you think Eric will ever leave Gaby?" Chi asked, and Breck shook her head. "Why not?" Chi asked.

"Because he loves his family."

"Then what does he have with you?"

Breck didn't answer, only took another sip.

"I think Eric loves you more than you give him credit for," Chi said. "He may think that this is all you want from him. If you don't tell him you want more, then he'll never know."

Gena walked in. "Oh, great. You guys get to drink while I watch the food and the kids." She picked up the packages and dumped the hot dogs in a pan to take outside. "The least you drunks could do is come outside and fill me in on the gossip." She nudged Breck on the arm while she kissed Chi.

"Breck is questioning her future with Eric." Chi summed up the conversation with that simple statement.

"What took you so long?" Gena said, sipping her wine and sitting down on a stool beside Chi.

"Not you too," Breck huffed.

Gena threw up her arms and said, "Hey, if you're happy, I'm happy. I'm not going to judge your relationship with Eric, *but*, it is what it is, and as long as there isn't a reason for him to change the situation, he's not going to."

"I never asked for anything more," Breck said.

"Maybe you should."

They ate dinner on the deck and watched the children play on the jungle gym. Sierra was very protective of Jordan, referring to him as her little brother. It was fun to watch her help him around the wooden gym and stand behind him to make sure he didn't fall. As the sun began to drop behind the trees, Breck and Jordan headed for home. Jordan fell asleep in the car, and Breck carried him into the house and put him into his bed before retiring to her room. She played a classical CD while she prepared for work the next morning. She paused when

she came across the afghan, the first of many gifts Eric
had showered on her. Hell, even the house was a gift.
Was this his way of making up for his absence? Breck
wondered. She had never thought Eric had tried to buy
her, but he knew he couldn't give her more of himself, so
he gave her more things.

Breck wrapped the afghan around her, lay flat on
the bed, and stared up at the ceiling. Despite being surrounded by Eric's presents, remnants of his thoughts,
she felt lonelier at that moment than she had ever felt in
her life.

SHE HATED mornings like this. She had slept through
the alarm but was awakened by a dream. Sitting up in
bed, she looked over at the clock on the nightstand,
moving the baby monitor out of her way. She cursed. It
was ten after eight.

"Shit." She threw off the sheet. The moment her feet
hit the floor, her head exploded. It was one of those
pounding headaches she got when she awoke suddenly
from a deep sleep. Squinting through the pain and holding her head, she stumbled to the bathroom and grabbed
the aspirin bottle from the medicine cabinet. Once she
took the pills, she brushed her teeth and then pulled her
sleep shirt over her head as she stepped in front of the
bathroom mirror. She washed her face quickly and then
dressed in the white cotton tunic and khaki stretch pants
she had laid out just hours before. Once she was satisfied with her appearance, she rushed downstairs to wake
Jordan.

She helped him brush the few teeth he had and dressed
him. They rushed downstairs, where Breck grabbed her
design bag and held on to Jordan's hand as they headed
out the door. He usually ate breakfast at Alyce's house if
he hadn't already eaten at home. In fact, Alyce always

encouraged her to wait so that he could eat with her children before they left for school.

She secured his tiny body in the car seat before she opened her door and jumped in. At Eric's urging Breck had finally traded in her car for a Land Rover. He felt it was safer for the baby to have a bigger car. The moment she pulled away from the curb, she knew something was wrong. She stopped the SUV and put it in park again while she jumped out with the engine still running. She walked around the vehicle and she saw the flat tire.

"Damn!" she yelled, and put her hands on her hips, shaking her head in disbelief. She jumped back into the SUV and returned it to the curb, then turned off the engine and walked to the back to get the spare tire and the iron rod.

It took her five tries at loosening the lug nuts to accept that she was not going to be able to change her own tire. She took out her cell phone and called Martin.

"Hello." It was Alyce's soft but alert voice.

"Hi, Alyce. It's me, Breck. Is Martin home?"

"You're late."

"I know," she said, shaking her head. "I have a flat."

"Hold on," Alyce said. Breck heard voices before Martin finally came to the phone.

"Having problems this morning?" Martin said. His good nature always cheered Breck up.

"Yes, can you help me?" Breck whined into the phone.

Martin laughed. "I tell you, there are just two times when a woman needs a man. When she wants something put in and when she wants something taken off."

"Martin!" Breck squealed.

"Yeah, yeah, yeah," he said. "Brian is with me. We'll stop by on our way to work."

Breck sighed. "Thanks, Martin." She flipped the

phone shut and reached for Jordan. They walked back into the house to wait.

It didn't take long for the two to arrive at Breck's house. While Martin proceeded to finish what Breck had started, Brian rang her doorbell to let her know that they were there. She walked out to the Land Rover with him and watched.

"Looks like you ran over a nail," Martin said after he had the tire off. He pointed to the nail embedded in the groove of the tire. "You can have that fixed. After I put your spare on, just take it to the service station on Race Street and tell Allen I sent you. He'll fix it and put it back on for you."

"Okay," Breck said, nodding. "I really appreciate this."

"Don't worry about it." Brian lifted the damaged tire and put it into the back of Breck's SUV.

"Make sure you take care of that this morning. You don't want to drive around on this donut with the baby in there," Martin said, rolling the thin, small tire to the other side of her truck.

Breck nodded, feeling like she had just gotten a lecture from her father.

"How have you been, gorgeous?" Brian asked, returning to stand beside her and giving her a quick hug. Breck smiled at him. Thanks to Gaby, she and Brian had no prohibitions about being friends, and he never pressured her about her relationship with Eric. She appreciated him more for that.

"Pretty good. No complaints." She nodded, folding her arms across her chest.

"Business going okay?"

Breck nodded again. "You haven't called me in a while," she said. "New girlfriend?" She nudged his arm playfully.

Brian grinned. "Was, but she dumped me."

"What's up with that, Brian?" Breck said. "Why can't a terrific guy like you seem to keep a girlfriend?"

"Well, hell. You dumped me for a married guy."

Ouch. Breck flinched and covered her face.

"Sorry about that," he said, rubbing her arm. "Eric's a good man."

Breck nodded and straightened up. Martin busied himself tightening the temporary tire and checking the other tires; he wasn't paying any attention to their conversation.

"Do you have any plans for this weekend?" Brian suddenly asked. The question caught Breck off guard and she turned to look at him. "I have two tickets to the Kirk Whalum, Rick Braun, and Boney James concert in New York City. Would you like to go?"

"That concert sold out within hours!" Breck screamed. "How did you get tickets?" She and Chi had tried to get tickets the day they went on sale but couldn't.

Brian beamed. "I know people."

Breck wondered whether she should accept his offer. On the one hand, she and Brian had become friends and he was safe because he knew about her relationship with Eric. But on the other hand, she didn't want to take advantage of his friendship.

Brian stepped forward, and she held her breath as he whispered in her ear, "What goes on between you and Eric is your business, and I'm not trying to come between that. I just have an extra ticket and I didn't want to go alone. That's it."

Breck exhaled, and her respect for Brian increased tenfold. "I would love to go with you," she finally said, feeling reassured that Brian was a good person to have in her corner even though she couldn't offer him more of her heart.

"Good," he said. "I'll call you with details."

After Martin and Brian left, Breck dropped Jordan off

with Alyce, took the tire to be fixed and changed, then headed to work. It was eleven o'clock by the time she strolled into the office and recounted the morning's activities to Chi.

Because she had arrived late, it was well after six o'clock before she was able to leave the office. Everyone else had left. When she left, she rushed to pick up Jordan. She hated the idea of imposing on Alyce. Madison was in half-day kindergarten now, but Alyce made no mention of returning to work. Breck figured she had settled into her life at home. Whenever Jordan stayed late, Breck made sure she paid Alyce for the overtime, even though she never asked for it.

She hadn't talked with Eric the entire day, but she was too busy to dwell on him and the headache that had nagged at her all day. After she and Jordan arrived home, she fixed a small soup-and-salad dinner before putting him into the bathtub. They played their usual water games before she hoisted him from the tub and into his favorite pair of pajamas. She read him the selected Dr. Seuss book of the night, and before she turned the last page he was asleep.

Groggily, she walked the flight of stairs to her bedroom and fell on top of the bed. Now she thought about Eric. It wasn't like him to not call at least once. Something must be wrong. She showered quickly, not wanting to miss his call. When she stepped from the shower, she picked up the telephone to check her voice mail, but the phone just buzzed.

She sighed and slid under the covers of her bed. She looked at her novel on the nightstand and decided against picking it up. She was in no mood to read tonight. She checked the alarm, making sure it was turned on this time, then turned off the lamp and went to sleep.

She awoke the next morning feeling optimistic. She

and Chi went for their usual lunchtime run, and while they jogged around the block, she told Chi about her impending date with Brian.

"This is a good thing," Chi said between breaths. Chi hadn't been running for as long as Breck, but she managed to keep up well. Breck slowed to accommodate her, but she didn't lose out on the feeling of having a good run.

"Don't get the wrong idea, Chi. We're just going to the concert. Nothing more."

"I know, but Brian is such a cutey, and he's available."

Breck laughed and waved her off as they rounded the corner, pumping their arms. The last quarter mile they tried to run harder, with Breck sometimes pulling out in front, but not by much. Now she stopped at the coffeehouse and waited for Chi to catch up. She only had to wait a few minutes. "Water?" she asked, opening the door of the coffeehouse. Chi nodded and they stepped into the room. Breck got them two bottled waters and fruit salads from the cooler, while Chi took a seat at one of the booths.

"Now, back to Brian," Chi said, twisting the cap off her water and taking a big drink.

"Don't get your hopes up about that. We're friends."

"Is Brian seeing room for opportunity here?"

"I doubt he would take it if he did. And what's with you? I thought you liked Eric."

"I do like Eric, but I also want to see you happy. I don't see you happy in the long run in this relationship." After they finished their salads, they returned upstairs, washed up, and changed back into their work clothes. David was still at lunch, but Marla was minding the phones.

Later that afternoon, Breck and Marla were finally able to get together to go over some designs. These days David took care of any projects that required travel. All the women in the office were now mothers and wanted to stay put. David was single and young, and the idea of flying all over the country at the company's expense seemed like fun to him. While they reviewed the sketches, Breck's phone beeped twice, her personal signal that it was an outside call. The digital display told her the call was from Eric's office number.

"Excuse me," she said as she reached down to answer the phone. "Hello," she said, a huge grin on her face.

"Hi, honey. How are you?"

"Good. One second," she covered the mouthpiece with her hand and turned toward Marla. "Can we continue in a minute?" Marla nodded and walked out of the office, closing the door behind her.

"I'm back," she said. "I missed you yesterday."

"I know. I was busy. We can do something tonight."

"Okay." She paused. "I hope you didn't make any plans for us this weekend. Brian invited me to go to the Kirk Whalum concert with him in New York."

Eric was so quiet she couldn't even hear him breathe.

"You're going to the concert with Brian?" he finally asked.

"Yes. Can you get a ticket and go with us?"

"I . . . I already have a ticket," he stuttered. "Gaby and I are going."

Breck's heart dropped into her stomach. "How long have you had tickets?"

"Since they went on sale."

"Oh." She swallowed. "Why didn't you ask me if I wanted to go?"

"Because Gaby said that she wanted to go."

"Oh, I see." Breck sat back in her chair and shook her head.

"How did you end up going to the concert with Brian?"

"He and Martin came over yesterday morning to fix my tire, and he asked me."

"What was wrong with your tire?" he asked.

"I had a flat. Why didn't you tell me you were going to the concert?"

"I didn't think it was important."

"How often do you and Gaby do things like this?"

"We've always done things like this, but I told you that."

Breck took a deep breath but didn't say anything. It was easy for her to think that Gaby and Eric were not involved in each other's lives. That way she could justify Eric's spending time with her. But now she was jealous. Eric and Gaby did have a regular marriage and did things that married people normally do. But Gaby was such a pesky woman. What on earth did he see in her?

She shook her head. Stop it, Breck. You can't compare Gaby to you. None of this is new information. He's had a marriage all along. You're the one who chose to ignore it. "You'll be gone for the whole weekend?" she asked.

"Yes. We'll be back Sunday night."

"And when were you going to tell me this?" She couldn't let it go. For some reason she felt betrayed. Eric hadn't even considered asking her to the concert. He could have arranged for all of them to go together. Hell, Gaby wouldn't have known what was going on. Oh, that's even more fucked-up, Breck, she thought, smacking herself on the forehead for even thinking it.

"I wasn't."

"Why not?" she asked, her voice raised.

"Why would you want to know?" Her heart beat harder and her breath became more erratic. Nothing he said pleased her, and she felt more and more like she was being disregarded. It didn't matter that nothing about what was happening in that moment was different from anything that had happened in their relationship the past three years. But for some reason, at that moment it made her mad.

"I think I should know exactly where I stand in your life. Why didn't you call me last night?"

"What is the problem, Breck?"

"Why didn't you call me last night?" she repeated. "You always call."

He sighed heavily. "Gaby and I spent the evening together. I got home late."

"Did you make love?" She held her breath while she waited for him to reply.

"Yes."

Breck hung up and hid her face in her hands. Why the hell did she ask that question? She knew better. She already knew Gaby was a bit cynical and irritating, and she had hoped that that carried over into their bedroom, diminishing Eric's desire to make love to her. But that theory had just been shredded. The illusions of Eric's marriage were easier to accept than the truth.

Her mind went back to Chi's advice. She should have told Eric how she felt, that she wanted more of a relationship. Three years ago it didn't matter. She was twenty-six years old and her business was flying high. She loved her life, being in love, and most of all, she loved her freedom. When did that change? Was it when she had Jordan? Having him ensured that she wouldn't be alone when Eric was with his family, but it also made her realize how empty her life really was.

Breck shook off the hurt and focused on her work. Work had always been the cure when life got to be too much. She picked up her phone and punched in Marla's extension. "You can come back in when you're ready," she said, and began flipping through the designs again.

BRIAN CALLED her Wednesday night with details for the trip. Considering the concert would last well into the night, they made plans to stay in New York for the evening. Brian took the liberty of making reservations for them. Breck giggled when he told her they would be staying in separate rooms.

"What's so funny?" he asked.

"Nothing, just something Chi said. Brian, are you aware that Eric will be in New York with his wife?"

"He called and told me Tuesday evening."

"Why did he call you?"

"He told me where he and Gaby would be staying so we can avoid running into each other."

"Was this his idea?" Her temper began to flare.

"Yes, it was, and I agreed. There's no need to cause unnecessary bullshit." That calmed her a bit.

Breck leaned back on the sofa. Even while they argued, Eric continued to think logically. As much as Breck hated to admit it, there were times when she had wished Gaby would find out more about them. That would possibly take the choice out of Eric's hands, and once and for all Breck would know where she stood with him. She would either live happily ever after with Eric or be free to move on.

But she was already free. Eric had never tried to tie her down or make her feel she couldn't terminate the relationship. He knew he had no rights to her. She was free to walk anytime she wanted to, and there was nothing he could do about it. Even that thought upset her. Why didn't he fight to keep her? Wouldn't a man fight for the woman he loved? Maybe that was what she wanted to know, that Eric would fight for her.

"Breck, you still there?" Brian asked, snapping her out of her musings.

"Yeah," she said softly.

"Listen, what goes down with you and Eric is your business. He's my friend and I love him, but I'm going to say this to you because I like you and I think you are a good person." He took a deep breath. "Eric and Gaby have a good thing going on over there. Sure, it could use some work, but they love each other. I can't see Eric leaving. I could be wrong, but he loves his wife and his son and he's committed to their marriage. I'm just as surprised as everyone else that he got involved with you. No offense to you, but I think you happened into his life when the differences between him and Gaby were at their peak. I think they are working through it."

Tears began to fill her eyes again. Brian had only reiterated what her mother had been warning her about for years. If she forced Eric to choose, he wouldn't choose her, but this too was nothing new. She'd said it herself years ago. The only difference now was that she wanted him to choose her.

"Are you okay?" Brian asked.

"Yeah, I'm fine," she said between sobs. She wiped the hot tears from her face.

"Do you want to cancel the New York trip?"

Breck shook her head. "No, I want to go," she said, even though she doubted she would enjoy herself.

After she hung up the phone, she lay flat on the sofa and continued to cry. Her worst fear had become a reality. Eric was easing out of her life, and there wasn't anything she could do about it. She couldn't stop him from choosing to be with his wife. She stood up and climbed the flight of stairs to Jordan's room. From his doorway she watched his breathing as he slept.

What would happen to Jordan if she and Eric broke up? Would Eric remain in his life? She turned to walk down the stairs but paused halfway when the doorbell rang. On the bottom floor she looked up and saw Eric standing on the other side of the door. She stood still and stared at him before she walked to the door to let him in. She inched the door open and then turned and walked away.

"I see you're still angry," he said, standing over her. He shoved his hands into his jeans pockets and leaned against the wall while Breck took a seat on the sofa and picked up a magazine to keep her hands occupied and her eyes on something other than him.

"I never said I was angry." Breck waved through the pages without even bothering to look at the words.

"You don't have to." He took his hands from his pockets and sat down in the chair opposite her.

"I see you called Brian to give him instructions," she said.

Eric leaned forward. "Not instructions. Just a heads-up."

"Why?" She stopped turning the pages and looked directly at him.

"I don't want anyone to get hurt."

"Does Gaby still suspect that we're having an affair?"

He shrugged. "No, but that's one of the reasons I've been spending more time at home."

Breck frowned. "That's a contradictory statement."

"How so?"

"Because you said that she doesn't suspect, yet you're spending more time at home because she may suspect. That's a contradiction." Eric sighed. "If you don't want to be with me anymore, just tell me," she said, tossing the magazine on the table.

"That's not what I want."

"Then I don't understand what's happening." She stood up, unable to sit any longer. "Things are changing."

"Things like what?"

"I don't know. It just seems that things are changing." She knew exactly what was changing but didn't know how to put it into words. How could she tell him *she* was changing?

"Is it because you want to date other people?"

Breck squinted. "I never said I wanted to date other people."

"You have a date with Brian."

"It's not a date."

"Then what is it?" He got up and walked toward her.

"He asked me to the concert as a friend, and I said yes. It's not a date."

"Oh, please, Breck. You know how Brian feels about you." He put his hands on his hips.

"You're jealous that I'm going out with Brian, but you admit to making love to your wife?"

"That's different."

"Oh, I forgot. You're married and I'm not. That makes everything okay." She rolled her eyes.

Eric shook his head and slumped down on the sofa. "We had this conversation a long time ago, and I really don't want to have it again. You know how I feel about you dating someone else. I can't stop you but I don't like it."

"Why can't you stop me?" she blurted. "Why can't you fight for me if you want me so badly?"

"What the hell are you talking about?"

Breck put her hands on her hips and turned away from him. "I don't consider this a date," she said, "and I don't know how much longer I can be in a relationship with someone who can't fight for me." Tears burned her eyes as she spoke.

She heard him breathe in deeply and exhale loudly before the room became deathly still and quiet. "Am I about to lose you?" he finally asked in almost a whimper.

"I don't know," she said, and wiped a tear from her eye. Eric stood up and took her in his arms. He turned her to face him and then kissed her until she responded and kissed him back. They walked to the sofa and lay down together, his arms wrapped tightly around her, her legs entwined with his. When he had to leave, he held her hand as he walked to the door and kissed her hard before he said good night.

TWENTY-THREE

THE SMOOTH sounds of jazz resounded throughout Radio City Music Hall in Manhattan. As much as Breck tried to focus on the music, she found it hard not to look around and try to spot Eric and Gaby in the crowd. She never found them and that was probably a good thing. The concert lasted three glorious hours, with an improvisational encore that went an additional thirty minutes. The crowd couldn't get enough of the talented trio.

After the concert, Breck and Brian walked around Manhattan toward Times Square, reveling in the bright marquee scrolling across the tall buildings. They dashed down a side street to an obscure restaurant in hopes of getting a quick drink before heading back to the hotel, but the host informed them that even at this late hour it would be two hours before they could be seated.

Occasionally during the concert Breck had glanced at Brian and admired how handsome he was. If things were different, she would have pursued him, she was sure of it. The opportunity might still be available for her to do so. Brian had never made an advance toward her, but if she and Eric did break up, Brian would be an excellent boyfriend. With Brian, Breck could have everything she couldn't have with Eric. He would be available. He could spend time with her and Jordan without having to rush off. Breck felt he would be totally devoted to her if she gave him the opportunity. All she had to do was be open to the possibility and she was sure

Brian would react to it. Eric was right: Breck did know that Brian continued to be interested in her, but when they went out Breck was careful not to give him false hope. Now, with things changing between her and Eric, maybe she should consider giving Brian a chance.

"How about a nightcap at the hotel instead?" Brian asked, breaking into her daydream.

Breck agreed and entwined her arm around his as they left the restaurant. Brian hailed a cab and they went straight back to the hotel.

"You want to sit in the bar?" Brian asked.

Breck shook her head. "Not really. I feel like kicking off my shoes and taking these clothes off. Let's go to my room."

They took the elevator to the fifth floor, Breck wondering what she would do once they stepped into her room. Would she seduce him? If she did, she knew there would be no turning back. She wouldn't be able to go back to Eric and tell him that she had slept with one of his best friends and expect him to accept it. It would tear apart her relationship with Eric and possibly Eric's friendship with Brian, if Eric chose to react harshly about it.

Outside Breck's room she took her key card from her clutch purse and unlocked the door. She stepped inside the lavishly decorated room with Brian following closely behind her. She tossed her purse onto the dresser and reached down and slid her shoes off, then threw herself on top of the bed, on her back, bouncing softly.

"Tired?" Brian asked, taking a seat at the desk opposite her bed.

"A little." She took a deep breath, her breasts falling flat as she exhaled. She rolled onto her side and rested her head in her hand. "Thank you for inviting me. I had a good time."

"Really?" Brian said, sitting back in the chair and crossing his legs. "No thoughts of you-know-who?"

"Maybe one or two. But I'm okay."

"Good." Brian nodded. "Still up for that drink?"

"Yep," Breck said, bouncing off the bed and heading for the bathroom.

"What would you like?" Brian asked, standing up and walking toward the door.

"Doesn't matter."

"Okay, I'll be right back."

"Take the key with you," Breck said. "I'm stepping into the shower." She grabbed her housecoat from the hanger, walked into the bathroom, and closed the door. She eagerly stepped out of the long, black, fitted skirt and pulled the spaghetti-strap shirt over her head. She unsnapped her strapless bra and let it fall to the floor before she turned on the faucet, tested the water, and stepped in.

"Umm." She sighed and let the water stream against her face and body. She had the massager on full-blast, and the water pelted her shoulders and neck. Her mind went to Eric, somewhere in the same city. As she lathered up, she wondered if he and Gaby had made it back to their hotel room or were out enjoying themselves. She should have stayed out longer with Brian instead of coming back to the room to pout. There were too many things to do in New York. She always loved spending time here, marveling at the bright lights in Times Square, seeing a play, or—Chi's favorite—shopping.

After her shower she dried off and rubbed oil over her body before slipping into the blue silk sleep shirt she'd packed. When she opened the door to the main room, Brian had returned and was sitting on the edge of the chair with a mixed drink in his hand. She glanced at the table and saw two bottles: one of Jack Daniel's and the other a twenty-ounce Coke. Beside them were a glass and a bucket of ice.

"Whoa, you look nice," Brian said, then poured the

mixture over a glass of ice and handed it to her. "Try that."

"Thank you," she said, and took a big gulp, then a deep breath while the whiskey tingled in her throat as it went down. "My good friend Jack." She coughed.

"Figured you might want some hair on your chest tonight," he joked, and then took a drink from his glass.

"Just might." Breck took a quick sip, then sat down on the bed and crossed her oiled legs.

"Feel better?" Brian asked, returning to the chair across the room.

Breck nodded. "I want to know what's up with you and the women in your life. And tell me the truth." He already knew about her life, so it was time for him to spill the beans about his.

"Why are you so interested in the women in my life?"

"Because I don't get it. You are a really nice person, and handsome and successful, but you have rotten luck with women."

Brian laughed. "I don't have rotten luck. I just haven't met the right one yet. It happens all the time."

"And what is the right one?"

"Someone like you."

Breck swallowed hard. "Someone like me? Why?"

"Breck, you're not a bad catch." Brian leaned forward and fixed himself another drink. "I'm going to respect what you have going on with Eric, but I've been sitting back waiting for you guys to break up."

That was her cue to stand up, walk over to him, and plant a big kiss on his lips. Tonight she could take a very proactive step toward having a more normal life and a normal relationship with a really wonderful man. Brian was offering himself, and all she had to do was get off the bed and go to him.

She took a sip of her drink.

After seeing she wasn't going to comment, Brian continued. "Eric is a great guy. I have nothing but love for him, and I can understand why he doesn't want to let you go. But the question I have for you is . . ." He paused. "Is that all you want?"

"Once upon a time it was. Not so much now." She still didn't move from the bed. Her fingers circled the rim of her glass, and her gold bracelet clanged loudly against it. She looked at the shiny bracelet dangling on her wrist—a wonderful reminder of her connection with Eric, much like a wedding or engagement ring would be. Since he'd bought the matching set, she had never seen Eric without his.

Brian nodded. "I'll just wait a little longer then."

THEY LEFT New York early the next morning. Breck didn't say much for the entire ride, though Brian's words remained fresh in her mind. He played continuous jazz on his CD player; he was as much a fan as Breck was, and the selection he'd brought with him was similar to what she had at home. It was interesting to know they had compatible taste in music.

The first stop they made was to Alyce's to pick up Jordan. They didn't stay long; Breck was mentally drained. She felt like she was on an emotional roller coaster, with no end in sight. She promised Alyce a full recap later in the week, and they left for home.

When they reached her house, Brian carried her overnight bag and took Jordan by the hand, walking him up the porch stairs to the door. The scene gave Breck an eerie picture of what life could be like with Brian. She shook off the image and walked ahead of them to unlock the door. Once inside, Jordan ran to his play area while Breck and Brian stood at the door.

"Well, I hope I didn't make you too uncomfortable,"

he said, dropping her bag just inside the door and shoving his hands deep into his pockets.

"No, you didn't. Why do you say that?"

"You were pretty quiet."

"I just have some thinking to do," she said, and reached up and kissed his cheek. "Thanks again for inviting me. I had a good time." He embraced her, and she felt sorry she couldn't give him more. When he finally released her, he stroked the side of her face. "Would I be out of line if I asked if it would be all right to call you sometime? Perhaps dinner and a movie?"

Breck smiled nervously. "No, you wouldn't be out of line, but I need to think about it." She didn't know where her relationship with Eric was going to be a month from now—or tomorrow, for that matter. But she did know for certain that she didn't want to create a rift between Brian and Eric.

Brian bent forward to kiss her softly on the cheek, then turned and left.

Breck joined Jordan in the play area. She picked him up and squeezed him hard. "Did you have fun at Aunt Alyce's house?" She kissed his plump cheeks.

"Yep." He nodded his little head wildly. "We had pizza."

"Ah, pizza. You like pizza."

"Yep," he said, still nodding. "Can I go outside?"

"Sure." Breck put him down on the floor and held his small hand while she walked him through the kitchen. She unlocked the back door and helped him onto the deck and down the stairs. Once his feet touched the last step, he leaped onto the grass, dropped Breck's hand, and ran to the sandbox. Breck sat on the deck and watched him, admiring the prominent features of his tiny face. He was looking more and more like Eric every day. How much of Eric's genes and personality would he inherit? she wondered. Would he have the same confident stride?

And what about his knack for taking charge? And she definitely couldn't forget Eric's cockiness.

Breck hurried into the house and grabbed her sketch pad from her office. She stepped back outside, sat down, and began sketching Jordan as he played silently in his sandbox.

TWENTY-FOUR

BRECK PLACED the overnight bag on the floor near the door. She was about to go upstairs to get the sleeping bags out of the second-floor closet when the doorbell rang. She turned and saw Eric standing on the other side. The door wasn't locked, so she motioned for him to come in while she ran up the stairs.

"Are you on your way to the club?" she yelled from the second floor. She pulled the bags from the shelf and hurried downstairs to join him. She stopped on the last step when she saw the sullen look on his face. "What's wrong?" She placed the sleeping bags on the floor near the door.

Eric took a deep breath before he answered. "Gaby is going to the club."

Breck's heart dropped. She couldn't do anything but stare at him. Then she shook her head, turned on her heel, and walked into the sitting room.

Here we go again, she thought, still shaking her head. After the New York trip she'd brushed aside the conflicting feelings she had about the relationship. Eric had come over the following night; they had made love and both ended up taking the next day off work. They spent most of that time talking and making love until it was time to pick up Jordan from Alyce's. They drove together to fetch him, and when they returned to the house, they had dinner together before Eric left. She had fallen in love with him all over again.

"So you're here to tell me not to go?" She turned around to face him now.

"It's a public place. I can't stop you from going. I'm here to let you know that Gaby will be there."

Breck shook her head and sat down on the sofa. She knew she couldn't go. "Why?" Breck asked. "Four years and not once has she bothered to come. Why all of a sudden now?"

Eric shrugged. "I don't know."

"And how do you feel about it?"

"I don't know."

"Sure you do." Breck stood up and walked toward him. "Are you happy that Gaby is finally willing to share this part of your life with you? This is what you've wanted all along, isn't it?"

Eric was quiet. His hands were jammed inside his pants pockets as he stared down at the floor.

Without even thinking, she swung and slapped him across the chest. "You know damn well there is no way I can go. If she takes one look at Jordan, she will know that he's your son!" she raved as the tears rolled from her eyes.

"What am I supposed to do? I can't tell her she can't go."

"Of course not, because I'm the one who's disposable!" Breck yelled. She paced the foyer, not knowing what to do with her hands. She wanted to hit him again or hit herself for thinking that everything was okay. She tried to blink away the tears, but they fell anyway.

"I think we should . . ." Her voice cracked. "Stop," she finished between sobs. Eric's eyes dropped to the floor. "Your wife is trying to be a part of your life. I'm not going to fight her." Breck felt like someone was squeezing her heart. It had never hurt so badly. Her hand closed around the bracelet she wore on her left wrist. Eric sat quietly, his silence only infuriating her. He wasn't going to fight for her; he was doing exactly what she knew he would do all along. He was going to just let her go.

"I love you, Breck. You have to believe that," he finally said, but he still could not look at her.

"I know you love me, but what good is that when you can't even fight for me or for what we have together? You should go," she said, sobbing. She pulled her knees to her chest and buried her face. She heard his footsteps coming toward her and she rushed from the sofa before he had the chance to touch her. She stood on the other side of the room, her arms wrapped across her body as she tried to hide her face and her tears.

"What do you want from me?" he asked angrily.

"Everything, damn it!" He looked at her wide-eyed. "I've never asked you for anything, and four years ago that was fine with me, but it's not anymore, Eric. We've just been living this one big fucking lie, and I can't take it anymore."

"Breck, I give you everything I have."

"No, you give me what's left over, and damn it, it's not good enough." She wiped her tears. "I've taken a back-seat for four fucking years! Everything is just fucking bullshit, and I'm the biggest fool for putting up with it." Her voice cracked as tears spilled from her eyes.

"You're not a fool," he said, reaching out to her, but she backed away from him.

"Don't touch me. Just go."

"Are you asking me to leave Gaby?"

"No," she replied. "I'm just saying I can't be involved with you any longer if you're married. I can't do this anymore."

He didn't try to touch her again. The next sound she heard was the door closing behind him. She sat down on the sofa, buried her face in her hands, and kept crying. Finally she reached for the phone beside the sofa and called Chi. She had known this day would come, but no matter how much she thought she had prepared for it, nothing can prepare you for a sliced heart.

The phone rang once. "Please be there," she mumbled softly. The phone rang twice. "Please, please, pick up."

"Hello," Chi answered, her voice sounding sleepy. Chi always did sleep late on weekends.

"Eric and I broke up."

"I'll be right there."

TWENTY-FIVE

FOR THREE months Eric tried to talk with her, charm her, and win her back. He'd come close to getting her into bed again, but each time she gathered her nerve to refuse him. She couldn't do it anymore. She couldn't accept what he was offering. She wasn't asking Eric to leave his wife, but the only way she would be with him again was if he did.

When they broke up, Eric had asked if he could come by every Tuesday night to have dinner with Jordan, and Breck had agreed.

She didn't ask how Gaby's night at the club went because she didn't want to know. She even stopped Alyce from telling her. If anything could be said about Gaby, it was that she was a smart woman. She didn't push and she didn't cause waves, but she'd succeeded in winning her husband back.

Once it became apparent that Breck and Eric had split, Chi and Alyce tried to push her toward Brian. Breck wasn't ready to dive into a courtship with Brian or anyone. Even though they were not together, Eric still had a lock on her heart.

Eric came over one Thursday evening, a sign that something was wrong—this was not his usual night. "Where's my bear hug?" he asked Jordan, grabbing him and tickling him as he carried him to the sofa, where the play continued. Jordan laughed heartily, as he always did whenever Eric was around.

"What's up?" Breck asked, interrupting their play.

"Later," he said, and continued to play with Jordan. Jordan's laughter made the house brighter than it had been in the three months since Breck and Eric had been estranged. Breck grabbed a book and walked outside to sit on the front-porch swing. She could hear the laughter. It made her feel good that Eric kept his promise and didn't neglect Jordan. It also made her heart long to have him near her permanently.

She read a chapter in her book before the laughter subsided and Eric led Jordan upstairs for his bath. She joined him for that, and after drying Jordan off, Eric wrapped the towel around him and carried him into his room, dressed him in his pajamas, and laid him down for his nightly story. Breck went into the upstairs sitting room and turned on the radio to listen to the nightly jazz on National Public Radio.

Eric strolled in a few minutes later and took a seat in the leather recliner. Breck sat in a love seat pretending to be reading, but she really didn't see a word on the page. "So, what's up?" she asked.

Eric stared at her before he answered. Normally, she would not have minded, but now his stare made her nervous. "Are you happy?" he finally asked.

She matched his stare. "No, are you?" She really didn't know if admitting it would make that much of a difference. They still couldn't do anything about the situation.

"Gaby and I had a fight," he said suddenly. "Before you ask me to leave, I think you should hear what I have to say."

Breck didn't think of asking him to leave. When they broke up, she realized that having him out of her bed didn't mean having him out of her life, since Jordan was a product of their union. Even though he stopped by to see Jordan, she enjoyed having him around. Privately, she ached and usually cried herself to sleep.

"I just need to know, Breck, do you love me?"

She dropped her book on her lap. "Why would you even ask me that? You know I do—"

Before she could finish, he leapt off the recliner and kissed her. Touching his lips again almost brought tears to her eyes, but she fought them and just touched his face. When he pulled away from her, he touched her forehead with his. "I've missed you so much," he said, kissing her again.

"I've missed you too," she said, holding his face.

"I have to tell you something," he said, sliding back from her. "As you know, Gaby went with me to the club." Breck dropped her eyes, and Eric took her hand and squeezed it. "She complained the entire time we were there. She refused to sleep on the floor. We had to get her a cot from the back room, but it was too dusty for her. She complained so miserably that we ended up leaving." He leaned forward with his head dropped as he stared at his open hands. "You made a very good observation. I'm not the same with the friends I share with Gaby. The life I have with you and Jordan and Martin and everyone at the club is the real me."

Breck didn't speak. This was nothing new. She was not the only one who knew that he couldn't be as happy in his life with Gaby as he was when he was in Mansfield. He was good, but he wasn't good enough to fool his closest friends.

"She's not going back and I don't want her to. She embarrassed me so horribly that I just went home and stared at everything I owned in that big-ass house. We have a chef who cooks our meals, we have maids who come every day to clean our toilets and wash our dirty laundry. We have tutors who come an hour a day to read to our son, we have this person and that person . . ." His voice trailed off while his hands waved through the air.

"We would never have a get-together, but we have plenty of dinner parties."

"But that's what you wanted," Breck managed to say. "That is the reason you left Mansfield."

"I thought that was what I wanted. When I left Mansfield, moved my mother away and my sister and brother moved away, I thought I would never go back. I met Gaby and she introduced me to a different life. We had dinner with the governor, and we were regulars on the society pages. We were it. I had arrived." Eric made a fist. "After Gaby and I married, I didn't see Martin and Brian for over a year." He paused. "The old saying: sometimes we return to where we came from so that we can be proud of where we are. I drove through Mansfield one day. Everywhere I looked, I saw vacant buildings, boarded-up homes, and thugs hanging out on the streets. I shook my head in disgust that I had come from there." He paused again, bit his lower lip, then continued. "Then it hit me. I spend millions of dollars developing land and buildings in areas that didn't need my money or my presence. The only thing Mansfield needed was money, and money would create jobs, and jobs would create livelihoods. We left Mansfield because nothing was there but trouble. If I could spend five hundred thousand dollars on a single cottage in Cape Cod, I could spend a fraction of that to rebuild a city block in Mansfield. So I got back in touch with Martin and Brian, and we started buying and building. We literally bought twenty-thousand-square-foot warehouses for fifty thousand dollars and turned them into multimillion-dollar buildings. Mansfield is now flourishing. Those same thugs now run businesses and work at the Boys and Girls Club, and some even own homes.

"I remember one of the guys we sold a house to just broke down and started crying, a young brother with three kids living in a run-down, pest-infested apartment hustling to make a dollar, now owning a house not far from yours. We started a microloan program and gave him a business loan, and he now owns the moving company that moved you into your house. Brother is doing great, and his kids come to the sleepovers every month. All he needed was a job and a chance, but I was too busy being Stephen to see it."

"How did Gaby react to your new vision?"

Eric shook his head. "She flat-out hated it. I had given some thought to following Martin and Brian back to Mansfield, but Gaby wouldn't hear of it. Her life is Boston, dinner parties, exotic travel, and she doesn't want the suburbs or anything that they represent. The more time I spent in Mansfield, the more I wanted to be there. I married a beautiful socialite who had no intention of becoming a Mansfield wife in charge of carpooling and Boys and Girls Club sleepovers. Gaby is Darius's mother and I love her. But I'm not in love with Gaby." He took a breath so deep, Breck felt him exhale on her face.

"What does this mean?" she said, her voice quivering.

"It means I married the wrong woman." He turned to look at her and touched her face.

"Eric, what are you saying?" Was he going to pack his bags and move in? Is that what this was all about? Hell, yes, she would take him. But even as she thought it, she couldn't help but feel low and cruel to the point that she wanted to slap herself. How shallow and self-centered she must be to wish someone else pain so that she could have the pleasure of having him in her life permanently. Eric was losing his family, and all she thought about was whether or not he was coming to her.

He walked closer to her, pulled her into his arms, and kissed her hard. Breck didn't want to let go, but the more she thought of what he was saying the more she felt like she was being ripped apart.

"I hate myself," she said, covering her face.

"Why?"

"Because I want you to be saying what I think you're saying, but I know other people are going to be hurt." She shook her head. "I know that you would want to try to save your marriage because that is the type of man you are and why I fell in love with you."

"I have tried to save it but I can't," he replied. Breck had waited so long for him to say those words. She threw herself into his arms and held on as tightly as she could. Had she finally won? But it wasn't an issue of winning because it had never been a game. She'd loved Eric from the start, and it had always been about that, never about winning.

Her eyes flowed with tears, but this time it was not because the pain was too unbearable. Eric knelt beside her and held her while she buried her face in his shoulder.

"Breck," he said softly. "Breck." He lifted her face to him. She opened her tear-drenched eyes and looked at him. "Will you have me?"

She almost choked as she threw herself into his arms again. That was such a ridiculous question.

He kissed her cheek. "I have to go. I will talk with you soon. I promise." He kissed her dry, chapped lips and wiped the tears from her face before he rose.

"Where are you going?"

"I'm going home. I need to talk to Gaby."

Breck held on to him a little longer and a little more tightly that night, knowing that the next time she saw him he would be hers. Eric was going to fight for her.

THAT NIGHT, Breck slept with Jordan even though he didn't know it. She needed to feel close to Eric, to hear his heartbeat. The closest thing to Eric she had was Jordan. She woke up at her usual time on Friday morning, even without the alarm, and immediately went into the exercise room to get on the treadmill she'd purchased after Jordan was born. She had a difficult time concentrating this morning, and for good reason: Eric was coming to live with her.

After her exercise, she took a quick shower and put on a pair of jeans and a button-down shirt before she trotted downstairs to begin breakfast.

She didn't feel like cooking at a time like this, so she took out a box of plain donuts, diced an apple, poured two glasses of orange juice, then went upstairs to wake Jordan.

Jordan knew the morning routine. With Breck's help, he performed it without question. He got up, brushed his teeth, and then he and Breck wiggled his little body into the clothes she'd set out for him the night before.

Breck was quiet as she watched him eat breakfast. She couldn't eat. She wanted to ask him how would he like it if Daddy came to live with them, but she decided against it. It would be great if they could tell Jordan together. She smiled wider than she had in a long time. She did drink her coffee while she glanced through the newspaper.

After Jordan finished his breakfast, she wiped the crumbs from his face and they left for Alyce's.

Enjoying a quiet ride to the office after dropping Jordan off, Breck allowed her thoughts to return to her conversation with Eric. He was leaving Gaby. He hadn't come right out and said those words, but that was what he meant when he asked her if she would she have him. She pulled into the office parking lot but sat in the car, trying to remember everything Eric had said, word for word. When she finally pulled herself together, she walked into the office humming. She was dazed. She didn't say good morning to anyone, and she didn't notice if anyone said good morning to her. She walked straight into her office and closed the door, something she rarely did.

She placed her sketches on her desk and sat down in her leather swivel chair.

"Are you okay?" Chi asked. She had opened the door slightly and poked her head inside.

Breck waved her in and immediately jumped up and closed the door behind her. "Eric is leaving Gaby."

"What?!" Chi exclaimed, and Breck immediately clamped her hand over her mouth.

"He came over last night and announced he was leaving. He wants to be with Jordan and me."

Chi said down in the chair in front of the desk. "Oh, my God," she said, putting her hand to her mouth as she thought. "I'm happy for you, but . . ."

Breck sighed and folded her hands across her chest. "I know. I had the same thought." She returned to her chair and leaned back. "It's a bittersweet moment, isn't it? My happiness will be at the expense of someone else."

After work Breck picked up Jordan and drove home. She couldn't wait to talk to Eric, but he hadn't called. He was probably at home packing, she thought. She wondered how Gaby would take it. Perhaps she would plead with him to stay and he would agree to give the marriage another try. She wouldn't be able to fault him for that.

"What's happening, Eric?" she said aloud as she sat at her drafting board later that night. When Jordan's bedtime came she had read him a story and, as usual, he was fast asleep before she got to the last page. She had returned the book to the shelf and left the door partly open. When she reached the sitting room, she sat with her legs tucked underneath her and waited for either the phone to ring or Eric to walk through the door with his bags. Neither happened.

Breck fell asleep on the sofa that night. When she woke up, she glanced at the digital clock on the satellite box. It was seven-thirty. She stood up, her body tensed and achy from the odd curves she'd slept in. Stretching and shaking the sleep from her body, she glanced around the house, collecting her thoughts, and realized she still hadn't heard from Eric.

She panicked. What if it had all been a hoax? He could have come over to get her sympathy and to get her back but without any real intention of furthering the relationship. They'd be back where they had started. Breck immediately dismissed that thought. Eric had never played games with her, and there was no reason for him to start now.

She reached for the cordless phone and punched in his cell-phone number. She couldn't be patient any longer. She let it ring several times before giving up. It was Saturday morning, but there was always a chance he would be in the office. There had to be a reason why he hadn't called her.

"Warren and Peterson." The phone was picked up on the first ring, and it was a woman's voice instead of Eric's. Breck paused before she spoke, but she thought she recognized the voice.

"Gloria?"

"Yes?"

Since when did she work on a Saturday? Breck thought. "Gloria, this is Breck. I thought I dialed Eric's direct line."

"You . . . you did, Breck. All of Eric's calls will be forwarded to me or Stephen until further notice." Gloria's voice trembled. That was odd. Had Eric been called away on business again? She was sure he would have called and told her, but maybe there was an emergency that required his immediate attention. Something could have happened to one of Gaby's parents or another relative. That would require Eric to leave town right away with Gaby and to be by her side to comfort her. These things always happened at times like this. Eric would feel compelled to stay with Gaby now. He would never leave her distraught.

Breck squinted. "Was there a family emergency?" she asked, hoping that she was wrong. She wanted Gloria to tell her that Eric was called away on business. The last thing she wanted to know was that he was home consoling Gaby and reconciling their marriage.

Gloria cleared her throat. It was a deliberate attempt to stall, and that made Breck uneasy.

"Breck . . ." Gloria paused, inhaled, exhaled. Breck could almost see the woman's chest rise and fall. "Eric was in an accident last night."

Breck dropped to her knees. Her heart stopped and her hands began to shake.

Please, God, please let him be all right, she prayed.

"Breck," Gloria whispered, "Eric was killed."

TWENTY-SIX

BRECK IMMEDIATELY dialed Chi with trembling hands and howled as soon as Chi picked up the phone. She couldn't talk, despite Chi's desperate attempts to get her to.

Her next thought was Jordan, and she ran upstairs to get him. She fell to the floor with him and bellowed. She cried so hard that she retched on the bedroom floor. When she felt it coming up again, she doubled over, still sitting on her knees, and expelled again. Jordan started to cry.

She heard the banging but she couldn't get up to answer it. She heard Chi and Gena call out to her and then use their extra key to open the door. The tears came hard, too hard for her to see anything in front of her. Jordan wailed even louder, and that got Chi and Gena's attention. Dragging Sierra with them, they shot up the stairs to find Breck curled on the floor in a fetal position near a pool of vomit.

They dashed into the room and grabbed Breck's arm to lift her up. Too weak to walk, she fell toward the floor again. The two women managed to drag her to her bedroom. Gena led the children out of the room, leaving Chi to play detective and find out what was going on.

"Breck, talk to me!" Chi shouted. "What happened?" She had grabbed a towel from the bathroom and wiped Breck's mouth and face.

Breck pulled her knees to her chest, crying and gasping.

AS WE LAY · 355

The next thing she heard were more footsteps hurrying up the stairs. They were hard and heavy—definitely not those of a woman.

Eric! She bolted from the floor and ran to the bedroom door. Gloria had been wrong. Eric was alive. She stepped into the doorway and right into Martin's arms. That was all Breck could remember before she passed out.

BRECK WOKE up in her bed. The soft blanket was pulled over her. She blinked several times before she could focus. Why was she lying in bed? What happened? She didn't remember getting into the bed. She looked around and saw Chi sitting comfortably in the chaise on the other side of the room, her head resting against its side.

"Jordan," Breck said weakly. Chi jumped up and rushed to the bed, then took Breck's hand and squeezed it. "Where's Jordan?" Breck murmured.

"He's fine. Gena took him home with her." Chi removed several strands of hair that had fallen over Breck's face. Breck looked into Chi's eyes. They were red, redder than Breck had ever seen them. Chi never cried. Breck was the emotional one, crying at everything, but Chi was solid, unaffected by trivial things.

"Martin and Alyce stopped by," Chi said, stroking her hair. "They said they'd be back." Breck didn't respond. Her body was numb, paralyzed. "I'm so sorry." Chi pulled her to her bosom and hugged her hard. Breck's body was limp, like a rag doll. "We'll get through this," Chi continued. "We're been through a lot together and we'll get through this. I promise."

Another promise. Eric had said that. It was the only promise he had ever made to her that he didn't keep.

"Don't say that!" Breck screamed. "Don't ever promise me anything. He was supposed to call me and he didn't. He promised."

Chi looked at her, horrified. "I'm sorry," she said,

which sent Breck into another round of tears until she collapsed against the pillow.

Eric was dead.

BRECK FELL in and out of consciousness. Every time she was awake she found someone new in the room, but she never stayed conscious enough to acknowledge their presence. After the last time she lost consciousness, she opened her eyes and saw her mother.

She reached out with both arms and her mother came to her and held her. They shed tears together.

"Eric—" Breck whimpered, but she couldn't finish. She just couldn't say it aloud.

"I know, baby, I know." Breck had never known how much she had needed her mother until that moment. Having her there gave Breck strength.

"Breck, honey," Camille said, separating herself. "We need you to try to eat for us. Do you think you can do that?"

Breck shook her head. "I'm not hungry," she said. Her tongue stuck to the roof of her mouth and tasted like bad medicine.

"I know you're not hungry, but you've been lying here for three days and we need you to eat. You need to get your strength back. Otherwise we're going to have to take you to the hospital."

Breck sank into the pillow. The thought of food repulsed her. She felt her stomach tighten up as if she were going to start vomiting again. She caught sight of Chi walking into the room with a tray of food, and she started to gag.

Her head pounded. She hadn't felt it before or perhaps she just didn't notice it. "Ow!" she cried, and grabbed her head. It hurt so badly, almost like something had just popped. "I can't!" she wailed.

"You've got to try, Breck. You are a strong woman. You can't break on us now. Jordan needs you. He can't lose both his parents."

Tears ran steadily down Breck's cheeks.

"Breck." Camille stood. She was not giving up, and she wasn't going to let Breck give up. "You've got to try to eat now." She motioned for Chi to bring the tray to her, and she took it and placed it on the nightstand. She picked up the bowl of soup and a spoon and directed it toward Breck's mouth.

"Open up now," she said, and Breck obeyed. "It's your favorite." Her mother had made her favorite chicken soup.

Breck swallowed, and Camille continued to spoon the soup into her mouth until it was gone, and then she had Breck chomp on several crackers before she fed her a bowl of Jell-O. "It's going to be okay," she said, stroking Breck's hair and pulling the strands from her face.

Breck nodded. "Where's Jordan?"

"He's still with Gena." Chi stepped from the shadows and sat down on the opposite side of the bed.

"Does he know about Eric?"

"No. We all felt it would be best if you told him." Chi squeezed Breck's hand. "Martin stopped by and told us the funeral is tomorrow morning."

Breck fought tears.

"Do you want to go to the funeral?" Chi asked.

It was a legitimate question. As far as everyone outside of Mansfield knew, she was a business acquaintance and good friend. She would be expected to attend. Eric Warren had caused her career to skyrocket. She knew she couldn't take Jordan. He didn't know the circumstances of his father's relationship with his mother. He would proudly boast that Eric was his father, in the innocent way that only a two-year-old can boast.

"I can't take Jordan to the funeral, but I want him to say good-bye," she said.

"We can talk to Martin about arranging a private viewing," her mother said. Breck looked at her, surprised that she would think of that. And why had she even bothered coming? She had never liked Eric or their relationship. She was probably gloating privately that this had happened as some sort of justice for having an affair.

Breck pushed her mother's hand away and suddenly felt repulsed by her and everyone in the room. They were all probably glad that this had happened. They had probably talked about her to one another while she was asleep.

"You're happy this has happened, aren't you?" She was seething. "You wanted this, didn't you? Admit it!" she yelled. She sat straight up in the bed and looked from her mother to Chi. "Well, Mother, you've got what you wanted. That married man is out of my life for good now." Her mother sat, agape, and stared at her.

"Breck, no one wanted this," Chi said, coming to Camille's rescue.

"The hell you didn't!" Breck screamed back at her, and bolted from the bed. "All I've ever heard from you two was how Eric was ruining my life. How the hell was he ruining my life when he was the best thing that ever happened to me? I've spent the last three months apart from him because I was listening to you and you," she said, pointing to Chi, then her mother. "And now he's gone and I can't have those three months back. I hate you!" She screamed and knocked the bowl of Jell-O out of her mother's hand, sending it soaring across the room before she dropped to the floor. "Get out of my house!" She sobbed hard, barely able to get the words out. Tears streamed from her eyes as her mother tried to scoop her slumped body off the floor. Camille finally gave up and sat on the floor with her and rocked her as Breck cried uncontrollably in her arms. Camille began to hum while she massaged her daughter's hair. Breck stopped fighting and let the tears fall freely from her eyes.

TWENTY-SEVEN

MARTIN WAS outraged when he found out that Gaby had declared Eric's funeral private. Although he was invited, it meant that most of the people who knew Eric in Mansfield would not be allowed to pay their final respects. He protested to Gaby and got her to agree to a public viewing separate from hers and a full day before. He then arranged a separate memorial in Mansfield. Gaby readily agreed, expressing to Martin that it would be best, considering the two worlds really didn't mix anyway.

Breck, her mother, Chi, Gena, Sierra, and Jordan arrived in Gena's truck. Breck and Jordan dressed identically in black and violet; Breck wore a black dress embroidered with violet flowers, and Jordan wore a violet handkerchief and matching bow tie. Deep violet was one of Eric's favorite colors.

At two Jordan had little concept of death, but he understood that his father had gone away and he was going to say good-bye. The little boy understood more than Breck had given him credit for, because he walked somberly throughout the house and had lost his appetite.

"But what about Men Only?" Jordan had asked as he stared at his father's photo still sitting on the mantel.

Breck swept him into her arms and set him on her lap. "You and I can start our own tradition."

"It won't be the same." He placed his head on Breck's shoulder.

"It won't be the same, but I bet we'll have fun." She hugged him tightly against her chest.

When they stepped from the truck Martin hugged all of them and led them to the viewing room. The casket was open, and Martin had warned Breck beforehand that Eric's face had swollen tremendously from the accident.

It was Martin who had gotten the sketchy details of the fatal accident from Gaby. Eric had been alone in his Range Rover and had apparently gone through a red light and been hit on the driver's side by a truck, only blocks from their home. He was pronounced dead at the scene. The driver of the truck walked away from the accident with no visible injuries. Details of the accident puzzled Breck. Eric had always been a careful driver, even refusing to use his cell phone while driving unless he had a hands-free microphone attached. She didn't understand how he could have been careless enough to go through a red light.

They walked slowly into the viewing room. Breck held on to Jordan's hand, and her mother took hold of his other hand. The room had the cold stench of death found only at a funeral home. They inched closer to the body lying at rest inside a grand white-and-gold casket suitable for a king. Flowers were everywhere—small ones, large ones, flowers of every shape and color.

Breck looked around for his favorite, wildflowers. Eric used to love to stop his car alongside the road and pick wildflowers. He'd brought her several bundles of wildflowers when she stayed at the townhome and then when she moved into the house. She had loved walking into the house and finding a bouquet he had put together on the kitchen table or placed in a vase in the sitting room or in her bedroom. Breck remembered arriving home one evening to find a trail of wildflowers starting on the front porch and ending in her bedroom, where Eric had a new nightgown from Victoria's Secret laid out on the bed, waiting for her.

She wanted to smile, but the urge quickly vanished when she saw Eric's body inside the casket. His face had swollen almost beyond recognition. This was not her Eric. This was a stranger. After one look in the casket, Chi turned and ran out of the room. Breck could hear her bawling in the lobby. Gena immediately joined her, taking Sierra with her. Breck held Jordan's hand tightly as her mouth dropped open. Her heart pounded so hard that her chest began to hurt.

Any sound she could have made was trapped inside her throat. She wanted to say something. Someone had played a terrible trick on her. This man's face was twice the size of Eric's and was dull, ashen, and darker, with grayish, dry lips. Eric's face always glowed, was always vibrant and smooth. Eric's lips were full and pinkish— kissable lips, she had called them. This was not Eric. The mortuary beauticians had tried hard to create a peaceful expression on his swollen face.

His hands were clasped in front of him. The only jewelry he wore was his wedding band. Breck looked for the white-gold bracelet but didn't see it. It was a simple symbol of their union, but Eric never took it off and neither did she. Now it was gone.

Jordan stepped onto a stool placed to the side of the casket and looked down at his father resting peacefully on a violet satin pillow. Without hesitation he touched the side of Eric's face. "Bye, Daddy," he whispered in a somber voice.

Breck hadn't known what to expect from Jordan. She didn't know if he fully understood death. She was going to read books to him and invited a psychologist friend to her home to help her explain it to him, but Jordan seemed to understand that this was good-bye. He held his hand to Eric's face and bit down on his lower lip, as if he was holding back tears.

He's trying to be strong for me, Breck thought, and tears wet her eyes.

THEY LEFT the funeral home thirty minutes later. Martin, Alyce, and Brian were planning to attend that service the following day, but Breck had declined, deciding to stay close to Jordan. Instead they had prepared a farewell memorial at the Boys and Girls Club and invited all of the neighborhood children and their parents.

Brian had arranged for the kids from the club to pay their final respects before Breck had gone for her viewing. Afterward, they had boarded a bus and returned to the club for the farewell party. Home videos were shown on the large movie projector in the gym, while the children sat around and watched. Some cried, while others hugged each other. Several collages of Eric's pictures from various events with the children covered the walls. When Breck and Jordan walked in, the children and their parents immediately hugged them and told her how much they'd missed her.

Some of the children had assumed that Breck and Eric were married to each other until Gaby's sudden visit. After Gaby's visit, Breck had never gone back.

"We hope you come back," one little girl whispered to her. "We miss you and Jordan." The sentiment made Breck cry—they didn't seem to care that she and Eric weren't married and that he had a wife.

Breck watched her mother as she made her way around the club, looking at the pictures and listening to the children. As she and Breck stood alone at the table of food the children's parents had brought in, her mother squeezed her hand. "I understand now why you loved him so much," she said. "He was a good man." Breck turned and hugged her mother. She only wished her mother had realized that when Eric was alive and had told him so.

Camille stayed in Mansfield another week before returning to Indianapolis. When she left, Breck felt she and her mother were closer than they had ever been. She saw a lot of herself in her mother that she had never seen before. Before she left, her mother talked to Breck about returning to Indianapolis so that Jordan could be closer to his family there. Breck seriously considered it but declined. The night before her mother left she told her, "I can't go back to Indianapolis." They were sitting on the sofa together. Breck had poured each of them a glass of wine. Jordan had already gone to bed, and they had the last few moments alone.

"Why not? We all miss you."

"I miss you too," Breck said, taking her mother's hand. "But Mansfield is my home now." She looked around her house. "This is where my heart is." Breck had a life in Mansfield that she had never had in Indianapolis. Now she knew how Eric felt when he spoke so eloquently of Mansfield to her so many years ago. She smiled, remembering those initial conversations.

"I'm very proud of you, Breck. You've done well here."

Breck fell into her mother's arms and hugged her tightly. A tear rolled down her cheek.

"Please say you'll come back often," Breck whispered in her ear. "I'll pay for it."

Her mother laughed. "Well, I can't refuse that offer." Camille pulled back and stroked the side of Breck's face, wiping the tear with her hand. "You take care of my grandson. He's a special boy. I feel it."

Breck smiled. "I know."

WHAT WOULD life in Mansfield be like without Eric? The hours seemed to drag and the days went on forever. The second week after Eric's death, Breck found herself walking zombielike around the house, trying desperately to piece her life back together and get things back to "normal." But what was normal? Eric had been so much a part of her life that things would never be normal.

Like children often do after tragedy, Jordan bounced back a lot better than she did. Breck wished she could be as resilient, but most nights she found herself wrapped in her favorite afghan, now even more special, crying herself to sleep.

Although she wasn't feeling ready to return to work, she did—she couldn't stand being alone at the house any longer knowing Eric would never ring the doorbell or call her and tell her that he was skipping a day of work to spend it with her. As much as she loved her house, she was beginning to hate being in it—every room smelled of Eric's cologne, even the basement. Some days she could still smell him when she was out for her lunchtime run. He was everywhere, and the only time she could escape his smell was when she was at the office. Eric had hardly ever come there, and that was the only place he hadn't left his scent.

Breck resumed her morning routine and dropped Jordan off with Alyce. The first day was the hardest, but Alyce made a point of cheering her up.

"We're having another baby," Alyce blurted out as she walked Jordan into the playroom.

"Oh, my!" Breck exclaimed and hugged her. "This is sudden."

"Well, we've known for a little while, but we felt it would best to wait, considering . . ." Her voiced trailed off and her eyes were glossy, but she didn't shed a tear.

Breck nodded and sighed heavily. She didn't want to cry again either. "I thought you said you didn't want any more children."

"I didn't, but having Jordan and Sierra around really made me want another one."

"Congratulations. I bet Martin is very excited."

"He is. He wanted another one too, though he would never admit it." She laughed. "Have you given any thoughts to having another one?" Breck looked at her as if she was crazy. Who would she have a baby with? Eric was the only man she had ever considered having a child with, and he had been dead for only a few short weeks. She hadn't thought about meeting someone and starting a family.

"I'm sorry," Alyce apologized quickly. "That was pretty insensitive, wasn't it?"

"It's okay," Breck said, clearing her thoughts and straightening her posture. "But I have to get going."

"Breck, before you go there's something I want to tell you." Alyce took her hand and walked with her to a couple of chairs that were placed on the porch, then motioned for her to sit down. "I don't know if I was a good friend to you or not. I probably wasn't as good a friend as I could have been because of my discomfort about your relationship with Eric."

Breck frowned. She had never noticed any discomfort from Alyce. "You and Martin have been wonderful to me," Breck interjected. "After I had Jordan, I don't know what I would have done if it were not for you."

"Thank you, but I know that I still could have been a better friend. I've said some things about you when you were not around that I probably shouldn't have said. I didn't approve of your relationship with Eric and I saw it as a threat at first. Getting to know you and seeing you and Eric together and coming to understand why you were together opened my eyes to some things about my own marriage."

Breck squinted. "I don't understand."

Alyce paused, choosing her words before she spoke. "We all thought Eric and Gaby had the perfect marriage and the perfect life and we were a little jealous of that."

"We?"

"Some of the other wives. The men could care less. Eric was just a damn good man, and he was damn good to his wife, and his family came first, always. He made us see the faults in our husbands, and we held them to his level. That was, of course, until you came along."

Still Breck didn't understand where she was going with the conversation.

"You made us realize that things were not as perfect as they seemed, and it also made us examine our relationships with our husbands. How much did I really know about Martin and the things he was passionate about? Was I sharing my life with him or someone else? Before you came along I took everything for granted and swore up and down that nothing like that would ever happen to me. When I looked at it more closely— witnessing your relationship with Eric forced me to do that—I realized that it very well could have happened. There were too many doors left open.

"It wasn't enough to say that I know Martin loves me and is devoted to me. I know Martin loves me, and I also knew that Eric loved Gaby and was devoted to her, but that didn't stop it from happening."

"So I taught you to distrust your husband?" Breck asked.

"No, no," Alyce said, touching her hand. "You taught me to appreciate him more. The one thing that could have stopped your and Eric's relationship from developing was if Gaby had been involved in Eric's life and shared his passion for Mansfield. It could have been any of our husbands and we knew that. I bet you one thing, after you came along we knew we had better involve ourselves in our husbands' lives and stop taking it for granted that they'd been at work all day and were coming home to us at night."

Breck sighed. "I didn't want anyone to think less of Eric because of me. He didn't deserve that."

"No, he didn't, and I don't think any of us do. At first we didn't understand why he was doing what he was doing, and it scared the hell out of us, but it became very clear. He was in love with you and Mansfield, but many years ago he'd decided that this wasn't good enough for him. He married a woman who was so far removed from here that, had it not been for you, we would have lost him long before we did. Gaby took him away but you brought him back. You got involved in his life and didn't just wait until he came home to you at night, and that made all the difference."

"I'm really not a bad person, and I know some of the other women are very wary of me."

"They're foolish," Alyce said, and patted her hand again. "I know that what you and Eric had was very real. It wasn't a game, and I wish that it had turned out differently for you. I really do." Alyce took Breck into her arms and hugged her tight. "What are you going to do?" she asked when they had parted again.

"Jordan and I are staying in Mansfield. This is our home. As far as dating, I just don't know. I don't have a desire to be with another man. I had the most perfect man for me. How can you top that?" She hugged Alyce again, then left before starting another round of tears. She drove the few short blocks to the office and rushed out of the car. She stormed into the office, bypassing Chi sitting at her desk without even speaking, and slammed her portfolio case onto her desk and hid her head in her hands. She needed to get this over with. This day needed to hurry up and end so that she could get back home. She was crazy to think she was ready to go back to work. She wasn't ready.

"Breck." She heard Chi calling her but didn't answer. She just sat with her hands covering her face. "Breck,"

Chi called again, and this time Breck peeked through her fingers to see Chi's long face staring back at her. "Are you okay?"

Breck shook her head but placed her hands flat on her desk and took a deep breath. "No." She paused and took another deep breath. "It feels so lonely and empty sometimes without him." She inhaled deeply.

"There's someone waiting to see you," Chi said. Breck thought quickly. She hadn't made any appointments. She thought for a few seconds but couldn't recall forgetting any. "He says he's one of Eric's lawyers," Chi continued. "He went downstairs to get a cup of coffee. He said there should be another attorney arriving as well."

"Eric's lawyers?" Breck whispered. "Why would one of Eric's lawyers be here?"

Chi shrugged.

Oh, shit, what is this about? Breck wondered as she leaned back in her chair. Her first panicked thought was that Gaby was suing her. She must have found out about the affair and that Eric had bought her the house, and now Gaby wanted to take it from her.

Chi returned to the front to see if the lawyer had returned. Breck heard noises and raised voices. She pushed away from her desk and hurried to the lobby. Chi stood in the reception area with Gena and an immaculately dressed white gentleman Breck had never seen before. He wore a stylish gray Armani suit with a cream-colored shirt and silk tie. At his side was a bulky black leather attaché case.

"What's going on?" she asked, walking toward the trio.

"Breck, this is Eric's attorney, Mr. Anthony Barone," Gena said, speaking casually. Evidently she had met him before. Mr. Barone extended his slender, well-tanned hand toward Breck, and she shook it.

"Morning," he said, and held on to Breck's hand longer than she had anticipated. "I'm sorry about your loss," he said, then tipped his head in condolence.

My loss? Breck said to herself. What did he know about my loss? And why was Gena here with him?

"Can we talk in your office?" Gena asked. She clutched a powerful leather briefcase in her hand, telling Breck this wasn't a social call.

"Sure." Breck motioned for them to follow her into her office. As she closed the door, Breck turned to look at Chi, who put her hands on her hips and glared.

Both attorneys took seats opposite Breck's desk. Mr. Barone flipped opened his leather-bound case and pulled out a large manila folder. "Two years ago, Mr. Warren and Ms. Price came to see me about drafting an irrevocable trust naming your son, Jordan Warren Larson, and his other son, Darius Cornelius Warren, as the sole beneficiaries."

"What?!" Breck exclaimed, immediately shooting a glance at Gena.

Mr. Barone momentarily stopped talking and looked from Breck to Gena.

"Let him finish," Gena insisted, and Breck looked again at Eric's attorney as he opened the folder and handed her a packet of several stapled pages.

"As you can see," Mr. Barone continued, "the trust purchased a life insurance policy for Mr. Warren. Upon his death, the proceeds will be used to pay for college education and life expenses for both sons. The trust also names myself and Ms. Price as executors."

Breck's mouth dropped open as she flipped through the pages. Breck heard Mr. Barone going on about numbers that were in the millions and percentages of this and shares of that. Everything had started to run together, and all she heard were mumbles, except for Mr. Barone's final statement. Eric specifically chose this type of trust so that Gaby would have less of a chance of disputing it and so its content would not become public record, as in the case of a will.

But for Breck it went much farther than that. Naming Darius and Jordan as cobeneficiaries of this trust meant one thing, and when Breck looked up from the papers she had only one question. "She knows now, doesn't she?" she asked, and all Gena needed to do was nod.

TWENTY-EIGHT

FIVE YEARS from the day she met him, five years of lying and sneaking and hiding, were over. Eric had just done what he could not do while he was alive. Forget shit hitting the fan; Breck knew her world was about to get turned upside down and inside out. Gaby and her family were not going to let this lie without a fight.

For days after the announcement, Chi and Sierra stayed with Breck, because Chi was too upset with Gena for keeping the secret. "How could she keep something like that from me?" Chi had said, storming into the house with Sierra and baggage in tow.

"Attorney-client privilege," Breck said, pouring each of them a glass of wine after they had put the children to bed. Breck understood perfectly well why Gena had not divulged the information or turned down the work. The trust would pay the lawyers a handsome annual salary. Gena would have been foolish to turn it down, but it also gave Eric a peace of mind that someone would sincerely be looking out for Jordan's best interest. According to Gena, that had been the deciding factor for her.

"But what about partner privileges?" Chi fumed. She downed her wine and poured herself another glass. Breck understood all too well how Chi felt, because she too felt betrayed, but by Eric. He had left her to fight this battle alone. She knew it was important for him to make sure Jordan would be taken care of, but there had to be a way to do that without turning everyone's world upside down from his grave.

"You know you can't stay mad at her about this," Breck said. "She did the right thing."

"I know, but I want her to know that she'd better not ever do anything like this again."

The telephone rang, and Chi said, "If that's Gena, tell her I went out." Breck laughed, seeing the pint-sized woman madder than she had ever seen her before.

"Hello," Breck said.

"Is this Breck Larson?" Breck didn't recognize the voice, which sounded like it belonged to an elderly woman. She hesitated before answering, not sure what to expect.

"Yes, it is."

"Ms. Larson, this is Sylvia Warren. I'm Eric's mother." Once again Breck felt her stomach slammed to the floor. She'd had so many surprises the past few days that she was sure her heart was going to stop.

At first Breck said nothing. What could she say? Eric had talked about his mother, sister, and brother repeatedly, but she had never met them.

"I hope I'm not disturbing you," the woman went on to say.

"No, not at all," Breck said, sitting down on the sofa. She cupped her hand over the phone and whispered to Chi who was sitting on the other end. Chi's eyebrows rose. "My condolences to you," Breck said into the receiver.

"Thank you, and likewise to you. I know it's sudden, and I don't mean to upset you. I apologize if I do."

She sounded nice enough, Breck thought; when would the yelling, accusations, and cursing start? "No, it's okay," Breck reassured her.

Sylvia paused as if she were searching for the right thing to say. The silence became extremely uncomfortable. Breck didn't know if she was expected to carry the

374 · DARLENE JOHNSON

conversation. "I don't recall meeting you at Eric's funeral," Sylvia finally said.

"I didn't go to the funeral. I attended the memorial in
Mansfield."

"I see. Eric always did love Mansfield. We should have
held the official service there." Ms. Warren paused again.
"I would like to meet my grandson." Hearing the sadness
in Sylvia's voice, Breck fought from crying. Chi came to
sit with her on the sofa.

"I would like that," Breck said.

"Good," she said, and Breck could hear a sigh of relief. "I was under the impression that you might resist."

"Why would I resist?"

"For the same reason I didn't know Eric had a second
child."

"It was because of the circumstances, Ms. Warren. If
things had been different, Eric and I would have done
things differently and you would have known. On behalf of myself and Eric, I apologize."

They arranged to meet the next day. Eric's sister and
brother were still in town, and they wanted to meet Jordan as well. Breck gave them directions to her house,
and Sylvia was thrilled to learn that Jordan was being
raised within a few blocks of where his father had lived
as a boy. Breck assured her that Mansfield was different
now, thanks to Eric's vision. Ms. Warren admitted that
it had been ten years since she'd visited Mansfield. She
had struggled to raise her three children there, and once
Eric bought her the home on Martha's Vineyard, she'd
never yearned to return.

At two o'clock the following afternoon, Sylvia, Eric's
sister, Karmen, her husband and two small children, and
Eric's brother, Christopher, appeared on her doorstep,
immaculately dressed and on time. Breck had her own
support system present as well. Chi, Gena, and Sierra
were at the house, waiting with her. Martin and Alyce

promised to stop by to offer more support if Breck needed it and to see the Warrens again. They had all been close friends years ago, and for Martin and Alyce it would be a reunion.

When Breck opened the door for them, she really didn't know what to do. Should she shake their hands or hug them? It was all so very awkward and strange. She wondered if Eric's spirit was somewhere nearby, smiling. He had always wanted this, they had talked about it before, but he couldn't figure out a way to make it happen while he was alive.

"Welcome," Breck said when everyone had stepped inside.

"I'm Eric's mother," Sylvia Warren said, extending her hand toward Breck. "You have a lovely home."

"Thank you. Please, come in." Breck escorted everyone into the sitting room. Jordan and Sierra played on the floor, and when Jordan's kin walked in the children stood up and turned to face them. Sylvia took one look at Jordan and stopped. She covered her mouth with her hand. Her legs became unsteady, and she appeared to be near collapse. Christopher and Karmen grabbed her by the forearms and walked her to the sofa.

"I really didn't know what to expect," Sylvia said, sitting down, her eyes still on Jordan. "He looks exactly like Eric." Tears flooded her eyes. She held her arms out to Jordan. He was reluctant at first, but Breck nudged him and he walked into his grandmother's waiting embrace.

Every adult in the room cried. Breck turned her head to keep Jordan from seeing her, but it didn't matter. The tears came and wouldn't stop. Chi walked to her and put her arms around her shoulders.

"I'm your grandma," Sylvia said, holding Jordan still to look into his face. Her face was wet with tears, and she tried to wipe them away as she spoke. "I'm your father's mother, and this is your Aunt Karmen and Uncle

Christopher." She took Karmen's and Christopher's hands and pulled them closer to her.

"I know," Jordan said. "My mommy told me about you. You want to see a picture of my father? It's my favorite." He wiggled from Sylvia's lap and then took her hand and walked her to the mantel. He pointed to the picture, and Sylvia lifted him into her arms so they could look at it together. It was a black-and-white snapshot taken when Eric held Jordan in his arms as a baby. Eric had lifted Jordan to his face and was about to kiss him when Breck snapped the photo.

"I was a baby," Jordan said.

"You're still a baby."

"But that's when I was a little baby."

Sylvia laughed. "You were a beautiful baby."

As promised, Martin and Alyce came to the house, and the meeting quickly became a celebration of Eric's life that, according to Sylvia, was very different from the gathering at Eric's home after his funeral. Breck took to Eric's sister, who was a few years her senior and who owned and operated a successful catering service in Washington, D.C. Her husband was in the Secret Service. A celebration of Eric's life wasn't complete without a drive through Mansfield. All of the women climbed into Gena's Ford Expedition and drove around the town. They stopped at the convention center and piled out of the truck, then walked around the building. Eric's mother traced his name embedded in slab of concrete on the side of the building.

As Breck stood beside Sylvia, once again she smelled Eric's scent. "I can't seem to get away from that smell," she said, crossing her arms across her chest.

"What smell is that?"

"Eric's cologne. Everywhere I go, I smell it."

Sylvia smiled. "That means he's with you. Cherish it, honey."

The Warrens were amazed by the changes that had occurred in Mansfield over the years. No one had imagined it becoming a thriving community, but they all knew it did so because of Eric's vision and his money.

When they left the convention center, they drove to the home Eric was raised in. Sylvia explained they had left it boarded up with dangling shingles and peeling paint; now it was one of the most beautiful homes in Mansfield.

"I never thought this house could be so beautiful," she said, shaking her head in disbelief. When they returned to Breck's house, Sylvia took Breck by the hand and held her back while the others walked ahead.

"I've missed two years of my grandson's life," she said. "If Eric hadn't died, I may not have met him. That angers me." She shoved her hands into her shirt pockets. "I never thought I would bury my son. Finding out about Jordan almost sent me to the grave beside him." She stopped talking and looked at the house and everything around them. "Learning about you was a shock. My son was an honorable family man." Breck swallowed hard and braced herself to be criticized for seducing Eric and turning him into a devil's pawn. Only a wicked woman could manipulate such an honorable man to do something so sinful.

"Eric called me a few days before he died and told me that he had something he needed to talk with me about," Sylvia continued. "Now, that was not like Eric. Usually he'd just come right out and say what was on his mind. I'm figuring that he was about to tell me about you and Jordan." Breck dropped her head and stared at a crack in the sidewalk. She wanted to confirm that that might have been the case. She thought about telling Sylvia that Eric had decided to leave Gaby, but she chose not to. That information would serve no purpose now.

"I believe Eric loved you very much." Sylvia stopped walking and looked around again. "I feel his spirit here. He did not have this with Gaby." She placed a hand to Breck's face and smiled at her. "My son was happy with you."

The women hugged, reassuring each other that everything would be okay. When they pulled apart, they started toward the house to join the others. "I plan to visit often, and I do expect to have a full relationship with my grandson," Sylvia added, her tone becoming stern. "Do you have a problem with that?"

Breck shook her head. Breck knew Sylvia's comments were not negotiable.

"Another thing." Sylvia turned to look directly at Breck. The soft expression she'd had earlier had disappeared. "The other side of Eric's family will not be as accepting, so expect a fight."

TWENTY-NINE

THE FIGHT began the next day, when Gaby barged into her office. The door flew open with a thunderous bang. Breck was at her desk on a conference call. Hearing the commotion in the other room, she immediately apologized, then disconnected the call.

"Where's that bitch?" Gaby screamed. "Breck, damn it!"

Breck stepped out of her office and walked toward the irate woman. Gaby lunged at her so quickly that Breck barely had time to step back. She grabbed a lock of Breck's hair and pulled it so hard that Breck's head snapped back and it almost sent her to the floor. The last thing Breck wanted to do was hit the floor and have Gaby sprawling on top of her.

Breck screamed while Chi and David tried to pry Gaby's hand from her hair.

"I'll teach your ass about fucking with someone's husband!" Gaby shouted, taking a swing at Breck as she stumbled. The punch landed solidly on her nose, and blood spurted all over her clothes and the floor. Breck knew she had to get free before she ended up taking another blow.

"I knew you were fucking," Gaby yelled. "I knew it!" She twisted to get out of David's arms while he tried to keep her from lunging at Breck again. "Here, you can have your fucking bracelet back." Gaby threw Eric's gold bracelet and it struck her hard in the eye. Breck put her bloody hand to her eye as a welt developed along the length of her face.

"You better leave before we call the police." Chi stepped in while David held Gaby's hands behind her back.

"What type of woman has a baby by a married man?" Gaby yelled, ignoring Chi's warning. "I'll see you in hell before I let your bastard son anywhere near my child! Eric's death rests on your head." Breck shot a quick look at her.

"Yeah, that's right," Gaby continued. "He told me about his plans. He was leaving, all right. He had just told me about his affair with you, but I knew that already. I was the one calling your house when he left for his so-called business trips. I knew he was fucking you, but then he told me about that bastard child he has with you. I told him that child will never see my son if I have anything to do with it. He got in his car, pulled off, and never made it off the fucking street."

Breck gasped. Eric had probably been coming to see her when he was killed.

"Let me go," Gaby protested. "I'm leaving." But David wasn't taking any chances of letting her go and kept a tight grip on her until she was completely out the door. He stayed behind her to make sure she left the building.

Everything made sense now; from the phone calls to Eric's distraction that cost him his life. Even if she wasn't directly responsible, Breck couldn't shake the feeling that she'd had some part in Eric's death. It was an accident, but if he had not been on his way to see her, he would be alive.

Her face swelled up and her nose still bled, but Breck needed to get out of there. She pushed Chi aside and ran out of the office and down the flight of stairs to her car. She slumped over the steering wheel and sobbed uncontrollably as blood poured from her nose and covered her pants.

EPILOGUE

FOR SOME people, not much can change in a year, but for Breck and Jordan, their world opened up and they welcomed a flood of people into their lives. Most of them were Eric's family, and he turned out to have a large extended family that he never talked about. The most surprising news was that his sister, Karmen, and her family moved back to Mansfield. Karmen quickly became an addition to the weekly girls' night out. Karmen tried unsuccessfully to get her mother to move back as well, but there was no chance of that, and privately Breck was glad: the bungalow on Martha's Vineyard was a nice retreat from Boston and Mansfield whenever Breck and Jordan went for a visit. They made biweekly visits that included an occasional overnight stay for Jordan.

Gaby began a campaign to keep Darius and Jordan separated by refusing to allow Sylvia visits with Darius as long as she had a relationship with Jordan. But Sylvia was just as strong-willed as Eric had been. She was determined to have a relationship with all of her grandchildren and threatened legal action against Gaby if she persisted in keeping Darius away.

Gaby then set out to destroy Breck's reputation, realizing that many of her clients were a direct result of Eric's influence. Gaby managed to kill three potential projects, but Breck's reputation preceded Gaby's declaration of war against her and her business remained strong.

After a year of verbal insults and telephone harassment,

382 · DARLENE JOHNSON

Gaby's vindictive crusade against the family suddenly stopped.

BRECK FIRST learned that Darius was sick from Sylvia, when she and Jordan arrived for the usual bi-weekly visit. "He's been sick a lot lately, so they're running tests on him," Sylvia said rather casually. Breck didn't think much of it—Darius was still at that age when children bring home germs from school, nothing a shot or antibiotics couldn't cure. It wasn't until the following week that Breck got the disturbing phone call from Karmen. Darius was not okay. He had been diagnosed with leukemia.

The news sent Breck spiraling into mental turmoil. Like any parent of a healthy child, she was thankful it was not her son who was sick. On the other hand, she pitied Gaby for the harsh blows life had dealt her over the past year. Breck understood Gaby's anger and her need to get back at her, but she also wanted to scream—enough was enough already, get over it and move on. Eric wasn't there to help her fight or to defend himself. There were times when Breck felt she didn't have the strength to keep it up. As long as it didn't cause any harm to Jordan, she let it be.

"We're all being tested to see if our bone marrow is a match," Karmen said during the same phone conversation. "All we can do is pray."

It didn't take long, only about a week, for the entire Aletor and Warren family to be tested and immediately ruled out. The donor plea then went out to the general public, but the odds of finding a match outside of the family were very slim.

"Are you going to have Jordan tested?" Chi asked her one night while they washed dishes together. Gena, Jordan, Sierra, and Nikki, one of Karmen's daughters who had become best friends with Sierra, were in the family room watching the latest Disney animated flick.

Breck continued to wipe the dish she was drying, moving the towel counterclockwise so many times that the plate began to squeak. She had agonized over this for the entire week. She had prayed that someone in the family would be deemed a match and she could keep Jordan away from Gaby.

Chi grabbed her hand. "Are you going to have Jordan tested?" she asked again.

Breck turned around and leaned her behind on the sink, still holding on to the dish. "Even if Jordan is a match, Gaby will never allow it to happen."

"She may not have a choice."

Breck sighed. Those two little boys had been through enough this year. They didn't need this, and they most certainly didn't need another loss.

"If it was Jordan, she would let him die," Breck said, shaking her head. She wanted to believe that Gaby would come to Jordan's aid, but she knew in her heart that Gaby would never offer any part of Darius to save his life. Justice, she would have cited.

"But it's not Jordan and you're not Gaby."

BRECK GOT the hospital and doctor's information from Karmen and together she and Chi took Jordan to be tested. She held his hand as they walked to a private room. Dangling on the little boy's left wrist was the bracelet that used to belong to his father. Breck had a few of the links removed so it fit snugly around Jordan's wrist. As Jordan grew older and bigger, the other links could be reattached.

While the plasma was being drawn from Jordan, Breck and Karmen walked to the hospital chapel to say a silent prayer before returning to the room.

In a matter of a few hours, they had the results—Jordan was a match. The doctor announced that siblings usually were, but the odds were reduced dramatically because the boys didn't share the same mother. Even before he told them the news, the doctor had placed a call to Gaby to alert her that a match had been found and they could do the surgery immediately.

"Get ready for World War Three," Karmen said while they waited for Gaby to arrive at the hospital.

GABY AND Darius arrived but not alone. Stephen accompanied her, and they walked into the hospital hand in hand. Gaby had inherited Eric's percentage of the business and she ran it alongside Stephen, but it seemed their relationship had gone beyond that of business partners. Stephen never appeared warm enough with anyone to allow physical contact, but Breck could definitely imagine a Gaby-and-Stephen union. The two were more closely matched than Gaby and Eric ever were.

I wonder what Eric would think of this, Breck thought when she saw them together. It seemed strange somehow that everyone's lives had moved on after Eric's death except hers. Chi and Gena were in the final stage of adopting Sierra's brother. They believed the siblings should be raised together. Also, in the past year Brian had gotten engaged. He hadn't pursued Breck like most people had expected he would when Eric died. Breck figured he was waiting for her to make the first move, but she never did. Still, she was surprised when he and his girlfriend became regulars at Frankie's and around Mansfield. It was the longest anyone had seen Brian with anyone.

She was a nice woman, with a ten-year-old son who fit in well at the Boys and Girls Club. Breck watched them together, and their relationship appeared as solid as hers was with Eric. She wasn't envious—how could she be? It was her loss.

BRECK WASN'T in the room when the doctors revealed who the donor was, but she heard the yelling. There was no way to miss the enraged Portuguese accent above the beeps and alarms of hospital machines. It was now up to Gaby to set aside her pride and give the okay for the surgery to take place. If she didn't, she would be signing her son's death certificate.

At Gaby's request, Breck was escorted into a meeting room and they were left alone. Breck stood close to the door, ready to make an exit if Gaby made an attempt to lunge at her. She was not going to let the woman hit her again and do nothing about it. This time she was going to defend herself.

When Breck looked into Gaby's face, she expected to see the same hard, tight, and angry woman she had encountered a year ago. But Gaby's face had softened and her eyes were red and puffy with worry. It was a vulnerable side of Gaby Breck had never seen. Gaby's tears were real, and the bags that had accumulated around her eyes proved she had stayed up nights, probably worrying that she would have to bury her son alongside his father.

Gaby didn't say anything at first. She just stared at Breck, which made Breck uneasy until she finally decided to break the silence herself.

"Listen, Gaby, I know you don't like me, and quite frankly I don't care if you ever like me. But this is not about you or me. This is about the kids. Since Eric's death, it has always been about the kids." She wanted to go on, and surprisingly she could have, because Gaby did not attempt to stop her. Gaby's eyes were moist with tears. She collapsed onto the chair, hid her head in her palms, and cried. Breck froze, unsure whether she was supposed to comfort her or stay a comfortable distance away. For all Breck knew, the moment she walked near her Gaby would slap her. But the harder Gaby cried, the more Breck realized that she was too weak and distraught to strike anyone in anger.

Breck took a deep breath, walked closer to her, and sat in the chair beside her. She gingerly placed her arm around Gaby's shoulder and waited for something to happen. Gaby continued to cry for a few moments, then stopped, sniffed back tears, and wiped her eyes.

"I didn't think you would have Jordan tested," she began. "I prayed that you would. I believe in God, but I don't remember ever praying before. I prayed every night." She fought back tears. "Darius is the only child I could ever have. But you probably already know that." She dried her eyes. "I hated you," she said, and Breck stiffened. "Mostly, I hated you because you gave Eric something I could never give him again, which was another child. He wanted another baby and I've always known that. It was one of the reasons he devoted so much time to the Boys and Girls Club." She fought through another round of tears. "And you lived in Mansfield," she said. "That was a part of his life I just couldn't fit into." Gaby straightened in her chair and wiped her tears.

"Eric loved you," Breck said, and that caused Gaby to smile.

"I know he loved me," she said, as if it were the most absurd thing Breck could have ever said. "I just couldn't share Mansfield with him, and that was the very essence of his spirit. The anger is gone." She stood and walked to the opposite side of the room.

Breck had a hard time believing that. If the anger was gone, then why did she remain such a bitch when it involved the children spending time together?

"Pride," Gaby said, as if she had read Breck's mind. "But I will not allow pride to cost me my son's life." She turned to face Breck again, and the two women stared into each other's eyes.

So strange that they would find themselves in this

room, brought together by a tragedy. Breck remembered what her mother had said to her and Eric when she was visiting during the pregnancy: "There's an order to things." Everything that happens has a reason, and in time those reasons are revealed.